英语专业

四级

12年

真题试卷详解

2001

1997

2005

1996

主编　申富英

编著　（以姓氏笔画为序）

申富英　刘保华　刘智华

吴瑾瑾　明　艳　崔文龙

戚桂敏　鹿艳丽

世界图书出版公司

西安　北京　广州　上海

图书在版编目(CIP)数据

英语专业四级12年真题试卷详解/申富英主编.—西安:世界图书出版西安公司,2008.3
ISBN 978－7－5062－9425－6

Ⅰ.英… Ⅱ.申… Ⅲ.英语—高等学校—水平考试—解题
Ⅳ.H319.6

中国版本图书馆CIP数据核字(2008)第019430号

英语专业四级12年真题试卷详解

主　　编	申富英	
丛书策划	李林海	
责任编辑	李林海	
视觉设计	吉人设计	

出版发行	世界图书出版西安公司
地　　址	西安市北大街85号
邮　　编	710003
电　　话	029－87214941　87233647(市场营销部)
	029－87232980(总编室)
传　　真	029－87279675
经　　销	全国各地新华书店
印　　刷	陕西奇彩印务有限责任公司
开　　本	787×1092　　1/16
印　　张	17.375
字　　数	340千字

版　　次	2008年3月第1版　2008年3月第1次印刷
书　　号	ISBN 978－7－5062－9425－6
定　　价	26.00元(本书配1张MP3)

前　　言

　　该书编录了过去 12 年的英语专业四级考试真题,对其做了总结梳理,希望读者能够从中领悟到考试真谛,有的放矢地备考,从容决胜四级考试。该丛书具有以下两个突出特点:

　　单项能力专项练,难点问题各个击破　英语专业四级考试如同一场战争,树立正确的战争观,采取正确的战略战术是打赢这场战争,取得最终胜利的关键。作者注意到英语专业四级考生各个单项方面的能力差别非常突出,他们在某一方面已经非常强,几乎没有了提高的余地,再反复训练似乎有浪费时间的嫌疑;而在别的方面则表现为能力的欠缺,知识的匮乏,应试技巧的缺失,有着非常大的提高和上升空间,因此在这方面强化训练,集中提高就显得非常必要了。所以作者一改传统的一套试卷接一套试卷的编排模式,分专项独立成册,冀考生能够从自己的实际情况出发,在重点弥补不足的前提下,将难点问题各个击破,然后达到整体提高考试成绩目的。

　　答题思路详细解析,重点内容循环往复　任何"只见树木,不见森林",只注意到眼前问题且"就是论事"人,很难想像在英语专业四级考试中,他们不会遇到困难。因此,针对重点难点内容,尤其是语法和词汇知识方面的重点难点内容,作者在为试题做精解时,坚持这样一个原则:不但告诉读者答案,而且告诉读者解题的思路与方法,要使读者不但知其然,而且知其所以然。

　　以上两个方面既是本书有别于其他图书的特点,更是作者编写此书的初衷。作者希望这本书能够帮助读者炼就不败金身,成就战无不胜之真英雄。

编　者
2008 年 1 月

Contents

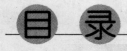

Contents

1996 年英语专业四级考试听力理解

Part Ⅱ Dictation

Listen to the following passage. Altogether the passage will be read to you four times. During the first reading, which will be read at normal speed, listen and try to understand the meaning. For the second and third readings, the passage will be read sentence by sentence, or phrase by phrase, with intervals of 15 seconds. The last reading will be read at normal speed again and during this time you should check your work. You will then be given 2 minutes to check through your work once more.

Please write the whole passage on ANSWER SHEET TWO.

Part Ⅲ Listening Comprehension

In Sections A, B and C you will hear everything once only. Listen carefully and then answer the questions that follow. Mark the correct response for each question in your ANSWER BOOKLET.

Section A   Statement

In this section you will hear eight statements. At the end of the statement you will be given 10 seconds to answer each of the following eight questions.

Now listen to the statements.

1. Joe went to court because he was a _____ .
   [A] law breaker   [B] trainee lawyer
   [C] friend of the judge   [D] traffic policeman
2. Where did the speaker think they were supposed to meet?
   [A] On the platform.   [B] On the train.
   [C] Near the stairs.   [D] At the information desk.
3. What is being described?
   [A] Telephone.   [B] Telegraph.

[C] Microfilm.   [D] Microscope.

4. How long was the coach delayed?

    [A] Three hours and forty five minutes.   [B] Five and a half hours.

    [C] Two hours and forty five minutes.   [D] Eight hours and fifteen minutes.

5. What does the speaker imply?

    [A] I want you to have a fully enjoyable holiday.

    [B] Your plans for the trip interest me a lot.

    [C] I think you should arrive according to the plan.

    [D] We are now making plans for your journey.

6. What does the speaker mean?

    [A] The shop told me this would happen.   [B] I didn't know it would be like this.

    [C] It became smaller but still fits me.   [D] The cardigan is well worth the price.

7. When will the writer's new book be published?

    [A] In the spring.   [B] In the summer.

    [C] In the autumn.   [D] In the winter.

8. What does the speaker mean?

    [A] Travelling by car is more dangerous than by air.

    [B] There are 300 air crashes each year in the US.

    [C] The air crashes each year kill about 50,000 people.

    [D] Travelling by plane is more dangerous than by car.

Section B   Conversation

    In this section, you will hear nine short conversations between two speakers. At the end of each conversation you will be given 10 seconds to answer each of the following nine questions.

    Now listen to the conversations.

9. What does the man mean?

    [A] It's really nice to have a change.

    [B] They ought to have been changed long ago.

    [C] The curtains are of a wrong colour.

    [D] The curtains are still quite good.

10. The woman's usual attitude towards films is _____ .

    [A] mixed   [B] fascinated

    [C] enthusiastic   [D] disinterested

11. According to the conversation, the woman's sister _____ .

    [A] was probably upset   [B] had little education

    [C] always writes like that   [D] usually never writes

12. The man's purpose in visiting was to _____ .

    [A] take a course   [B] see the city

    [C] go to the park   [D] take a rest

13. What does the man indicate?

[A] Most people like the museum.　　[B] It is difficult to get up early.

[C] There might be varied opinions.　　[D] It is a problem to get there.

14. What does the woman mean?

[A] She does not really need his help.

[B] She has not started thinking about it yet.

[C] She is very grateful to the man for his advice.

[D] She has already talked with the man.

15. Which of the following best describes the woman's reaction?

[A] Overjoyed.　　[B] Confused.

[C] Surprised.　　[D] Supportive.

16. The woman is going to the supermarket tomorrow because _____ .

[A] the supermarket is closing down after Christmas

[B] the man is going to help her with shopping

[C] tomorrow is the only day she is free before Christmas

[D] she wants to get enough food for the holiday period

17. John is going to France because _____ .

[A] he'll start a new business in properties　　[B] he has been left property there

[C] he's made a fortune with his uncle　　[D] his uncle wants his company there

Section C　News Broadcast

Question 18 is based on the following news. At the end of the news item, you will be given 10 seconds to answer the question.

Now listen to the news.

18. What happened to the schoolboy?

[A] He forgot to lock the cold store door.

[B] He was forced to work throughout the night.

[C] He caught cold while working at the butcher's.

[D] He was locked up by accident in a cold store.

Questions 19 & 20 are based on the following news. At the end of the news item, you will be given 20 seconds to answer the two questions.

Now listen to the news.

19. Mr. Warren Christopher _____ .

[A] believes there is hope for peace

[B] will report to the UN on Thursday

[C] will hold more talks before leaving the region

[D] is not sure that the peace process will succeed

20. With whom did Mr. Christopher NOT meet?

[A] The Syrian President.　　[B] The PLO leader.

[C] The Jordanian President.　　　　[D] The Israeli Prime Minister.

Questions 21 & 22 are based on the following news. At the end of the news item, you will be given 20 seconds to answer the two questions.

Now listen to the news.

21. The number of the escaped prisoners is _____ .

　　[A] 6　　　　[B] 5　　　　[C] 1　　　　[D] 7

22. Following the prison breakout, the Government is to _____ .

　　[A] restructure the prison service　　　　[B] discipline some prison officers

　　[C] recruit more security staff　　　　[D] look into security conditions

Questions 23 to 25 are based on the following news. At the end of the news item, you will be given 30 seconds to answer the three questions.

Now listen to the news.

23. The aim of the agreement is to _____ .

　　[A] encourage trade in the region　　　　[B] crack down on drug smuggling

　　[C] save the declining fishing industry　　　　[D] strengthen cross-border police presence

24. Which group of people is now taking advantage of the agreement?

　　[A] Canadian police.　　　　[B] Businessmen.

　　[C] Drug traffickers.　　　　[D] Customs officers.

25. The percentage of cocaine brought through the coast has increased by _____ .

　　[A] 10%　　　　[B] 50%　　　　[C] 60%　　　　[D] 70%

1997年英语专业四级考试听力理解

Part Ⅱ   Dictation

Listen to the following passage. Altogether the passage will be read to you four times. During the first reading, which will be read at normal speed, listen and try to understand the meaning. For the second and third readings, the passage will be read sentence by sentence, or phrase by phrase, with intervals of 15 seconds. The last reading will be read at normal speed again and during this time you should check your work. You will then be given 2 minutes to check through your work once more.

Please write the whole passage on ANSWER SHEET TWO.

Part Ⅲ   Listening Comprehension

In Sections A, B and C you will hear everything once only. Listen carefully and then answer the questions that follow. Mark the correct response for each question in your answer sheet.

Section A   Statement

In this section you will hear nine statements. At the end of the statement you will be given 10 seconds to answer each of the following nine questions.

1. What does the speaker mean?
   [A] John was unhappy with his dormitory.   [B] John's dormitory wasn't full.
   [C] John didn't meet me at the door.   [D] There wasn't any vacant room.

2. What does the statement imply?
   [A] We are sorry that we both failed.   [B] Mary is envious of Jane's success.
   [C] We are amazed by the fact.   [D] Jane is envious of Mary's success.

3. The speaker thinks that _____ .
   [A] writing is his favourite course
   [B] he prefers other courses to composition
   [C] one particular course is better than writing

[D] he doesn't like any course, least of writing

4. What does the speaker imply?

    [A] He didn't finish the exercises yesterday.

    [B] The exercises were handed in yesterday.

    [C] He knew the exercises should be handed in today.

    [D] He doesn't need to hand in the exercises today.

5. The speaker was _____ minutes late.

    [A] 50   [B] 15   [C] 30   [D] 10

6. What does the statement mean?

    [A] The speaker didn't attend the exam.   [B] The speaker didn't do the spelling.

    [C] The speaker was good at spelling.   [D] The speaker ignored his spelling.

7. According to the statement, the house is _____.

    [A] badly built   [B] noisy inside

    [C] very dirty   [D] in disorder

8. David decided to take the express train because _____.

    [A] he was in a hurry to get home   [B] he did not enjoy flying at all

    [C] he needed time to be on his own   [D] he had booked a seat on the train

9. The weather last weekend was _____.

    [A] warm and dry   [B] cold and wet

    [C] cool and crisp   [D] sunny and lovely

Section B   Conversation

    In this section. you will hear seven short conversations between two speakers. At the end of each conversation you will be given 10 seconds to answer each of the following seven questions.

10. Between getting up and her meeting, the woman had about _____.

    [A] 6 hours   [B] 40 minutes

    [C] 4 hours   [D] 30 minutes

11. The conversation probably took place in _____.

    [A] Rome   [B] Paris

    [C] London   [D] Madrid

12. What does the woman mean?

    [A] She hasn't read the passage.   [B] She doesn't understand it either.

    [C] She cannot read it in darkness.   [D] She suggests that the man read it.

13. What does the woman mean?

    [A] The job is advertised in English.

    [B] The advertisement is in an English paper.

    [C] She offers the man English and computer skills.

    [D] English and computer skills are essential for the job.

14. Vincent solved his problem by _____.

[A] going directly to the boss [B] talking to his parents

[C] asking his mother to speak to his boss [D] telling his boss' mother about it

15. What had the woman assumed?

[A] They had received a broken computer. [B] She knew how to repair the computer.

[C] The computer couldn't be fixed. [D] They'd have to buy another one.

16. The couple had previously planned to _____ .

[A] go boating [B] play golf [C] go cycling [D] play tennis

Section C News Broadcast

Question 17 is based on the following news. At the end of the news item, you will be given 10 seconds to answer the question.

Now listen to the news.

17. What are the attitudes of the local residents?

[A] They protested against detaining boat people.

[B] They protested against letting them stay forever.

[C] They urged Vietnam to accept the boat people.

[D] They urged Britain to accept the boat people.

Questions 18 and 19 are based on the following news. At the end of the news item. you will be given 20 seconds to answer the two questions.

Now listen to the news.

18. NATO troops will join in _____ .

[A] Cold War [B] training exercises

[C] Western armies [D] Eastern armies

19. Soldiers from _____ countries will participate.

[A] 17 [B] 30 [C] 13 [D] 43

Questions 20 to 22 are based on the following news. At the end of the news item, you will be given 30 seconds to answer the three questions.

Now listen to the news.

20. Who sponsored the conference on population?

[A] Cairo. [B] The United Nations.

[C] The World Bank. [D] The World Health Organization.

21. The current rate of annual increase in the world population is about _____ .

[A] 9 million [B] 5.7 million

[C] 90 million [D] 20 million

22. Which of the following concerning the document is NOT true?

[A] The document will cover the next two decades.

[B] The document will win support from the delegates.

[C] The document will serve as a guideline.

[D] The document will be completed after the conference.

Questions 23 to 25 are based on the following news. At the end of the news item, you will be given 30 seconds to answer the three questions.

Now listen to the news.

23. The news item reported a(n) _____ .

    [A] air crash   [B] traffic accident

    [C] lorry crash   [D] ferry accident

24. It was reported to have occurred _____ .

    [A] inside Manila's port   [B] in Singapore

    [C] near the Manila Bay   [D] in Malaysia

25. There were _____ people on board.

    [A] 30   [B] 400

    [C] 110   [D] 120

1998 年英语专业四级考试听力理解

Part Ⅱ   Dictation

Listen to the following passage. Altogether the passage will be read to you four times. During the first reading, which will be read at normal speed, listen and try to understand the meaning. For the second and third readings, the passage will be read sentence by sentence, or phrase by phrase, with intervals of 15 seconds. The last reading will be read at normal speed again and during this time you should check your work. You will then be given 2 minutes to check through your work once more.

Please write the whole passage on ANSWER SHEET TWO.

Part Ⅲ   Listening Comprehension

In Sections A, B and C you will hear everything once only. Listen carefully and then answer the questions that follow. Mark the correct response for each question on your answer sheet.

Section A   Statement

In this section you will hear eight statements. At the end of the statement you will be given 10 seconds to answer each of the following eight questions.

1. The speaker is talking to a _____ .
   [A] doctor   [B] pharmacist
   [C] mechanic   [D] waiter

2. What is the speaker's attitude?
   [A] He couldn't agree any more.   [B] He agrees completely.
   [C] He agrees partially.   [D] He couldn't stand it any more.

3. How much did Mr. awson pay for the sweater?
   [A] $30.   [B] $13.
   [C] $80.   [D] $18.

4. What does 'staying healthy' mean today?

[A] You should often go to a doctor.   [B] Going to a doctor regularly helps.

[C] Keeping fit and strong all the time.   [D] You should never go to a doctor.

5. Where is the speaker?

   [A] In a bank.   [B] In a restaurant.

   [C] In an office.   [D] In a shop.

6. The speaker regretted having _____ .

   [A] missed the game   [B] gone to the game

   [C] won the game   [D] missed the bet

7. What does the speaker think about teachers?

   [A] Teachers get much satisfaction from work.

   [B] Teachers get little satisfaction from work.

   [C] Few teachers are satisfied with their work.

   [D] Few teachers are satisfied with their salary.

8. The speaker is comparing two _____ .

   [A] research projects   [B] political declarations

   [C] kinds of candies   [D] political events

Section B Conversation

In this section, you will hear nine short conversations between two speakers. At the end of each conversation you will be given 10 seconds to answer each of the following nine questions.

9. Who is the caller?

   [A] John Smith.   [B] Max Thomas.

   [C] Max Green.   [D] John Thomas.

10. The conversation takes place between _____ .

   [A] a host and a guest   [B] two neighbours

   [C] a doctor and a patient   [D] a hotel clerk and a guest

11. What did the man do last weekend?

   [A] He went skiing.   [B] He studied.

   [C] He did nothing.   [D] He did shopping.

12. What do you guess they'll do?

   [A] Go to the class at once.   [B] Make it in the dorm.

   [C] Skip over the work.   [D] Find out the assignment.

13. James is going to _____ .

   [A] buy a car   [B] stay at home

   [C] go to the party   [D] solve the problem

14. The man advised the woman to _____ .

   [A] find her way around   [B] enjoy herself thoroughly

   [C] remember her culture   [D] see the differences

15. The woman is supposed to be a(n)_____ .

[A] shop assistant   [B] job applicant

[C] interviewer   [D] receptionist

16. What did the woman do this morning?

    [A] She had the cooker changed.   [B] She had her cooker repaired.

    [C] She bought a new cooker.   [D] She returned her new cooker.

17. The woman intends to _____ .

    [A] offer the man a lift   [B] go with the man by bus

    [C] borrow the man's car   [D] check if he has a car

Section C　News Broadcast

Question 18 is based on the following news. At the end of the news item, you will be given 10 *seconds to answer the question.*

Now listen to the news.

18. Which of the following statements is TRUE?

    [A] Heavy rains and storms caused rivers to overflow.

    [B] Flooding forced evacuation in seven counties.

    [C] Flooding damaged homes and cut off electricity.

    [D] Heavy rains and flooding kept banks closed.

Question 19 is based on the following news. At the end of the news item, you will be given 10 *seconds to answer the question.*

Now listen to the news.

19. Who is going to make a visit?

    [A] The Iranian Foreign Minister.

    [B] The Iraqi Foreign Minister.

    [C] A senior Iraqi advisor.

    [D] A senior Iranian advisor.

Questions 20 and 21 are based on the following news. At the end of the news item, you will be given 20 *seconds to answer the questions.*

Now listen to the news.

20. The Senate bill aims to _____ within the next seven years.

    [A] end the country's huge public debts

    [B] cut government spendings on health

    [C] end the large budget deficit

    [D] cut some educational programmes

21. Congressional leaders have to work out a compromise because _____ .

    [A] a similar bill has been passed

    [B] the President might oppose the plan

    [C] the Senate bill was passed by 57 to 42

    [D] the White House is facing opposition

Question 22 is based on the following news. At the end of the news item, you will be given 10 seconds to answer the question.

  Now listen to the news.

22. Australia reacted towards the French test by _____ .

  [A] recalling her ambassador to Paris

  [B] describing the test as insignificant

  [C] expressing her regret

  [D] expressing disapproval

  Question 23 is based on the following news. At the end of the news item, you will be give 10 seconds to answer the question.

  Now listen to the news.

23. The Indian police were reported to have discovered _____ .

  [A] a large amount of money   [B] a large plastic bomb

  [C] similar explosives   [D] the bodies of many victims

  Questions 24 and 25 are based on the following news. At the end of the news item, you will be given 20 seconds to answer the questions.

  Now listen to the news.

24. The 6-day negotiations between the PLO and Israel are mainly about _____ .

  [A] the extension of Palestinian self-rule

  [B] the establishment of Jewish settlement

  [C] the arrangement of PLO troops

  [D] the reconstruction of Hebron

25. What progress has been made in their negotiations?

  [A] Israeli troops can stay on in the West Bank.

  [B] Israel has released thousands of prisoners.

  [C] PLO and Israel have made a final agreement.

  [D] Agreement has been reached on the future of Hebron.

1999 年英语专业四级考试听力理解

Part Ⅱ   Dictation

Listen to the following passage. Altogether the passage will be read to you four times. During the first reading, which will be read at normal speed, listen and try to understand the meaning. For the second and third readings, the passage will be read sentence by sentence, or phrase by phrase, with intervals of 15 seconds. The last reading will be read at normal speed again and during this time you should check your work. You will then be given 2 minutes to check through your work once more.

Please write the whole passage on Answer Sheet Two.

Part Ⅲ   Listening Comprehension

In Sections A, B and C you will hear everything once only. Listen carefully and then answer the questions that follow. Mark the correct answer to each question on your answer sheet.

Section A   Statement

In this section you will hear eight statements. At the end of each statement you will be given 10 seconds to answer each of the following eight questions.

1. How well did the speaker do in the test?
   [A] He answered the last four questions.
   [B] He answered the last few questions first.
   [C] He answered only some of the questions.
   [D] He answered all the questions except the first.

2. Jane thinks that Swiss cheese _____ .
   [A] tastes the best
   [B] tastes very bad
   [C] is better than butter cheese
   [D] is no better than other cheese

3. John went to _____ first.
   [A] the cinema
   [B] the repair shop

[C] the gas station   [D] the service station

4. Betty wishes to _____ .

   [A] send away the cleaning lady   [B] replace the cleaning lady

   [C] keep the cleaning lady   [D] do the house cleaning

5. How much did Fred pay for his car?

   [A] He paid half the price the salesman asked.

   [B] He paid twice as much as the salesman asked.

   [C] He paid the price the salesman asked.

   [D] He needn't have paid that much for the car.

6. Permanent education is practical because _____ .

   [A] there are no limits at all   [B] there are no age limits

   [C] no one is getting really too old   [D] no one wants to learn at old age

7. According to the speaker, the most difficult thing is _____ .

   [A] traveling from place to place   [B] keeping away from crowds

   [C] making holiday plans   [D] finding a place with many people

8. William lost his job because _____ .

   [A] he was always sick   [B] he usually went to work late

   [C] he made a mistake in his work   [D] he got angry with his boss

Section B   Conversation

   In this section, you will hear eight short conversations between two speakers. At the end of each conversation you will be given 10 seconds to answer each of the following eight questions.

9. Mark refused to take the job because _____ .

   [A] the working hours were not suitable   [B] the job was not well paid

   [C] he had to do a lot of travelling   [D] the job was quite difficult

10. What do they think about the restaurant?

   [A] The service there is not good.   [B] The food might not be good.

   [C] The waiter is not hospitable.   [D] The restaurant is too small.

11. Which language does Mary speak well?

   [A] Chinese.   [B] French.

   [C] Japanese.   [D] English.

12. The woman believes that John _____ .

   [A] was playing a joke   [B] was leaving Boston

   [C] was moving to Boston   [D] was selling his house himself

13. The woman should have arrived by _____ .

   [A] 10 : 45   [B] 10 : 40

   [C] 10 : 55   [D] 11 : 00

14. What do we learn from the conversation?

   [A] John is not sick.   [B] John is feeling better.

[C] Jack hasn't been sick.   [D] Jack has not got better.

15. The tone of the man is that of _____ .

     [A] surprise   [B] sarcasm

     [C] disappointment   [D] humour

16. The two speakers are probably _____ .

     [A] in a parking ground   [B] at a ferry-crossing

     [C] in a traffic jam   [D] at a petrol station

Section C   News Broadcast

Questions 17 and 18 are based on the following news. At the end of the news item, you will be given 20 seconds to answer the questions.

Now listen to the news.

17. Some Haitians are on strike in order to _____ .

     [A] get proper medical treatment   [B] ask for their political rights

     [C] protest against the US decision   [D] demand food supply aid from USA

18. The strikers are denied entry into the US because _____ .

     [A] AIDS virus has been found among them

     [B] they can not get political asylum in the US

     [C] the US government has refused to take them

     [D] they don't accept proper medical treatment

Question 19 is based on the following news. At the end of the news item, you will be given 10 seconds to answer the question.

Now listen to the news.

19. The US auto-makers decided to stop their action because _____ .

     [A] Japanese auto-makers promised to stop dumping cars in the US

     [B] the Government promised to solve the US-Japan trade imbalance

     [C] three US companies have ended the US-Japan trade imbalance

     [D] Japan agreed to sell cars at the agreed prices inside the US

Questions 20 and 21 are based on the following news. At the end of the news item, you will be given 20 seconds to answer the questions.

Now listen to the news.

20. Where did the storms first strike?

     [A] The eastern US.   [B] The Gulf of Mexico.

     [C] The Canadian border.   [D] Some areas in Cuba.

21. The storms have resulted in the following EXCEPT _____ .

     [A] death and damage   [B] disruption of air services

     [C] destruction of crops   [D] relocation of people

Question 22 is based on the following news. At the end of the news item, you will be given 10 seconds to answer the question.

Now listen to the news.

22. According to the news, France was strongly criticized for _____ .

　　[A] conducting five nuclear tests on Wednesday

　　[B] carrying out a series of nuclear tests in the Pacific

　　[C] getting disappointing results in the nuclear program

　　[D] refusing to sign a global treaty banning nuclear tests

　　Questions 23 is based on the following news. At the end of the news item, you will be given 10 seconds to answer the question.

　　Now listen to the news.

23. The news item is mainly about _____ .

　　[A] air traffic problems　　　　　　　[B] safety improvement

　　[C] the number of flights　　　　　　 [D] flight training courses

　　Questions 24 and 25 are based on the following news. At the end of the news item, you will be given 20 seconds to answer the questions.

　　Now listen to the news.

24. What is the purpose of the meeting in Luxembourg?

　　[A] To control patrol boats on the River Danube.

　　[B] To end economic sanctions against Serbia.

　　[C] To step up economic sanctions against Serbia.

　　[D] To send police officers to search the river.

25. International efforts against Serbia have been ineffective because _____ .

　　[A] ships carrying illegal supplies still sail along the river

　　[B] more illegal goods have been carried over land

　　[C] local authorities didn't attempt to stop illegal goods

　　[D] there has been disagreement over economic sanctions

2000 年英语专业四级考试听力理解

Part Ⅱ　　Dictation

Listen to the following passage. Altogether the passage will be read to you four times. During the first reading, which will be read at normal speed, listen and try to understand the meaning. For the second and third readings, the passage will be read sentence by sentence, or phrase by phrase, with intervals of 15 seconds. The last reading will be read at normal speed again and during this time you should check your work. You will then be given 2 minutes to check through your work once more.

Please write the whole passage on ANSWER SHEET TWO.

Part Ⅲ　　Listening Comprehension

In Sections A, B and C you will hear everything ONCE ONLY. Listen carefully and then answer the questions that follow. Mark the best answer to each question on your answer sheet.

Section A　　Statement

In this section you will hear nine statements. At the end of the statement you will be given 10 seconds to answer each of the following nine questions.

1. What is said about Harry's brother?
   [A] He is happy with his job.
   [B] He is a very ambitious man.
   [C] He is too ambitious to be an engine driver.
   [D] He doesn't like to be an engine driver.

2. What do you learn about Ms. Ellis?
   [A] She has been waiting.
   [B] She is examining her patient.
   [C] She is seeing her doctor.
   [D] She wouldn't mind waiting.

3. Joan is probably a _____ .
   [A] nurse
   [B] doctor
   [C] lawyer
   [D] saleswoman

4. The speaker sees Mary wear _____ different silk scarves in a week.

    [A] 2   [B] 5

    [C] 7   [D] 6

5. Where will the passengers change trains to go to Gilford?

    [A] East Croydon.   [B] Victoria.

    [C] Southeast.   [D] Red Hill.

6. What is the speaker probably doing?

    [A] Interviewing a clerk.   [B] Writing a job ad.

    [C] Dismissing a clerk.   [D] Making inquiries.

7. What does the speaker mean?

    [A] Emily is neither honest nor trustworthy.

    [B] Emily used to be honest only.

    [C] Emily used to be trustworthy only.

    [D] Emily is more than honest and trustworthy.

8. When does the next train leave?

    [A] 6 : 56.   [B] 7 : 00.

    [C] 7 : 28.   [D] 8 : 38.

9. What was wrong with Malcolm?

    [A] He had trouble working hard.   [B] He didn't know where to go.

    [C] He never went anywhere.   [D] He worked hard but never succeeded.

Section B   Conversation

In this section, you will hear eight short conversations between two speakers. At the end of each conversation you will be given 10 seconds to answer each of the following eight questions.

10. What's the probable relationship between the two speakers?

    [A] Teacher and student.   [B] Doctor and patient.

    [C] Lawyer and client.   [D] Boss and secretary.

11. What is the weather usually like in November?

    [A] Hotter than the present weather.   [B] More humid than the present weather.

    [C] Drier than the present weather.   [D] Cooler than the present weather.

12. What conclusion can we draw from this conversation?

    [A] Public buses are fast and cheap.

    [B] Parking is becoming a big problem.

    [C] Subway trains are even safer than taxis.

    [D] Taxis are more convenient than buses.

13. What are the two speakers talking about?

    [A] Fixing the woman's computer.

    [B] Ordering some new parts by Friday.

    [C] Getting the new parts ready by Friday.

[D] Sending the woman's computer for repair.

14. What can we learn from the conversation?

[A] Neither of them has a favourable opinion of the service.

[B] The woman is having a terrible time serving in the restaurant.

[C] Both agree it's time for the restaurant to fire some staff.

[D] The man thinks the restaurant is all right, but the woman doesn't.

15. Who will pay for the call?

[A] The man.   [B] The operator.

[C] The man's sister.   [D] The man and his sister.

16. What does the man think of the woman's choice of clothing?

[A] He thinks her choice is good.   [B] He thinks her choice is terrible.

[C] He doesn't like the colour.   [D] He doesn't like the style.

17. What happened to Mr. Hunt's project?

[A] It was fairly successful.   [B] It was hard and futile.

[C] It failed for lack of fund.   [D] It stopped for lack of land.

Section C   News Broadcast

Question 18 is based on the following news. At the end of the news item, you will be given 10 seconds to answer the question.

Now listen to the news.

18. According to the news, NATO and Russia _____ .

[A] have finalized a charter on their new relationship

[B] still have differences in military and political issues

[C] will hold a fifth round of talks in Luxembourg

[D] made no progress in this round of talks

Questions 19 and 20 are based on the following news. At the end of the news item, you will be given 20 seconds to answer the two questions.

Now listen to the news.

19. _____ people were killed during the air crash.

[A] 61   [B] 51   [C] 41   [D] 10

20. According to the news, the plane crashed _____ .

[A] shortly before it landed   [B] minutes after it took off

[C] after it cleared the mountains   [D] at the foot of the mountains

Questions 21 and 22 are based on the following news. At the end of the news item, you will be given 20 seconds to answer the two questions.

Now listen to the news.

21. Which of the following is NOT listed as a terrorist group by the US?

[A] The pro-Iranian Hezbollah.   [B] The Palestinian group Hamas.

[C] The Irish Republican Army.   [D] The Basque separatist group ETA.

22. The affected groups will be prevented from _____ .

   [A] entering the United States legally

   [B] freezing US financial assets abroad

   [C] receiving support from other countries

   [D] giving weapons to other terrorist groups

   Question 23 is based on the following news. At the end of the news item, you will be given 10 seconds to answer the question.

   Now listen to the news.

23. Israeli Prime Minister Benjamin Netanyahu _____ .

   [A] has been prosecuted by the Justice Ministry

   [B] may be prosecuted by the Justice Ministry

   [C] has been prosecuted by the police

   [D] will be prosecuted on Monday

   Questions 24 and 25 are based on the following news. At the end of the news item, you will be given 20 seconds to answer the two questions.

   Now listen to the news.

24. The winners of the reported elections are _____ .

   [A] the left-wing Conservatives   [B] the left-wing Socialists

   [C] the centre-right Conservatives   [D] the centre-right Socialists

25. If the left secures the parliamentary majority, _____ .

   [A] Chirac will share his presidential power with Jospin

   [B] Jospin will share his prime ministerial power with Chirac

   [C] Jospin will become prime minister, and Chirac will remain

   [D] Jospin will become prime minister, and Chirac will resign

2001 年英语专业四级考试听力理解

Part II   Dictation

Listen to the following passage. Altogether the passage will be read to you four times. During the first reading, which will be read at normal speed, listen and try to understand the meaning. For the second and third readings, the passage will be read sentence by sentence, or phrase by phrase, with intervals of 15 seconds. The last reading will be read at normal speed again and during this time you should check your work. You will then be given 2 minutes to check through your work once more.

Please write the whole passage on Answer Sheet Two.

Part III   Listening Comprehension

In Sections A, B and C you will hear everything once only. Listen carefully and then answer the questions that follow. Mark the correct answer to each question on your answer sheet.

Section A   Statement

In this section you will hear nine statements. At the end of each statement you will be given 10 seconds to answer the question.

1. The speaker likes teaching because of _____ .
   [A] its interesting nature   [B] the good salaries
   [C] contact with the young   [D] more summer holidays

2. What does the speaker mean?
   [A] Bad living conditions are due to the poor city.
   [B] Bad planning is responsible for poor living conditions.
   [C] Living conditions are bad because the city is too big.
   [D] Small cities have better living conditions than large ones.

3. What does the statement mean?
   [A] Many people are concerned about their security.

[B] Social security bears no relation to population.

[C] Most social security problems are caused by a few people.

[D] Too many people may result in social security problems.

4. Passengers must check in to board Flight 998 by _____ .

   [A] 10 : 30 am   [B] 10 : 00 am

   [C] 11 : 30 am   [D] 11 : 00 am

5. The speaker is probably a(n) _____ .

   [A] insurance agent   [B] fireman

   [C] salesman   [D] policeman

6. The speaker thinks that _____ .

   [A] Ian achieved a lot as an athlete

   [B] Ian's blind eye prevented him from athletics

   [C] Ian's success depended on his childhood experience

   [D] Ian trained so hard in athletics as to lose one eye

7. Mrs. Clark is worried about her _____ .

   [A] husband's health   [B] husband's work

   [C] husband's illness   [D] own health

8. The relationship between Susan and Jenny is _____ .

   [A] neutral   [B] friendly

   [C] unclear   [D] strained

9. What do we learn about Jack?

   [A] He is well-known for hard work.

   [B] He is pretty busy working.

   [C] He has overworked and hurt his sight.

   [D] He doesn't like to have dinner with us.

Section B   Conversation

   In this section, you will hear nine short conversations between two speakers. At the end of each conversation you will be given 10 seconds to answer the question.

10. What are they mainly talking about?

   [A] Graduation date.   [B] Vacation plans.

   [C] School courses.   [D] Job hunting.

11. The conversation probably takes place in _____ .

   [A] a library   [B] a bookstore

   [C] the classroom   [D] a department store

12. The relationship between the two speakers is probably _____ .

   [A] man and wife   [B] lawyer and client

   [C] customer and waitress   [D] colleagues

13. We can infer from the conversation that the man is a(n) _____ .

[A] plumber   [B] construction worker

[C] office boy   [D] porter

14. What will the man probably do next?

     [A] Turn off the tape recorder.   [B] Turn up the tape recorder.

     [C] Call the doctor.   [D] Continue to play.

15. How does Lisa feel about her work?

     [A] Satisfied.   [B] Frustrated.

     [C] Annoyed.   [D] Confident.

16. The woman is going to the _____ .

     [A] library   [B] theatre

     [C] research institute   [D] laboratory

17. Jackson changed his job because he _____ .

     [A] hurt himself during his work   [B] was not satisfied with his pay

     [C] wanted to work harder   [D] found the job too hard

18. What does the woman say about the film?

     [A] It is hard to pronounce the name.   [B] It is not going to be well received.

     [C] She has temporarily forgotten its name.   [D] She has never heard of the name.

Section C   News Broadcast

Questions 19 and 20 are based on the following news. At the end of the news item, you will be given 20 seconds to answer the questions.

Now listen to the news.

19. Nigeria returned to the Commonwealth after _____ .

     [A] she had sentenced minority rights activists to death

     [B] the military had resumed control of the country

     [C] power had been handed over to an elected president

     [D] she had negotiated with Commonwealth leaders

20. The Commonwealth consists of _____ countries which were former British colonies.

     [A] 54   [B] 29

     [C] 9   [D] 95

Questions 21 and 22 are based on the following news. At the end of the news item, you will be given 20 seconds to answer the questions.

Now listen to the news.

21. The space shuttle Discovery completed a _____ mission upon its return to the Kennedy Space Centre.

     [A] 11-day   [B] 94-day

     [C] 10-day   [D] 49-day

22. When the spacecraft was going to land, _____ .

     [A] it produced a lot of noise   [B] there were scattered showers

[C] people could see it high in the sky   [D] people could neither see nor hear it

Questions 23 and 24 are based on the following news. At the end of the news item, you will be given 20 seconds to answer the questions.

Now listen to the news.

23. How many people died during the collision?

    [A] Two.   [B] Eighteen.

    [C] Three.   [D] Five.

24. Three Albanians were arrested for _____ .

    [A] attacking the patrol boat   [B] smuggling in refugees

    [C] causing the accident   [D] injuring refugees

Question 25 is based on the following news. At the end of the news item, you will be given 10 seconds to answer the question.

Now listen to the news.

25. The news item is mainly about _____ .

    [A] efforts to salvage Sun Vista

    [B] negotiation with the ship's owner

    [C] threats Sun Vista poses to passing ships

    [D] a newspaper's comment on Sun Vista

2002 年英语专业四级考试听力理解

Part Ⅱ Dictation

Listen to the following passage. Altogether the passage will be read to you four times. During the first reading, which will be read at normal speed, listen and try to understand the meaning. For the second and third readings, the passage will be read sentence by sentence, or phrase by phrase, with intervals of 15 seconds. The last reading will be read at normal speed again and during this time you should check your work. You will then be given 2 minutes to check through your work once more.

Please write the whole passage on ANSWER SHEET TWO.

Part Ⅲ Listening Comprehension

In Sections A, B and C you will hear everything once only. Listen carefully and then answer the questions that follow. Mark the correct answer to each question on your answer sheet.

Section A Statement

In this section you will hear eight statements. At the end of each statement you will be given 10 seconds to answer the question.

1. The speaker is most probably a(n) _____.
   - [A] architect
   - [B] construction worker
   - [C] tourist guide
   - [D] housing agent

2. What does the statement mean?
   - [A] Travel is much faster and convenient now than before.
   - [B] People are now travelling much more than in old days.
   - [C] Travelling to far-away places has become very common.
   - [D] It used to take two more weeks to travel by coach than now.

3. The speaker feels sorry because _____.
   - [A] he can't attend tomorrow's dinner

[B] his wife can't attend tomorrow's dinner

[C] the couple can't attend tomorrow's dinner

[D] the couple would be unable to cook the dinner

4. Where is the speaker?

[A] In the zoo.　　　　　　　　　　[B] In the classroom.

[C] In the library.　　　　　　　　　[D] At a meeting.

5. What does the statement mean?

[A] One's success is largely dependent on intelligence.

[B] Low motivation may lead to poor performance.

[C] Motivated people are more likely to succeed.

[D] Both motivation and intelligence are important.

6. What does the speaker suggest?

[A] We should read word by word to get his meaning.

[B] We should read line by line to get his meaning.

[C] We should try to find the hidden meaning.

[D] We should try to find the lines and read them aloud.

7. How much does the overcoat cost at the regular price?

[A] £ 120.　　　　　　　　　　　　[B] £ 15.

[C] £ 60.　　　　　　　　　　　　　[D] £ 45.

8. What does the speaker mean?

[A] The sports meet has been cancelled.

[B] The sports meet has been held despite the rain.

[C] The time has been set for the sports meet.

[D] When the sports meet will be held is yet to be known.

Section B　Conversation

In this section, you will hear nine short conversations between two speakers. At the end of each conversation you will be given 10 seconds to answer the question.

9. What are the speakers probably going to do?

[A] To persuade Mary to spend more time on her lessons.

[B] To help Mary to prepare for the upcoming concert.

[C] To talk with Mary about going to the concert.

[D] To ask Mary to stop worrying about the exam.

10. What can we learn about the man?

[A] He firmly believes in UFOs.

[B] He is doubtful about UFOs.

[C] He is sure many people have seen UFOs.

[D] He thinks many people have lied about UFOs.

11. Which of the following has the man never been interested in?

[A] Electronic music.   [B] Civil engineering.

[C] Electronics.   [D] Electronic engineering.

12. What does the man mean?

[A] The milk is safe to drink.   [B] The milk is not safe to drink.

[C] She shouldn't have bought the milk.   [D] He wouldn't have milk for breakfast.

13. How many people were caught in the fire?

[A] 6.   [B] 5.

[C] 4.   [D] 7.

14. What can we learn from the conversation?

[A] The woman will attend her course at 7：45.

[B] The woman will be late for the blood test.

[C] The woman will have her blood tested before the first class.

[D] The woman decides to miss the first class for her blood test.

15. What is the probable relationship between the two speakers?

[A] Salesman and customer.   [B] Expert on jewelry and his wife.

[C] Estate agent and client.   [D] Husband and wife.

16. How does the man probably feel?

[A] Nervous.   [B] Uninterested.

[C] Confident.   [D] Upset.

17. What do we know about Bill?

[A] He is thoughtful.   [B] He is forgetful.

[C] He is careless.   [D] He is helpful.

Section C   News Broadcast

Questions 18 and 19 are based on the following news. At the end of the news item, you will be given 20 seconds to answer the questions.

Now, listen to the news.

18. Which of the following is NOT a condition for the reduction of debts?

[A] Poverty elimination.   [B] Good government.

[C] Fight against corruption.   [D] Poor living standard.

19. By cancelling the debts owed to her, Britain intends to _____ a similar scheme proposed by the International Monetary Fund.

[A] reject   [B] restart

[C] follow   [D] review

Questions 20 and 21 are based on the following news. At the end of the news item, you will be given 20 seconds to answer the questions.

Now, listen to the news.

20. What happened during the accident?

[A] A train hit another train.   [B] A train killed 23 people.

[C] A train went off its tracks.   [D] A train was trapped inside the station.

21. Which of the following statements best describes the condition of the passengers?

    [A] No one was fatally injured.

    [B] There were many heavy casualties.

    [C] No one was hurt during the accident.

    [D] Someone was killed during the accident.

    Questions 22 and 23 are based on the following news. At the end of the news item, you will be given 20 seconds to answer the questions.

    Now, listen to the news.

22. The civil servants held a strike to protest _____.

    [A] spending cuts   [B] reform measures

    [C] pay cuts   [D] low pay

23. The civil servants' strike was staged _____ the general strike.

    [A] a few days after   [B] a few days before

    [C] a few weeks after   [D] a few weeks before

    Questions 24 and 25 are based on the following news. At the end of the news item, you will be given 20 seconds to answer the questions.

    Now, listen to the news.

24. Which is the main idea of the news?

    [A] Industrial relations in Germany.   [B] The German energy industry.

    [C] Coalition in the government.   [D] Closure of nuclear reactors.

25. The decision to shut down nuclear reactors resulted from the demand from _____.

    [A] the Government   [B] the energy industry

    [C] a party in the coalition   [D] a declining need for nuclear energy

2003 年英语专业四级考试听力理解

Part Ⅱ　Dictation

Listen to the following passage. Altogether the passage will be read to you four times. During the first reading, which will be read at normal speed, listen and try to understand the meaning. For the second and third readings, the passage will be read sentence by sentence, or phrase by phrase, with intervals of 15 seconds. The last reading will be read at normal speed again and during this time you should check your work. You will then be given 2 minutes to check through your work once more.

Please write the whole passage on ANSWER SHEET TWO.

Part Ⅲ　Listening Comprehension

In Sections A, B and C you will hear everything ONCE ONLY. Listen carefully and then answer the questions that follow. Mark the correct answer to each question on your answer sheet.

Section A　Statement

In this section you will hear seven statements. At the end of each statement you will be given 10 seconds to answer the question.

1. Which is NOT true about the listener?
   [A] He works hard.　　　　　　　　[B] He drinks a lot.
   [C] He smokes a lot.　　　　　　　　[D] He is healthy.

2. How did the speaker feel when he heard the news?
   [A] He was satisfied.　　　　　　　　[B] He was annoyed.
   [C] He was astonished.　　　　　　　[D] He was relieved.

3. When does the next coach leave?
   [A] At 9：10.　　　　　　　　　　　[B] At 9：15.
   [C] At 9：20.　　　　　　　　　　　[D] At 9：05.

4. The speaker thinks that Jane might have _____.

[A] a better marriage   [B] a better career

[C] a better education   [D] a better family life

5. What does the statement mean?

   [A] I am too happy to be helpful in any way.

   [B] I am willing but unable to help you.

   [C] I shall be very glad to offer my help.

   [D] I promise to think about how to help you.

6. What does the statement imply?

   [A] The man was wearing clean clothes.

   [B] The man was wearing improper clothes.

   [C] The man was wearing fanciful clothes.

   [D] The man was wearing dirty clothes.

7. What does the speaker mean?

   [A] I believe I can find you in other places as well.

   [B] I had no idea that I could find you here.

   [C] I believe that I can only find you in this place.

   [D] This is not the place for me to meet you.

Section B   Conversation

   In this section, you will hear ten short conversations between two speakers. At the end of each conversation you will be given 10 seconds to answer the question.

8. What is the probable relationship between the two speakers?

   [A] Salesman and customer.   [B] Doctor and nurse.

   [C] Doctor and patient.   [D] Patient and patient.

9. What does the man think of his writing?

   [A] Writing will not be easy.   [B] Writing will be less difficult.

   [C] Writing has been boring.   [D] Writing has been enjoyable.

10. What can we learn from the conversation?

    [A] Cold is a kind of serious illness.   [B] Cold will go away quickly.

    [C] You should go to see a doctor.   [D] You needn't do anything about it.

11. What did the man assume previously?

    [A] She would go to the bookstore.   [B] She would not go to the bookstore.

    [C] She would go to the bookstore later.   [D] She would go to another bookstore.

12. What do we know about the flight?

    [A] There will be a short delay.   [B] There will be a long delay.

    [C] The flight has been canceled.   [D] The condition is still uncertain.

13. What does the man say about Linda?

    [A] She is forgetful.   [B] She is considerate.

    [C] She is forgiving.   [D] She is careless.

14. What does the woman mean?

　　[A] She doesn't believe he can do it.　　[B] She agrees with the man.

　　[C] She expects to see him soon.　　[D] She will go to the library.

15. What does the man think of the woman's choice of clothing?

　　[A] He thinks her choice is good.　　[B] He thinks her choice is terrible.

　　[C] He doesn't like the colour.　　[D] He doesn't like the style.

16. Sam refused to take the job because _____.

　　[A] the working hours were unsuitable　　[B] the job was not well paid

　　[C] he had to do a lot of travelling　　[D] the job was quite difficult

17. The man sounds _____.

　　[A] surprised　　[B] ignorant

　　[C] humorous　　[D] disappointed

Section C   News Broadcast

Questions 18 and 19 are based on the following news. At the end of the news item, you will be given 20 seconds to answer the questions.

Now, listen to the news.

18. The UN resolution is about international efforts in tightening control on _____.

　　[A] terrorism activities　　[B] terrorists' networks

　　[C] weapons for terrorists　　[D] funding for terrorism

19. What does the UN resolution specifically require states to do?

　　[A] To establish a financial network.　　[B] To revise their banking laws.

　　[C] To increase their police force.　　[D] To curb regional terror activities.

Questions 20 and 21 are based on the following news. At the end of the news item, you will be given 20 seconds to answer the questions.

Now, listen to the news.

20. Altogether how many people were injured during the violence?

　　[A] 1.　　[B] 2.

　　[C] 13.　　[D] 14.

21. How long has the violence lasted?

　　[A] For one day.　　[B] For two days.

　　[C] For the whole summer.　　[D] For one year.

Question 22 is based on the following news. At the end of the news item, you will be given 10 seconds to answer the question.

Now, listen to the news.

22. After the terrorist attacks in the United States, insurance rates soared as much as _____.

　　[A] 100%　　[B] 200%

　　[C] 500%　　[D] 1000%

Questions 23 and 24 are based on the following news. At the end of the news item, you will

be given 20 *seconds to answer the questions.*

Now, listen to the news.

23. Eight foreign aid workers were arrested in Afghanistan because of their _____ activities.

    [A] political　　　　　　　　　　　　[B] espionage

    [C] religious　　　　　　　　　　　　[D] relief

24. Which of the following is NOT mentioned as one of the penalties?

    [A] A fine.　　　　　　　　　　　　　[B] Expulsion.

    [C] A jail term.　　　　　　　　　　　[D] Death sentence.

Question 25 is based on the following news. At the end of the news item, you will be given

10 *seconds to answer the question.*

Now, listen to the news.

25. According to the report, how many people are HIV-positive?

    [A] 22 million.　　　　　　　　　　　[B] 36 million.

    [C] 25 million.　　　　　　　　　　　[D] 58 million.

2004 年英语专业四级考试听力理解

Part Ⅱ   Dictation

Listen to the following passage. Altogether the passage will be read to you four times. During the first reading, which will be read at normal speed, listen and try to understand the meaning. For the second and third readings, the passage will be read sentence by sentence, or phrase by phrase, with intervals of 15 seconds. The last reading will be read at normal speed again and during this time you should check your work. You will then be given 2 minutes to check through your work once more.

Please write the whole passage on ANSWER SHEET TWO.

Part Ⅲ   Listening Comprehension

In Sections A, B and C you will hear everything ONCE ONLY. Listen carefully and then answer the questions that follow. Mark the correct answer to each question on your answer sheet.

Section A   Statement

In this section you will hear eight statements. At the end of each statement you will be given 10 seconds to answer each question.

1. Where is Lily working now?
   [A] In the police department.　　　　　[B] In a drama society.
   [C] In a university.　　　　　　　　　　[D] In a primary school.

2. Passengers must check in to board Flight 5125 by _____.
   [A] 11 : 00　　　[B] 11 : 20　　　[C] 11 : 30　　　[D] 11 : 50

3. Which of the following statements is true?
   [A] There is a strike across the country.
   [B] Many trains have been cancelled.
   [C] A few trains have been cancelled.
   [D] There is a strike in the North Region.

4. The death and missing numbers in the floods are respectively _____.

    [A]60/9   [B]16/9   [C]9/60   [D]9/16

5. What is John supposed to do on Sunday?

    [A]Call the office.   [B]Revise his paper.

    [C]Solve the problem.   [D]Hand in the paper.

6. What do we know about Mary Jackson?

    [A]She is the speaker's friend.   [B]She likes stories.

    [C]She is an author.   [D]She gave a gift.

7. What do we know about the speaker?

    [A]The speaker can get good tips.   [B]The speaker pays for the meals.

    [C]The speaker can get good wages. [D]The speaker lives comfortably.

8. What will the speaker probably do next?

    [A]To buy some medicine.   [B]To buy a new cupboard.

    [C]To ignore the matter.   [D]To investigate the matter.

Section B   Conversation

    In this section, you will hear nine short conversations between two speakers. At the end of each conversation you will be given 10 seconds to answer each question.

9. When will they discuss the agenda?

    [A]Before dinner.   [B]During dinner.

    [C]After dinner.   [D]Tomorrow.

10. What can be inferred about the woman?

    [A]She'll be travelling during the vacation.

    [B]She'll be working during the vacation.

    [C]She's looking forward to going home.

    [D]She will offer her help to Jane.

11. What is the cause of their complaint?

    [A]The place.   [B]The heat.

    [C]The workload.   [D]The facilities.

12. What can be concluded about Janet?

    [A]She has come to the party.

    [B]She is hosting the party.

    [C]She hasn't turned up.

    [D]She is planning a party.

13. Where does the conversation probably take place?

    [A]In a hotel.   [B]At a bus station.

    [C]In a restaurant.   [D]At an airport.

14. What does the woman intend to do?

    [A]Get a job on campus.   [B]Get her resume ready.

[C] Visit the company.   [D] Apply for a job with PICC.

15. What are the man and woman doing?

    [A] Listening to the radio.   [B] Looking at the photos.

    [C] Watching television.   [D] Reading a newspaper.

16. What does the man mean?

    [A] He hopes the party will be successful.

    [B] He will see the woman around five.

    [C] He is eager to help the woman.

    [D] He is unenthusiastic about the party.

17. What is NOT a change to the literature class?

    [A] Class location.   [B] Class times.

    [C] Class length.   [D] Class size.

Section C   News Broadcast

Questions 18 and 19 are based on the following news. At the end of the news item, you will be given 20 seconds to answer the questions.

    Now, listen to the news.

18. The journalist was brought to court because _____.

    [A] he was working for a British newspaper

    [B] he published an untrue story

    [C] the story was published in Britain

    [D] he was working with other foreign journalists

19. How did the lawyer defend for the journalist?

    [A] He was an American journalist.

    [B] He worked for a British newspaper.

    [C] His story was published elsewhere.

    [D] Foreigners are not subject to local laws.

Questions 20 and 21 are based on the following news. At the end of the news item, you will be given 20 seconds to answer the questions.

    Now, listen to the news.

20. Afghanistan's first match will be against _____.

    [A] Mongolia   [B] South Korea

    [C] Iran   [D] Qatar

21. Which of the following statements is NOT true?

    [A] The announcement was made by AFA.

    [B] Afghanistan was a founding member of AFC.

    [C] Afghanistan had been in chaos for long.

    [D] The football players were under 23.

Questions 22 and 23 are based on the following news. At the end of the news item, you will

be given 20 *seconds to answer the questions*.

    Now, *listen to the news*.

22. The expected life-span of Beijing residents has gone up by _____ compared with that a decade earlier.

    [A] 1. 5 years   [B] 1. 4 years   [C] 1. 2 years   [D] 1. 1 years

23. The _____ mortality rate had gone up greatly during the past 10 years.

    [A] infant   [B] maternal

    [C] male   [D] middle-aged

    Questions 24 and 25 are based on the following news. *At the end of the news item*, *you will be given 20 seconds to answer the questions*.

    Now, *listen to the news*.

24. According to Pakistan's President, the chances of the two countries going to war were _____.

    [A] great   [B] small

    [C] growing   [D] greater than before

25. Recent tensions between the two countries were a direct result of _____.

    [A] their border conflicts   [B] their military build-up

    [C] killings in the two countries   [D] their mutual distrust

2005 年英语专业四级考试听力理解

Part Ⅰ Dictation

Listen to the following passage. Altogether the passage will be read to you four times. During the first reading, which will be read at normal speed, listen and try to understand the meaning. For the second and third readings, the passage will be read sentence by sentence, or phrase by phrase, with intervals of 15 seconds. The last reading will be read at normal speed again and during this time you should check your work. You will then be given 2 minutes to check through your work once more.

Please write the whole passage on ANSWER SHEET ONE.

Part Ⅱ Listening Comprehension

In Sections A, B and C you will hear everything ONCE ONLY. Listen carefully and then answer the questions that follow. Mark the correct answer to each question on your answer sheet.

Section A Conversation

In this section you will hear several conversations. Listen to the conversations carefully and then answer the questions that follow.

Questions 1 to 3 are based on the following conversation. At the end of the conversation, you will be given 15 seconds to answer the questions.

Now listen to the conversation.

1. According to the conversation, Mr. Johnson is NOT very strong in _____.

   [A] history [B] geography [C] mathematics [D] art

2. Mr. Johnson thinks that _____ can help him a lot in the job.

   [A] logic [B] writing [C] history [D] mathematics

3. Mr. Johnson would like to work as a(n) _____

   [A] adviser [B] computer programmer

   [C] product designer [D] school teacher

Questions 4 to 7 are based on the following conversation. At the end of the conversation, you will be given 20 seconds to answer the questions.

Now listen to the conversation.

4. What is the main purpose of the research?

　　[A] To make preparations for a new publication.

　　[B] To learn how couples spend their weekends.

　　[C] To know how housework is shared.

　　[D] To investigate what people do at the weekend.

5. What does the man do on Fridays?

　　[A] He goes to exercise classes.　　　　　　[B] He goes sailing.

　　[C] He goes to the cinema.　　　　　　　　[D] He stays at home.

6. On which day does the couple always go out?

　　[A] Friday.　　　　　　　　　　　　　　[B] Saturday.

　　[C] Sunday.　　　　　　　　　　　　　　[D] Any weekday.

7. Which personal detail does the man give?

　　[A] Surname.　　　　　　　　　　　　　[B] First name.

　　[C] Address.　　　　　　　　　　　　　[D] Age.

Questions 8 to 10 are based on the following conversation. At the end of the conversation, you will be given 15 seconds to answer the questions.

Now listen to the conversation.

8. Parcel Express needs the following details about the sender EXCEPT _____.

　　[A] name　　　　　　　　　　　　　　[B] address

　　[C] receipt　　　　　　　　　　　　　[D] phone number

9. Parcels must be left open mainly for _____.

　　[A] customs' check　　　　　　　　　　[B] security check

　　[C] convenience's sake　　　　　　　　[D] the company's sake

10. The woman's last inquiry is mainly concerned with _____.

　　[A] the time needed for sending the parcel

　　[B] the flight time to New York

　　[C] the parcel destination

　　[D] parcel collection

Section B　Passages

In this section, you will hear several passages. Listen to the passages carefully and then answer the questions that follow.

Questions 11 to 13 are based on the following announcement. At the end of the announcement, you will be given 15 seconds to answer the questions.

Now listen to the announcement.

11. Where is the train to Nanjing now standing?

[A] At Platform 7.   [B] At Platform 8.

[C] At Platform 9.   [D] At Platform 13.

12. Which train will now leave at 11：35?

     [A] The train to Jinan.   [B] The train to Zhengzhou.

     [C] The train to Tianjin.   [D] The train to Hangzhou.

13. Which train has now been cancelled?

     [A] The train to Jinan.   [B] The train to Zhengzhou.

     [C] The train to Tianjin.   [D] The train to Hangzhou.

Questions 14 to 16 are based on the following passage. At the end of the passage, you will be given 15 seconds to answer the questions.

     Now listen to the passage.

14. The museum was built in memory of those _____.

     [A] who died in wars   [B] who worked to help victims

     [C] who lost their families in disasters   [D] who fought in wars

15. Henry Durant put forward the idea because he _____.

     [A] had once fought in a war in Italy

     [B] had been wounded in a war

     [C] had assisted in treating the wounded

     [D] had seen the casualties and cruelties of war

16. Which of the following statements about the symbols is INCORRECT?

     [A] Both are used as the organization's official symbols.

     [B] Both are used regardless of religious significance.

     [C] The red cross was the organization's original symbol.

     [D] The red crescent was later adopted for use in certain regions.

Questions 17 to 20 are based on the following passage. At the end of the passage, you will be given 20 seconds to answer the questions.

     Now listen to the passage.

17. How should cheerleading be viewed according to the passage?

     [A] It is just a lot of cheering.   [B] It mainly involves yelling.

     [C] It mainly involves dancing.   [D] It is competitive in nature.

18. How do the cheerleaders perform their jobs?

     [A] They set fireworks for their team.

     [B] They put on athletic shows.

     [C] They run around the spectators.

     [D] They yell for people to buy drinks.

19. Why do the cheerleaders sometimes suffer physical injuries?

     [A] Because they try dangerous acts to catch people's attention.

     [B] Because they shout and yell so their voice becomes hoarse.

     [C] Because they go to the pyramid and the hills to perform.

[D] Because they dance too much every day for practice.

20. Which of the following statements is NOT true?

 [A] The first cheerleader was a man named John Campbell.

 [B] Cheerleaders' contests are only held at the state level.

 [C] Before 1930 there were no women cheerleaders.

 [D] The first cheerleading occurred in 1898.

Section C   News Broadcast

In this section you will hear several news items. Listen to them carefully and then answer the questions that follow.

Questions 21 to 22 are based on the following news. At the end of the news item, you will be given 10 seconds to answer the questions.

Now listen to the news.

21. How many of the emigrants died after being thrown into the sea?

 [A] 15 of them.   [B] 3 of them.

 [C] 100 of them.   [D] Dozens of them.

22. The illegal emigrants came from _____.

 [A] Italy   [B] Africa

 [C] the Mediterranean region   [D] places unknown

Question 23 is based on the following news. At the end of the news item, you will be given 5 seconds to answer the question.

Now listen to the news.

23. What does the news item mainly report?

 [A] China will send three people into space in a week.

 [B] Three Chinese astronauts will spend a week in space.

 [C] The Shenzhou Ⅵ will be launched next year.

 [D] Shenzhou Ⅴ circled the earth for two days.

Questions 24 and 25 are based on the following news. At the end of the news item, you will be given 10 seconds to answer the questions.

Now listen to the news.

24. Which of the following has NOT been affected by the wildfires?

 [A] Houses.   [B] Land.   [C] Skies.   [D] Cars.

25. The fires were thought to have been started _____.

 [A] purposefully   [B] accidentally

 [C] on the Mexican border   [D] in southern California

Questions 26 to 28 are based on the following news. At the end of the news item, you will be given 15 seconds to answer the question.

Now listen to the news.

26. _____ ranks second among leading tourism nations.

[A] France   [B] The United States
[C] Spain   [D] Italy

27. It is predicted that by 2020 China will receive _____ visitors.
    [A] 77 million   [B] 130 million
    [C] 36. 8 million   [D] 100 million

28. According to a Xinhua report, last year saw a _____ per cent increase in the number of Chinese traveling abroad.
    [A] 16. 6   [B] 30   [C] 100   [D] 37

   Questions 29 and 30 are based on the following news. At the end of the news item, you will be given 10 seconds to answer the questions.

   Now listen to the news.

29. What would happen to the Argentine officers?
    [A] They would be arrested by Spanish authorities.
    [B] They would be tried in an Argentine court.
    [C] They would be sent to Spain for trial.
    [D] They would be tortured or murdered.

30. What accusation would the Argentine officers face?
    [A] Violation of human rights.
    [B] Involvement in illegal actions.
    [C] Planning anti-government activities.
    [D] Being part of the military rule.

2006 年英语专业四级考试听力理解

Part I   Dictation

Listen to the following passage. Altogether the passage will be read to you four times. During the first reading, which will be read at normal speed, listen and try to understand the meaning. For the second and third readings, the passage will be read sentence by sentence, or phrase by phrase, with intervals of 15 seconds. The last reading will be read at normal speed again and during this time you should check your work. You will then be given 2 minutes to check through your work once more.

Please write the whole passage on ANSWER SHEET ONE.

Part II   Listening Comprehension

In Sections A, B and C you will hear everything ONCE ONLY. Listen carefully and then answer the questions that follow. Mark the correct answer to each question on your answer sheet.

Section A   Conversation

In this section you will hear several conversations. Listen to the conversations carefully and then answer the questions that follow.

Questions 1 to 3 are based on the following conversation. At the end of the conversation, you will be given 15 seconds to answer the questions.

Now listen to the conversation.

1. How did Mark get there?
   [A] By train and by car.   [B] By plane and by coach.
   [C] By train and by bus.   [D] By bus and by plane.
2. Mark used to wear all the following EXCEPT _____.
   [A] short hair   [B] glasses   [C] moustache   [D] beard
3. Where is the meeting of new students to be held?
   [A] In the third room on the right.   [B] In the Common Room.

[C] In a room at the other end.　　　　　　[D] In Room 501.

Questions 4 to 6 are based on the following conversation. At the end of the conversation, you will be given 15 seconds to answer the questions.

Now listen to the conversation.

4. What did Steve originally plan to do?

[A] To go to a park near the beach.　　　　[B] To stay at home.

[C] To see a new film.　　　　　　　　　　[D] To do some study.

5. Maggie finally decided to go to see a film because _____.

[A] there was no park nearby

[B] the weather wasn't ideal for a walk

[C] it would be easier to go to a cinema

[D] Steve hadn't seen the film yet

6. Where did they plan to meet?

[A] Outside the Town Hall.　　　　　　　　[B] Near the bank.

[C] In Steve's place.　　　　　　　　　　　[D] At the cinema.

Questions 7 to 10 are based on the following conversation. At the end of the conversation, you will be given 20 seconds to answer the questions.

Now listen to the conversation.

7. The following details are true about the new device EXCEPT _____.

[A] it has a clolour　　　　　　　　　　　[B] it has a moving image

[C] is costs less money　　　　　　　　　[D] it is not on the market

8. Why didn't Bill want one of them?

[A] He wanted to buy one from Japan.

[B] He wasn't sure about its quality.

[C] He thought it was for business use.

[D] He thought it was expensive.

9. Which of the following statements is INCORRECT about the woman?

[A] She had never read the magazine herself.

[B] She knew who usually read the magazine.

[C] She was quite interested in the new device.

[D] She agreed with Bill at the end of the conversation.

10. The conversation is mainly about _____.

[A] a new type of telephone

[B] the cost of telephone

[C] some features of the magazine

[D] the readership of the magazine

Section B　Passages

In this section, you will hear several passages. Listen to the passages carefully and then an-

swer the questions that follow.

Questions 11 to 13 are based on the following announcement. At the end of the announcement, you will be given 15 seconds to answer the questions.

Now listen to the announcement.

11. In the old days dogs were used for the following EXCEPT _____.
    [A] hunting other animals   [B] driving sheep
    [C] guarding chickens   [D] keeping thieves away

12. Which of the following is CORRECT?
    [A] Dogs are now treated as part of a family.
    [B] Dogs still perform all the duties they used to do.
    [C] People now keep dogs for the same reasons as before.
    [D] Only old people are seen walking their dogs.

13. The passage is mainly about _____.
    [A] what dogs can do   [B] how to keep dogs
    [C] dogs and their masters   [D] reasons for keeping dogs

Questions 14 to 17 are based on the following passage. At the end of the passage, you will be given 20 seconds to answer the questions.

Now listen to the passage.

14. According to the passage, the working conditions in the new place _____.
    [A] are the same as the speaker is used to
    [B] are expected to be rather poor
    [C] are just as adequate
    [D] are not yet clear

15. What is the speaker going to do in the new place?
    [A] Traveling.   [B] Studying.
    [C] Settling down.   [D] Teaching.

16. The speaker expects _____.
    [A] fewer choices of food   [B] many ways to do washing
    [C] modern lighting facilities   [D] new types of drinking water

17. From the passage we can learn that the speaker _____.
    [A] is unprepared for the new post
    [B] is unclear about the conditions there
    [C] is ready for all the difficulties there
    [D] is eager to know more about the post

Questions 18 to 20 are based on the following passage. At the end of the passage, you will be given 15 seconds to answer the questions.

Now listen to the passage.

18. According to the passage, when are children first expected to study hard?
    [A] Before 6 years of age.

[B]Between 6 and 10.

[C]After 10 years of age.

[D]After 12 years of age.

19. Parents who abuse their children tend to have the following problems EXCEPT _____.

[A]religious problems

[B]emotional problems

[C]financial problems

[D]marriage problems

20. Which of the following statements is CORRECT?

[A]Boys and girls are equally energetic.

[B]Parents have higher expectations for boys.

[C]Some parents lack skills to deal with their kids.

[D]Some parents are ill-educated and ill-tempered.

Section C News Broadcast

In this section you will hear several news items. Listen to them carefully and then answer the questions that follow.

Questions 21 to 22 are based on the following news. At the end of the news item, you will be given 10 seconds to answer the questions.

Now listen to the news.

21. What has happened to the Cubans?

[A]They set foot in Florida.　　　　[B]They were drowned.

[C]They were flown to the U.S.　　　[D]They were sent back to Cuba.

22. How did the Cubans try to enter the U.S.?

[A]In a small boat.　　　　　　　　[B]In an old truck.

[C]By swimming.　　　　　　　　　[D]By driving.

Question 23 is based on the following news. At the end of the news item, you will be given 5 seconds to answer the question.

Now listen to the news.

23. How many cities will have air quality monitoring systems installed by the end of this year?

[A]42 cites.　　[B]220 cites.　　[C]150 cites.　　[D]262 cites.

Questions 24 and 25 are based on the following news. At the end of the news item, you will be given 10 seconds to answer the questions.

Now listen to the news.

24. Altogether how many people were reported missing?

[A]68.　　　　[B]90.　　　　[C]150.　　　　[D]40.

25. Which of the following details is INCORRECT?

[A]The two ferries sank on different days.

[B]The accidents were caused by storms.

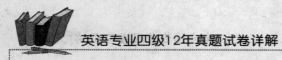

[C] The two ferries sank on the same river.

[D] More people were rescued from the first ferry.

Question 26 is based on the following news. At the end of the news item, you will be given 5 seconds to answer the question.

Now listen to the news.

26. What is the news item mainly about?

[A] Indonesian government policies.

[B] Australia's support to the UN assistance mission.

[C] Opening of an Australian consulate in East Timor.

[D] Talks between Australia and Indonesia.

Questions 27 and 28 are based on the following news. At the end of the news item, you will be given 10 seconds to answer the questions.

Now listen to the news.

27. The news item is mainly about a joint venture between _____.

[A] a US company and a UK company

[B] a Swiss company and a UK company

[C] Two Taiwanese companies

[D] a mainland company and US company

28. Who will provide the distribution network in the joint venture?

[A] Unilever.   [B] Nestlé.

[C] PepsiCo.   [D] Coca Cola.

Questions 29 and 30 are based on the following news. At the end of the news item, you will be given 10 seconds to answer the questions.

Now listen to the news.

29. Who staged the protest on Saturday?

[A] The soldiers.   [B] The peace camp.

[C] The militants.   [D] The hardliners.

30. Which of the following details about the news is INCORRECT?

[A] 13 soldiers were killed last week.

[B] 100,000 people participated in the protest.

[C] the protesters demanded a pullout from Gaza.

[D] The Primer Minister rejected the pullout plan.

2007 年英语专业四级考试听力理解

Part Ⅰ　　Dictation

Listen to the following passage. Altogether the passage will be read to you four times. During the first reading, which will be done at normal speed, listen and try to understand the meaning. For the second and third readings, the passage will be read sentence by sentence, or phrase by phrase, with intervals of 15 seconds. The last reading will be done at normal speed again and during this time you should check your work. You will then be given 2 minutes to check through your work once more.

Please write the whole passage on ANSWER SHEET ONE.

Part Ⅱ　　Listening Comprehension

In Sections A, B and C you will hear everything ONCE ONLY. Listen carefully and then answer the questions that follow. Mark the correct answer to each question on your answer sheet.

Section A　　Conversation

In this section you will hear several conversations. Listen to the conversations carefully and then answer the questions that follow.

Questions 1 to 3 are based on the following conversation. At the end of the conversation, you will be given 15 seconds to answer the questions.

Now listen to the conversation.

1. Which of the following is NOT needed for the LOST PROPERTY FORM?
　　[A] Name.　　　　　　　　　　[B] Nationality.
　　[C] Address.　　　　　　　　　[D] Phone number.

2. From the conversation we know that Mark Adams comes from _____.
　　[A] Essex　　　　　　　　　　[B] Edinburgh
　　[C] London　　　　　　　　　[D] the US

3. What will Mark Adams do the day after tomorrow?

[A] To come to the office again.

[B] To wait for the phone call.

[C] To call the office.

[D] To write to the office.

Questions 4 to 7 are based on the following conversation. At the end of the conversation, you will be given 20 seconds to answer the questions.

Now listen to the conversation.

4. Members of the club are required to _____.

[A] register when they arrive

[B] bring up to three guests

[C] register their guests

[D] show membership cards on arrival

5. Which of the following details about the changing rooms is NOT correct?

[A] There is a charge for the use of the locker.

[B] Showers are installed in the changing rooms.

[C] Lockers are located in the changing rooms.

[D] Lockers are used to store personal belongings.

6. According to the club's rules, members can play _____.

[A] for 30 minutes only   [B] for one hour only

[C] within the booked time only [D] longer than the booked time

7. Which of the following details is NOT correct?

[A] Players can eat in the club room.

[B] Players have to leave the club by ten o'clock.

[C] The courts are closed earlier than the club room.

[D] Players can use both the club room and the courts.

Questions 8 to 10 are based on the following conversation. At the end of the conversation, you will be given 15 seconds to answer the questions.

Now listen to the conversation.

8. At the university Mr. Robinson specialized in _____.

[A] maths   [B] physics

[C] water management   [D] geography

9. Mr. Robinson worked for the Indian Government because of _____.

[A] university links   [B] government agreements

[C] company projects   [D] degree requirements

10. After Mr. Robinson returned from India, he _____.

[A] changed jobs several times

[B] went to live in Manchester

[C] did similar work as in India

[D] became head of a research team

Section B   Passages

In this section, you will hear several passages. Listen to the passages carefully and then answer the questions that follow.

Questions 11 to 13 are based on the following talk. At the end of the talk, you will be given 15 seconds to answer the questions.

Now listen to the talk.

11. According to the talk, the owner of a bike has to _____.
    [A] register his bike immediately
    [B] put his bike on a list at one
    [C] have it stamped with a number
    [D] report to the police station

12. The speaker in the talk recommends _____.
    [A] two locks for an expensive bike
    [B] a good lock for an expensive bike
    [C] cheap locks for cheap bikes
    [D] good locks for cheap bikes

13. What is the main idea of the talk?
    [A] How to have the bike stamped.
    [B] How to protect your bike.
    [C] How to buy good locks.
    [D] How to report your lost bike to the police.

Questions 14 to 17 are based on the following talk. At the end of the talk, you will be given 20 seconds to answer the questions.

Now listen to the talk.

14. Which course(s) runs or run for one hour each time?
    [A] Conversation class.   [B] Writing Skills class.
    [C] Examinations Skills class.   [D] All of the three classes.

15. Which course(s) does not do NOT require enrolment beforehand?
    [A] Conversation class.   [B] Writing Skills class.
    [C] Examinations Skills class.   [D] All of the three classes.

16. Which course(s) is (are) designed especially for students of economics and social science?
    [A] Conversation class.   [B] Writing Skills class.
    [C] Examinations Skills class.   [D] All of the three classes.

17. Which course(s) is (are) the shortest?
    [A] Conversation class.   [B] Writing Skills class.
    [C] Examinations Skills class.   [D] All the language courses.

Questions 18 to 20 are based on the following passage. At the end of the passage, you will

be given 15 seconds to answer the questions.

   Now listen to the passage.

18. How old was Leonard da Vinci when he moved to Milan?

   [A]25.   [B]30.   [C]35.   [D]40.

19. Throughout his life, Leonardo da Vinci worked as all the following EXCEPT _____.

   [A]a painter   [B]an engineer   [C]an architect   [D]a builder

20. Where did Leonardo da Vinci die?

   [A]In France.   [B]In Milan.   [C]In Florence.   [D]In Tuscany.

Section C   News Broadcast

   In this section you will hear several news items. Listen to them carefully and then answer the questions that follow.

   Questions 21 and 22 are based on the following news. At the end of the news item, you will be given 10 seconds to answer the questions.

   Now listen to the news.

21. Who had to leave the Gaza Strip and the West Bank?

   [A]The Israeli army.   [B]The Jewish settlers.

   [C]The Palestinians.   [D]The Israeli Prime Minister.

22. How many settlements would have to be removed altogether in the Gaza Strip and the West Bank?

   [A]2.   [B]4.   [C]21.   [D]25.

   Questions 23 and 24 are based on the following news. At the end of the news item, you will be given 10 seconds to answer the questions.

   Now listen to the news.

23. Which of the following is NOT mentioned in the news?

   [A]The agreement has to be approved by Romania.

   [B]The agreement has to be approved by Bulgaria.

   [C]The agreement has to be approved by some EU states.

   [D]The agreement has to be approved by all the EU states.

24. Romania and Bulgaria cannot join the EU in 2007 unless they carry out reforms in the following areas EXCEPT _____.

   [A]manufacturing   [B]border control

   [C]administration   [D]justice

   Questions 25 and 26 are based on the following news. At the end of the news item, you will be given 10 seconds to answer the questions.

   Now listen to the news.

25. What is the theme of the forum?

   [A]Business leadership.

   [B]Global business community.

[C]Economic prospects in China.

[D]Business and government in China.

26. According to the news, the first forum was held _____.

    [A]10 years ago.   [B]3 years ago.

    [C]in 1999.   [D]in 2001.

Questions 27 and 28 are based on the following news. At the end of the news item, you will be given 10 seconds to answer the questions.

Now listen to the news.

27. About _____ of the 15,000 visitors on the opening day of Hong Kong Disneyland came from the mainland.

    [A]4,000   [B]5,000   [C]6,000   [D]7,000

28. According to the news, residents in _____ showed least interest in visiting the theme park.

    [A]Beijing   [B]Guangzhou   [C]Shanghai   [D]Hong Kong

Questions 29 and 30 are based on the following news. At the end of the news item, you will be given 10 seconds to answer the questions.

Now listen to the news.

29. What is the news mainly about?

    [A]Religious violence.   [B]Refugee issues.

    [C]A ferry disaster.   [D]A rescue operation.

30. The ferry boat was designed to carry _____ passengers.

    [A]198   [B]200   [C]290   [D]500

1996 年英语专业四级考试语法与词汇

Part IV   Grammar & Vocabulary

41. You won't get a loan _____ you can offer some security.

    [A] lest   [B] in case   [C] unless   [D] other than

42. _____ time, he'll make a first-class tennis player.

    [A] Having   [B] Given   [C] Giving   [D] Had

43. I _____ the party much more if there hadn't been quite such a crowd of people there.

    [A] would enjoy   [B] will have enjoyed

    [C] would have enjoyed   [D] will be enjoying

44. This company has now introduced a policy _____ pay rises are related to performance at work.

    [A] which   [B] where   [C] whether   [D] what

45. He wasn't asked to take on the chairmanship of the society, _____ insufficiently popular with all members.

    [A] having considered   [B] was considered

    [C] was being considered   [D] being considered

46. This may have preserved the elephant from being wiped out as well as other animals _____ in Africa.

    [A] hunted   [B] hunting   [C] that hunted   [D] are hunted

47. The office has to be shut down _____ funds.

    [A] being a lack of [B] from lack of   [C] to a lack of   [D] for lack of

48. In international matches, prestige is so important that the only thing that matters is to avoid _____.

    [A] from being beaten   [B] being beaten

    [C] beating   [D] to be beaten

49. As it turned out to be a small house party, we _____ so formally.

    [A] need not have dressed up   [B] must not have dressed up

    [C] did not need to dress up   [D] must not dress up

50. Western Nebraska generally receives less snow than _____ Eastern Nebraska.

    [A] in   [B] it receives in   [C] does   [D] it does in

51. _____ no cause for alarm, the old man went back to his bedroom.

   [A] There was   [B] Since   [C] Being   [D] There being

52. The brilliance of his satires was _____ make even his victims laugh.

   [A] so as to   [B] such as to   [C] so that   [D] such that

53. If he _____ in that way for much longer he will find himself in the bankruptcy court.

   [A] carries on   [B] carries off   [C] carried by   [D] carried away

54. Although the false banknotes fooled many people, they did not _____ to close examination.

   [A] look up   [B] pay up   [C] keep up   [D] stand up

55. He must give us more time, _____ we shall not be able to make a good job of it.

   [A] consequently   [B] otherwise   [C] therefore   [D] doubtlessly

56. When there was a short _____ in the conversation, I asked if anyone would like anything to drink.

   [A] blank   [B] space   [C] pause   [D] wait

57. You can do it if you want to, but in my opinion it's not worth the _____ it involves.

   [A] effort   [B] strength   [C] attempt   [D] force

58. The main road through Littlebury was blocked for three hours today after an accident _____ two lorries.

   [A] involving   [B] including   [C] combining   [D] containing

59. Very few scientists _____ with completely new answers to the world's problems.

   [A] come to   [B] come round   [C] come on   [D] come up

60. Hotel rooms must be _____ by noon, but luggage may be left with the porter.

   [A] departed   [B] abandoned   [C] vacated   [D] displaced

61. Half the excuses she gives are not true, but she always seems to _____ them.

   [A] get on with   [B] get away with   [C] get up from   [D] get in on

62. The _____ physicist has been challenged by others in his field.

   [A] respectable   [B] respectful   [C] respective   [D] respecting

63. With hundreds of works left behind, Picasso is regarded as a very _____ artist.

   [A] profound   [B] productive   [C] prosperous   [D] plentiful

64. The city suffered _____ damage as a result of the earthquake.

   [A] considered   [B] considerate   [C] considerable   [D] considering

65. Undergraduate students have no _____ to the rare books in the school library.

   [A] access   [B] entrance   [C] way   [D] path

1997 年英语专业四级考试语法与词汇

Part IV   Grammar & Vocabulary

41. How can I ever concentrate if you _____ continually _____ me with silly questions?

    [A] have. . . interrupted   [B] had. . . interrupted

    [C] are. . . interrupting   [D] were. . . interrupting

42. When you have finished with that video tape, don't forget to put it in my drawer, _____?

    [A] do you   [B] will you   [C] don't you   [D] won't you

43. He left orders that nothing _____ touched until the police arrived here.

    [A] should be   [B] ought to be   [C] must be   [D] would be

44. Mr. White works with a chemicals import & export company, but he _____ for this industrial fair, since he is on leave.

    [A] has worked   [B] works   [C] has been working   [D] is working

45. The physicist has made a discovery, _____ of great importance to the progress of science and technology.

    [A] I think which is   [B] that I think is

    [C] which I think is   [D] which I think it is

46. _____, he is ready to accept suggestions from different sources.

    [A] Instead of his contributions   [B] For all his notable contributions

    [C] His making notable contributions [D] However his notable contributions

47. The team can handle whatever _____.

    [A] that needs handling   [B] which needs handling

    [C] it needs handling   [D] needs to be handled

48. Come and see me whenever _____.

    [A] you are convenient   [B] you will be convenient

    [C] it is convenient to you   [D] it will be convenient to you

49. It was as a physician that he represented himself, and _____ he was warmly received.

    [A] as such   [B] such as   [C] as that   [D] so that

50. I have never been to London, but that is the city _____.

    [A] where I like to visit most   [B] I'd most like to visit

    [C] which I like to visit mostly   [D] where I'd like most to visit

51. I was to have made a speech if _____ .

    [A] I was not called away   [B] nobody would have called me away

    [C] I had not been called away   [D] nobody called me away

52. I felt that I was not yet _____ to travel abroad.

    [A] too strong   [B] strong enough   [C] so strong   [D] enough strong

53. The plane found the spot and hovered close enough to _____ that it was a car.

    [A] ensure   [B] examine   [C] verify   [D] testify

54. The encouraging factor is that the _____ majority of people find the idea of change acceptable.

    [A] numerous   [B] vast   [C] most   [D] massive

55. The increase in student numbers _____ many problems for the universities.

    [A] forces   [B] presses   [C] provides   [D] poses

56. Please _____ from smoking until the aeroplane is airborne.

    [A] refrain   [B] prevent   [C] resist   [D] restrain

57. Reporters and photographers alike took great _____ at the rude way the actor behaved during the interview.

    [A] annoyance   [B] offence   [C] resentment   [D] irritation

58. Topics for composition should be _____ to the experiences and interests of the students.

    [A] concerned   [B] dependent   [C] connecting   [D] relevant

59. The novel contains some marvellously revealing _____ of rural life in the 19th century.

    [A] glances   [B] glimpses   [C] glares   [D] gleams

60. Sometimes the student may be asked to write about his _____ to a certain book or article that has some bearing on the subject being studied.

    [A] reaction   [B] comment

    [C] impression   [D] comprehension

61. Picking flowers in the park is absolutely _____ .

    [A] avoided   [B] prohibited   [C] rejected   [D] repelled

62. Tony has not the least _____ of giving up his research work.

    [A] intention   [B] interest   [C] wish   [D] desire

63. Two of the children have to sleep in one bed, but the other three have _____ ones.

    [A] similar   [B] singular   [C] different   [D] separate

64. Am I to understand that his new post _____ no responsibility with it at all?

    [A] keeps   [B] supports   [C] carries   [D] possesses

65. Animals that could not _____ themselves to the changed environment perished and those that could survived.

    [A] change   [B] adapt   [C] modify   [D] conform

English

1998 年英语专业四级考试语法与词汇

Part Ⅳ   Grammar & Vocabulary

41. John is _____ hardworking than his sister, but he failed in the exam.

 [A] no less   [B] no more   [C] not less   [D] no so

42. She remembered several occasions in the past _____ she had experienced a similar feeling.

 [A] which   [B] before   [C] that   [D] when

43. If your car _____ any attention during the first 12 months, take it to an authorised dealer.

 [A] shall need   [B] should need   [C] would need   [D] will need

44. The indoor swimming pool seems to be a great deal more luxurious than _____.

 [A] is necessary   [B] being necessary   [C] to be necessary   [D] it is necessary

45. _____, he can now only watch it on TV at home.

 [A] Obtaining not a ticket for the match   [B] Not obtaining a ticket for the match

 [C] Not having obtained a ticket for the match [D] Not obtained a ticket for the match

46. The children prefer camping in the mountains _____ an indoor activity.

 [A] to   [B] than   [C] for   [D] with

47. Language belongs to each member of the society, to the cleaner _____ to the professor.

 [A] as far as   [B] the same as   [C] as much as   [D] as long as

48. _____ he needed money for a new car, he decided not to borrow it from the bank.

 [A] Much as   [B] Much though   [C] As much   [D] Though much

49. The Clarks haven't decided yet which hotel _____.

 [A] to stay   [B] is to stay   [C] to stay at   [D] is for staying

50. His strong sense of humour was _____ make everyone in the room burst out laughing.

 [A] so as to   [B] such as to   [C] so that   [D] such that

51. _____ enough time and money, the researchers would have been able to discover more in this field.

 [A] Giving   [B] To give   [C] Given   [D] Being given

52. You _____ Mark anything. It was none of his business.

 [A] needn't have told   [B] needn't tell

 [C] mustn't have told   [D] mustn't tell

53. The membership card entitled him _____ certain privileges in the club.

[A] on   [B] in   [C] at   [D] to

54. Obviously, the Chairman's remarks at the conference were _____ and not planned.

[A] substantial   [B] spontaneous   [C] simultaneous   [D] synthetic

55. For the success of the project, the company should _____ the most of the opportunities at hand.

[A] obtain   [B] grasp   [C] catch   [D] make

56. Failure to follow the club rules _____ him from the volleyball team.

[A] disfavoured   [B] dispelled   [C] disqualified   [D] dismissed

57. The discovery of new oil-fields in various parts of the country filled the government with _____ hope.

[A] eternal   [B] infinite   [C] ceaseless   [D] everlasting

58. At first the company refused to purchase the equipment, but this decision was _____ revised.

[A] subsequently   [B] successively   [C] predominantly   [D] preliminarily

59. The local police are authorized to _____ anyone's movements as they think fit.

[A] pause   [B] halt   [C] repel   [D] keep

60. Have you ever received _____ of what has happened to her?

[A] the word   [B] words   [C] word   [D] the words

61. Twelve is to three _____ four is to one.

[A] what   [B] as   [C] that   [D] like

62. Things went well for her during her early life, but in her middle age her _____ seemed to change.

[A] affair   [B] luck   [C] event   [D] chance

63. Although I spoke to her about the matter several times, she took little _____ of what I said.

[A] remark   [B] warning   [C] notice   [D] attention

64. The scheme was _____ when it was discovered it would be very costly.

[A] resigned   [B] surrendered   [C] released   [D] abandoned

65. Yesterday my aunt bought some new _____ for her flat at the seaside.

[A] furniture   [B] furnitures   [C] possession   [D] possessions

1999 年英语专业四级考试语法与词汇

Part Ⅳ   Grammar & Vocabulary

41. After _____ seemed an endless wait, it was her turn to enter the personnel manager's office.

　　[A] that　　　　　　[B] there　　　　　　[C] what　　　　　　[D] it

42. The three men tried many times to sneak across the border into the neighbouring country, _____ by the police each time.

　　[A] had been captured　　　　　　　[B] being always captured

　　[C] only to be captured　　　　　　　[D] unfortunately captured

43. Professor Johnson is said _____ some significant advance in his research in the past year.

　　[A] having made　　[B] making　　[C] to have made　　[D] to make

44. Fat cannot change into muscle _____ muscle changes into fat.

　　[A] any more than　　[B] no more than　　[C] no less than　　　[D] much more than

45. It is not so much the language _____ the cultural background that makes the book difficult to understand.

　　[A] but　　　　　　[B] nor　　　　　　[C] as　　　　　　[D] like

46. There ought to be less anxiety over the perceived risk of mountain climbing than _____.

　　[A] exists　　　　　[B] exist　　　　　[C] existing　　　　　[D] to exist

47. I've never been to Lhasa, but that's the city _____.

　　[A] I'd most like to visit　　　　　　[B] which I like to visit mostly

　　[C] where I like to visit　　　　　　[D] I'd like much to visit

48. He _____ unwisely, but he was at least trying to do something helpful.

　　[A] may have acted　　　　　　　　[B] must have acted

　　[C] should act　　　　　　　　　　[D] would act

49. If you have really been studying English for so long, it's about time you _____ able to write letters in English.

　　[A] should be　　　[B] were　　　[C] must be　　　[D] are

50. He's _____ as a "bellyacher"—he's always complaining about something.

　　[A] who is known　　　　　　　　[B] whom is known

　　[C] what is known　　　　　　　　[D] which is known

51. _____, he always tries his best to complete it on time.

　　[A] However the task is hard　　　　[B] However hard the task is

　　[C] Though hard the task is　　　　　[D] Though hard is the task

52. Much as _____, I couldn't lend him the money because I simply didn't have that much spare cash.

　　[A] I would have liked to　　　　　[B] I would like to have

　　[C] I should have to like　　　　　　[D] I should have liked to

53. My cousin likes eating very much, but he isn't very _____ about the food he eats.

　　[A] special　　　　[B] peculiar　　　　[C] particular　　　　[D] specific

54. Your advice would be _____ valuable to him, who is now at a loss as to what to do first.

　　[A] exceedingly　　　[B] excessively　　　[C] extensively　　　[D] exclusively

55. More often than not, it is difficult to _____ the exact meaning of a Chinese idiom in English.

　　[A] exchange　　　　[B] transfer　　　　[C] convey　　　　[D] convert

56. She refused to _____ the door key to the landlady until she got back her deposit.

　　[A] hand in　　　[B] hand out　　　[C] hand down　　　[D] hand over

57. The scientists have absolute freedom as to what research they think is best to _____.

　　[A] engage　　　　[B] devote　　　　[C] seek　　　　[D] pursue

58. The Olympic Games _____ in 776 B. C. in Olympia, a small town in Greece.

　　[A] originated　　　[B] stemmed　　　[C] derived　　　[D] descended

59. We should always bear in mind that _____ decisions often result in serious consequences.

　　[A] urgent　　　[B] instant　　　[C] prompt　　　[D] hasty

60. The fact that the management is trying to reach agreement _____ five separate unions has led to long negotiations.

　　[A] over　　　　[B] upon　　　　[C] in　　　　[D] with

61. The chairman of the company said that new techniques had _____ improved their production efficiency.

　　[A] violently　　　[B] severely　　　[C] extremely　　　[D] radically

62. The local authorities realized the need to make _____ for elderly people in their housing programmes.

　　[A] preparation　　　[B] requirement　　　[C] specification　　　[D] provision

63. The guest team was beaten by the host team 2 _____ 4 in last year's CFA Cup Final.

　　[A] over　　　　[B] in　　　　[C] to　　　　[D] against

64. The police let him go, because they didn't find him guilty _____ the murder.

　　[A] of　　　　[B] in　　　　[C] over　　　　[D] on

65. As a developing country, we must keep _____ with the rapid development of the world economy.

　　[A] move　　　[B] step　　　[C] speed　　　[D] pace

2000 年英语专业四级考试语法与词汇

Part Ⅳ Grammar & Vocabulary

41. Acute hearing helps most animals sense the approach of thunderstorms long before people _____ .

[A] do   [B] hear   [C] do them   [D] hearing it

42. This is an illness that can result in total blindness _____ left untreated.

[A] after   [B] if   [C] since   [D] unless

43. The central provinces have floods in some years, and _____ .

[A] drought in others   [B] droughts are others

[C] while other droughts   [D] others in drought

44. Do help yourself to some fruit, _____ you?

[A] can't   [B] don't   [C] wouldn't   [D] won't

45. There _____ nothing more for discussion, the meeting came to an end half an hour earlier.

[A] to be   [B] to have been   [C] being   [D] be

46. My mother can't get _____ because she has rheumatism.

[A] about   [B] on   [C] through   [D] in

47. I was very much put _____ by Mark's rude behavior; it really annoyed me.

[A] over   [B] off   [C] up   [D] by

48. You _____ Jim anything about it. It was none of his business.

[A] needn't have told [B] needn't tell [C] mustn't have told [D] mustn't tell

49. All of us would have enjoyed the party much more if there _____ quite such a crowd of people there.

[A] weren't   [B] hasn't been   [C] hadn't been   [D] wouldn't be

50. Firms that use computers have found that the number of staff _____ is needed for quality control can be substantially reduced.

[A] whose   [B] as   [C] what   [D] that

51. _____ at in this way, the present economic situation doesn't seem so gloomy.

[A] Looking   [B] Looked   [C] Having looked   [D] To look

52. Many people are _____ to insect bites, and some even have to go to hospital.

[A] insensitive   [B] allergic   [C] sensible   [D] infected

53. When you're driving on a motorway, you must obey the signs telling you to get into the right _____.

    [A] way   [B] track   [C] road   [D] lane

54. The motorist had to _____ to avoid knocking the old woman down in the middle of the road.

    [A] swerve   [B] twist   [C] depart   [D] swing

55. In winter drivers have trouble stopping their cars from _____ on icy roads.

    [A] skating   [B] skidding   [C] sliding   [D] slipping

56. This project would _____ a huge increase in defense spending.

    [A] result   [B] assure   [C] entail   [D] accomplish

57. The chances of a repetition of these unfortunate events are _____ indeed.

    [A] distant   [B] slim   [C] unlikely   [D] narrow

58. We should make a clear _____ between 'competent' and 'proficient' for the purposes of our discussion.

    [A] separation   [B] division   [C] distinction   [D] difference

59. In the present economic _____ we can make even greater progress than previously.

    [A] air   [B] mood   [C] area   [D] climate

60. *Rite of Passage* is a good novel by any standards; _____, it should rank high on any list of science fiction.

    [A] consistently   [B] consequently   [C] invariably   [D] fortunately

61. The diversity of tropical plants in the region represents a seemingly _____ source of raw materials, of which only a few have been utilized.

    [A] exploited   [B] controversial   [C] inexhaustible   [D] remarkable

62. While he was in Beijing, he spent all his time _____ some important museums and buildings.

    [A] visiting   [B] traveling   [C] watching   [D] touring

63. You must let me have the annual report without _____ by ten o'clock tomorrow morning.

    [A] failure   [B] hesitation   [C] trouble   [D] fail

64. As the director can't come to the reception, I'm representing the company _____.

    [A] on his account   [B] on his behalf   [C] for his part   [D] in his interest

65. Dreams are _____ in themselves, but, when combined with other data, they can tell us much about the dreamer.

    [A] uninformative   [B] startling   [C] harmless   [D] uncontrollable

2001 年英语专业四级考试语法与词汇

Part Ⅳ   Grammar & Vocabulary

41. I can't go—for one thing, I have no money, and _____, I have too much work.

   [A] what's more   [B] as well   [C] for another   [D] in addition

42. Even as a girl, _____ to be her life, and theater audiences were to be her best teachers.

   [A] performing by Melissa were

   [B] it was known that Melissa's performances were

   [C] knowing that Melissa's performances were

   [D] Melissa knew that performing was

43. _____ him tomorrow?

   [A] Why not to call on   [B] Why don't call on

   [C] Why not calling on   [D] Why not call on

44. There is no doubt _____ the company has made the right decision on the sales project.

   [A] why   [B] that   [C] whether   [D] when

45. Intellect is to the mind _____ sight is to the body.

   [A] what   [B] as   [C] that   [D] like

46. _____ I sympathize, I can't really do very much to help them out of the difficulties.

   [A] As long as   [B] As   [C] While   [D] Even

47. The patient's progress was very encouraging as he could _____ get out of bed without help.

   [A] nearly   [B] hardly   [C] merely   [D] barely

48. He was _____ to tell the truth even to his closest friend.

   [A] too much of a coward   [B] too much the coward

   [C] a coward enough   [D] enough of a coward

49. Barry had an advantage over his mother _____ he could speak French.

   [A] since that   [B] in that   [C] at that   [D] so that

50. You needn't worry _____ regards the cost of the operation.

   [A] with   [B] which   [C] as   [D] about

51. _____ is not a serious disadvantage in life.

   [A] To be not tall   [B] Not to be tall   [C] Being not tall   [D] Not being tall

52. During the famine, many people were _____ to going without food for days.

 [A] sunk [B] reduced [C] forced [D] declined

53. The computer can be programmed to _____ a whole variety of tasks.

 [A] assign [B] tackle [C] realize [D] solve

54. The team's efforts to score were _____ by the opposing goalkeeper.

 [A] frustrated [B] prevented [C] discouraged [D] accomplished

55. I only know the man by _____ but I have never spoken to him.

 [A] chance [B] heart [C] sight [D] experience

56. Being colour-blind, Sally can't make a _____ between red and green.

 [A] difference [B] distinction [C] comparison [D] division

57. You must insist that students give a truthful answer _____ with the reality of their world.

 [A] relevant [B] simultaneous [C] consistent [D] practical

58. In order to raise money, Aunt Nicola had to _____ with some of her most treasured possessions.

 [A] divide [B] separate [C] part [D] abandon

59. The car was in good working _____ when I bought it a few months ago.

 [A] order [B] form [C] state [D] circumstance

60. The customer expressed her _____ for that broad hat.

 [A] disapproval [B] distaste [C] dissatisfaction [D] dismay

61. In order to repair barns, build fences, grow crops, and care for animals a farmer must indeed be _____.

 [A] restless [B] skilled [C] strong [D] versatile

62. His expenditure on holidays and luxuries is rather high in _____ to his income.

 [A] comparison [B] proportion [C] association [D] calculation

63. Although he has become rich, he is still very _____ of his money.

 [A] economic [B] thrifty [C] frugal [D] careful

64. As the manager was away on a business trip, I was asked to _____ the weekly staff meeting.

 [A] preside [B] introduce [C] chair [D] dominate

65. The _____ of the word is unknown, but it is certainly not from Greek.

 [A] origin [B] generation [C] descent [D] cause

2002 年英语专业四级考试语法与词汇

Part Ⅳ   Grammar & Vocabulary

41. She did her work _____ her manager had instructed.

    [A] as   [B] until   [C] when   [D] though

42. _____ of the twins was arrested, because I saw both at a party last night.

    [A] None   [B] Both   [C] Neither   [D] All

43. For some time now, world leaders _____ out the necessity for agreement on arms reduction.

    [A] had been pointing   [B] have been pointing

    [C] were pointing   [D] pointed

44. Have you ever been in a situation _____ you know the other person is right yet you cannot agree with him?

    [A] by which   [B] that   [C] in where   [D] where

45. We've just installed two air-conditioners in our apartment, _____ should make great differences in our life next summer.

    [A] which   [B] what   [C] that   [D] they

46. AIDS is said _____ the number-one killer of both men and women over the past few years in that region.

    [A] being   [B] to be   [C] to have been   [D] having been

47. She managed to save _____ she could out of her wages to help her brother.

    [A] how little money   [B] so little money

    [C] such little money   [D] what little money

48. Fool _____ Jane is, she could not have done such a thing.

    [A] who   [B] as   [C] that   [D] like

49. The experiment requires more money than _____.

    [A] have been put in   [B] being put in   [C] has been put in   [D] to be put in

50. _____ for the fact that she broke her leg, she might have passed the exam.

    [A] Had it not been   [B] Hadn't it been   [C] Was it not   [D] Were it not

51. "What courses are you going to do next semester?"

    "I don't know. But it's about time _____ on something."

    [A] I'd decide   [B] I decided   [C] I decide   [D] I'm deciding

52. The police have offered a large _____ for information leading to the robber's arrest.

    [A] award [B] compensation [C] prize [D] reward

53. I arrived at the airport so late that I _____ missed the plane.

    [A] only [B] quite [C] narrowly [D] seldom

54. The popularity of the film shows that the reviewers' fears were completely _____.

    [A] unjustified [B] unjust [C] misguided [D] unaccepted

55. The head of the Museum was _____ and let us actually examine the ancient manuscripts.

    [A] promising [B] agreeing [C] pleasing [D] obliging

56. The multinational corporation was making a take-over _____ for a property company.

    [A] application [B] bid [C] proposal [D] suggestion

57. The party's reduced vote was _____ of lack of support for its policies.

    [A] indicative [B] positive [C] revealing [D] evident

58. There has been a _____ lack of communication between the union and the management.

    [A] regretful [B] regrettable [C] regretting [D] regretted

59. The teacher _____ expects his students to pass the university entrance examination.

    [A] confidentially [B] proudly [C] assuredly [D] confidently

60. The _____ family in Chinese cities now spends more money on housing than before.

    [A] normal [B] average [C] usual [D] general

61. The new colleague _____ to have worked in several big corporations before he joined our company.

    [A] confesses [B] declares [C] claims [D] confirms

62. During the reading lesson, the teacher asked students to read a few _____ from the novel.

    [A] pieces [B] essays [C] fragments [D] extracts

63. During the summer holiday season it is difficult to find a(n) _____ room in the hotels here.

    [A] empty [B] vacant [C] free [D] deserted

64. The old couple will never _____ the loss of their son.

    [A] get over [B] get away [C] get off [D] get across

65. Scientific research results can now be quickly _____ to factory production.

    [A] used [B] applied [C] tried [D] practiced

2003 年英语专业四级考试语法与词汇

Part IV Grammar & Vocabulary

41. Agriculture is the country's chief source of wealth, wheat _____ by far the biggest cereal crop.

[A] is   [B] been   [C] be   [D] being

42. Jack _____ from home for two days now, and I am beginning to worry about his safety.

[A] has been missing [B] has been missed [C] had been missing [D] was missed

43. Above the trees are the hills, _____ magnificence the river faithfully reflects on the surface.

[A] where   [B] of whose   [C] whose   [D] which

44. Who _____ was coming to see me in my office this afternoon?

[A] you said   [B] did you say   [C] did you say that [D] you did say

45. —Does Alan like hamburgers?

—Yes. So much _____ that he eats them almost every day.

[A] for   [B] as   [C] to   [D] so

46. Your ideas, _____, seem unusual to me.

[A] like her   [B] like hers

[C] similar to her   [D] similar to herself

47. The opening ceremony is a great occasion. It is essential _____ for that.

[A] for us to be prepared   [B] that we are prepared

[C] of us to be prepared   [D] our being prepared

48. Time _____, the celebration will be held as scheduled.

[A] permit   [B] permitting   [C] permitted   [D] permits

49. _____ I like economics, I like sociology much better.

[A] As much as   [B] So much   [C] How much   [D] Much as

50. It is futile to discuss the matter further, because _____ going to agree upon anything today.

[A] neither you nor I are   [B] neither you nor me is

[C] neither you nor I am   [D] neither me nor you are

51. They overcame all the difficulties and completed the project two months ahead of time, _____ is something we had not expected.

[A] which   [B] it   [C] that   [D] what

52. He is quite worn out from years of hard work. He is not the man _____ he was twenty years ago.

     [A] which   [B] that   [C] who   [D] whom

53. She would have been more agreeable if she had changed a little bit, _____?

     [A] hadn't she   [B] hasn't she   [C] wouldn't she   [D] didn't she

54. At three thousand feet, wide plains begin to appear, and there is never a moment when some distant mountain is not _____.

     [A] on view   [B] at a glance   [C] on the scene   [D] in sight

55. The first two stages in the development of civilized man were probably the invention of weapons and the discovery of fire, although nobody knows exactly when he acquired the use of the _____.

     [A] latter   [B] latest   [C] later   [D] last

56. It will take us twenty minutes to get to the railway station, _____ traffic delays.

     [A] acknowledging   [B] affording   [C] allowing for   [D] accounting for

57. He will have to _____ his indecent behaviour one day.

     [A] answer to   [B] answer for   [C] answer back   [D] answer about

58. With _____ exceptions, the former president does not appear in public now.

     [A] rare   [B] unusual   [C] extraordinary   [D] unique

59. We have been hearing _____ accounts of your work.

     [A] favoured   [B] favourable   [C] favourite   [D] favouring

60. During the summer holiday season there are no _____ rooms in this seaside hotel.

     [A] empty   [B] blank   [C] deserted   [D] vacant

61. Drive straight ahead, and then you will see a _____ to the Shanghai-Nanjing Expressway.

     [A] sign   [B] mark   [C] signal   [D] board

62. Whenever possible, Ian _____ how well he speaks Japanese.

     [A] shows up   [B] shows around   [C] shows off   [D] shows out

63. The tenant left nothing behind except some _____ of paper, cloth, etc.

     [A] sheets   [B] scraps   [C] pages   [D] slices

64. Shares on the stock market have _____ as a result of a worldwide economic downturn.

     [A] turned   [B] changed   [C] floated   [D] fluctuated

65. I think you can take a(n) _____ language course to improve your English.

     [A] intermediate   [B] middle   [C] medium   [D] mid

2004 年英语专业四级考试语法与词汇

Part Ⅳ   Grammar & Vocabulary

51. That trumpet player was certainly loud. But I wasn't bothered by his loudness _____ by his lack of talent.
    [A] so much as   [B] rather than   [C] as   [D] than

52. _____, I'll marry him all the same.
    [A] Was he rich or poor   [B] Whether rich or poor
    [C] Were he rich or poor   [D] Be he rich or poor

53. The government has promised to do _____ lies in its power to ease the hardships of the victims in the flood-stricken area.
    [A] however   [B] whichever   [C] whatever   [D] wherever

54. _____ if I had arrived yesterday without letting you know beforehand?
    [A] Would you be surprised   [B] Were you surprised
    [C] Had you been surprised   [D] Would you have been surprised

55. If not _____ with the respect he feels due to him, Jack gets very ill-tempered and grumbles all the time.
    [A] being treated   [B] treated   [C] be treated   [D] having been treated

56. It is imperative that students _____ their term papers on time.
    [A] hand in   [B] would hand in   [C] have to hand in   [D] handed in

57. The less the surface of the ground yields to the weight of a fully-loaded truck, _____ to the truck.
    [A] the greater stress is   [B] greater is the stress
    [C] the stress is greater   [D] the greater the stress is

58. The Minister of Finance is believed _____ of imposing new taxes to raise extra revenue.
    [A] that he is thinking   [B] to be thinking
    [C] that he is to think   [D] to think

59. Issues of price, place, promotion, and product are _____ conventional concerns in planning marketing strategies.
    [A] these of the most   [B] most of those
    [C] among the most   [D] among the many of

60. _____ both sides accept the agreement _____ a lasting peace be established in this region.

　［A］Only if, will　　　　　　［B］If only, would

　［C］Should, will　　　　　　［D］Unless, would

61. Mr. Wells, together with all the members of his family, _____ for Europe this afternoon.

　［A］are to leave　　［B］are leaving　　［C］is leaving　　［D］leave

62. It was suggested that all government ministers should _____ information on their financial interests.

　［A］discover　　　　［B］uncover　　　　［C］tell　　　　［D］disclose

63. As my exams are coming next week, I'll take advantage of the weekend to _____ on some reading.

　［A］catch up　　　　［B］clear up　　　　［C］make up　　　　［D］pick up

64. I'm surprised they are no longer on speaking terms. It's not like either of them to bear a _____.

　［A］disgust　　　　　［B］curse　　　　　［C］grudge　　　　　［D］hatred

65. Mary hopes to be _____ from hospital next week.

　［A］dismissed　　　　［B］discharged　　　　［C］expelled　　　　［D］resigned

66. Once a picture is proved to be a forgery, it becomes quite _____.

　［A］invaluable　　　　［B］priceless　　　　［C］unworthy　　　　［D］worthless

67. Jimmy earns his living by _____ works of art in the museum.

　［A］recovering　　　　［B］restoring　　　　［C］renewing　　　　［D］reviving

68. I couldn't sleep last night because the tap in the bathroom was _____.

　［A］draining　　　　　［B］dropping　　　　［C］spilling　　　　［D］dripping

69. The book gives a brief _____ of the course of his research up till now.

　［A］outline　　　　　［B］reference　　　　［C］frame　　　　　［D］outlook

70. She was standing outside in the snow, _____ with cold.

　［A］spinning　　　　　［B］shivering　　　　［C］shaking　　　　［D］staggering

71. All the rooms on the second floor have nicely _____ carpets, which are included in the price of the house.

　［A］adapted　　　　　［B］equipped　　　　［C］suited　　　　　［D］fitted

72. He plays tennis to the _____ of all other sports.

　［A］eradication　　　　［B］exclusion　　　　［C］extension　　　　［D］inclusion

73. She answered with an _____ "No" to the request that she attend the public hearing.

　［A］eloquent　　　　　［B］effective　　　　［C］emotional　　　　［D］emphatic

74. Everyone who has visited the city agrees that it is _____ with life.

　［A］vibrant　　　　　［B］violent　　　　　［C］energetic　　　　［D］full

75. We met Mary and her husband at a party two months ago. _____ we've had no further communication.

　［A］Thereof　　　　　［B］Thereby　　　　［C］Thereafter　　　　［D］Thereabouts

2005 年英语专业四级考试语法与词汇

Part Ⅳ   Grammar & Vocabulary

51. If you explained the situation to your solicitor, he _____ able to advise you much better than I can.

    [A] would be   [B] will have been   [C] was   [D] were

52. _____, Mr. Wells is scarcely in sympathy with the working class.

    [A] Although he is a socialist   [B] Even if he is a socialist
    [C] Being a socialist   [D] Since he is a socialist

53. His remarks were _____ annoy everybody at the meeting.

    [A] so as to   [B] such as to   [C] such to   [D] as much as to

54. James has just arrived, but I didn't know he _____ until yesterday.

    [A] will come   [B] was coming   [C] had been coming   [D] came

55. _____ conscious of my moral obligations as a citizen.

    [A] I was and always will be   [B] I have to be and always will be
    [C] I had been and always will be   [D] I have been and always will be

56. Because fuel supplies are finite and many people are wasteful, we will have to install _____ solar heating device in our home.

    [A] some type of   [B] some types of a   [C] some type of a   [D] some types of

57. I went there in 1984, and that was the only occasion when I _____ the journey in exactly two days.

    [A] must take   [B] must have made   [C] was able to make   [D] could make

58. I know he failed his last test, but really he's _____ stupid.

    [A] something but [B] anything but   [C] nothing but   [D] not but

59. Do you know Tim's brother? He is _____ than Tim.

    [A] much more sportsman   [B] more of a sportsman
    [C] more of sportsman   [D] more a sportsman

60. That was not the first time he _____ us. I think it's high time we _____ strong actions against him.

    [A] betrayed...take   [B] had betrayed...took
    [C] has betrayed...took   [D] has betrayed...take

61. What's the chance of _____ a general election this year?

 [A] there being [B] there to be

 [C] there be [D] there going to be

62. The meeting was put off because we _____ a meeting without John.

 [A] objected having [B] were objected to having

 [C] objected to have [D] objected to having

63. _____ you _____ further problems with your printer, contact your dealer for advice.

 [A] If;had [B] Have;had [C] Should;have [D] In case;had

64. He asked me to lend him some money, which I agreed to do, _____ that he paid me back the following week.

 [A] on occasion [B] on purpose [C] on condition [D] only if

65. Children who stay away from school do _____ for different reasons.

 [A] them [B] / [C] it [D] theirs

66. —Why are you staring?

 —I've never seen _____ tree before.

 [A] kind of [B] that kind of [C] such kind [D] such

67. There are still many problems ahead of us, but by this time next year we can see light at the end of the _____.

 [A] battle [B] day [C] road [D] tunnel

68. We realized that he was under great _____, so we took no notice of his bad temper.

 [A] excitement [B] stress [C] crisis [D] nervousness

69. The director tried to get the actors to _____ to the next scene by hand signals.

 [A] move on [B] move off [C] move out [D] move along

70. His ideas are invariably condemned as _____ by his colleagues.

 [A] imaginative [B] ingenious [C] impractical [D] theoretical

71. Thousands of people turned out into the streets to _____ against the local authorities' decision to build a highway across the field.

 [A] contradict [B] reform [C] counter [D] protest

72. The majority of nurses are women, but in the higher ranks of the medical profession women are in a _____.

 [A] minority [B] scarcity [C] rarity [D] minimum

73. Professor Johnson's retirement _____ from next January.

 [A] carries into effect [B] takes effect [C] has effect [D] puts into effect

74. The president explained that the purpose of taxation was to _____ government spending.

 [A] finance [B] expand [C] enlarge [D] budget

75. The heat in summer is no less _____ here in this mountain region.

 [A] concentrated [B] extensive [C] intense [D] intensive

76. Taking photographs is strictly _____ here, as it may damage the precious cave paintings.

 [A] forbidden [B] rejected [C] excluded [D] denied

77. Mr. Brown's condition looks very serious and it is doubtful if he will _____.

　　[A] pull back　　　[B] pull up　　　　[C] pull through　　　[D] pull out

78. Since the early nineties, the trend in most businesses has been toward on-demand, always-available products and services that suit the customer's _____ rather than the company's.

　　[A] benefit　　　　[B] availability　　　[C] suitability　　　[D] convenience

79. The priest made the _____ of the cross when he entered the church.

　　[A] mark　　　　　[B] signal　　　　　[C] sign　　　　　　[D] gesture

80. This spacious room is _____ furnished with just a few articles in it.

　　[A] lightly　　　　[B] sparsely　　　　[C] hardly　　　　　[D] rarely

2006 年英语专业四级考试语法与词汇

Part IV　Grammar & Vocabulary

51. _____ dull he may be, he is certainly a very successful top executive.

　　[A] Although　　　[B] Whatever　　　[C] As　　　　　　[D] However

52. If only I _____ play the guitar as well as you.

　　[A] would　　　　[B] could　　　　　[C] should　　　　　[D] might

53. The party, _____ I was the guest of honor, was extremely enjoyable.

　　[A] by which　　　[B] for which　　　[C] to which　　　　[D] at which

54. It is high time _____ cutting down the rainforests.

　　[A] stopped　　　　[B] had to stop　　　[C] shall stop　　　[D] stop

55. The student said there were a few points in the essay he _____ impossible to comprehend.

　　[A] has found　　　[B] was finding　　　[C] had found　　　[D] would find

56. Loudspeakers were fixed in the hall so that everyone _____ an opportunity to hear the speech.

　　[A] ought to have　　[B] must have　　　[C] may have　　　　[D] should have

57. I am surprised _____ this city is a dull place to live in.

　　[A] that you should think　　　　　[B] by what you are thinking

　　[C] that you would think　　　　　[D] with what you were thinking

58. Susan is very hardworking, but her pay is not _____ for her work.

　　[A] enough good　　　　　　　　　[B] good enough

　　[C] as good enough　　　　　　　　[C] good as enough

59. It is imperative that the government _____ more investment into the shipbuilding industry.

　　[A] attracts　　　　[B] shall attract　　　[C] attract　　　　[D] has to attract

60. Land belongs to the city; there is _____ thing as private ownership of land.

　　[A] no such a　　　[B] not such　　　　[C] not such a　　　[D] no such

61. My daughter has walked eight miles today. We never guessed that she could walk _____ far.

　　[A] /　　　　　　　[B] such　　　　　　[C] that　　　　　　[D] as

62. The statistics _____ that living standards in the area have improved drastically in recent times.

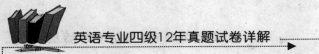

[A] proves   [B] is proving   [C] are proving   [D] prove

63. There are only ten apples left in the baskets, _____ the spoilt ones.

    [A] not counting   [B] not to count   [C] don't count   [D] having not counted

64. It was _____ we had hoped.

    [A] more a success than   [B] a success more than

    [C] as much of a success as   [D] a success as much as

65. There used to be a petrol station near the park, _____?

    [A] didn't it   [B] doesn't there   [C] usedn't it?   [D] didn't there

66. It is an offence to show _____ against people of different races.

    [A] distinction   [B] difference   [C] separation   [D] discrimination

67. A great amount of work has gone into _____ the Cathedral to its previous splendour.

    [A] refreshing   [B] restoring   [C] renovating   [D] renewing

68. The thieves fled with the local police close on their _____.

    [A] backs   [B] necks   [C] toes   [D] heels

69. The economic recession has meant that job _____ is a rare thing.

    [A] security   [B] safety   [C] protection   [D] secureness

70. Many people nowadays save money to _____ for their old age.

    [A] cater   [B] supply   [C] provide   [D] equip

71. The tone of the article _____ the writer's mood at the time.

    [A] reproduced   [B] reflected   [C] imagined   [D] imitated

72. This is not the right _____ to ask for my help; I am far too busy even to listen!

    [A] moment   [B] situation   [C] opportunity   [D] circumstance

73. The job of a student accommodation officer _____ a great many visits to landladies.

    [A] concerns   [B] offers   [C] asks   [D] involves

74. Our family doctor's clinic _____ at the junction of two busy roads.

    [A] rests   [B] stands   [C] stays   [D] seats

75. She was so fat that she could only just _____ through the door.

    [A] assemble   [B] appear   [C] squeeze   [D] gather

76. After the heavy rain, a builder was called to repair the roof, which was _____.

    [A] leaking   [B] trickling   [C] dripping   [D] floating

77. The reception was attended by _____ members of the local community.

    [A] excellent   [B] conspicuous   [C] prominent   [D] noticeable

78. Share prices on the Stock Exchange plunged sharply in the morning but _____ slightly in the afternoon.

    [A] regained   [B] recovered   [C] restored   [D] revived

79. His _____ brain has worked away on the idea of a universal cure.

    [A] rich   [B] quick   [C] productive   [D] fertile

80. The couple has donated a not _____ amount of money to the foundation.

    [A] inconsiderable   [B] inconsiderate   [C] inaccurate   [D] incomparable

2007 年英语专业四级考试语法与词汇

Part Ⅳ   Grammar & Vocabulary

51. There are as good fish in the sea _____ ever came out of it.

    [A] than   [B] like   [C] as   [D] so

52. *All the President's Men* _____ one of the important books for historians who study the Watergate Scandal.

    [A] remain   [B] remains   [C] remained   [D] is remaining

53. "You _____ borrow my notes provided you take care of them." I told my friend.

    [A] could   [B] should   [C] must   [D] can

54. If only the patient _____ a different treatment instead of using the antibiotics, he might still be alive now.

    [A] had received [B] received   [C] should receive [D] were receiving

55. Linda was _____ the experiment a month ago, but she changed her mind at the last minute.

    [A] to start   [B] to have started   [C] to be starting   [D] to have been starting

56. She _____ fifty or so when I first met her at the conference.

    [A] must be   [B] had been   [C] could be   [D] must have been

57. It is not _____ much the language as the background that makes the book difficult to understand.

    [A] that   [B] as   [C] so   [D] very

58. The committee has anticipated the problems that _____ in the road construction project.

    [A] arise   [B] will arise   [C] arose   [D] have arisen

59. The student said there were a few points in the essay he _____ impossible to comprehend.

    [A] had found   [B] finds   [C] has found   [D] would find

60. He would have finished his college education, but he _____ to quit and find a job to support his family.

    [A] had had   [B] has   [C] had   [D] would have

61. The research requires more money than _____.

    [A] have been put in   [B] has been put in   [C] being put in   [D] to be put in

62. Overpopulation poses a terrible threat to the human race. Yet it is probably _____ a threat to the human race than environmental destruction.

    [A] no more   [B] not more   [C] even more   [D] much more

63. It is not uncommon for there _____ problems of communication between the old and the young.

    [A] being   [B] would be   [C] be   [D] to be

64. _____ at in his way, the situation doesn't seem so desperate.

    [A] Looking   [B] Looked   [C] Being looked   [D] To look

65. It is absolutely essential that William _____ his study in spite of learning difficulties.

    [A] will continue   [B] continued   [C] continue   [D] continues

66. The painting he bought at the street market the other day was a _____ forgery.

    [A] man-made   [B] natural   [C] crude   [D] real

67. She's always been kind to me—I can't just turn _____ on her now that she needs my help.

    [A] my back   [B] my head   [C] my eye   [D] my shoulder

68. The bar in the club is for the _____ use of its members.

    [A] extensive   [B] exclusive   [C] inclusive   [D] comprehensive

69. The tuition fees are _____ to students coming from low-income families.

    [A] approachable   [B] payable   [C] reachable   [D] affordable

70. The medical experts warned the authorities of the danger of diseases in the _____ of the earthquake.

    [A] consequence   [B] aftermath   [C] result   [D] effect

71. This sort of rude behavior in public hardly _____ a person in your position.

    [A] becomes   [B] fits   [C] supports   [D] improves

72. I must leave now. _____, if you want that book I'll bring it next time.

    [A] Accidentally   [B] Incidentally   [C] Eventually   [D] Naturally

73. After a long delay, she _____ replying to my e-mail.

    [A] got away with [B] got back at   [C] got by   [D] got round to

74. Personal computers are no longer something beyond the ordinary people; they are _____ available these days.

    [A] promptly   [B] instantly   [C] readily   [D] quickly

75. In my first year at the university, I learnt the _____ of journalism.

    [A] basics   [B] basic   [C] elementary   [D] elements

76. According to the new tax law, any money earned over that level is taxed at the _____ of 59 per cent.

    [A] ratio   [B] percentage   [C] proportion   [D] rate

77. Thousands of _____ at the stadium came to their feet to pay tribute to an outstanding performance.

    [A] audience   [B] participants   [C] spectators   [D] observers

78. We stood still, gazing out over the limitless _____ of the desert.

    [A] space   [B] expanse   [C] stretch   [D] land

79. Doctors often _____ uneasiness in the people they deal with.

    [A] smell   [B] hear   [C] sense   [D] touch

80. Mary sat at the table, looked at the plate and _____ her lips.

    [A] smacked   [B] opened   [C] parted   [D] separated

1996 年英语专业四级考试阅读理解

Part VI Reading Comprehension

In this part there are four passages followed by questions or unfinished statements, each with four suggested answers marked A, B, C and D. Choose the one that you think is the correct answer.

Mark your choice in the ANSWER BOOKLET.

TEXT A

In the past thirty years many social changes have taken place in Britain. The greatest of these have probably been in the economic lives of women.

The changes have been significant, but, because tradition and prejudice can still handicap women in their working careers and personal lives, major legislation to help promote equality of opportunity and pay was passed during the 1970s.

At the heart of women's changed role in society has been the rise in the number of women at work, particularly married women. As technology and society permit highly effective and generally acceptable methods of family planning there has been a decline in family size. Women as a result are involved in child-rearing for a much shorter time and related to this, there has been a rapid increase in the number of women with young children who return to work when the children are old enough not to need constant care and attention.

Since 1951 the proportion of married women who work has grown from just over a fifth to a half. Compared with their counterparts elsewhere on the Continent, British women comprise a relatively high proportion of the work-force, about two-fifths, but on average they work fewer hours, about 31 a week. There is still a significant difference between women's average earnings and men's, but the equal pay legislation which came into force at the end of 1975 appears to have helped to narrow the gap between women's and men's basic rates.

As more and more women joined the work-force in the 1960s and early 1970s there was an increase in the collective incomes of women as a whole and a major change in the economic role of large numbers of housewives. Families have come to rely on married women's earnings as an essential part of their income rather than as "pocket money". At the same time social roles within the family are more likely to be shared, exchanged or altered.

66. The general idea of the passage is about _____.

[A] social trends in contemporary Britain

[B] changes in women's economic status

[C] equal opportunity and pay in Britain

[D] women's roles within the family

67. According to the author, an increasing number of married women are able to work because _____.

[A] their children no longer require their care

[B] there are more jobs available nowadays

[C] technology has enabled them to find acceptable jobs

[D] they spend far less time on child care than before

TEXT B

Nature's Gigantic Snowplough

On January 10, 1962, an enormous piece of glacier broke away and tumbled down the side of a mountain in Peru. A mere seven minutes later, when cascading ice finally came to a stop ten miles down the mountain, it had taken the lives of 4,000 people.

This disaster is one of the most <u>devastating</u> examples of a very common event: an avalanche of snow or ice. Because it is extremely cold at very high altitudes, snow rarely melts. It just keeps piling up higher and higher. Glaciers are eventually created when the weight of the snow is so great that the lower layers are pressed into solid ice. But most avalanches occur long before this happens. As snow accumulates on a steep slope, it reaches a critical point at which the slightest vibration will send it sliding into the valley below.

Even an avalanche of light power can be dangerous, but the Peruvian catastrophe was particularly terrible because it was caused by a heavy layer of ice. It is estimated that the ice that broke off weighed three million tons. As it crashed down the steep mountainside like a gigantic snowplough, it swept up trees, boulders and tons of topsoil, and completely crushed and destroyed the six villages that lay in its path.

At present there is no way to predict or avoid such enormous avalanches, but, luckily, they are very rare. Scientists are constantly studying the smaller, more common avalanches, to try to understand what causes them. In the future, perhaps dangerous masses of snow and ice can be found and removed before they take human lives.

68. The first paragraph catches the reader's attention with a _____.

[A] first-hand report   [B] dramatic description

[C] tall tale   [D] vivid word picture

69. In this passage devastating means _____.

[A] violently ruinous   [B] spectacularly interesting

[C] stunning   [D] unpleasant

70. The passage is mostly about _____.

[A] avalanches   [B] glaciers   [C] Peru   [D] mountains

English

I was born in Tuckahoe, Tallbot County, Maryland. I have no accurate knowledge of my age, never having seen any authentic record containing it. By far the larger part of the slaves know as little of their age as horses know of theirs, and it is the wish of most masters within my knowledge to keep their slaves thus ignorant. I do not remember having ever met a slave who could tell of his birthday. They seldom come nearer to it than planting-time, harvesting, springtime, or falltime. A lack of information concerning my own was a source of unhappiness to me even during childhood. The white children could tell their ages, I could not tell why I ought to be deprived of the same privilege. I was not allowed to make any inquiries of my master concerning it. He considered all such inquiries on the part of a slave improper and impertinent. The nearest estimate I can give makes me now between twenty-seven and twenty-eight years of age. I come to this, from hearing my master say, some time during 1853, I was about seventeen years old.

My mother was named Harriet Bailey. She was the daughter of Isaac and Betsey Bailey, both coloured, and quite dark. My mother was of a darker complexion than either my grandmother or grandfather.

My father was a white man. He was admitted to be such by all I ever heard speak of my parentage. The opinion was also whispered that my master was my father; but of the correctness of this opinion, I know nothing; the means of knowing was withheld from me. My mother and I were separated when I was but an infant—before I knew her as my mother. It is a common custom, in the part of Maryland from which I ran away, to part children from their mothers at a very early age. Frequently, before the child has reached its twelfth month, its mother is taken from it, and hired out on some farm a considerable distance off, and the child is placed under the care of an older woman, too old for field labour. For what this separation is done, I do not know, unless it be to hinder the development of the child's affection towards its mother.

71. The author did not know exactly when he was born because _____.

　　[A] he did not know who his mother was

　　[B] there was no written evidence of it

　　[C] his master did not tell his father

　　[D] nobody on his farm knew anything about it

72. In the mid-nineteenth century, slaves often _____.

　　[A] marked their birthdays by the season

　　[B] did not really care how old they were

　　[C] forgot the exact time when they were born

　　[D] pretended not to know each other's birthdays

73. The author's mother told him _____.

　　[A] his father was black　　　　　　　[B] his father was white

　　[C] nothing about his father　　　　　　[D] his master was his father

74. According the passage, when the author was very young his mother _____.

    [A] ran away   [B] was light-skinned

    [C] had several children   [D] was sent to work elsewhere

75. The author had not spent much time with his _____.

    [A] mother   [B] master

    [C] grandfather   [D] grandmother

76. The author was most probably raised _____.

    [A] by his grandparents   [B] by an old woman slave

    [C] with his master's support   [D] together with other children

TEXT D

Please Recycle That Bobsled Run (大雪橇滑道)

For the 1992 Winter Games, French organizers constructed a new motorway, parking lots and runs for skiing in the Alps. Environmentalists screamed "Disaster!". Thus warned, the Norwegians have adopted "green" advice and avoided great blots on the landscape. The speed-skating rink was built to look like an overturned ship, and placed so as not to disturb a bird sanctuary. Dug into a mountainside, the hockey arena is well concealed and energy efficient. The bobsled run is built out of wood not metal and hidden among trees. No wonder the president of the International Olympic Committee has called these the first "Green Games."

Lillehammer's opening ceremonies featured a giant Olympic Torch burning biogas produced by rotting vegetation. During construction, builders were threatened with $7,500 fines for felling trees unnecessarily. Rare trees were carefully transplanted from hillsides. Food is being served on potato-based plates that will be fed, in turn, to pigs. Smoking has been banned outdoors as well as in, with enforcement by polite requests.

Environmentalists have declared partial victory: though Coca-Cola's plan to decorate the town with banners has been scaled back, there are still too many billboards for strict green tastes. Perhaps, but after the Games, athlete housing will be converted into vacation homes or shipped to the northlands for student dormitories. Bullets will be plucked from biathlon targets and recycled to keep the lead from poisoning ground water. And these tricks won't be forgotten. Embarrassed by environmental protests, the I.O.C. claims that green awareness is now entrenched—along with sport and culture—as a permanent dimension of the Olympic Charter.

Indeed, Sydney was successful in becoming host for the 2000 Summer Games in part on the strength of its endorsement from Greenpeace. Aspiring host cities are picking up the code. Salt Lake City, bidding for the 2002 Games, may opt to use the bobsled run that Calgary built for the '88 Games. After that, who could deny that recycling is an Olympic movement?

77. Which of the following countries has not paid enough attention to the "green" issues?

    [A] Norway.   [B] France.   [C] America.   [D] Australia.

78. In which area did the environmentalists fail in Lillehammer?

    [A] Energy.   [B] Smoking.   [C] Housing.   [D] Advertising.

79. Which of the following describes the I. O. C. 's attitude towards the environmentalists' protests?

    [A] Trying to commit themselves.   [B] Showing indifference and contempt.

    [C] Arguing for practical difficulties.   [D] Negotiating for gradual changes.

80. The 2002 Games might be held in _____ .

    [A] Oslo   [B] Calgary

    [C] Sydney   [D] Salt Lake City

1997 年英语专业四级考试阅读理解

Part Ⅵ　Reading Comprehension

In this section there are four passages followed by fifteen questions or unfinished statements, each with four suggested answers marked A, B, C and D. Choose the one that you think is the correct answer.

Mark your choice in your answer sheet.

TEXT　A

　　University teaching in the United Kingdom is very different at both undergraduate and graduate levels from that of many overseas countries.

　　An undergraduate course consists of a series of lectures, seminars and tutorials and, in science and engineering, laboratory classes, which in total account for about 15 hours per week. Arts students may well find that their official contact with teachers is less than this average, while science and engineering students may expect to be timetabled for up to 20 hours per week. Students studying for a particular degree will take a series of lecture courses which run in parallel at a fixed time in each week and may last one academic term or the whole year. Associated with each lecture course are seminars, tutorials and laboratory classes which draw upon, analyze, illustrate or amplify the topics presented in the lectures. Lecture classes can vary in size from 20 to 200 although larger-sized lectures tend to decrease as students progress into the second and third year and more options become available. Seminars and tutorials are on the whole much smaller than lecture classes and in some departments can be on a one-to-one basis (that is, one member of staff to one student). Students are normally expected to prepare work in advance for seminars and tutorials and this can take the form of researching a topic for discussion, by writing essays or by solving problems. Lectures, seminars and tutorials are all one hour in length, whilst laboratory classes usually last either 2 or 3 hours. Much emphasis is put on how to spend as much time if not more studying by themselves as being taught. In the UK it is still common for people to say that they are "reading" for a degree! Each student has a tutor whom they can consult on any matter whether academic or personal. Although the tutor will help, motivation for study is expected to come from the student.

66. According to the passage, science and engineering courses seem to be more ＿＿＿＿ than

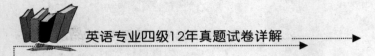

arts courses.

[A] motivating [B] varied [C] demanding [D] interesting

67. Which of the following is the length of lectures or seminars or tutorials?

[A] 1 hour [B] 2 hours [C] 3 hours [D] 15 hours

68. In British universities teaching and learning are carried out in _____.

[A] a variety of ways [B] laboratory classes

[C] seminars and tutorials [D] lectures and tutorials

TEXT B

Who said the only way to learn about a country you can't visit is by reading a book? Dan Eckberg's television students at Hopkins High School know better. They're seeing countries and learning about cultures with the aid of electronic communications.

Using computers, satellite hookups, and telephone hotlines, Eckberg's students have already followed a team of cyclists 11,500 miles across the continent of Africa, sat atop Mount Kilimanjaro, and sweltered in the Sahara Desert.

This winter they'll interact with an expedition exploring Central America in search of the classic Maya culture.

You can join them.

How? By following Eckberg and his class as they track the adventures of Dan and Steve Buettner, two world-class bicyclists from U. S. A. Starting last month these two bicyclists, joined by archaeologists and a technical support team, are interacting with students via the Internet, the worldwide computer network.

From classroom or home computer, students can make research proposals to the Buettners or the archaeologists at the various Central American locations they've been exploring as part of their MayaQuest expedition.

"We hope that someone will ask a question that can't readily be answered," says Hopkins High School student Barry Anderson, "and through the online activities, an answer will be found—a discovery!"

Having students "discover" why a civilization as advanced as the Maya collapsed in the 9th century is one key goal for the leaders of the MayaQuest expedition. The more important goal is using interactive learning to discover the cause of the decline and compare it to issues we face today—natural disasters, environmental problems, and war.

Ten lesson plans—on topics ranging from the Maya language to the Maya creation myth—have been developed for the interactive expedition.

"Through a combination of live call-in television and the Internet," says Eckberg, "we're hoping to build excitement and engagement in learning in our school."

69. Dan Eckberg and his students learn about Africa by _____.

[A] reading books [B] watching video tapes

[C] Interacting via the Internet [D] cycling 11,500 miles

70. Which of the following activities is NOT involved in Dan Eckberg and his students' expedition?

[A] Going to visit various Central American locations.

[B] Getting information through electronic communications.

[C] Discussing different topics on the Maya civilization.

[D] Forming research proposals and discovering the answers.

TEXT C

Most earthquakes occur within the upper 15 miles of the earth's surface. But earthquakes can and do occur at all depths to about 460 miles. Their number decreases as the depth increases. At about 460 miles one earthquake occurs only every few years. Near the surface earthquakes may run as high as 100 in a month, but the yearly average does not vary much. In comparison with the total number of earthquakes each year, the number of disastrous earthquakes is very small.

The extent of the disaster in an earthquake depends on many factors. If you carefully build a toy house with an Erector set, it will still stand no matter how much you shake the table. But if you build a toy house with a pack of cards, a slight shake of the table will make it fall. An earthquake in Agadir, Morocco, was not strong enough to be recorded on distant instruments, but it completely destroyed the city. Many stronger earthquakes have done comparatively little damage. If a building is well constructed and built on solid ground, it will resist an earthquake. Most deaths in earthquakes have been due to faulty building construction or poor building sites. A third and very serious factor is panic. When people rush out into narrow streets, more deaths will result.

The United Nations has played an important part in reducing the damage done by earthquakes. It has sent a team of experts to all countries known to be affected by earthquakes. Working with local geologists and engineers, the experts have studied the nature of the ground and the type of most practical building code for the local area. If followed, these suggestions will make disastrous earthquakes almost a thing of the past.

There is one type of earthquake disaster that little can be done about. This is the disaster caused by seismic sea waves, or *tsunamis*. (These are often called tidal waves, but the name is incorrect. They have nothing to do with tides.) In certain areas, earthquakes take place beneath the sea. These submarine earthquakes sometimes give rise to seismic sea waves. The waves are not noticeable out at sea because of their long wave length. But when they roll into harbours, they pile up into walls of water 6 to 60 feet high. The Japanese call them "*tsunamis*", meaning "harbour waves", because they reach a sizable height only in harbours.

Tsunamis travel fairly slowly, at speeds up to 500 miles an hour. An adequate warning system is in use to warn all shores likely to be reached by the waves. But this only enables people to leave the threatened shores for higher ground. There is no way to stop the oncoming wave.

71. Which of the following CANNOT be concluded from the passage?

　[A] The number of earthquakes is closely related to depth.

　[B] Roughly the same number of earthquakes occur each year.

　[C] Earthquakes are impossible at depths over 460 miles.

　[D] Earthquakes are most likely to occur near the surfaces.

72. The destruction of Agadir is an example of _____.

　[A] faulty building construction

　[B] an earthquake's strength

　[C] widespread panic in earthquakes

　[D] ineffective instruments

73. The United Nations' experts are supposed to _____.

　[A] construct strong buildings　　　[B] put forward proposals

　[C] detect disastrous earthquakes　　[D] monitor earthquakes

74. The significance of the slow speed of tsunamis is that people may _____.

　[A] notice them out at sea　　　　　[B] find ways to stop them

　[C] be warned early enough　　　　　[D] develop warning systems

TEXT D

One of the good things for men in women's liberation is that men no longer have to pay women the old-fashioned courtesies.

In an article on the new manners, Ms. Holmes says that a perfectly able woman no longer has to act helplessly in public as if she were a model. For example, she doesn't need help getting in and out of cars. "Women get in and out of cars twenty times a day with babies and dogs. Surely they can get out by themselves at night just as easily."

She also says there is no reason why a man should walk on the outside of a woman on the sidewalk. "Historically, the man walked on the inside so he caught the garbage thrown out of a window. Today a man is supposed to walk on the outside. A man should walk where he wants to. So should a woman. If, out of love and respect, he actually wants to take the blows, he should walk on the inside—because that's where attackers are all hiding these days."

As far as manners are concerned, I suppose I have always been a supporter of women's liberation. Over the years, out of a sense of respect, I imagine, I have refused to trouble women with outdated courtesies.

It is usually easier to follow rules of social behaviour than to depend on one's own taste. But rules may be safely broken, of course, by those of us with the gift of natural grace. For example, when a man and woman are led to their table in a restaurant and the waiter pulls out a chair, the woman is expected to sit in the chair. That is according to Ms. Ann Clark. I have always done it the other way, according to my wife.

It came up only the other night. I followed the hostess to the table, and when she pulled the chair out I sat on it, quite naturally, since it happened to be the chair I wanted to sit in.

"Well," my wife said, when the hostess had gone, "you did it again."

"Did what?" I asked, utterly confused.

"Took the chair."

Actually, since I'd walked through the restaurant ahead of my wife, it would have been awkward, I should think, not to have taken the chair. I had got there first, after all.

Also, it has always been my custom to get in a car first, and let the woman get in by herself. This is a courtesy I insist on as the stronger sex, out of love and respect. In times like these, there might be attackers hidden about. It would be unsuitable to put a woman in a car and then shut the door on her, leaving her at the mercy of some bad fellow who might be hiding in the back seat.

75. It can be concluded from the passage that _____.

　[A] men should walk on the inside of a sidewalk

　[B] women are becoming more capable than before

　[C] in women's liberation men are also liberated

　[D] it's safe to break rules of social behaviour

76. The author was "utterly confused" because he _____.

　[A] took the chair out of habit

　[B] was trying to be polite

　[C] was slow in understanding

　[D] had forgotten what he did

77. He "took the chair" for all the following reasons EXCEPT that _____.

　[A] he got to the chair first

　[B] he happened to like the seat

　[C] his wife ordered him to do so

　[D] he'd walked ahead of his wife

78. The author always gets in a car before a woman because he _____.

　[A] wants to protect her

　[B] doesn't need to help her

　[C] chooses to be impolite to her

　[D] fears attacks on him

79. The author is _____ about the whole question of manners and women's liberation.

　[A] joking 　　　　[B] satirical 　　　[C] serious 　　　　[D] critical

80. Which of the following best states the main idea of the passage?

　[A] Manners ought to be thrown away altogether.

　[B] In manners one should follow his own judgement.

　[C] Women no longer need to be helped in public.

　[D] Men are not expected to be courteous to women.

1998 年英语专业四级考试阅读理解

Part Ⅵ   Reading Comprehension

In this section there are four passages followed by questions or unfinished statements, each with four suggested answers marked A, B, C and D. Choose the one that you think is the correct answer.

Mark your choice on your answer sheet.

TEXT A

People have been painting pictures for at least 30,000 years. The earliest pictures were painted by people who hunted animals. They used to paint pictures of the animals they wanted to catch and kill. Pictures of this kind have been found on the walls of caves in France and Spain. No one knows why they were painted there. Perhaps the painters thought that their pictures would help them to catch these animals. Or perhaps human beings have always wanted to tell stories in pictures.

About 5,000 years ago the Egyptians and other people in the Near East began to use pictures as a kind of writing. They drew simple pictures or signs to represent things and ideas, and also to represent the sounds of their language. The signs these people used became a kind of alphabet.

The Egyptians used to record information and to tell stories by putting picture-writing and pictures together. When an important person died, scenes and stories from his life were painted and carved on the walls of the place where he was buried. Some of these pictures are like modern comicstrip (连环漫画) stories. It has been said that Egypt is the home of the comic strip. But, for the Egyptians, pictures still had magic power. So they did not try to make their way of writing simple. The ordinary people could not understand it.

By the year 1,000 BC, people who lived in the area around the Mediterranean Sea had developed a simpler system of writing. The signs they used were very easy to write, and there were fewer of them than in the Egyptian system. This was because each sign, or letter, represented only one sound in their language. The Greeks developed this system and formed the letters of the Greek alphabet. The Romans copied the idea, and the Roman alphabet is now used all over the world.

These days, we can write down a story, or record information, without using pictures. But we still need pictures of all kinds: drawings, photographs, signs and diagrams. We find them everywhere: in books and newspapers, in the street, and on the walls of the places where we live and work. Pictures help us to understand and remember things more easily, and they can make a story much more interesting.

66. Pictures of animals were painted on the walls of caves in France and Spain because _____.

　　[A] the hunters wanted to see the pictures

　　[B] the painters were animal lovers

　　[C] the painters wanted to show imagination

　　[D] the pictures were thought to be helpful

67. The Greek alphabet was simpler than the Egyptian system for all the following reasons EXCEPT that _____.

　　[A] the former was easy to write

　　[B] there were fewer signs in the former

　　[C] the former was easy to pronounce

　　[D] each sign stood for only one sound

68. Which of the following statements is TRUE?

　　[A] The Egyptian signs later became a particular alphabet.

　　[B] The Egyptians liked to write comic-strip stories.

　　[C] The Roman alphabet was developed from the Egyptian one.

　　[D] The Greeks copied their writing system from the Egyptians.

69. In the last paragraph, the author thinks that pictures _____.

　　[A] should be made comprehensible

　　[B] should be made interesting

　　[C] are of much use in our life

　　[D] are disappearing from our life

TEXT　B

Human beings have used tools for a very long time. In some parts of the world you can still find tools that people used more than two million years ago. They made these tools by hitting one stone against another. In this way they broke off pieces from one of the stones. These chips of stone were usually sharp on one side. People used them for cutting meat and skin from dead animals, and also for making other tools out of wood. Human beings needed to use tools because they did not have sharp teeth like other meat-eating animals, such as lions and tigers. Tools helped people to get food more easily.

Working with tools also helped to develop human intelligence. The human brain grew bigger, and human beings began to invent more and more tools and machines. The stone chip was one of the first tools that people used, and perhaps it is the most important. Some scientists say

that it was the key to the success of mankind.

Since 1960 a new kind of tool has appeared. This is the silicon chip—a little chip of silicon crystal（硅晶体）. It is smaller than a finger-nail, but it can store more than a million 'bits' of information. It is an electronic brain.

Every year these chips get cleverer, but their size gets smaller, and their cost gets less. They are used in watches, calculators and intelligent machines that we can use in many ways.

In the future we will not need to work with tools in the old way. Machines will do everything for us. They will even talk and play games with us. People will have plenty of spare time. But what will they do with it?

Human beings used stone chips for more than two million years, but human life changed very little in that time. We have used silicon chips for only a few years, but life is changing faster every day. What will life be like twenty years from now? What will the world be like two million years from now?

70. The stone chip is thought to be the most important tool because it _____.

　　[A] was one of the first tools

　　[B] developed human capabilities

　　[C] led to the invention of machines

　　[D] was crucial to the development of mankind

71. At the end of the passage the author seems to suggest that life in future is _____.

　　[A] disastrous　　　[B] unpredictable.　　[C] exciting　　　[D] colourful

TEXT C

A century ago in the United States, when an individual brought suit against a company, public opinion tended to protect that company. But perhaps this phenomenon was most striking in the case of the railroads. Nearly half of all negligence（过失）cases decided through 1896 involved railroads. And the railroads usually won.

Most of the cases were decided in state courts, when the railroads had the climate of the times on their sides. Government supported the railroad industry; the progress railroads represented was not to be slowed down by requiring them often to pay damages to those unlucky enough to be hurt working for them.

Court decisions always went against railroad workers. A Mr. Farwell, an engineer, lost his right hand when a switchman's negligence ran his engine off the track. The court reasoned that since Farwell had taken the job of an engineer voluntarily at good pay, he had accepted the risk. Therefore the accident, though avoidable had the switchmen acted carefully, was a "pure accident." In effect a railroad could never be held responsible for injury to one employee caused by the mistake of another.

In one case where a Pennsylvania Railroad worker had started a fire at a warehouse and the fire had spread several blocks, causing widespread damage, a jury found the company responsible for all the damage. But the court overturned the jury's decision because it argued that the railroad's negligence was the immediate cause of damage only to the nearest buildings. Beyond them the connection was too remote to consider.

As the century wore on, public sentiment began to turn against the railroads—against their economic and political power and high fares as well as against their callousness（无情）toward individuals.

72. Which of the following is NOT true in Farwell's case?

[A] Farwell was injured because he negligently ran his engine off the track.

[B] Farwell would not have been injured if the switchman had been more careful.

[C] The court argued that the victim had accepted the risk since he had willingly taken his job.

[D] The court decided that the railroad should not be held responsible.

73. What must have happened after the fire case was settled in court?

[A] The railroad compensated for the damage to the immediate buildings.

[B] The railroad compensated for all the damage by the fire.

[C] The railroad paid nothing for the damaged building.

[D] The railroad worker paid for the property damage himself.

74. The following aroused public resentment EXCEPT _____.

[A] political power   [B] high fares   [C] economic loss   [D] indifference

75. What does the passage mainly discuss?

[A] Railroad oppressing individuals in the US.

[B] History of the US railroads.

[C] Railroad workers' working rights.

[D] Law cases concerning the railroads.

TEXT D

Hawaii's native minority is demanding a greater degree of sovereignty over its own affairs. But much of the archipelago's political establishment, which include the White Americans who dominated until the second world war and people of Japanese, Chinese and Filipino origin, is opposed to the idea.

The islands were annexed by the US in 1898 and since then Hawaii's native peoples have fared worse than any of its other ethnic groups. They make up over 60 per cent of the state's homeless, suffer higher levels of unemployment and their life span is five years less than the average Hawaiians. They are the only major US native group without some degree of autonomy.

But a sovereignty advisory committee set up by Hawaii's first native governor, John Waihee, has given the natives' cause a major boost by recommending that the Hawaiian natives decide by themselves whether to re-establish a sovereign Hawaiian nation.

However, the Hawaiian natives are not united in their demands. Some just want greater autonomy within the state—as enjoyed by many American Indian natives over matters such as education. This is a position supported by the Office of Hawaiian Affairs（OHA）, a state agency set up in 1978 to represent the natives' interests and which has now become the moderate face of the native sovereignty movement. More ambitious is the Ka Lahui group, which declared itself a new nation in 1987 and wants full, official independence from the US.

But if Hawaiian natives are given greater autonomy, it is far from clear how many people this will apply to. The state authorities only count as native those people with more than 50 per cent Hawaiian blood.

Native demands are not just based on political grievances, though. They also want their claim on 660,000 hectares of Hawaiian crown land to be accepted. It is on this issue that native groups are facing most opposition from the state authorities. In 1993, the state government paid the OHA US $ 136 million in back rent on the crown land and many officials say that by accepting this payment the agency has given up its claims to legally own the land. The OHA has vigorously disputed this.

76. Hawaii's native minority refers to _____.

[A] Hawaii's ethnic groups

[B] people of Filipino origin

[C] the Ka Lahui group

[D] people with 50% Hawaiian blood

77. Which of the following statements is true of the Hawaiian natives?

[A] Sixty percent of them are homeless or unemployed.

[B] Their life span is 5 years shorter than average Americans.

[C] Their life is worse than that of other ethnic groups in Hawaii.

[D] They are the only native group without sovereignty.

78. Which of the following is NOT true of John Waihee?

[A] He is Hawaii's first native governor.

[B] He has set up a sovereignty advisory committee.

[C] He suggested the native people decide for themselves.

[D] He is leading the local independence movement.

79. Which of the following groups holds a less radical attitude on the matter of sovereignty?

[A] American Indian natives.

[B] Office of Hawaiian Affairs.

[C] The Ka Lahui group.

[D] The Hawaiian natives.

80. Various native Hawaiians demand all the following EXCEPT _____.

[A] a greater autonomy within the state

[B] more back rent on the crown land

[C] a claim on the Hawaiian crown land

[D] full independence from the US

1999 年英语专业四级考试阅读理解

Part Ⅵ   Reading Comprehension

In this section there are four passages followed by questions or unfinished statements, each with four suggested answers marked A, B, C and D. Choose the one that you think is the correct answer.

Mark your choice on your answer sheet.

TEXT   A

Surprisingly, no one knows how many children receive education in English hospitals, still less the content or quality of that education. Proper records are just not kept.

We know that more than 850,000 children go through hospital each year, and that every child of school age has a legal right to continue to receive education while in hospital. We also know there is only one hospital teacher to every 1,000 children in hospital.

Little wonder the latest survey concludes that the extent and type of hospital teaching available differ a great deal across the country. It is found that half the hospitals in England which admit children have no teacher. A further quarter have only a part-time teacher. The special children's hospitals in major cities do best; general hospitals in the country and holiday areas are worst off.

From this survey, one can estimate that fewer than one in five children have some contact with a hospital teacher—and that contact may be as little as two hours a day. Most children interviewed were surprised to find a teacher in hospital at all. They had not been prepared for it by parents or their own school. If there was a teacher they were much more likely to read books and do math or number work; without a teacher they would only play games.

Reasons for hospital teaching range from preventing a child falling behind and maintaining the habit of school to keeping a child occupied, and the latter is often all the teacher can do. The position and influence of many teachers was summed up when parents referred to them as "the library lady" or just "the helper".

Children tend to rely on concerned school friends to keep in touch with school work. Several parents spoke of requests for work being ignored or refused by the school. Once back at school, children rarely get extra teaching, and are told to catch up as best they can.

Many short-stay child-patients catch up quickly. But schools do very little to ease the anxiety about falling behind expressed by many of the children interviewed.

66. The author points out at the beginning that _____.

   [A] every child in hospital receives some teaching

   [B] not enough is known about hospital teaching

   [C] hospital teaching is of poor quality

   [D] the special children's hospital are worst off

67. It can be inferred from the latest survey that _____.

   [A] hospital teaching across the country is similar

   [B] each hospital has at least one part-time teacher

   [C] all hospitals surveyed offer education to children

   [D] only one-fourth of the hospitals have full-time teachers

68. Children in hospital usually turn to _____ in order to catch up with their school work.

   [A] hospital teachers   [B] schoolmates   [C] parents   [D] school teachers

69. We can conclude from the passage that the author is _____.

   [A] unfavourable towards children receiving education in hospitals

   [B] in favour of the present state of teaching in hospitals

   [C] unsatisfied with the present state of hospital teaching

   [D] satisfied with the results of the latest survey

TEXT B

Computer people talk a lot about the need for other people to become "computer-literate", in other words, to learn to understand computers and what makes them tick. Not all experts agree, however, that this is a good idea.

One pioneer, in particular, who disagrees is David Tebbutt, the founder of Computertown UK. Although many people see this as a successful attempt to bring people closer to the computer, David does not see it that way. He says that Computertown UK was formed for just the opposite reason, to bring computers to the people and make them "people-literate".

David first got the idea when he visited one of America's best-known computer "guru" figure, Bob Albrecht, in the small university town of Palo Alto in Northern California. Albrecht had started a project called Computertown USA in the local library, and the local children used to call round every Wednesday to borrow some time on the computers there, instead of borrowing library books. Albrecht was always on hand to answer any questions and to help the children discover about computers in their own way.

Over here, in Britain, Computertowns have taken off in a big way, and there are now about 40 scattered over the country. David Tebbutt thinks they are most successful when tied to a computer club. He insists there is a vast and important difference between the two, although they complement each other. The clubs cater for the enthusiasts, with some computer knowledge already, who get together and eventually form an expert computer group. This frightens away non-experts, who are happier going to Computertowns where there are computers available for them to experiment on, with experts available to encourage them and answer any questions; they are not told what to do, they find out.

David Tebbutt finds it interesting to see the two different approaches working side by side. The computer experts have to learn not to tell people about computers, but have to be able to explain the answers to the questions that people really want to know. In some Computertowns there are question sessions, rather like radio phone-ins, where the experts listen to a lot of questions and then try to work out some structure to answer them. People are not having to learn computer jargons, but the experts are having to translate computer mysteries into easily understood terms; the computers are becoming "people-literate."

70. According to David Tebbutt, the purpose of Computertown UK is to _____.

　　[A] train people to understand how computers work

　　[B] make more computers available to people

　　[C] enable more people to fix computers themselves

　　[D] help people find out more about computers

71. We learn from the passage that Computertown USA was a _____.

　　[A] town　　　　　　　[B] project　　　　　[C] library　　　　　[D] school

72. Which of the following statements is INCORRECT?

　　[A] Computertowns in the UK have become popular.

　　[B] Computertowns and clubs cater for different people.

　　[C] Computertowns are more successful than clubs.

　　[D] It's better that Computertowns and clubs work together.

73. Which of the following is NOT an advantage of Computertowns?

　　[A] Experts give lectures and talks on computers.

　　[B] Experts are on hand to answer people's questions.

　　[C] People are left to discover computers on their own.

　　[D] There are computers around for people to practise on.

TEXT C

There must be few questions on which responsible opinion is so utterly divided as on that of how much sleep we ought to have. There are some who think we can leave the body to regulate these matters for itself. "The answer is easy," says Dr. A. Burton. "With the right amount of sleep you should wake up fresh and alert five minutes before the alarm rings." If he is right many people must be undersleeping, including myself. But we must remember that some people have a greater inertia than others. This is not meant rudely. They switch on slowly, and they are reluctant to switch off. They are alert at bedtime and sleepy when it is time to get up, and this may have nothing to do with how fatigued their bodies are, or how much sleep they must take to lose their fatigue.

Other people feel sure that the present trend is towards too little sleep. To quote one medical opinion, "Thousands of people drift through life suffering from the effects of too little sleep; the reason is not that they can't sleep. Like advancing colonists, we do seem to be grasping ever more of the land of sleep for our waking needs, pushing the boundary back and reaching, apparently, for a point in our evolution where we will sleep no more. This in itself, of course, need not be a bad thing. What could be disastrous, however, is that we should press too quickly towards this goal, sacrificing sleep only to gain more time in which to jeopardize our civilization by actions and decisions made weak by fatigue.

Then, to complete the picture, there are those who believe that most people are persuaded to sleep too much. Dr H. Roberts, writing in *Every Man in Health*, asserts: "It may safely be stated that, just as the majority eat too much, so the majority sleep too much." One can see the point of this also. It would be a pity to retard our development by holding back those people who are gifted enough to work and play well with less than the average amount of sleep, if indeed it does them no harm. If one of the trends of evolution is that more of the life span is to be spent in gainful waking activity, then surely these people are in the van of this advance.

74. The author seems to indicate that _____.

[A] there are many controversial issues like the right amount of sleep

[B] among many issues the right amount of sleep is the least controversial

[C] people are now moving towards solving many controversial issues

[D] the right amount of sleep is a topic of much controversy among doctors

75. The author disagrees with Dr. Burton because _____.

[A] few people can wake up feeling fresh and alert

[B] some people still feel tired with enough sleep

[C] some people still feel sleepy with enough sleep

[D] some people go to bed very late at night

76. In the last paragraph the author points out that _____.

[A] sleeping less is good for human development

[B] people ought to be persuaded to sleep less than before

[C] it is incorrect to say that people sleep too little

[D] those who can sleep less should be encouraged

77. We learn from the passage that the author _____.

[A] comments on three different opinions

[B] favours one of the three opinions

[C] explains an opinion of his own

[D] revises someone else's opinion

TEXT D

Migration is usually defined as "permanent or semipermanent change of residence." This broad definition, of course, would include a move across the street or across a city. Our concern is with movement between nations, not with internal migration within nations, although such movements often exceed international movements in volume. Today, the motives of people who move short distances are very similar to those of international migrants.

Students of human migration speak of "push" and "pull" factors, which influence an individual's decision to move from one place to another. Push factors are associated with the place of origin. A push factor can be as simple and mild a matter as difficulty in finding a suitable job, or as traumatic as war, or severe famine. Obviously, refugees who leave their homes with guns pointed at their heads are motivated almost entirely by push factors (although pull factors do influence their choice of destination).

Pull factors are those associated with the place of destination. Most often these are economic, such as better job opportunities or the availability of good land to farm. The latter was an important factor in attracting settlers to the United States during the 19th century. In general, pull factors add up to an apparently better chance for a good life and material well-being than is offered by the place of origin. When there is a choice between several attractive potential destinations, the deciding factor might be a non-economic consideration such as the presence of relatives, friends, or at least fellow countrymen already established in the new place who are willing to help the newcomers settle in. Considerations of this sort lead to the development of migration flow.

Besides push and pull factors, there are what the sociologists call "intervening obstacles". Even if push and/or pull factors are very strong they still may be outweighed by intervening obstacles, such as the distance of the move, the trouble and cost of moving, the difficulty of entering the new country, and the problems likely to be encountered on arrival.

The decision to move is also influenced by "personal factors" of the potential migrant. The same push-pull factors and obstacles operate differently on different people, sometimes because they are at different stages of their lives, or just because of their varying abilities and personalities. The prospect of packing up everything and moving to a new and perhaps very strange environment may appear interesting and challenging to an unmarried young man and appallingly difficult to a slightly older man with a wife and small kids. Similarly, the need to learn a new language and customs may excite one person and frighten another.

Regardless of why people move, migration of large numbers of people causes conflict. The United States and other western countries have experienced adjustment problems with each new wave of immigrants. The newest arrivals are usually given the lowest-paid jobs and are resented by native people who may have to compete with them for those jobs. It has usually taken several decades for each group to be accepted into the mainstream of society in the host country.

78. The author thinks that pull factors _____.

    [A] are all related to economic considerations

    [B] are not as decisive as push factors

    [C] include a range of considerations

    [D] are more important than push factors

79. People's decisions to migrate might be influenced by all the following EXCEPT _____.

[A] personalities　　[B] education　　　[C] marital status　　[D] abilities

80. The purpose of the passage is to discuss _____.

　[A] the problems of international migrants

　[B] the motives of international migrants

　[C] migration inside the country

　[D] migration between countries

English

2000 年英语专业四级考试阅读理解

Part Ⅵ   Reading Comprehension

In this section there are four passage followed by questions or unfinished statements, each with four suggested answers marked A, B, C and D. Choose the one that you think is the best answer.

Mark your answers on your answer sheet.

TEXT   A

Clearly if we are to participate in the society in which we live we must communicate with other people. A great deal of communicating is performed on person-to-person basis by the simple means of speech. If we travel in buses, buy things in shops, or eat in restaurants, we are likely to have conversations where we give information or opinions, receive news or comment, and very likely have our views challenged by other members of society.

Face-to-face contact is by no means the only form of communication and during the last two hundred years the art of *mass communication* has become one of the dominating factors of contemporary society. Two things, above others, have caused the enormous growth of the communication industry. Firstly, inventiveness has led to advances in printing, telecommunications, photography, radio and television. Secondly, speed has revolutionized the transmission and reception of communications so that local news often takes a back seat to national news, which itself is often almost eclipsed by international news.

No longer is the possession of information confined to a privileged minority. In the last century the wealthy man with his own library was indeed fortunate, but today there are public libraries. Forty years ago people used to flock to the cinema, but now far more people sit at home and turn on the TV to watch a programme that is being channeled into millions of homes.

Communication is no longer merely concerned with the transmission of information. The modern communication industry influences the way people live in society and broadens their horizons by allowing access to information, education and entertainment. The printing, broadcasting and advertising industries are all involved with informing, educating and entertaining.

Although a great deal of the material communicated by the mass media is very valuable to the individual and to the society of which he is a part, the vast modern network of communications is open to abuse. However, the mass media are with us for better, for worse, and there is no turning back.

66. In the first paragraph the writer emphasizes the _____ of face-to-face contact in social settings.

    [A] nature   [B] limitation   [C] usefulness   [D] creativity

67. It is implied in the passage that _____.

    [A] local news used to be the only source of information

    [B] local news still takes a significant place

    [C] national news is becoming more popular

    [D] international news is the fastest transmitted news

68. Which of the following statements is INCORRECT?

    [A] To possess information used to be a privilege.

    [B] Public libraries have replaced private libraries.

    [C] Communication means more than transmission.

    [D] Information influences ways of life and thinking.

69. From the last paragraph we can infer that the writer is _____.

    [A] indifferent to the harmful influence of the mass media

    [B] happy about the drastic changes in the mass media

    [C] pessimistic about the future of the mass media

    [D] concerned about the wrong use of the mass media

TEXT B

The men and women of Anglo-Saxon England normally bore one name only. Distinguishing epithets were rarely added. These might be patronymic, descriptive or occupational. They were, however, hardly surnames. Heritable names gradually became general in the three centuries following the Norman Conquest in 1066. It was not until the 13th and 14th centuries that surnames became fixed, although for many years after that, the degree of stability in family names varied considerably in different parts of the country.

British surnames fall mainly into four broad categories: *patronymic*, occupational, descriptive and local. A few names, it is true, will remain puzzling: foreign names, perhaps, crudely translated, adapted or abbreviated; or artificial names.

In fact, over fifty per cent of genuine British surnames derive from place names of different kinds, and so they belong to the last of our four main categories. Even such a name as Simpson may belong to this last group, and not to the first, had the family once had its home in the ancient village of that name. Otherwise, Simpson means "the son of Simon", as might be expected.

Hundreds of occupational surnames are at once familiar to us, or at least recognisable after a little thought: Archer, Carter, Fisher, Mason, Thatcher, Taylor, to name but a few. Hundreds of others are more obscure in their meanings and testify to the amazing specialisation in medieval arts, crafts and functions. Such are "Day", (Old English for breadmaker) and "Walker" (a fuller whose job it was to clean and thicken newly made cloth).

All these vocational names carry with them a certain gravity and dignity, which descriptive names often lack. Some, it is true, like "Long", "Short" or "Little", are simple. They may be taken quite literally. Others require more thinking: their meanings are slightly different from the modern ones. "Black" and "White" implied dark and fair respectively. "Sharp" meant genuinely discerning, alert, acute rather than quick-witted or clever.

Place-names have a lasting interest since there is hardly a town or village in all England that has not at some time given its name to a family. They may be picturesque, even poetical; or they may be pedestrian, even trivial. Among the commoner names which survive with relatively little change from old-English times are "Milton" (middle enclosure) and "Hilton" (enclosure on a hill).

70. Surnames are said to be _____ in Anglo-Saxon England.

　　[A] common 　　　　[B] vocational 　　　　[C] unusual 　　　　[D] descriptive

71. We learn from the first paragraph that _____ for many years after the 13th and 14th centuries.

　　[A] family names became descriptive and occupational

　　[B] people in some areas still had no surnames

　　[C] some people kept changing their surnames

　　[D] all family names became fixed in England

72. "Patronymic" in the second paragraph is closest in meaning to "formed from _____".

　　[A] the name of one's father 　　　　[B] the family occupation

　　[C] one's family home 　　　　　　　[D] one's family history

73. Which of the following sentences is an opinion rather than a fact?

　　[A] Hundreds of occupational names are at once familiar to us.

　　[B] "Black" and "White" implied "dark" and "fair" respectively.

　　[C] Vocational names carry with them a certain gravity and dignity.

　　[D] Every place in England has given its name to a family.

TEXT C

Since the early 1930s, Swiss banks had prided themselves on their system of banking secrecy and numbered accounts. Over the years, they had successfully withstood every challenge to this system by their own government who, in turn, had been frequently urged by foreign governments to reveal information about the financial affairs of certain account holders. The result of this policy of secrecy was that a kind of mystique had grown up around Swiss banking. There was a widely-held belief that Switzerland was irresistible to wealthy foreigners, mainly because of its numbered accounts and bankers' reluctance to ask awkward questions of depositors. Contributing to the mystique was the view, carefully propagated by the banks themselves, that if this secrecy was ever given up, foreigners would fall over themselves in the rush to withdraw money, and the Swiss banking system would virtually collapse overnight.

To many, therefore, it came like a bolt out of the blue, when, in 1977, the Swiss banks announced they had signed a pact with the Swiss National Bank (the Central Bank). The aim of the agreement was to prevent the improper use of the country's bank secrecy laws, and its effect was to curb severely the system of secrecy.

The rules which the banks had agreed to observe made the opening of numbered accounts subject to much closer scrutiny than before. The banks would be required, if necessary, to identify the origin of foreign funds going into numbered and other accounts. The idea was to stop such accounts being used for dubious purposes. Also, they agreed not to accept funds resulting from tax evasion or from crime.

The pact represented essentially a tightening up of banking rules. Although the banks agreed to end relations with clients whose identities were unclear or who were performing improper acts, they were still not obliged to inform of a client to anyone, including the Swiss government. To some extent, therefore, the principle of secrecy had been maintained.

74. Swiss banks took pride in _____.

[A] the number of their accounts

[B] withholding client information

[C] being mysterious to the outsiders

[D] attracting wealthy foreign clients

75. According to the passage, the widely-held belief that Switzerland was irresistible to wealthy foreigners was _____ by banks themselves.

[A] denied   [B] criticized   [C] reviewed   [D] defended

76. In the last paragraph, the writer thinks that _____.

[A] complete changes had been introduced into Swiss banks

[B] Swiss banks could no longer keep client information

[C] changes in the bank policies had been somewhat superficial

[D] more changes need to be considered and made

TEXT D

Coketown was a town of red brick, or of brick that would have been red if the smoke and the ashes had allowed it; but as matters stood it was a town of unnatural red and black like the painted face of a savage. It was a town of machinery and tall chimneys, out of which smoke trailed themselves for ever and ever. It had a black canal in it, and a river that ran purple with ill-smelling dye, and vast piles of buildings full of windows where there was a rattling and a trembling all day long, and where the piston of the steam-engine worked monotonously up and down like the head of an elephant in a state of madness. The town contained several large streets all very like one another, and many small streets still more like one another, inhabited by people equally like one another.

A sunny midsummer day. There was such a thing sometimes, even in Coketown. Seen from a distance in such weather, Coketown lay covered in a haze of its own. You only knew the town was there, because you knew there could have been no such blotch upon the view without a town.

The streets were hot and dusty on the summer day, and the sun was so bright that it even shone through the haze over Coketown, and could not be looked at steadily. Workers emerged from low underground doorways into factory yards, and sat on posts and steps, wiping their faces and contemplating coals. The whole town seemed to be frying in oil. There was a stifling smell of hot oil everywhere. The atmosphere of those places was like the breath of hell, and their inhabitants wasting with heat, toiled languidly in the desert. But no temperature made the mad elephants more mad or more sane. Their wearisome heads went up and down at the same rate, in hot weather and in cold, wet weather and dry, fair weather and foul. The measured motion of their shadows on the walls, was the substitute Coketown had to show for the shadows of rustling woods; while for the summer hum of insects, it could offer all the year round, from the dawn of Monday to the night of Saturday, the whirr of shafts and wheels.

77. Which of the following adjectives is NOT appropriate to describe Coketown?

　　[A] dull 　　　　　　[B] dirty 　　　　　　[C] noisy 　　　　　　[D] savage

78. From the passage we know that Coketown was mainly a(n) _____ town.

　　[A] industrial 　　　　[B] agricultural 　　　[C] residential 　　　　[D] commercial

79. Only _____ were not affected by weather.

　　[A] the workmen 　　　　　　　　　　[B] the inhabitants

　　[C] the steam-engines 　　　　　　　　[D] the rustling woods

80. Which is the author's opinion of Coketown?

　　[A] Coketown should be replaced by woods.

　　[B] The town was seriously polluted.

　　[C] The town had too much oil in it.

　　[D] The town's atmosphere was traditional.

2001 年英语专业四级考试阅读理解

Part VI   Reading Comprehension

In this section there are four passages followed by questions or unfinished statements, each with four suggested answers marked A, B, C and D. Choose the one that you think is the best answer.

Mark your answers on your answer sheet.

TEXT   A

The train clattered over points and passed through a station.

Then it began suddenly to slow down, presumably in obedience to a signal. For some minutes it crawled along, then stopped; presently it began to move forward again. Another up-train passed them, though with less vehemence than the first one. The train gathered speed again. At that moment another train, also on a down-line, swerved inwards towards them, for a moment with almost alarming effect. For a time the two trains ran parallel, now one gaining a little, now the other. Mrs. McGillicuddy looked from her window through the windows of the parallel carriages. Most of the blinds were down, but occasionally the occupants of the carriages were visible. The other train was not very full and there were many empty carriages.

At the moment when the two trains gave the illusion of being stationary, a blind in one of the carriages flew up with a snap. Mrs. McGillicuddy looked into the lighted first-class carriage that was only a few feet away.

Then she drew her breath in with a gasp and half-rose to her feet.

Standing with his back to the window and to her was a man. His hands were round the throat of a woman who faced him, and he was slowly, remorselessly, strangling her. Her eyes were staring from their sockets, her face was purple. As Mrs. McGillicuddy watched, fascinated, the end came; the body went limp and crumpled in the man's hands.

At the same moment, Mrs. McGillicuddy's train slowed down again and the other began to gain speed. It passed forward and a moment or two later it had vanished from sight.

Almost automatically Mrs. McGillicuddy's hand went up to the communication cord then paused, irresolute. After all, what use would it be ringing the cord of the train in which she was travelling? The horror of what she had seen at such close quarters, and the unusual circumstances, made her feel paralysed. Some immediate action was necessary—but what?

The door of her compartment was drawn back and a ticket collector said, "Ticket, please."

66. When Mrs. McGillicuddy's train passed through a station, it _____.

    [A] gained speed suddenly   [B] kept its usual speed

    [C] changed its speed   [D] stopped immediately

67. Mrs. McGillicuddy seems to be a(an) _____ person.

    [A] observant   [B] interested   [C] nosy   [D] nervous

68. What she saw in the parallel train made her feel _____.

    [A] excited   [B] anxious   [C] worried   [D] horrified

69. She didn't ring the communication cord immediately because _____.

    [A] she was very much afraid

    [B] there was no point of doing so

    [C] she was too shocked to move

    [D] the ticket collector came in

TEXT B

I am one of the many city people who are always saying that given the choice we would prefer to live in the country away from the dirt and noise of a large city. I have managed to convince myself that if it weren't for my job I would immediately head out for the open spaces and go back to nature in some sleepy village buried in the country. But how realistic is the dream?

Cities can be frightening places. The majority of the population live in massive tower blocks, noisy, dirty and impersonal. The sense of belonging to a community tends to disappear when you live fifteen floors up. All you can see from your window is sky, or other blocks of flats. Children become aggressive and nervous—cooped up at home all day, with nowhere to play; their mothers feel isolated from the rest of the world. Strangely enough, whereas in the past the inhabitants of one street all knew each other, nowadays people on the same floor in tower blocks don't even say hello to each other.

Country life, on the other hand, differs from this kind of isolated existence in that a sense of community generally binds the inhabitants of small villages together. People have the advantage of knowing that there is always someone to turn to when they need help. But country life has disadvantages too. While it is true that you may be among friends in a village, it is also true that you are cut off from the exciting and important events that take place in cities. There's little possibility of going to a new show or the latest movie. Shopping becomes a major problem, and for anything slightly out of the ordinary you have to go on an expedition to the nearest large town. The citydweller who leaves for the country is often oppressed by a sense of unbearable stillness and quiet.

What, then, is the answer? The country has the advantage of peace and quiet, but suffers from the disadvantage of being cut off; the city breeds a feeling of isolation, and constant noise batters the senses. But one of its main advantages is that you are at the centre of things, and that life doesn't come to an end at half past nine at night. Some people have found (or rather bought) a compromise between the two: they have expressed their preference for the "quiet life" by leaving the suburbs and moving to villages within commuting distance of large cities. They generally have about as much sensitivity as the plastic flowers they leave behind—they are polluted with strange ideas about change and improvement which they force on to the unwilling original inhabitants of the villages.

What then of my dreams of leaning on a cottage gate and murmuring "morning" to the locals as they pass by. I'm keen on the idea, but you see there's my cat, Toby. I'm not at all sure that he would take to all that fresh air and exercise in the long grass. I mean, can you see him mixing with all those hearty males down the farm? No, he would rather have the electric imitation-coal fire any evening.

70. We get the impression from the first paragraph that the author _____.
    [A] used to live in the country
    [B] used to work in the city
    [C] works in the city
    [D] lives in the country

71. In the author's opinion, the following may cause city people to be unhappy EXCEPT _____.
    [A] a strong sense of fear
    [B] lack of communication
    [C] housing conditions
    [D] a sense of isolation

72. The passage implies that it is easy to buy the following things in the country EXCEPT _____.
    [A] daily necessities   [B] fresh fruits
    [C] designer clothes   [D] fresh vegetables

73. According to the passage, which of the following adjectives best describes those people who work in large cities and live in villages?
    [A] Original.   [B] Quiet.   [C] Arrogant.   [D] Insensitive.

74. Do you think the author will move to the country?
    [A] Yes, he will do so.   [B] No, he will not do so.
    [C] It is difficult to tell.   [D] He is in two minds.

TEXT C

Traditionally, the woman has held a low position in marriage partnerships. While her husband went his way she had to wash, stitch and sew. Today the move is to liberate the woman, which may in the end strengthen the marriage union.

Perhaps the greatest obstacle to friendship in marriage is the amount a couple usually see of each other. Friendship in its usual sense is not tested by the strain of daily, year-long co-habitation. Couples need to take up separate interests (and friendship) as well as mutually shared ones, if they are not to get used to the more attractive elements of each other's personalities.

Married couples are likely to exert themselves for guests—being amusing, discussing with passion and point—and then to fall into dull exhausted silence when the guests have gone.

As in all friendship, a husband and wife must try to interest each other, and to spend sufficient time sharing absorbing activities to give them continuing common interests. But at the same time they must spend enough time on separate interests with separate people to preserve and develop their separate personalities and keep their relationship fresh.

For too many highly intelligent working women, home represents chore obligations, because the husband only tolerates her work and does not participate in household chores. For too many highly intelligent working men, home represents dullness and complaints—from an over-dependent wife who will not gather courage to make her own life.

In such an atmosphere, the partners grow further and further apart, both love and liking disappearing. For too many couples with children, the children are allowed to command all time and attention, allowing the couple no time to develop liking and friendship, as well as love, allotting them exclusive parental roles.

75. According to the passage, which of the following statements is CORRECT?

[A] Friendship in marriage means daily, year-long cohabitation.

[B] Friendship can be kept fresh by both separate and shared interests.

[C] Friendship in marriage is based on developing similar interests.

[D] Friendship in marriage is based on developing separate interests.

76. The passage suggests that married couples become _____.

[A] unfriendly with guests   [B] uninterested in guests

[C] hostile when guests have left   [D] quiet when guests have left

77. The passage seems to indicate at the end that children _____.

[A] help couples reinforce their friendship

[B] make no impact on the quality of friendship

[C] may pose obstacles in marital friendship

[D] command less time and care than expected

TEXT D

Sending a child to school in England is a step which many parents do not find easy to take. In theory, at least, the problem is that there are very many choices to make. Let us try to list some of the alternatives between which parents are forced to decide. To begin with, they may ask themselves whether they would like their child to go to a single-sex school or a co-educational school. They may also consider whether he should go to a school which is connected to a particular church or religious group, or whether the school should have no such connections. Another decision is whether the school should be one of the vast majority financed by the State or one of the very small but influential minority of private schools, though this choice is, of course, only available to the small number of those who can pay. Also connected with the question of money is whether the child should go to a boarding school or live at home. Then there is the question of what the child should do at school. Should it be a school whose curriculum lays emphasis, for instance, on necessary skills, such as reading, writing and mathematics, or one which pays more attention to developing the child's personality, morally, emotionally and socially. Finally, with dissatisfaction with conventional education as great as it is in some circles in England and certainly in the USA, the question might even arise in the parents' minds as to whether the child should be compelled to go to school at all. Although in practice, some parents may not think twice about any of these choices and send their child to the only school available in the immediate neighbourhood, any parent who is interested enough can insist that as many choices as possible be made open to him, and the system is theoretically supposed to provide them.

78. Parents find choosing a school hard because _____ .
    [A] there is a limited number of choices
    [B] some schools are very expensive
    [C] some schools are government schools
    [D] they are faced with a variety of offers

79. According to the passage, some parents, if allowed, might let their children stay at home because they _____ .
    [A] don't find conventional education satisfactory
    [B] don't know how to choose among different schools
    [C] intend to educate their children themselves
    [D] find conventional education too expensive to pay for

80. What is implied at the very end of the passage?
    [A] Most parents are unconcerned about the choices available to them.
    [B] Interested parents can request more school choices be open to them.
    [C] The educational system may not provide as many choices as expected.
    [D] Most parents usually send their children to the schools nearby.

2002 年英语专业四级考试阅读理解

Part Ⅵ   Reading Comprehension

In this section there are four passages followed by questions or unfinished statements, each with four suggested answers marked A, B, C and D. Choose the one that you think is the best answer.

Mark your answers on your answer sheet.

TEXT   A

Many of the home electric goods which are advertised as liberating the modern woman tend to have the opposite effect, because they simply change the nature of work instead of eliminating it. Machines have a certain novelty value, like toys for adults. It is certainly less tiring to put clothes in a washing machine, but the time saved does not really amount to much: the machine has to be watched, the clothes have to be carefully sorted out first, stains removed by hand, buttons pushed and water changed, clothes taken out, aired and ironed. It would be more liberating to pack it all off to a laundry and not necessarily more expensive, since no ***capital investment*** is required. Similarly, if you really want to save time you do not make cakes with an electric mixer, you buy one in a shop. If one compares the image of the woman in the women's magazine with the goods advertised by those periodicals, one realizes how useful a projected image can be commercially. A careful balance has to be struck: if you show a labour-saving device, follow it up with a complicated recipe on the next page; on no account hint at the notion that a woman could get herself a job, but instead foster her sense of her own usefulness, emphasizing the creative aspect of her function as a housewife. So we get cake mixes where the cook simply adds an egg herself, to produce "that lovely home-baked flavour the family love", and knitting patterns that can be made by hand, or worse still, on knitting machines, which became tremendously fashionable when they were first introduced. Automatic cookers are advertised by pictures of pretty young mothers taking their children to the park, not by professional women presetting the dinner before leaving home for work.

66. According to the passage, many of the home electric goods which are supposed to liberate women _____.

   [A] remove unpleasant aspects of housework

[B] save the housewife very little time

[C] save the housewife's time but not her money

[D] have absolutely no value for the housewife

67. According to the context, "capital investment" refers to money _____.

[A] spent on a washing machine

[B] borrowed from the bank

[C] saved in the bank

[D] lent to other people

68. The goods advertised in women's magazines are really meant to _____.

[A] free housewives from housework

[B] encourage housewives to go out to work

[C] turn housewives into excellent cooks

[D] give them a false sense of fulfillment

TEXT B

The "standard of living" of any country means the average person's share of the goods and services which the country produces. A country's standard of living, therefore, depends first and foremost on its capacity to produce wealth. "Wealth" in this sense is not money, for we do not live on money but on things that money can buy: "goods" such as food and clothing, and "services" such as transport and entertainment.

A country's capacity to produce wealth depends upon many factors, most of which have an effect on one another. Wealth depends to a great extent upon a country's natural resources, such as coal, gold, and other minerals, water supply and so on. Some regions of the world are well supplied with coal and minerals, and have a fertile soil and a favourable climate; other regions possess none of them.

Next to natural resources comes the ability to turn them to use. Some countries are perhaps well off in natural resources, but suffered for many years from civil and external wars, and for this and other reasons have been unable to develop their resources. Sound and stable political conditions, and freedom from foreign invasion enable a country to develop its natural resources peacefully and steadily, and to produce more wealth than another country equally well served by nature but less well ordered. Another important factor is the technical efficiency of a country's people. Industrialized countries that have trained numerous skilled workers and technicians are better placed to produce wealth than countries whose workers are largely unskilled.

A country's standard of living does not only depend upon the wealth that is produced and consumed within its own borders, but also upon what is indirectly produced through international trade. For example, Britain's wealth in foodstuffs and other agricultural products would be much less if she had to depend only on those grown at home. Trade makes it possible for her surplus manufactured goods to be traded abroad for the agricultural products that would otherwise be lacking. A country's wealth is, therefore, much influenced by its manufacturing capacity，provided that other countries can be found ready to accept its manufactures.

69. The standard of living in a country is determined by _____.

[A] its goods and services

[B] the type of wealth produced

[C] how well it can create wealth

[D] what an ordinary person can share

70. A country's capacity to produce wealth depends on all the factors EXCEPT _____.

[A] people's share of its goods

[B] political and social stability

[C] qualities of its workers

[D] use of natural resources

71. According to the passage, _____ play an equally important role in determining a country's standard of living.

[A] farm products　　　　　　　　　[B] industrial goods

[C] foodstuffs　　　　　　　　　　　[D] export & import

TEXT C

How we look and how we appear to others probably worries us more when we are in our teens or early twenties than at any other time in our life. Few of us are content to accept ourselves as we are, and few are brave enough to ignore the trends of fashion.

Most fashion magazines or TV advertisements try to persuade us that we should dress in a certain way or behave in a certain manner. If we do, they tell us, we will be able to meet new people with confidence and deal with every situation confidently and without embarrassment. Changing fashion, of course, does not apply just to dress. A barber today does not cut a boy's hair in the same way as he used to, and girls do not make up in the same way as their mothers and grandmothers did. The advertisers show us the latest fashionable styles and we are constantly under pressure to follow the fashion in case our friends think we are odd or dull.

What causes fashions to change? Sometimes convenience or practical necessity or just the fancy of an influential person can establish a fashion. Take hats, for example. In cold climates, early buildings were cold inside, so people wore hats indoors as well as outside. In recent times, the late President Kennedy caused a depression in the American hat industry by not wearing hats: more America men followed his example.

There is also a cyclical pattern in fashion. In the 1920s in Europe and America, short skirts became fashionable. After World War Two, they dropped to ankle length. Then they got shorter and shorter until the miniskirt was in fashion. After a few more years, skirts became longer again.

Today, society is much freer and easier than it used to be. It is no longer necessary to dress like everyone else. Within reason, you can dress as you *like* or do your hair the way you *like* instead of the way you *should* because it is the fashion. The popularity of jeans and the "untidy" look seems to be a reaction against the increasingly expensive fashions of the top fashion houses.

At the same time, appearance is still important in certain circumstances and then we must choose our clothes carefully. It would be foolish to go to an interview for a job in a law firm wearing jeans and a sweater; and it would be discourteous to visit some distinguished scholar looking as if we were going to the beach or a nightclub. However, you need never feel depressed if you don't look like the latest fashion photo. Look around you and you'll see that no one else does either!

72. The author thinks that people are _____.
    [A] satisfied with their appearance
    [B] concerned about appearance in old age
    [C] far from neglecting what is in fashion
    [D] reluctant to follow the trends in fashion
73. Fashion magazines and TV advertisements seem to link fashion to _____.
    [A] confidence in life   [B] personal dress
    [C] individual hair style   [D] personal future
74. Causes of fashions are _____.
    [A] uniform   [B] varied   [C] unknown   [D] inexplicable
75. Present-day society is much freer and easier because it emphasizes _____.
    [A] uniformity   [B] formality   [C] informality   [D] individuality
76. Which is the main idea of the last paragraph?
    [A] Care about appearance in formal situations.
    [B] Fashion in formal and informal situations.
    [C] Ignoring appearance in informal situations.
    [D] Ignoring appearance in all situations.

TEXT D

Massive changes in all of the world's deeply cherished sporting habits are underway. Whether it's one of London's parks full of people playing softball, and Russians taking up rugby, or the Superbowl rivaling the British Football Cup Final as a televised spectator event in Britain, the patterns of players and spectators are changing beyond recognition. We are witnessing a globalization of our sporting culture.

That annual bicycle race, the *Tour de France*, much loved by the French is a good case in point. Just a few years back it was a strictly continental affair with France, Belgium and Holland, Spain and Italy taking part. But in recent years it has been dominated by Colombian mountain climbers, and American and Irish riders.

The people who really matter welcome the shift toward globalization. Peugeot, Michelin and Panasonic are multi-national corporations that want worldwide returns for the millions they invest in teams. So it does them literally a world of good to see this unofficial world championship become just that.

This is undoubtedly an economic-based revolution we are witnessing here, one made possible by communications technology, but made to happen because of marketing considerations. Sell the game and you can sell Coca Cola or Budweiser as well.

The skilful way in which American football has been sold to Europe is a good example of how all sports will develop. The aim of course is not really to spread the sport for its own sake, but to increase the number of people interested in the major money-making events. The economics of the Superbowl are already astronomical. With seats at US $ 125, gate receipts alone were a staggering $ 10,000,000. The most important statistic of the day, however, was the $ 100,000,000 in TV advertising fees. Imagine how much that becomes when the eyes of the world are watching.

So it came as a terrible shock, but not really as a surprise, to learn that some people are now suggesting that soccer change from being a game of two 45 - minute halves, to one of four 25 - minute quarters. The idea is unashamedly to capture more advertising revenue, without giving any thought for the integrity of a sport which relies for its essence on the flowing nature of the action.

Moreover, as sports expand into world markets, and as our choice of sports as consumers also grows, so we will demand to see them played at a higher and higher level. In boxing we have already seen numerous, dubious world title categories because people will not pay to see anything less than a "World Title" fight, and this means that the title fights have to be held in different countries around the world!

77. Globalization of sporting culture means that _____.

    [A] more people are taking up sports

    [B] traditional sports are getting popular

    [C] many local sports are becoming international

    [D] foreigners are more interested in local sports

78. Which of the following is NOT related to the massive changes?

    [A] Good economic returns   [B] Revival of sports

    [C] Communications technology   [D] Marketing strategies

79. What is the author's attitude towards the suggestion to change soccer into one of four 25 - minute quarters?

    [A] Favourable.   [B] Unclear.   [C] Reserved.   [D] Critical.

80. People want to see higher-level sports competitions mainly because _____.

    [A] they become more professional than ever

    [B] they regard sports as consumer goods

    [C] there exist few world-class championships

    [D] sports events are exciting and stimulating

2003 年英语专业四级考试阅读理解

Part Ⅵ Reading Comprehension

In this section there are four passages followed by questions or unfinished statements, each with four suggested answers marked A, B, C and D. Choose the one that you think is the best answer.

Mark your answers on your answer sheet.

TEXT A

The way in which people use social space reflects their social relationships and their ethnic identity. Early immigrants to America from Europe brought with them a collective style of living, which they retained until late in the 18th century. Historical records document a group-oriented existence, in which one room was used for eating, entertaining guests, and sleeping. People ate soups from a communal pot, shared drinking cups, and used a common pit toilet. With the development of ideas about individualism, people soon began to shift to the use of individual cups and plates; the eating of meals that included meat, bread, and vegetables served on separate plates; and the use of private toilets. They began to build their houses with separate rooms to entertain guests—living rooms, separate bedrooms for sleeping, separate work areas—kitchen, laundry room, and separate bathrooms.

In Mexico, the meaning and organization of domestic space is strikingly different. Houses are organized around a *patio*, or courtyard. Rooms open onto the patio, where all kinds of domestic activities take place. Individuals do not have separate bedrooms. Children often sleep with parents, and brothers or sisters share a bed, emphasizing familial interdependence. Rooms in Mexican houses are locations for multiple activities that, in contrast, are rigidly separated in the United States.

66. Changes in living styles among early immigrants were initially brought about by _____.

    [A] rising living standards   [B] new concepts

    [C] new customs   [D] new designs of houses

67. Which of the following is NOT discussed in the passage?

    [A] Their concepts of domestic space.

    [B] Their social relationships.

[C] The functions of their rooms.

[D] The layout of their houses.

TEXT B

There are superstitions attached to numbers; even those ancient Greeks believed that all numbers and their multiples had some mystical significance.

Those numbers between 1 and 13 were in particular to have a powerful influence over the affairs of men.

For example, it is commonly said that luck, good or bad, comes in threes; if an accident happens, two more of the same kind may be expected soon afterwards. The arrival of a letter will be followed by two others within a certain period.

Another belief involving the number three has it that it is unlucky to light three cigarettes from the one match. If this happens, the bad luck that goes with the deed falls upon the person whose cigarette was the last to be lit. The ill-omen linked to the lighting of three things from one match or candle goes back to at least the 17th century and probably earlier. It was believed that three candles alight at the same time would be sure to bring bad luck; one, two, or four, were permissible, but never just three.

Seven was another significant number, usually regarded as a bringer of good luck. The ancient astrologers believed that the universe was governed by seven planets; students of Shakespeare will recall that the life of man was divided into seven ages. Seven horseshoes nailed to a house will protect it from all evil.

Nine is usually thought of as a lucky number because it is the product of three times three. It was much used by the Anglo Saxons in their charms for healing.

Another belief was that great changes occurred every 7th and 9th of a man's life. Consequently, the age of 63 (the product of nine and seven) was thought to be a very perilous time for him. If he survived his 63rd year he might hope to live to a ripe old age.

Thirteen, as we well know, is regarded with great awe and fear.

The common belief is that this derives from the fact that there were 13 people at Christ's Last Supper. This being the eve of his betrayal, it is not difficult to understand the significance given to the number by the early Christians.

In more modern times 13 is an especially unlucky number of a dinner party, for example. Hotels will avoid numbering a floor the 13th; the progression is from 12 to 14, and no room is given the number 13. Many home owners will use 12 1/2 instead of 13 as their house number.

Yet oddly enough, to be born on the 13th of the month is not regarded with any fear at all, which just shows how irrational we are in our superstitious beliefs.

68. According to the passage, which of the following groups of numbers will certainly bring good luck to people?

[A] 3 and 7.   [B] 3 and 9.   [C] 7 and 9.   [D] 3 and 13.

69. The ill luck associated with 13 is supposed to have its origin in _____.

[A] legend   [B] religion

[C] popular belief   [D] certain customs

70. What is the author's attitude towards people's superstitious beliefs?

    [A] He is mildly critical.

    [B] He is strongly critical.

    [C] He is in favour of them

    [D] His attitude is not clear.

TEXT C

Women's minds work differently from men's. At least, that is what most men are convinced of. Psychologists view the subject either as a matter of frustration or a joke. Now the biologists have moved into this minefield, and some of them have found that there are real differences between the brains of men and women. But being different, they point out hurriedly, is not the same as being better or worse.

There is, however, a definite structural variation between the male and female brain. The difference is in a part of the brain that is used in the most complex intellectual processes — the link between the two halves of the brain.

The two halves are linked by a trunkline of between 200 and 300 million nerves, the corpus callosum. Scientists have found quite recently that the *corpus callosum* in women is always larger and probably richer in nerve fibres than it is in men. This is the first time that a structural difference has been found between the brains of women and men and it must have some significance. The question is "What?", and, if this difference exists, are there others? Research shows that present-day women think differently and behave differently from men. Are some of these differences biological and inborn, a result of evolution? We tend to think that is the influence of society that produces these differences. But could we be wrong?

Research showed that these two halves of the brain had different functions, and that the corpus callosum enabled them to work together. For most people, the left half is used for wordhandling, analytical and logical activities; the right half works on pictures, patterns and forms. We need both halves working together. And the better the connections, the more harmoniously the two halves work. And, according to research findings, women have the better connections.

But it isn't all that easy to explain the actual differences between skills of men and women on this basis. In schools throughout the world girls tend to be better than boys at "language subjects" and boys better at maths and physics. If *these differences* correspond with the differences in the hemispheric trunkline, there is an unalterable distinction between the sexes.

We shan't know for a while, partly because we don't know of any precise relationship between abilities in school subjects and the functioning of the two halves of the brain, and we cannot understand how the two halves interact via the *corpus callosum*. But this striking difference must have some effect and, because the difference is in the parts of the brain involved in intellect, we should be looking for differences in intellectual processing.

71. Which of the following statements is CORRECT?

[A] Biologists are conducting research where psychologists have given up.

[B] Brain differences point to superiority of one sex over the other.

[C] Results of scientific research fail to support popular belief.

[D] The structural differences in the brain between the sexes has long been known.

72. According to the passage it is commonly believed that brain differences are caused by _____ factors.

[A] biological　　　[B] psychological　　　[C] physical　　　[D] social

73. "These differences" in paragraph 5 refer to those in _____.

[A] skills of men and women

[B] school subjects

[C] the brain structure of men and women

[D] activities carried out by the brain

74. At the end of the passage the author proposes more work on _____.

[A] the brain structure as a whole

[B] the functioning of part of the brain

[C] the distinction between the sexes

[D] the effects of the corpus callosum

75. What is the main purpose of the passage?

[A] To outline the research findings on the brain structure.

[B] To explain the link between sex and brain structure.

[C] To discuss the various factors that cause brain differences.

[D] To suggest new areas in brain research

TEXT D

Information is the primary commodity in more and more industries today.

By 2005, 83% of American management personnel will be knowledge workers. Europe and Japan are not far behind.

By 2005, half of all knowledge workers (22% of the labour force) will choose "flextime, flexplace" arrangements, which allow them to work at home, communicating with the office via computer networks.

In the United States, the so-called "*digital divide*" seems to be disappearing. In early 2000, a poll found, that, where half of white households owned computers, so did fully 43% of African-American households, and their numbers were growing rapidly. Hispanic households continued to lag behind, but their rate of computer ownership was expanding as well.

Company-owned and industry-wide television networks are bringing programming to thousands of locations. Business TV is becoming big business.

Computer competence will approach 100% in US urban areas by the year 2005, with Europe and Japan not far behind.

80% of US homes will have computers in 2005, compared with roughly 50% now.

In the United States, 5 of the 10 fastest-growing careers between now and 2005 will be computer related. Demand for programmers and systems analysts will grow by 70%. The same trend is accelerating in Europe, Japan, and India.

By 2005, nearly all college texts and many high school and junior high books will be tied to Internet sites that provide source material, study exercises, and relevant news articles to aid in learning. Others will come with CD-ROMs that offer similar resources.

Internet links will provide access to the card catalogues of all the major libraries in the world by 2005. It will be possible to call up on a PC screen millions of volumes from distant libraries. Web sites enhance books by providing pictures, sound, film clips, and flexible indexing and search utilities.

Implications: Anyone with access to the Internet will be able to achieve the education needed to build a productive life in an increasingly high-tech world. Computer learning may even reduce the growing American prison population.

Knowledge workers are generally better paid than less-skilled workers. Their wealth is raising overall prosperity.

Even entry-level workers and those in formerly unskilled positions require a growing level of education. For a good career in almost any filed, computer competence is a must. This is one major trend raising the level of education required for a productive role in today's work force. For many workers, the opportunity for training is becoming one of the most desirable benefits any job can offer.

76. Information technology is expected to have impact on all the following EXCEPT _____.

[A] American management personnel

[B] European management personnel

[C] American people's choice of career

[D] traditional practice at work

77. "Digital divide" in the 4th paragraph refers to _____.

[A] the gap in terms of computer ownership

[B] the tendency of computer ownership

[C] the dividing line based on digits

[D] the ethnic distinction among American household

78. Which of the following statements is INCORRECT according to the passage?

[A] By 2005 all college and school study materials will turn electronic.

[B] By 2005 printed college and school study materials will be supplemented with electronic material.

[C] By 2005 some college and school study materials will be accompanied by CD-ROMs.

[D] By 2005 Internet links make worldwide library search a possibility.

79. Which of the following areas is NOT discussed in the passage?

[A] Future careers. [B] Nature of future work.

[C] Ethnic differences. [D] Schools and libraries.

80. At the end of the passage, the author seems to emphasize _____ in an increasingly high-tech world.

[A] the variety of education

[B] the content of education

[C] the need for education

[D] the function of education

2004 年英语专业四级考试阅读理解

Part Ⅵ Reading Comprehension

In this section there are four passages followed by questions or unfinished statements, each with four suggested answers marked A, B, C and D. Choose the one that you think is the best answer.

Mark your answers on your answer sheet.

TEXT A

It often happens that a number of applicants with almost identical qualifications and experience all apply for the same position. In their educational background, special skills and work experience, there is little, if anything, to choose between half a dozen candidates. How then does the employer make a choice? Usually on the basis of an interview.

There are many arguments for and against the interview as a selection procedure. The main argument against it is that it results in a wholly subjective decision. As often as not, employers do not choose the best candidate, they choose the candidate who makes a good first impression on them. Some employers, of course, reply to this argument by saying that they have become so experienced in interviewing staff that they are able to make a sound assessment of each candidate's likely performance.

The main argument in favour of the interview—and it is, perhaps, a good argument—is that an employer is concerned not only with a candidate's ability, but with the suitability of his or her personality for the particular work situation. Many employers, for example, will overlook occasional inefficiencies from their secretary provided she has a pleasant personality.

It is perhaps true to say, therefore, that the real purpose of an interview is not to assess the assessable aspects of each candidate but to make a guess at the more intangible things, such as personality, character and social ability. Unfortunately, both for the employers and applicants for jobs, there are many people of great ability who simply do not interview well. There are also, of course, people who interview extremely well, but are later found to be very unsatisfactory employees.

Candidates who interview well tend to be quietly confident, but never boastful; direct and straightforward in their questions and answers; cheerful and friendly, but never over-familiar;

and sincerely enthusiastic and optimistic. Candidates who interview badly tend to be at either end of the spectrum of human behaviour. They are either very shy or over-confident. They show either a lack of enthusiasm or an excess of it. They either talk too little or never stop talking. They are either over-polite or rudely abrupt.

66. We can infer from the passage that an employer might tolerate his secretary's occasional mistakes, if the latter is _____.

　　[A] direct　　　　　[B] cheerful　　　　　[C] shy　　　　　[D] capable

67. What is the author's attitude towards the interview as a selection procedure?

　　[A] Unclear.　　　　[B] Negative.　　　　[C] Objective.　　　　[D] Indifferent.

68. According to the passage, people argue over the interview as a selection procedure mainly because they have _____.

　　[A] different selection procedures

　　[B] different purposes in the interview

　　[C] different standards for competence

　　[D] different experiences in interviews

69. The purpose of the last paragraph is to indicate _____.

　　[A] a link between success in interview and personality

　　[B] connections between work abilities and personality

　　[C] differences in interview experience

　　[D] differences in personal behaviour

TEXT　B

Every year thousands of people are arrested and taken to court for shop-lifting. In Britain alone, about HK $ 3,000,000's worth of goods are stolen from shops every week. This amounts to something like HK $ 150 million a year, and represents about 4 per cent of the shops' total stock. As a result of this "shrinkage" as the shops call it, the honest public has to pay higher prices.

Shop-lifters can be divided into three main categories: the professionals, the deliberate amateurs, and the people who just can't help themselves. The professionals do not pose much of a problem for the store detectives, who, assisted by closed circuit television, two-way mirrors and various other technological devices, can usually cope with them. The professionals tend to go for high value goods in parts of the shops where security measures are tightest. And, in any case, they account for only a small percentage of the total losses due to shop-lifting.

The same applies to the deliberate amateur who is, so to speak, a professional in training. Most of them get caught sooner or later, and they are dealt with severely by the courts.

The real problem is the person who gives way to a sudden temptation and is in all other respects an honest and law-abiding citizen. Contrary to what one would expect, this kind of shop-lifter is rarely poor. He does not steal because he needs the goods and cannot afford to pay for them. He steals because he simply cannot stop himself. And there are countless others who, because of age, sickness or plain absent-mindedness, simply forget to pay for what they take from the shops. When caught, all are liable to prosecution, and the decision whether to send for the police or not is in the hands of the store manager.

In order to prevent the quite incredible growth in shop-lifting offences, some stores, in fact, are doing their best to separate the thieves from the confused by prohibiting customers from taking bags into the store. However, what is most worrying about the whole problem is, perhaps, that it is yet another instance of the innocent majority being penalized and inconvenienced because of the actions of a small minority. It is the aircraft hijack situation in another form. Because of the possibility of one passenger in a million boarding an aircraft with a weapon, the other 999,999 passengers must subject themselves to searches and delays. Unless the situation in the shops improves, in ten years' time we may all have to subject ourselves to a body-search every time we go into a store to buy a tin of beans!

70. Why does the honest public have to pay higher prices when they go to the shops?

[A] There is a "shrinkage" in market values.

[B] Many goods are not available.

[C] Goods in many shops lack variety.

[D] There are many cases of shop-lifting.

71. The third group of people steal things because they _____ work.

[A] are mentally ill

[B] are quite absent-minded

[C] can not resist the temptation

[D] can not afford to pay for goods

72. According to the passage, law-abiding citizens _____.

[A] can possibly steal things because of their poverty

[B] can possibly take away goods without paying

[C] have never stolen goods from the supermarkets

[D] are difficult to be caught when they steal things

73. Which of the following statements is NOT true about the main types of shop-lifting?

[A] A big percentage of the total losses are caused by the professionals.

[B] The deliberate amateurs will be punished severely if they get caught.

[C] People would expect that those who can't help themselves are poor.

[D] The professionals don't cause a lot of trouble to the store detectives.

74. The aircraft hijack situation is used in order to show that _____.

[A] "the professionals do not pose much of a problem for the stores"

[B] some people "simply forget to pay for what they take from the shops"

[C] "the honest public has to pay higher prices"

[D] the third type of shop-lifters are dangerous people

TEXT C

My bones have been aching again, as they often do in humid weather. They ache like history: things long done with, that still remain as pain. When the ache is bad enough it keeps me from sleeping. Every night I yearn for sleep, I strive for it; yet it flutters on ahead of me like a curtain. There are sleeping pills, of course, but the doctor has warned me against them.

Last night, after what seemed hours of damp turmoil, I got up and crept slipperless down the stairs, feeling my way in the faint street light that came through the window. Once safely arrived at the bottom, I walked into the kitchen and looked around in the refrigerator. There was nothing much I wanted to eat: the remains of a bunch of celery, a blue-tinged heel of bread, a lemon going soft. I've fallen into the habits of the solitary; my meals are snatched and random. Furtive snacks, furtive treats and picnics. I made do with some peanut butter, scooped directly from the jar with a forefinger: why dirty a spoon?

Standing there with the jar in one hand and my finger in my mouth, I had the feeling that someone was about to walk into the room—some other woman, the unseen, valid owner—and ask me what in hell I was doing in her kitchen. I've had it before, the sense that even in the course of my most legitimate and daily actions—peeling a banana, brushing my teeth—I am trespassing.

At night the house was more than ever like a stranger's. I wandered through the front room, the dining room, the parlour, hand on the wall for balance. My various possessions were floating in their own pools of shadow, denying my ownership of them. I looked them over with a burglar's eye, deciding what might be worth the risk of stealing, what on the other hand I would leave behind. Robbers would take the obvious things—the silver teapot that was my grandmother's, perhaps the hand-painted china. The television set. Nothing I really want.

75. The author could not fall asleep because _____.

　[A] it was too damp in the bedroom

　[B] she had run out of sleeping pills

　[C] she was in very poor health

　[D] she felt very hungry

76. The author did not like the food in the refrigerator because it was NOT _____.

　[A] fresh　　　　　[B] sufficient　　　　[C] nutritious　　　　[D] delicious

77. By "At night the house was more than ever like a stranger's" (Line 1, Para. 4), the author probably means that _____.

　[A] the house was too dark at night

　[B] there were unfamiliar rooms in the house

　[C] she felt much more lonely at night

　[D] the furniture there didn't belong to her

TEXT D

The chief problem in coping with foreign motorists is not so much remembering that they are different from yourself, but that they are enormously variable. Cross a frontier without adjusting and you can be in deep trouble.

One of the greatest gulfs separating the driving nations is the Atlantic Ocean. More precisely, it is the mental distance between the European and the American motorist, particularly the South American motorist. Compare, for example, an English driver at a set of traffic lights with a Brazilian.

Very rarely will an Englishman try to anticipate the green light by moving off prematurely. You will find the occasional sharpie who watches for the amber to come up on the adjacent set of lights. However, he will not go until he receives the lawful signal. Brazilians view the thing quite differently. If, in fact, they see traffic lights at all, they regard them as a kind of roadside decoration.

The natives of North America are much more disciplined. They demonstrate this in their addiction to driving in one lane and sticking to it—even if it means settling behind some great truck for many miles.

To prevent other drivers from falling into reckless ways, American motorists try always to stay close behind the vehicle in front, which can make it impossible, when all the vehicles are moving at about 55 mph, to make a real lane change. European visitors are constantly falling into this trap. They return to the Old World still flapping their arms in frustration because while driving in the States in their car they kept failing to get off the highway when they wanted to and were swept along to the next city.

However, one nation above all others lives scrupulously by its traffic regulations—the Swiss. In Switzerland, if you were simply to anticipate a traffic light, the chances are that the motorist behind you would take your number and report you to the police. What is more, the police would visit you; and you would be convicted.

The Swiss take their rules of the road so seriously that a driver can be ordered to appear in court and charged for speeding on hearsay alone, and very likely found guilty. There are slight regional variations among the French, German and Italian speaking areas, but it is generally safe to assume that any car bearing a CH sticker will be driven with a high degree of discipline.

78. The fact that the Brazilians regard traffic lights as a kind of roadside decoration suggests that _____.

    [A] traffic lights are part of street scenery

    [B] they simply ignore traffic lights

    [C] they want to put them at roadsides

    [D] there are very few traffic lights

79. The second and third paragraphs focus on the difference between _____.

    [A] the Atlantic Ocean and other oceans

［B］English drivers and American drivers

［C］European drivers and American drivers

［D］European drivers and South American drivers

80. The phrase "anticipate the green light" (Line 1, Para. 3) is closest in meaning to
_____.

　［A］"wait for the green light to be on"

　［B］"forbid others to move before the green light"

　［C］"move off before the green light is on"

　［D］"follow others when the green light is on"

2005 年英语专业四级考试阅读理解

Part Ⅵ   Reading Comprehension

In this section there are four reading passages followed by twenty questions or unfinished statements, each with four suggested answers marked A, B, C and D. Choose the one that you think is the best answer.

Mark your answers on your answer sheet.

TEXT A

It was 1961 and I was in the fifth grade. My marks in school were miserable and, the thing was, I didn't know enough to really care. My older brother and I lived with Mom in a dingy multi-family house in Detroit. We watched TV every night. The background noise of our lives was gunfire and horses' hoof from "Wagon Train" or "Cheyenne", and laughter from "I love Lucy" or "Mister Ed". After supper, we'd sprawl on Mom's bed and stare for hours at the tube.

But one day Mom changed our world forever. She turned off the TV. Our mother had only been able to get through third grade. But she was much brighter and smarter than we boys knew at the time. She had noticed something in the suburban houses she cleaned-books. So she came home one day, snapped off the TV, sat us down and explained that her sons were going to make something of themselves. "You boys are going to read two books every week," she said. "And you're going to write me a report on what you read."

We moaned and complained about how unfair it was. Besides, we didn't have any books in the house other than Mom's Bible. But she explained that we would go where the books were: "I'll drive you to the library."

So pretty soon there were these two peevish boys sitting in her white 1959 Oldsmobile on their way to Detroit Public Library. I wandered reluctantly among the children's books. I loved animals, so when I saw some books that seemed to be about animals, I started leafing through them.

The first book I read clear through was *Chip the Dam Builder*. It was about beavers. For the first in my life I was lost in another world. No television program had ever taken me so far away from my surroundings as did this verbal visit to a cold stream in a forest and these animals building a home.

It didn't dawn on me at the time, but the experience was quite different from watching TV. There were images forming in my mind instead of before my eyes. And I could return to them again and again with the flip of a page.

Soon I began to look forward to visiting this hushed sanctuary from my other world. I moved from animals to plants, and then to rocks. Between the covers of all those books were whole worlds, and I was free to go anywhere in them. Along the way a funny thing happened: I started to know things. Teachers started to notice it too. I got to the point where I couldn't wait to get home to my books.

Now my older brother is an engineer and I am chief of pediatric neurosurgery at John Hopkins Children's Center in Baltimore. Sometimes I still can't believe my life's journey, from a failing and indifferent student in a Detroit public school to this position, which takes me all over the world to teach and perform critical surgery.

But I know where the journey began-the day Mom snapped off the TV set and put us in her Oldsmobile for that drive to the library.

81. We can learn from the beginning of the passage that _____.

[A] the author and his brother had done poorly in school

[B] the author had been very concerned about his school work

[C] the author had spent much time watching TV after school

[D] the author had realized how important schooling was

82. Which of the following is NOT true about the author's family?

[A] He came from a middle-class family.

[B] He came from a single-parent family.

[C] His mother worked as a cleaner.

[D] His mother had received little education.

83. The mother was _____ to make her two sons switch to reading books.

[A] hesitant   [B] unprepared   [C] reluctant   [D] determined

84. How did the two boys feel about going to the library at first?

[A] They were afraid.   [B] They were reluctant.

[C] They were indifferent.   [D] They were eager to go.

85. The author began to love books for the following reasons EXCEPT that _____.

[A] he began to see something in his mind

[B] he could visualize what he read in his mind

[C] he could go back to read the books again

[D] he realized that books offered him new experience

TEXT B

Predicting the future is always risky. But it's probably safe to say that at least a few historians will one day speak of the 20th century as America's "Disney era". Today, it's certainly difficult to think of any other single thing that represents modern America as powerfully as the company that created Mickey Mouse. Globally, brands like Coca-Cola and McDonald's may be more widely known, but neither concludes 20th-century America in quite the same way as Disney.

The reasons for Disney's success are quite a lot, but ultimately the credit belongs to one person—the man who created the cartoon and built the company from nothing, Walt Disney. Ironically, he could not draw particularly well. But he was a genius in other respects. In business, his greatest skills were his insight and his management ability. After setting himself up in Hollywood, he single-handedly pioneered the concepts of branding and merchandising—something his company still does brilliantly today.

But what really distinguished Disney was his ability to identify with his audiences. Disney always made sure his films portrayed the "little boy". He achieved this by creating characters that reflected the hopes and fears of ordinary people.

Disney's other great virtue was the fact that his company—unlike other big corporations—had a human face. His Hollywood studio-the public heard-operated just like a democracy, where everyone was on firstname terms and had a say in how things should be run. He was also regarded as a great patriot because not only did his cartoons celebrate America, but, during World War II, studios made training films for American soldiers.

The reality, of course, was not so perfect. As the public would later learn, Disney's patriotism had an unpleasant side. After a strike by cartoonists in 1941, he agreed to work for the FBI secretly, identifying and spying on colleagues whom he suspected were anti-government.

But, apart from his affiliations with the FBI, Disney was more or less the genuine article. A new book, *The Magic Kingdom*: *Walt Disney and the American Way of Life*, confirms that he was very definitely on the side of ordinary people. In the 30s and 40s he voted for Franklin Roosevelt, believing he was a leader of the workers. Also, Disney was not an apologist for the FBI, as some have suggested. In fact, he was suspicious of large, bureaucratic organizations, as is evidenced in films like *That Darned Cat*.

By the time he died in 1966, Walt Disney was as famous as Thomas Edison and the Wright Brothers. To business people and filmmakers, he was a role model; to the public at large, he was "Uncle Walt"—the man who had entertained them all their lives, the man who represented all that was good about America.

86. Walt Disney is believed to possess the following abilities EXCEPT _____.

   [A] painting   [B] creativity   [C] management   [D] merchandising

87. According to the passage, what was the pleasant side of Disney's patriotism?

   [A] He sided with ordinary Americans in his films.

   [B] He supported America's war efforts in his own way.

   [C] He had doubts about large, bureaucratic organizations.

   [D] He voted for Franklin Roosevelt in the 30s and 40s.

88. In the sixth paragraph the sentence "Disney was more or less the genuine article" means

that _____.

[A] Disney was a creative and capable person

[B] Disney once agreed to work for the FBI

[C] Disney ran his company in a democratic way

[D] Disney was sympathetic with ordinary people

89. The writer's attitude toward Walt Disney can best be described as _____.

[A] sympathetic   [B] objective   [C] critical   [D] skeptical

TEXT   C

Why do you listen to music? If you should put this question to a number of people, you might receive answers like these: "I like the beat of music", "I look for attractive tunefulness", "I am moved by the sound of choral singing", "I listen to music for many reasons but I could not begin to describe them to you clearly." Answers to this question would be many and diverse, yet almost no one would reply, "Music means nothing to me." To most of us, music means something; it evokes some response. We obtain some satisfaction in listening to music.

For many, the enjoyment of music does not remain at a standstill. We feel that we can get more satisfaction from the musical experience. We want to make closer contact with music in order to learn more of its nature; thus we can range more broadly and freely in the areas of musical style, form, and expression. This book explores ways of achieving these objectives. It deals, of course, with the techniques of music, but only in order to show how technique is directed toward expressive aims in music and toward the listener's musical experience. In this way, we may get an idea of the composer's intentions, for indeed, the composer uses every musical device for its power to communicate and for its contribution to the musical experience.

Although everyone hears music differently, there is a common ground from which all musical experiences grow. That source is *sound* itself. Sound is the raw material of music. It makes up the body and substance of all musical activity. It is the *point of departure* in the musical experience.

The kinds of sound that can be used for musical purposes are amazingly varied. Throughout the cultures of the world, East and West, a virtually limitless array of sounds has been employed in the service of musical expression. Listen to Oriental theatre music, then to an excerpt from a Wagner work; these two are worlds apart in their qualities of sound as well as in almost every other feature, yet each says something of importance to some listeners. Each can stir a listener and evoke a response in him. All music, whether it is the pulsation of primitive tribal drums or the complex coordination of voices and instruments in an opera, has this feature: *it is based upon the power of sound to stir our senses and feelings.*

Yet sound alone is not music. Something has to happen to the sound. It must move forward in time. Everything that takes place musically involves the movement of sound. If we hear a series of drumbeats, we receive an impression of movement from one stroke to the next.

When sounds follow each other in a pattern of melody, we receive an impression of movement from one tone to the next. All music moves; and because it moves, it is associated with a fundamental truth of existence and experience. We are stirred by impressions of movement because our very lives are constantly in movement. Breathing, the action of the pulse, growth, decay, the change of day and night, as well as the constant flow of physical action-these all testify to the fundamental role that movement plays in our lives. Music appeals to our desire and our need for movement.

90. The author indicates at the beginning of the passage that _____.

    [A] people listen to music for similar reasons

    [B] reasons for listening to music are varied

    [C] some people don't understand music at all

    [D] purposes for listening to music can be specified

91. We can infer from the second paragraph that the book from which this excerpt is taken is mainly meant for _____.

    [A] listeners   [B] composers   [C] musicians   [D] directors

92. According to the passage, enjoying music is not an end in itself because people hope to _____ through listening.

    [A] learn more musical devices

    [B] know more about composers

    [C] communicate more effectively

    [D] understand music better

93. What is the common ground for musical experience to develop?

    [A] Material.   [B] Listening.   [C] Sound.   [D] Activity.

94. The importance of movement in music is explained by comparing it to _____.

    [A] a pattern of melody   [B] a series of drumbeats

    [C] physical movement   [D] existence and experience

TEXT D

Psychologists agree that I. Q. contributes only about 20 percent of the factors that determine success. A full 80 percent comes from other factors, including what I call *emotional intelligence*. Following are two of the major qualities that make up emotional intelligence, and how they can be developed:

1. *Self-awareness*. The ability to recognize a feelings as it happens is the keystone of emotional intelligence. People with greater certainty about their emotions are better pilots of their lives.

Developing self-awareness requires tuning in to what neurologist Antonio Damasio calls "gut feelings". Gut feelings can occur without a person being consciously aware of them. For example, when people who fear snakes are shown a picture of a snake, sensors on their skin will detect sweat, a sign of anxiety, even though the people say they do not feel fear. The sweat shows up even when a picture is presented so rapidly that the subject has no conscious awareness of seeing it.

Through deliberate effort we can become more aware of our gut feelings. Take someone who is annoyed by a rude encounter for hours after it occurred. He may be unaware of his irritability and surprised when someone calls attention to it. But if he evaluates his feelings, he can change them.

Emotional self-awareness is the building block of the next fundamental of emotional intelligence: being able to shake off a bad mood.

2. *Mood Management*. Bad as well as good moods *spice* life and build character. The key is balance.

We often have little control over *when* we are swept by emotion. But we can have some say in ***how long*** that emotion will last. Psychologist Dianne Tice asked more than 400 men and women about their strategies for escaping foul moods. Her research, along with that of other psychologists, provides valuable information on how to change a bad mood.

Of all the moods that people want to escape, rage seems to be the hardest to deal with. When someone in another car cuts you off on the highway, your reflexive thought may be, *That jerk! He could have hit me! I can't let him get away with that!* The more you stew, the angrier you get. Such is the stuff of hypertension and reckless driving.

What should you do to relieve rage? One myth is that ventilating will make you feel better. In fact, researchers have found that's one of the worst strategies. A more effective technique is "reframing", which means consciously reinterpreting a situation in a more positive light. In the case of the driver who cuts you off, you might tell yourself: *Maybe he had some emergency.* This is one of the most potent ways, Tice found, to put anger to rest.

Going off alone to cool down is also an effective way to refuse anger, especially if you can't think clearly. Tice found that a large proportion of men cool down by going for a drive-a finding that inspired her to drive more defensively. A safer alternative is exercise, such as taking a long walk. Whatever you do, don't waste the time pursuing your train of angry thoughts. Your aim should be to distract yourself.

The techniques of reframing and distraction can alleviate depression and anxiety as well as anger. Add to them such relaxation techniques as deep breathing and meditation and you have an arsenal of weapons against bad moods.

95. What are gut feelings?

[A] They are feelings one is born with.

[B] They are feelings one may be unaware of.

[C] They are feelings of fear and anxiety.

[D] They are feelings felt by sensible people.

96. According to the author, the importance of knowing one's gut feelings is that _____.

[A] one can develop them

[B] one can call others' attention to them

[C] one may get rid of them

[D] one may control them

97. The word "spice" in Paragraph Six is closest in meaning to "_____".

[A] add interest to

[B] lengthen

[C] make dull

[D] bring into existence

98. On mood control, the author seems to suggest that we _____.

[A] can control the occurrence of mood

[B] are often unaware of what mood we are in

[C] can determine the duration of mood

[D] lack strategies for controlling moods

99. The essence of "reframing" is _____.

[A] to forget the unpleasant situation

[B] to adopt a positive attitude

[C] to protect oneself properly

[D] to avoid road accidents

100. What is the best title for the passage?

[A] What is emotional intelligence?

[B] How to develop emotional intelligence.

[C] Strategies for getting rid of foul moods.

[D] How to control one's gut feelings.

2006 年英语专业四级考试阅读理解

Part Ⅴ   Reading Comprehension

In this section there are several reading passages followed by twenty questions or unfinished statements, each with four suggested answers marked A, B, C and D. Choose the one that you think is the best answer.

Mark your answers on your answer sheet.

TEXT   A

In the case of mobile phones, change is everything. Recent research indicates that the mobile phone is changing not only our culture, but our very bodies as well.

First, let's talk about culture. The difference between the mobile phone and its parent, the fixed-line phone, is that a mobile number corresponds to a person, while a landline goes to a place. If you call my mobile, you get me. If you call my fixed-line phone, you get whoever answers it.

This has several implications. The most common one, however, and perhaps the thing that has changed our culture forever, is the "meeting" influence. People no longer need to make firm plans about when and where to meet. Twenty years ago, a Friday night would need to be arranged in advance. You needed enough time to allow everyone to get from their place of work to the first meeting place. Now, however, a night out can be arranged on the run. It is no longer "see you there at 8", but "text me around 8 and we'll see where we all are".

Texting changes people as well. In their paper, "*Insights into the Social and Psychological Effects of SMS Text Messaging*", two British researchers distinguished between two types of mobile phone users: the "talkers" and the "texters"—those who prefer voice to text messages and those who prefer text to voice.

They found that the mobile phone's individuality and privacy gave texters the ability to express a whole new outer personality. Texters were likely to report that their family would be surprised if they were to read their texts. This suggests that texting allowed texters to present a setf-image that differed from the one familiar to those who knew them well.

Another scientist wrote of the changes that mobiles have brought to body language. There are two kinds that people use while speaking on the phone. There is the "speakeasy": the

head is held high, in a self-confident way, chatting away. And there is the "spacemaker": these people focus on themselves and keep out other people.

Who can blame them? Phone meetings get cancelled or reformed and camera-phones intrude on people's privacy. So, it is understandable if your mobile makes you nervous. But perhaps you needn't worry so much. After all, it is good to talk.

81. When people plan to meet nowadays, they _____.

    [A] arrange the meeting place beforehand

    [B] postpone fixing the place till the last minute

    [C] seldom care about when and where to meet

    [D] still love to work out detailed meeting plans

82. According to the two British researchers, the social and psychological effects are mostly likely to be seen on _____.

    [A] talkers   [B] the "speakeasy"

    [C] the "spacemaker"   [D] texters

83. We can infer from the passage that the texts sent by texters are _____.

    [A] quite revealing   [B] well written

    [C] unacceptable by others   [D] shocking to others

84. According to the passage, who is afraid of being heard while talking on the mobile?

    [A] Talkers.   [B] The "speakeasy".

    [C] The "spacemaker".   [D] Texters.

85. An appropriate tide for the passage might be _____.

    [A] The SMS Effect.

    [B] Cultural Implications of Mobile Phone Use.

    [C] Changes in the Use of the Mobile.

    [D] Body Language and the Mobile Phone.

TEXT B

Over the last 25 years, British society has changed a great deal—or at least many parts of it have. In some ways, however, very little has changed, particularly where attitudes are concerned. Ideas about social class—whether a person is "working-class" or "middle-class"—are one area in which changes have been extremely slow.

In the past, the working-class tended to be paid less than middle-class people, such as teachers and doctors. As a result of this and also of the fact that workers' jobs were generally much less secure, distinct differences in life-styles and attitudes came into existence. The typical working man would collect his wages on Friday evening and then, it was widely believed, having given his wife her "housekeeping", would go out and squander the rest on beer and betting.

The stereotype of what a middle-class man did with his money was perhaps nearer the truth. He was—and still is—inclined to take a longer-term view. Not only did he regard buying a house as a top priority, but he also considered the education of his children as extremely important. Both of these provided him and his family with security. Only in very few cases did workers have the opportunity (or the education and training) to make such long-term plans.

Nowadays, a great deal has changed. In a large number of cases factory workers earn as much, if not more, than their middle-class supervisors. Social security and laws to improve job-security, combined with a general rise in the standard of living since the mid-fifties of the 20th century, have made it less necessary than before to worry about "tomorrow". Working-class people seem slowly to be losing the feeling of inferiority they had in the past. In fact there has been a growing tendency in the past few years for the middle-classes to feel slightly a-shamed of their position.

The changes in both life-styles and attitudes are probably most easily seen amongst younger people. They generally tend to share very similar tastes in music and clothes, they spend their money in having a good time, and save for holidays or longer-term plans when necessary. There seems to be much less difference than in previous generations. Nevertheless, we still have a wide gap between the well-paid (whatever the type of job they may have) and the low-paid. As long as this gap exists, there will always be a possibility that new conflicts and jealousies will emerge, or rather that the old conflicts will re-appear, but between different groups.

86. Which of the following is seen as the cause of class differences in the past?

    [A] Life style and occupation.

    [B] Attitude and income.

    [C] Income and job security.

    [D] Job security and hobbies.

87. The writer seems to suggest that the description of _____ is closer to truth.

    [A] middle-class ways of spending money

    [B] working-class ways of spending the weekend

    [C] working-class drinking habits

    [D] middle-class attitudes

88. According to the passage, which of the following is NOT a typical feature of the middle-class?

    [A] Desiring for security.

    [B] Making long-term plans.

    [C] Having priorities in life.

    [D] Saving money.

89. Working-class people's sense of security increased as a result of all the following factors EXCEPT _____.

    [A] better social security

    [B] more job opportunities

    [C] higher living standard

    [D] better legal protection

90. Which of the following statements is INCORRECT?

[A] Changes are slowly taking place in all sectors of the British society.

[B] The gap between working-class and middle-class young people is narrowing.

[C] Differences in income will remain but those in occupation will disappear.

[D] Middle-class people may sometimes feel inferior to working-class people.

TEXT C

For several days I saw little of Mr. Rochester. In the morning he seemed much occupied with business, and in the afternoon gentlemen from the neighborhood called and sometimes stayed to dine with him. When his foot was well enough, he rode out a great deal.

During this time, all my knowledge of him was limited to occasional meetings about the house, when he would sometimes pass me coldly, and sometimes bow and smile. His changes of manner did not offend me, because I saw that I had nothing to do with the cause of them.

One evening, several days later, I was invited to talk to Mr. Rochester after dinner. He was sitting in his armchair, and looked not quite so severe, and much less gloomy. There was a smile on his lips, and his eyes were bright, probably with wine. As I was looking at him, he suddenly turned, and asked me, "Do you think I'm handsome. Miss Eyre?"

The answer somehow slipped from my tongue before I realized it: "No, sir."

"Ah, you really are unusual! You are a quiet, serious little person, but you can be almost rude."

"Sir, I'm sorry. I should have said that beauty doesn't matter, or something like that."

"No, you shouldn't! I see, you criticize my appearance, and then you stab me in the back. You have honesty and feeling. There are not many girls like you. But perhaps I go too fast. Perhaps you have awful faults to counterbalance your few good points."

I thought to myself that he might have too. He seemed to read my mind, and said quickly, "Yes, you're right. I have plenty of faults. I went the wrong way when I was twenty-one, and have never found the right path again. I might have been very different. I might have been as good as you, and perhaps wiser. I am not a bad man, take my word for it, but I have done wrong. It wasn't my character, but circumstances which were to blame. Why do I tell you all this? Because you're the sort of person people tell their problems and secrets to, because you're sympathetic and give them hope."

It seemed he had quite a lot to talk to me. He didn't seem to like to finish the talk quickly, as was the case for the first time.

"Don't be afraid of me. Miss Eyre." He continued. "You don't relax or laugh very much, perhaps because of the effect Lowood school has had on you. But in time you will be more natural with me, and laugh, and speak freely. You're like a bird in a cage. When you get out of the cage, you'll fly very high. Good night."

91. At the beginning Miss Eyre's impressions of Mr. Rochester were all EXCEPT _____.

[A] busy   [B] sociable   [C] friendly   [D] changeable

92. In "... and all my knowledge of him was limited to occasional meetings about the house,..." (the second paragraph), the word about means _____.

　　[A] around　　　　　　[B] on　　　　　　　[C] outside　　　　　[D] concerning

93. Why did Mr. Rochester say "... and then you stab me in the back!" (the seventh paragraph)?

　　[A] Because Jane had intended to kill him with a knife.

　　[B] Because Jane had intended to be more critical.

　　[C] Because Jane had regretted having talked to him.

　　[D] Because Jane had said something else to correct herself.

94. From what Mr. Rochester told Miss Eyre, we can conclude that he wanted to _____.

　　[A] tell her all his troubles

　　[B] tell her his life experience

　　[C] change her opinion of him

　　[D] change his circumstances

95. At the end of the passage, Mr. Rochester sounded _____.

　　[A] rude　　　　　　　[B] cold　　　　　　　[C] friendly　　　　　[D] encouraging

TEXT D

The ideal companion machine—the computer—would not only look, feel, and sound friendly but would also be programmed to behave in a pleasant manner. Those qualities that make interaction with other people enjoyable would be imitated as closely as possible, and the machine would appear to be charming, and easygoing. Its informal conversational style would make interaction comfortable, and yet the machine would remain slightly unpredictable and therefore interesting. In its first encounter it might be somewhat hesitant, but as it came to know the user it would progress to a more relaxed and intimate style. The machine would not be a passive participant but would add its own suggestions, information, and opinions; it would sometimes take the initiative in developing or changing the topic and would have a personality of its own.

Friendships are not made in a day, and the computer would be more acceptable as a friend if it imitated the gradual changes that occur when one person is getting to know another. At an appropriate time it might also express the kind of affection that stimulates attachment and intimacy. The whole process would be accomplished in a subtle way to avoid giving an impression of over-familiarity that would be likely to produce irritation. After experiencing a wealth of powerful, well-timed friendship indicators, the user would be very likely to accept the computer as far more than a machine and might well come to regard it as a friend.

An artificial relationship of this type would provide many of the benefits that people obtain from interpersonal friendships. The machine would participate in interesting conversation that could continue from previous discussions. It would have a familiarity with the user's life as revealed in earlier contact, and it would be understanding and good-humored. The computer's own personality would be lively and impressive, and it would develop in response to that of the user. With features such as these, the machine might indeed become a very attractive social partner.

96. Which of the following is NOT a feature of the ideal companion machine?

　　[A] Active in communication.

　　[B] Attractive in personality.

　　[C] Enjoyable in performance.

　　[D] Unpredictable in behavior.

97. The computer would develop friendships with humans in a(n) _____ way.

　　[A] quick　　　[B] unpredictable　　　[C] productive　　　[D] inconspicuous

98. Which of the following aspects is NOT mentioned when the passage discusses the benefits of artificial relationships?

　　[A] Being able to pick up an interesting conversation.

　　[B] Being sensitive to earlier contact.

　　[C] Being ready to learn about the person's life.

　　[D] Having a pleasant and adaptable personality.

99. Throughout the passage, the author is _____ in his attitude towards the computer.

　　[A] favourable　　　[B] critical　　　[C] vague　　　[D] hesitant

100. Which might be the most appropriate title of the passage?

　　[A] Artificial Relationships.

　　[B] How to Form Intimate Relationships.

　　[C] The Affectionate Machine.

　　[D] Humans and Computers.

2007 年英语专业四级考试阅读理解

Part Ⅴ   Reading Comprehension

In this section there are several reading passages followed by twenty questions or unfinished statements, each with four suggested answers marked A, B, C and D. Choose the one that you think is the best answer.

Mark your answers on your answer sheet.

TEXT   A

If you like the idea of staying with a family, living in house might be the answer. Good landladies—those who are superb cooks and launderers, are figures as popular in fiction as the bad ones who terrorize their guests and overcharge them at the slightest opportunity. The truth is probably somewhere between the two extremes. If you are lucky, the food will be adequate, some of your laundry may be done for you and you will have a reasonable amount of comfort and companionship. For the less fortune, house rules may restrict the freedom to invite friends to visit, and shared cooking and bathroom facilities can be frustrating and row-provoking if tidy and untidy guests are living under the same roof.

The same disadvantages can apply to flat sharing, with the added difficulties that arise from deciding who pays for what, and in what proportion. One person may spend hours on the phone, while another rarely makes calls. If you want privacy with a guest, how do you persuade the others to go out; how do you persuade them to leave you in peace, especially if you are student and want to study?

Conversely, flat sharing can be very cheap, there will always be someone to talk to and go out with, and the chores, in theory, can be shared.

81. According to the passage, landladies are _____.

    [A] usually strict   [B] always mean

    [C] adequately competent   [D] very popular with their guest

82. What is the additional disadvantage of flat sharing?

    [A] Problems of sharing and paying.

    [B] Differences in living habits.

    [C] Shared cooking and bathroom facilities.

［D］ Restriction to invite friends to visit.

83. What is NOT mentioned as a benefit of flat sharing?

　　［A］ Rent is affordable

　　［B］ There is companionship.

　　［C］ Housework can be shared.

　　［D］ There is peace and quiet.

TEXT　B

（1） Travelling through the country a couple of weeks ago on business, I was listening to the talk of the late UK writer Douglas Adams' master work "The Hitchhiker's Guide to the Galaxy" on the radio and thought—I know, I'll pick up the next hitchhikers I see and ask them what the state of real hitching is today in Britain.

（2） I drove and drove on main roads and side roads for the next few days and never saw a single one.

（3） When I was in my teens and 20s, hitchhiking was a main form of long-distance transport. The kindness or curiosity of strangers took me all over Europe, North America, Asia and southern Africa. Some of the lift-givers became friends, many provided hospitality on the road.

（4） Not only did you find out much more about a country than when traveling by train or plane, but there was that element of excitement about where you would finish up that night. Hitchhiking featured importantly in Western culture. It has books and songs about it. So what has happened to it?

（5） A few years ago, I asked the same question about hitching in a column of a newspaper. Hundreds of people from all over the world responded with their view on the state of hitchhiking.

（6） Rural Ireland was recommended as a friendly place for hitching, as was Quebec, Canada "if you don't mind being criticized for not speaking French".

（7） But while hitchhiking was clearly still alive and well in some places, the general feeling was that throughout much of the west it was doomed.

（8） With so much news about crime in the media, people assumed that anyone on the open road without the money for even a bus ticket must present a danger. But do we need to be so wary both to hitch and to give a lift?

（9） In Poland in the 1960s, according to a Polish woman who e-mailed me, "the authorities introduced the Hitchhiker's Booklet. The booklet contained coupons for drivers, so each time a driver picked somebody, he or she received a coupon. At the end of the season, drivers who had picked up the most hikers were rewarded with various prizes. Everyone was hitchhiking then".

（10） Surely this is a good idea for society. Hitchhiking would increase respect by breaking down barriers between strangers. It would help fight global warming by cutting down on fuel consumption as hitchhikers would be using existing fuels. It would also improve educational standards by delivering instant lessons in geography, history, politics and sociology.

（11） A century before Douglas Adams wrote his "Hitchhiker's Guide", another adventure story writer, Robert Louis Stevenson, gave us what should be the hitchhiker's motto: "To travel hopefully is a better thing than to arrive." What better time than putting a holiday weekend into practice. Either put it to the test yourself, or help out someone who is trying to travel hopefully with thumb outstretched.

84. In which paragraph(s) does the writer comment on his experience of hitchhiking?

　　[A] (3).　　　　　　　　　　　　　　[B] (4).

　　[C] (3) and (4).　　　　　　　　　　[D] (4) and (5).

85. What is the current situation of hitchhiking?

　　[A] It's popular in some parts of the world.

　　[B] It's popular throughout the west.

　　[C] It's popular only in North America.

　　[D] It's still popular in Poland.

86. What is the writer's attitude towards the practice in Poland?

　　[A] Critical.　　　　　　　　　　　　[B] Unclear.

　　[C] Somewhat favourable.　　　　　　[D] Strongly favourable.

87. The writer has mentioned all the following benefits of hitchhiking EXCEPT _____.

　　[A] promoting mutual respect between strangers

　　[B] increasing one's confidence in strangers

　　[C] protecting environment

　　[D] enrich one's knowledge

88. "Either put it to the test yourself..." in Paragraph (11) means _____.

　　[A] to experience the hopefulness

　　[B] to read Adams' book

　　[C] to offer someone a lift

　　[D] to be a hitchhiker

TEXT C

I am afraid to sleep. I have been afraid to sleep for the last few weeks. I am so tired that, finally, I do sleep, but only for a few minutes. It is not a bad dream that wakes me; it is the reality I took with me into sleep. I try to think of something else.

Immediately the woman in the marketplace comes into my mind.

I was on my way to dinner last night when I saw her. She was selling skirts. She moved with the same ease and loveliness I often saw in the women of Laos. Her long black hair was as shiny as the black silk of the skirts she was selling. In her hair, she wore three silk ribbons, blue, green, and white. They reminded me of my childhood and how my girlfriends and I used to spend hours braiding ribbons into our hair.

I don't know the word for "ribbons", so I put my hand to my own hair and, with three fingers against my head, I looked at her ribbons and said "Beautiful." She lowered her eyes and said nothing. I wasn't sure if she understood me (I don't speak Laotian very well).

I looked back down at the skirts. They had designs on them: squares and triangles and circles of pink and green silk. They were very pretty. I decided to buy one of those skirts, and I began to bargain with her over the price. It is the custom to bargain in Asia. In Laos bargaining is done in soft voices and easy moves with the sort of quiet peacefulness.

She smiled, more with her eyes than with her lips. She was pleased by the few words I was able to say in her language, although they were mostly numbers, and she saw that I understood something about the soft playfulness of bargaining. We shook our heads in disagreement over the price; then, immediately, we made another offer and then another shake of the head. She was so pleased that unexpectedly, she accepted the last offer I made. But it was too soon. The price was too low. She was being too generous and wouldn't make enough money. I moved quickly and picked up two more skirts and paid for all three at the price set; that way I was able to pay her three times as much before she had a chance to lower the price for the larger purchase. She smiled openly then, and, for the first time in months, my spirit lifted. I almost felt happy.

The feeling stayed with me while she wrapped the skirts in a newspaper and handed them to me. When I left, though, the feeling left, too. It was as though it stayed behind in the marketplace. I felt tears in my throat. I wanted to cry. I didn't, of course.

I have learned to defend myself against what is hard; without knowing it, I have also learned to defend myself against what is soft and what should be easy.

I get up, light a candle and want to look at the skirts. They are still in the newspaper that the woman wrapped them in. I remove the paper, and raise the skirts up to look at them again before I pack them. Something falls to floor. I reach down and feel something cool in my hand. I move close to the candlelight to see what I have. There are five long silk ribbons in my hand, all different colours. The woman in the marketplace! She has given these ribbons to me!

There is no defense against a generous spirit, and this time I cry, and very hard, as if I could make up for all the months that I didn't cry.

89. According to the writer, the woman in the marketplace _____.

[A] refused to speak to her   [B] was pleasant and attractive

[C] was selling skirts and ribbons   [D] recognized her immediately

90. Which of the following is NOT correct?

[A] The writer was not used to bargaining.

[B] People in Asia always bargain when buying things.

[C] Bargaining in Laos was quiet and peaceful.

[D] The writer was ready to bargain with the woman.

91. The writer assumed that the woman accepted the last offer mainly because the woman

_____.

[A] thought that the last offer was reasonable

[B] thought she could still make much money

[C] was glad that the writer knew their way of bargaining

[D] was tired of bargaining with the writer any more

92. Why did the writer finally decide to buy three skirts?

[A] The skirts were cheap and pretty.

[B] She liked the patterns on the skirts.

[C] She wanted to do something as compensation.

[D] She was fed up with further bargaining with the woman.

93. When the writer left the marketplace, she wanted to cry, but did not because _____.

[A] she had learned to stay cool and unfeeling

[B] she was afraid of crying in public

[C] she had learned to face difficulties bravely

[D] she had to show in public that she was strong

94. Why did the writer cry eventually when she looked at the skirts again?

[A] She suddenly felt very sad.　　　　[B] She liked the ribbons so much.

[C] She was overcome by emotion.　　　[D] She felt sorry for the woman.

TEXT D

The kids are hanging out. I pass small bands of students, on my way to work these mornings. They have become a familiar part of the summer landscape.

These kids are not old enough for jobs. Nor are they rich enough for camp. They are school children without school. The calendar called the school year ran out on them a few weeks ago. Once supervised by teachers and principals, they now appear to be "self care".

Passing them is like passing through a time zone. For much of our history, after all, Americans arranged the school year around the needs of work and family. In 19th-century cities, schools were open seven or eight hours a day, 11 months a year. In rural America, the year was arranged around the growing season. Now, only 3 percent of families follow the agricultural model, but nearly all schools are scheduled as if our children went home early to milk the cows and took months off to work the crops. Now, three-quarters of the mothers of school-age children work, but the calendar is written as if they were home waiting for the school bus.

The six-hour day, the 180-day school year is regarded as something holy. But when parents work an eight-hour day and a 240-day year, it means something different. It means that many kids go home to empty houses. It means that, in the summer, they hang out.

"We have a huge mismatch between the school calendar and realities of family life, "says Dr. Ernest Boyer, head of the Carnegie Foundation for the Advancement of Teaching.

Dr. Boyer is one of many who believe that a radical revision of the school calendar is inevitable. "School, whether we like it or not, is educational. It always has been. "

His is not popular idea. Schools are routinely burdened with the job of solving all our social problems. Can they be asked to meet the needs of our work and family lives?

It may be easier to promote a longer school year on its educational merits and, indeed, the educational case is compelling. Despite the complaints and studies about our kids' lack of learning, the United State still has a shorter school year than any industrial nation. In most of Europe, the school year is 220 days. In Japan, it is 240 days long. While classroom time alone doesn't produce a well-educated child, learning takes time and more learning takes more time. The long summers of forgetting take a toll.

The opposition to a longer school year comes from families that want to and can provide other experiences for their children. It comes from teachers. It comes from tradition. And surely from kids. But the most important part of the conflict has been over the money.

95. Which of the following is an opinion of the author's?

[A] "The kids are hanging out. "

[B] "They are school children without school. "

[C] "These kids are not old enough for jobs. "

[D] "The calendar called the school year ran out on them a few weeks ago. "

96. The current American school calendar was developed in the 19th century according to _____.

[A] the growing season on nation's farm

[B] the labour demands of the industrial age

[C] teachers' demands for more vacation time

[D] parents' demands for other experiences for their kids

97. The author thinks that the current school calendar _____.

[A] is still valid   [B] is out of date

[C] can not be revised   [D] can not be defended

98. Why was Dr. Boyer's idea unpopular?

[A] He argues for the role of school in solving social problems.

[B] He supports the current school calendar.

[C] He thinks that school year and family life should be considered separately.

[D] He strongly believes in the educational role of school.

99. "The long summers of forgetting take a toll" in the last paragraph but one means that _____.

[A] long summer vacation slows down the progress of learning

[B] long summer vacation has been abandoned in Europe

[C] long summers result in less learning time

[D] long summers are a result of tradition

100. The main purpose of the passage is _____.

[A] to describe how American children spend their summer

[B] to explain the needs of the modern working families

[C] to discuss the problems of the current school calendar

[D] to persuade parents to stay at home to look after their kids

TAPESCRIPTS
听力材料

1996年英语专业四级考试听力理解

Part II   Dictation

Listen to the following passage. Altogether the passage will be read to you four times. During the first reading, which will be read at normal speed, listen and try to understand the meaning. For the second and third readings, the passage will be read sentence by sentence, or phrase by phrase, with intervals of 15 seconds. The last reading will be read at normal speed again and during this time you should check your work. You will then be given 2 minutes to check through your work once more.

Please write the whole passage on ANSWER SHEET TWO.

The Medicine Man

Among the Indians of North America, the medicine man was a very important person. / He could cure illnesses and he could speak to the spirits. / The spirits were the supernatural forces that controlled the world. / The Indians believed that bad spirits made people ill. / So when people were ill, the medicine man tried to help them by using magic. / He spoke to the good spirits and asked for their help. / Many people were cured because they thought that the spirits were helping them. / But really these people cured themselves. / Sometimes your own mind is the best doctor for you. / The medicine men were often successful for another reason, too. / They knew about plants that really can cure illnesses. / A lot of modern medicines are made from plants that were used by medicine men hundreds of years ago. /

The second and third readings. You should begin writing now.

The last reading. Now, you have two minutes to check through your work.

(*a 2-minute interval*)

This is the end of the Dictation.

Part III   Listening Comprehension

In Sections A, B and C you will hear everything once only. Listen carefully and then answer the questions that follow. Mark the correct response for each question in your ANSWER BOOKLET.

Section A   Statement

In this section you will hear eight statements. At the end of the statement you will be given 10 seconds to answer each of the following eight questions.

Now listen to the statements.

1. Joe Clark, twenty-two years of age, appeared in court in the New York suburb yesterday. He was there to face a traffic charge.

2. I'm sorry I'm late, but I was waiting for you at the information desk upstairs. It's lucky I thought to look for you here on the platform.

3. This is a very complex system. It can send messages over long distances by means of electric or radio signals, and print them at the other end.

4. The elderly woman was planning to take the 5 : 30 coach. Unfortunately, due to poor road conditions which made safe driving impossible, it departed at a quarter past eight.

5. Let me know as soon as you have fixed your travel plans. I'd like to make sure you're properly looked after on arrival.

6. Just look at this cardigan, it has shrunk so much I can't wear it any more.

7. That famous writer's new book is coming out in September. However, we probably won't be able to find it in the library until December.

8. Statistics show that 300 people are killed in air crashes in the United States every year, but about 50,000 people are killed in car accidents.

Section B　Conversation

In this section, you will hear nine short conversations between two speakers. At the end of each conversation you will be given 10 seconds to answer each of the following nine questions.

Now listen to the conversations.

9. WOMAN: I'm going to take down those curtains and put up new ones.

   MAN: Why? What's wrong with them?

10. MAN: You should go to see the new movie. They're going to hold it over for another two weeks.

   WOMAN: Mm . . . Normally I wouldn't, but as you recommend it so strongly . . .

11. WOMAN: I got a letter from my sister. It's so badly written that I can hardly make out what exactly she is trying to say.

   MAN: Maybe you should call her up to find out what's troubling her.

12. WOMAN: The rain is going to continue till tomorrow. I wanted to take you to see the park, but it's too wet for that, and it's obvious we can't walk around to visit the sights that you've suggested, Jack. Too bad.

   MAN: Yes, it's a shame.

13. WOMAN: There is a special discount at the museum on weekends before 10 a. m. We could use the opportunity since there are so many of us.

   MAN: Mm . . . depending on what most of us want to see.

14. MAN: Do you know what you want to do when you finish your degree?

   WOMAN: I'll ask you if I ever need your advice.

15. MAN: I'm a free man from today on. Nobody will tell me what I should do and what I shouldn't any more.

   WOMAN: You don't mean you've quit that well-paid job you've held for so long?

16. WOMAN: I must go to the supermarket tomorrow. It's the last day it's open till after the Christmas holidays.

   MAN: Sure, we don't want to be out of anything. Want a hand?

17. MAN: Do you know John is going to move to France next month? His wealthy uncle has left all his property there for him to inherit.

   WOMAN: I wish I could come into a fortune like that one day.

Section C   News Broadcast

Question 18 *is based on the following news. At the end of the news item, you will be given* 10 *seconds to answer the question.*

Now listen to the news.

A fifteen-year-old schoolboy, Peter Emerson of Stratford-on-Avon, was recovering at home yesterday after being trapped all night in a cold store at the butcher's shop where he works after school. The door swung shut as he was putting meat into the store. He realized that he was left all alone after he had shouted and kicked the door and no one answered. He kept warm by jumping and running for about ten of the fourteen hours.

Questions 19 & 20 *are based on the following news. At the end of the news item, you will be given* 20 *seconds to answer the two questions.*

Now listen to the news.

Secretary of State Warren Christopher has wrapped up his latest trip to the Middle East, saying the peace process is progressing. Mr. Christopher says he will leave the region Thursday, assured that the picture is much less gloomy than suggested by recent reports. During two days of talks Mr. Christopher met with Israeli Prime Minister Yitzhak Rabin and Foreign Minister Shimon Pérés in Israel and with PLO Chairman Yasser Arafat in the Gaza Strip. He also met with Syrian President Hafez al-Assad in Damascus.

Questions 21 & 22 *are based on the following news. At the end of the news item, you will be given* 20 *seconds to answer the two questions.*

Now listen to the news.

Prison service staff here in Britain have been severely criticized in an official report for the escape of five IRA prisoners and an armed robber from Whitemoor Prison, Cambridgeshire. Bomb-making equipment was subsequently discovered at the jail. The government has announced a major review of prison security throughout England and Wales. A new task force will be set up under the Home Office; and the detailed list of recommendations is expected to be issued by the end of the year.

Questions 23 *to* 25 *are based on the following news. At the end of the news item, you will be given* 30 *seconds to answer the three questions.*

Now listen to the news.

The Canadian police say that the new North American Free Trade Agreement which is to open frontiers across the continent has been exploited by drug smugglers from South America. The Mafia can now move drugs across the continent with minimum supervision. Police estimate 60% of the cocaine which came through Canada this year has been brought through the east coast. Last year it was 10%. Police say the Mafia are benefiting from the declining fishing industry. There are more boats available to move the drugs.

1997 年英语专业四级考试听力理解

Part Ⅱ Dictation

Listen to the following passage. Altogether the passage will be read to you four times. During the first reading, which will be read at normal speed, listen and try to understand the meaning. For the second and third readings, the passage will be read sentence by sentence, or phrase by phrase, with intervals of 15 seconds. The last reading will be read at normal speed again and during this time you should check your work. You will then be given 2 minutes to check through your work once more.

Please write the whole passage on ANSWER SHEET TWO.

Legal Age for Marriage

Throughout the United States, the legal age for marriage shows some difference. / The most common age without parents' consent is eighteen for both females and males. / However, persons who are underage in their home state can get married in another state, / and then return to the home state legally married. /

Each state issues its own marriage license. / Both residents and nonresidents are qualified for such a license. / The fees and ceremonies vary greatly from state to state. / Most states, for instance, have a blood test requirement, but a few do not. / Most states permit either a civil or religious ceremony, / but a few require the ceremony to be religious. / In most states, a waiting period is required before the license is issued. / This period is from one to five days depending on the state. / A three-day wait is the most common. / In some states, there's no required waiting period. /

The second and third readings. You should begin writing now.

The last reading. Now, you have two minutes to check through your work.

(a 2-minute interval)

This is the end of the Dictation.

Part Ⅲ Listening Comprehension

In Sections A, B and C you will hear everything once only. Listen carefully and then answer the questions that follow. Mark the correct response for each question in your answer sheet.

Section A Statement

In this section you will hear nine statements. At the end of the statement you will be given 10 seconds to answer each of the following nine questions.

1. John met me at the door and said that his dormitory wasn't full, but in fact it was.
2. We just can't get over the fact that Jane failed while Mary succeeded.
3. At the moment there is no course I enjoy more than composition.
4. If I had known the exercises should be handed in today, I'd have finished them yesterday.
5. I woke up at 8:30, knowing that the appointment was at 9:45, but despite all of my plans I still got there at 10:00.

· 149 ·

6. If only he had paid more attention to his spelling in the examination.

7. Come in, John. Please excuse the mess. We only moved in here a month ago, and we're in the middle of house decoration.

8. David decided to take the overnight express train to Rome. Usually he would have gone by plane, but now he wanted to have some time on his own before he got back home.

9. My students went camping last weekend. They had a wonderful time, and they stayed warm and dry in spite of the weather.

Section B   Conversation

In this section. you will hear seven short conversations between two speakers. At the end of each conversation you will be given 10 *seconds to answer each of the following seven questions.*

10. MAN: Why did you get up at 6:40? I thought your meeting wasn't until 10:30.

    WOMAN: I wanted to visit the park before I left. It's the first time I've seen it.

11. WOMAN: London is a gorgeous city. From here you can see the Palace guards.

    MAN: Wait until we get to Paris and Madrid, and don't forget about Rome.

12. MAN: Do you have any idea what this passage is about?

    WOMAN: I'm as much in the dark as you are.

13. MAN: I'd like to apply for the position you advertised in China Daily.

    WOMAN: A good command of English and computing is a must as far as the position is concerned.

14. WOMAN: I see that Vincent is smiling again.

    MAN: Yes. He decided to speak to his boss's mother about his problems at work rather than to go directly to his boss.

15. MAN: We got the computer repaired last week.

    WOMAN: Oh, so it could be fixed.

16. WOMAN: There was a storm warning on the radio this morning. Did you happen to be listening?

    MAN: No, but what a shame. I guess we'll have to change our sailing plans. Would you rather play golf or go cycling?

Section C   News Broadcast

Question 17 *is based on the following news. At the end of the news item*, *you will be given* 10 *seconds to answer the question.*

Now listen to the news.

The authorities in Hong Kong have released a second group of Vietnamese boat people from detention after Vietnam refused to accept them. The group of sixteen have been detained since 1991 when they entered Hong Kong. The release last month of more than one hundred boat people in Hong Kong caused protest from local residents opposing any move to allow the boat people to stay permanently. There are still some 24,000 Vietnamese boat people in detention camps in Hong Kong.

Questions 18 *and* 19 *are based on the following news. At the end of the news item. you will be given 20 seconds to answer the two questions.*

Now listen to the news.

NATO troops are to join their former Cold War enemies in training exercises in Poland this week. The drills, which will begin on 17th, are the first major joint exercises of western and eastern armies under NATO's partnership. Some 900 soldiers from 13 countries will take part. NATO says it would be a good way to share peace-keeping experiences and develop a common understanding of operational procedures.

Questions 20 to 22 are based on the following news. At the end of the news item, you will be given 30 seconds to answer the three questions.

Now listen to the news.

A twenty-year action plan for cutting the rate of world population growth is expected to win wide approval today in Cairo. Delegates at the UN-sponsored conference on population completed final talks on the plan Monday. The document is non-binding, but it will serve as a guideline for countries and donor states that fund health care and family-planning programs. The world population of 5.7 billion currently is growing at more than 90 million a year.

Questions 23 to 25 are based on the following news. At the end of the news item, you will be given 30 seconds to answer the three questions.

Now listen to the news.

In the Philippines, a ferry carrying at least 400 people has sunk after an apparent collision with a cargo ship. There were no immediate reports of casualties. The accident occurred at about 11:30 a.m. local time at the mouth of the Manila Bay shortly after the ferry left Manila's port. A Philippine Coast Guard spokesman said the ferry had been hit by 12,000-ton Singapore-registered cargo vessel. Further details were not immediately available.

1998 年英语专业四级考试听力理解

Part Ⅱ   Dictation

Listen to the following passage. Altogether the passage will be read to you four times. During the first reading, which will be read at normal speed, listen and try to understand the meaning. For the second and third readings, the passage will be read sentence by sentence, or phrase by phrase, with intervals of 15 seconds. The last reading will be read at normal speed again and during this time you should check your work. You will then be given 2 minutes to check through your work once more.

Please write the whole passage on ANSWER SHEET TWO.

The Railways in Britain

The success of early railways, such as the lines between big cities,/ led to a great increase in railway building in Victorian times. / Between 1835 and 1865, about 25,000 kilometers of track were built,/ and over one hundred railway companies were created. /

Railway travel transformed people's lives. / Trains were first designed to carry goods. /

English

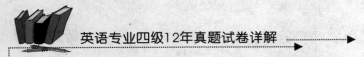

However, a law in the 19th century forced railway companies to run one cheap train a day,/ which stopped at every station, and cost only a penny a mile. / Soon working-class passengers found they could afford to travel by rail. / Cheap Day Excursion trains became popular, and seaside resorts grew rapidly. /

The railways also provided thousands of new jobs: / building carriages, running the railways, and repairing the tracks. /

That local time was abolished. / And clocks showed the same time all over the country. /

The second and third readings. You should begin writing now.

The last reading. Now, you have two minutes to check through your work.

(a 2-minute interval)

This is the end of the Dictation.

Part III Listening Comprehension

In Sections A, B and C you will hear everything once only. Listen carefully and then answer the questions that follow. Mark the correct response for each question on your answer sheet.

Section A Statement

In this section you will hear eight statements. At the end of the statement you will be given 10 seconds to answer each of the following eight questions.

1. I need some aspirin, please. I'd also like to get this prescription filled.

2. Wow, that's terrific. I couldn't agree more.

3. Mr. Dawson bought a thirty-dollar sweater for eighteen dollars on 13th of July.

4. Staying healthy today means more than just going to a doctor when you're ill.

5. I really don't want any dessert or coffee. Just bring me the bill, please.

6. If I had gone to the game, you bet I would have enjoyed seeing our team win.

7. Some people make more money than teachers, but few get as much satisfaction from their work.

8. Although there are some similarities in the platforms of both candidates, the differences between them are considerably wide.

Section B Conversation

In this section, you will hear nine short conversations between two speakers. At the end of each conversation you will be given 10 seconds to answer each of the following nine questions.

9. WOMAN: Hilton Hotel. May I help you?

   MAN: Mr. John Thomas, Room 13, please.

   WOMAN: I'll put you through. Oh, sorry, Mr. Thomas isn't in at the moment.

   MAN: Can I leave a message?

   WOMAN: Certainly.

   MAN: Have him call Max Green at six. It's important.

10. WOMAN: Good morning, did you sleep well last night?

    MAN: Yes, the room was fine.

    WOMAN: Are you checking out this morning?

MAN:　　　 Yes, I'm leaving around ten.

11. MAN:　　 Did you do anything last weekend?

　　WOMAN:　 Not much. What did you do?

　　MAN:　　 I had planned to go skiing or do some shopping, but wound up studying.

12. WOMAN:　 Hey, John, were you in the literature class yesterday?

　　MAN:　　 No, I couldn't make it. Weren't you there either?

　　WOMAN:　 No, I wasn't. I was hoping you could tell me the reading assignment.

13. MAN:　　 Are we going to the party this evening?

　　WOMAN:　 Well, I wonder if James can make it from home.

　　MAN:　　 He's got a car now.

　　WOMAN:　 Sounds like no problem, then.

14. WOMAN:　 I'm going to India next month. Is there any advice you'd like to give me on my first trip?

　　MAN:　　 Well, see as much as you can, because its a country with a very different culture from ours.

15. WOMAN:　 When shall I come again?

　　MAN:　　 Well, I'm afraid we must wait till all the applications are in. And if we decide to put your name on our short list, we will let you know.

16. WAN:　　 What's wrong with your new electric cooker? Let me see if I can fix it.

　　WOMAN:　 Oh, I had the shop replace it with a new one this morning.

17. WOMAN:　 Look, it's getting late, and we'd better be leaving together. Have you got a car, Mr. Smith?

　　WAN:　　 No, thanks. There's a bus.

Section C　News Broadcast

Question 18 is based on the following news. At the end of the news item, you will be given 10 seconds to answer the question.

　　Now listen to the news.

Heavy rains and overflowing rivers have caused extensive flooding in some parts of the US mid-west and in eastern regions of the US as well. Melting snow and new snowfall in the mid-west states of Iowa, Michigan and Indiana have driven rivers over their banks, and have cut off electricity to thousands of customers. In the eastern states of Pennsylvania and New Jersey and West Virginia, flooding has damaged homes and forced evacuations in several counties.

　　Question 19 is based on the following news. At the end of the news item, you will be given 10 seconds to answer the question.

　　Now listen to the news.

Official Iranian news agency, quoting a senior Foreign Ministry official, has said preparations were being made for the Foreign Minister Dr. Ali Ahbar Velayati to visit Iraq. No specific date was given. The news was carried the day after a preparatory team led by his senior advisor, Ali Karum ended a four-day visit to the Iraqi capital Baghdad. In an interview carried on

Tehran Radio, Ali Karum said an Iraqi delegation will be travelling to Tehran shortly to follow up on the talks.

Questions 20 and 21 are based on the following news. At the end of the news item, you will be given 20 seconds to answer the questions.

Now listen to the news.

The US Senate has passed a landmark bill aimed at ending the country's huge budget deficits within the next seven years. It would cut government spending by more than 900 billion dollars. Health, education, and hundreds of other programs will be hit. The bill was passed last week by the House of Representatives. And congressional leaders now have to work out a compromise. A BBC Washington correspondent says the stage is now set for a confrontation with the White House. President Clinton has threatened to veto the Republican plans.

Question 22 is based on the following news. At the end of the news item, you will be given 10 seconds to answer the question.

Now listen to the news.

France has carried out the first of a planned series of nuclear tests in the south Pacific despite strong international opposition. The French Defense Ministry said the device exploded at an underground site beneath Mururoa Atoll yielded less than twenty kilotons.

Australian scientists described it as fairly small compared with previous tests. There's been swift reaction from several countries. New Zealand and Chile have recalled their ambassadors to Paris in protest. Australia condemned the test and the US expressed its regret.

Before the nuclear device was exploded, the French President, Jacques Chirac said his country might carry out fewer than the eight tests originally planned.

Question 23 is based on the following news. At the end of the news item, you will be give 10 seconds to answer the question.

Now listen to the news.

Indian police have found a large cache of plastic explosives in Bombay—the type used in last month's serial bombings that killed more than 300 people. Police say they seized nearly 2,000 kilograms of explosives from a marshy region north of Bombay. About 1,300 kilograms of similar explosives were discovered in the area last week. Police also arrested 14 more people in connection with the bombings.

Questions 24 and 25 are based on the following news. At the end of the news item, you will be given 20 seconds to answer the questions.

Now listen to the news.

Israel and the PLO, after six days of intensive negotiations, meet again later today for what they say they hope will be the final initialing of an agreement on extending Palestinian self-rule in the West Bank. The two sides had been optimistic about reaching agreement yesterday. But last-minute hitches arose over the timetable for releasing thousands of prisoners and arrangements for the redeployment of Israeli troops. The BBC Jerusalem correspondent says it appears the two sides have made progress on one of the most difficult issues of all—the future of

Hebron, the only town in the West Bank where there is a community of Jewish settlers.

1999 年英语专业四级考试听力理解

Part Ⅱ　Dictation

Listen to the following passage. Altogether the passage will be read to you four times. During the first reading, which will be read at normal speed, listen and try to understand the meaning. For the second and third readings, the passage will be read sentence by sentence, or phrase by phrase, with intervals of 15 seconds. The last reading will be read at normal speed again and during this time you should check your work. You will then be given 2 minutes to check through your work once more.

Please write the whole passage on Answer Sheet Two.

United Nations' Day

The 24th of October is celebrated as United Nations' Day. / It is a day that belongs to everyone, / and it is celebrated in most countries of the world. / Some countries celebrate for a week instead of a day. /

In many parts of the world, schools have special programs for the day. / Boys and girls in some communities decorate a UN tree. / In other communities, young people put on plays about the UN. / Some libraries exhibit children's art works from around the world. / Schools celebrate with the songs and dances of other countries/ or give parties where foods of other countries are served. /

No matter how the day is celebrated, / the purpose of these celebrations is to help everyone understand the UN, / and the important roles it plays in world affairs. /

The UN encourages people to learn about other lands and their customs. / In this way, people can get a better understanding and appreciation of peoples all over the world. /

The second and third readings. You should begin writing now.

The last reading. Now, you have two minutes to check through your work.

(a 2-minute interval)

This is the end of the Dictation.

Part Ⅲ　Listening Comprehension

In Sections A, B and C you will hear everything once only. Listen carefully and then answer the questions that follow. Mark the correct answer to each question on your answer sheet.

Section A　Statement

In this section you will hear eight statements. At the end of each statement you will be given 10 seconds to answer each of the following eight questions.

1. During this morning's test, I couldn't do the last four questions, but I did the first five.

2. According to Jane, there's no better cheese than Swiss cheese in our local supermarket.

3. Before going to the gas station to have his tank filled, John had his emergency brake checked and fixed at the service station near the local cinema.

4. Betty would rather that her husband didn't send away the cleaning lady, but he will anyway.

5. Fred would have paid twice as much as he did for his car if the salesman had asked more, as he really needed the car.

6. The idea of permanent education is practical, because people are never really too old to go on learning. Of course, there are certain limits, but these are not age limits.

7. It is getting much easier to travel nowadays, but increasingly harder to get away from people, and now that is perhaps the most difficult thing for holiday makers.

8. According to Tom, William lost his job not because he was always sick and usually went to work late, but because he made a big error in last month's accounting, and the boss was angry with him.

Section B Conversation

In this section, you will hear eight short conversations between two speakers. At the end of each conversation you will be given 10 seconds to answer each of the following eight questions.

9. WOMAN: Do you know that Mark turned down that job offer by a travel agency?

   WAN: Yeah, the hours were convenient, but he wouldn't have been able to make ends meet.

10. WAN: Can we eat somewhere else? Very few small restaurants like this serve good food.

    WOMAN: I know, but there isn't anywhere else in this town. Look! the waiter is coming over for our order.

11. WOMAN: Mary is fluent in English and she's just started to learn Japanese.

    WAN: I hear she also knows a few words in Chinese and French.

12. WAN: John must have been joking when he said that he was going to live in Boston.

    WOMAN: Don't be so sure. He told me that he was looking for an agent to sell his house.

13. WOMAN: Excuse me, I wonder if the bus would come at all. It's already a quarter to eleven.

    WAN: Oh, I'm afraid you have just missed the last one which left 5 minutes ago.

14. WOMAN: Hi, John, haven't seen you for quite a few days. I heard you've been sick. How are you feeling now?

    WAN: They must have confused me with my brother, Jack. Anyway, he is feeling better now.

15. WOMAN: At the rate it is being used, the photocopier is not going to make it through the rest of the year.

    WAN: The year?! It's supposed to be good for four!

16. WAN: Look at all those cars and trucks lined up for the ferry. There must be at least 40 ahead of ours.

    WOMAN: True, I think it would take a quite while for us to be on board.

Section C News Broadcast

Questions 17 and 18 are based on the following news. At the end of the news item, you will be given 20 seconds to answer the questions.

Now listen to the news.

Haitian hunger strikers at the US naval base at Guantanamo Bay, Cuba, have begun refusing all fluids and medical treatments. 15 of the 267 Haitians at the base, say they are prepared to die if necessary to force the US to admit the rest of them. The Haitians are eligible to pursue political asylum in the US, but have been barred from entry because most have the AIDS virus. The Clinton Administration says they would lift the ban on their entry, but it is not known when.

Question 19 is based on the following news. At the end of the news item, you will be given 10 seconds to answer the question.

Now listen to the news.

The top three US auto-makers have decided not to proceed with plans to file a trade complaint against Japanese auto-makers. General Motors, Ford and Chrysler had planned to accuse Japanese companies of dumping cars below market prices in the US, but they dropped the idea, citing a pledge by the Clinton Administration to address the US-Japan trade imbalance.

Questions 20 and 21 are based on the following news. At the end of the news item, you will be given 20 seconds to answer the questions.

Now listen to the news.

About 100 people are now known to have died in what has been described as the worst storms ever to hit the eastern US this century. The hurricane-force winds first struck the Gulf of Mexico, and have now spread across the Canadian border, continuing to bring record snowfalls, severe flooding, and causing millions of dollars of damage. All major airports have now reopened and airlines are beginning to cope with a backlog of thousands of stranded passengers. The storm also paralyzed areas of Cuba, where several people were killed and property and crops destroyed.

Question 22 is based on the following news. At the end of the news item, you will be given 10 seconds to answer the question.

Now listen to the news.

France has carried out another underground nuclear test in the South Pacific. It is the fifth in the region since September. The test was conducted at the Muroroa Atoll on Wednesday. Paris has come under strong criticism for its nuclear testing programme, especially from Asia-Pacific countries. A State Department spokeswoman in Washington expressed disappointment at the latest French test. France has promised to sign a global test-ban treaty after it completes its current series of nuclear tests in the Pacific.

Question 23 is based on the following news. At the end of the news item, you will be given 10 seconds to answer the question.

Now listen to the news.

The association representing British airline pilots says that there is an urgent need to raise levels of air safety throughout the world. In the statement, the association, known as BALBA, warns that unless air safety improves travelers face a perilous future. The association also said that the standard of training must be raised among flight crews and air traffic controllers as the sky has become ever more crowded.

Questions 24 and 25 are based on the following news. At the end of the news item, you will be given 20 seconds to answer the questions.

Now listen to the news.

The Western European Union, the defense organization linking most countries of the European Community, is meeting in Luxemberg to discuss ways to reinforce economic sanctions against the Serbs by tightening controls on the River Danube. It is expected to approve proposals to send patrol boats manned by armed police and customs officers with powers to search and turn back ships suspected of breaking the sanctions. International efforts to isolate Serbia have been undermined by ships carrying oil and other illegal supplies from the Black Sea region along the Danube into the former Yugoslavia, often ignoring attempts by the local authorities to stop them. It is reported that most of the illegal traffic of goods is believed to be arriving in Serbia over land from Greece and former Yugoslavian Republic of Macedonia.

2000 年英语专业四级考试听力理解

Part Ⅱ   Dictation

Listen to the following passage. Altogether the passage will be read to you four times. During the first reading, which will be read at normal speed, listen and try to understand the meaning. For the second and third readings, the passage will be read sentence by sentence, or phrase by phrase, with intervals of 15 seconds. The last reading will be read at normal speed again and during this time you should check your work. You will then be given 2 minutes to check through your work once more.

Please write the whole passage on ANSWER SHEET TWO.

What We Know About Language

Many things about language are a mystery and will remain so. / However, we now do know something about it. /

First, we know that all human beings have a language of some sort. / No human race anywhere on earth is so backward/ that it has no language of its own at all. /

Second, there is no such thing as a primitive language. / There are many people whose cultures are undeveloped, / but the languages they speak are by no means primitive. / In all the languages existing in the world today, / there are complexities that must have been developed for years. /

Third, we know that all languages are perfectly adequate. / Each is a perfect means of expressing its culture. /

And finally, we know that language changes over time, / which is natural and normal if a language is to survive. / The language which remains unchanged is nothing but dead. /

The second and third readings. You should begin writing now.

The last reading. Now, you have two minutes to check through your work.

(*a 2-minute interval*)

This is the end of the Dictation.

Part Ⅲ   Listening Comprehension

In Sections A, B and C you will hear everything ONCE ONLY. Listen carefully and then answer the questions that follow. Mark the best answer to each question on your answer sheet.

Section A   Statement

In this section you will hear nine statements. At the end of the statement you will be given 10 seconds to answer each of the following nine questions.

1. Harry's brother would not remain an engine driver if he were ambitious.

2. Would you mind waiting a few minutes? Ms. Ellis is being examined by her physician at the moment.

3. Joan is in hospital. I'd like to send her a handbag she can use later in the law office where she is employed.

4. Mary and I work in the same office. We're on five days and off two days in a week. Every time I see her, she's wearing a different silk scarf.

5. Welcome aboard Southeast Service to Red Hill, East Croydon and Victoria with changes in Red Hill for Gilford.

6. What we need here is a clerk who is careful and considerate. Let's write that in the ad. — Carefulness and consideration are a must.

7. I used to think Emily was honest and trustworthy. But now I know better.

8. The first train to Greenhill leaves at 6:28. There's a train every hour on the hour and every twenty-eight minutes past the hour.

9. The trouble is no matter how hard he tried, Malcolm didn't seem to get anywhere.

Section B   Conversation

In this section, you will hear eight short conversations between two speakers. At the end of each conversation you will be given 10 seconds to answer each of the following eight questions.

10. WOMAN: What do you think, am I OK?

    WAN: Well, there's some inflammation it seems to me. I want to have a thorough check-up and do some tests.

11. WAN: It's hot. I wish it would rain and cool off.

    WOMAN: This is unusual for November. I don't remember it ever being so hot and dry in November before.

12. WAN: Many people prefer taking public buses or the subway, or even taxis because parking is getting to be a real headache in some parts of the city.

    WOMAN: That doesn't surprise me.

13. WOMAN: Hello, good morning. I'm calling to check on the status of my computer.

    WAN: Well, the new parts have just come in. So it should be ready by Friday.

14. WOMAN: My goodness! The service in the restaurant is really terrible, a lot worse than before.

    WAN: Right. It's high time they got rid of half the staff here if you ask me.

15. WAN: Operator, I booked a long distance collect call to my sister in Switzerland 25 minutes ago, but I haven't got a reply yet.

    WOMAN: Sorry, I'll ring it for you right now.

16. WOMAN: I'll wear this blue jacket. I like the color on me, don't you think so?

    WAN: I think it looks terrific on you, really.

17. WOMAN: How did Mr. Hunt's project turn out? I heard he had trouble with the financing, and he then couldn't get the land he wanted.

    WAN: It's true. He did have difficulties at first. But all in all, the project couldn't have turned out better.

Section C   News Broadcast

Question 18 is based on the following news. At the end of the news item, you will be given 10 seconds to answer the question.

Now listen to the news.

NATO and Russia are reporting some progress in efforts to finalize a charter governing their post-Cold War relationship. But they stressed more work must be done to settle their differences in military and political issues. A fifth round of talks between Russian Foreign Minister and NATO's Secretary General ended Tuesday in Luxembourg.

Questions 19 and 20 are based on the following news. At the end of the news item, you will be given 20 seconds to answer the two questions.

Now listen to the news.

A Boeing-727 aircraft with 51 passengers and 10 crew on board has crashed into a mountainside just outside the Columbian capital Bogota. Police and rescue workers said everyone was killed when the plane exploded, scattering wreckage over a wide area. The crash happened shortly after takeoff when the plane was unable to gain enough height to clear the mountains. The aircraft belonged to Ecuador Airline but it had been chartered by Air France for the route from Bogota to the Ecuadorian capital Quito.

Questions 21 and 22 are based on the following news. At the end of the news item, you will be given 20 seconds to answer the two questions.

Now listen to the news.

The US has designated 30 international groups as terrorist organizations, barring them from receiving money, weapons or other support from US citizens. The new terrorist list includes a Palestinian group Hamas, the pro-Iranian Hezbollah, Cambodia's Khmer Rouge, the Basque separatist group ETA, Sri Lanka's Tamil Tigers, and the Peruvian-based Shining Path, and Tupac Amaru Revolutionary Movement. The list does not include the Irish Republican Army, or the Palestinian Liberation Organization. US Secretary of State Madeleine Albright says the affected groups will have their US visas revoked and the US financial assets frozen.

Question 23 is based on the following news. At the end of the news item, you will be given 10 seconds to answer the question.

Now listen to the news.

Israeli prosecutors are reviewing charges against Prime Minister Benjamin Netanyahu after Israeli police called for his indictment. Justice Ministry officials say they hope the decision on whether to bring charges against the Israeli leader will be announced Sunday. The case stems from the appointment of Roni Bar-On as Israeli's Attorney General. Critics charged the appointment was part of a conspiracy to end the trial of Netanyahu's political ally.

Questions 24 and 25 are based on the following news. At the end of the news item, you will be given 20 seconds to answer the two questions.

Now listen to the news.

The combined left-wing opposition in France has defeated President Jacques Chirac's ruling Conservative Coalition in the first round of the country's parliamentary elections. Projections by French television give the Socialist-led opposition 40% of the vote; and Mr. Chirac's centre-right coalition 37%. If the left secures a majority of seats in Parliament, Socialist leader Lionel Jospin would likely become Prime Minister in a power-sharing arrangement with President Chirac.

2001 年英语专业四级考试听力理解

Part II   Dictation

Listen to the following passage. Altogether the passage will be read to you four times. During the first reading, which will be read at normal speed, listen and try to understand the meaning. For the second and third readings, the passage will be read sentence by sentence, or phrase by phrase, with intervals of 15 seconds. The last reading will be read at normal speed again and during this time you should check your work. You will then be given 2 minutes to check through your work once more.

Please write the whole passage on Answer Sheet Two.

Characteristics of a Good Reader

To improve your reading habits,/ you must understand the characteristics of a good reader./ First, the good reader usually reads rapidly./ Of course, he does not read every piece of material at the same rate,/ but whether he is reading a newspaper or a chapter in a physics text,/ his reading rate is relatively fast./ He has learned to read for ideas rather than words one at a time./

Next, the good reader can recognize and understand general ideas and specific details./ Thus he is able to comprehend the material/ with a minimum of effort and a maximum of interest./

Finally, the good reader has in his command several special skills,/ which he can apply to reading problems as they occur. / For the college student, the most helpful of these skills include/ making use of the various aids to understanding that most textbooks provide/ and skim-reading for a general survey. /

The second and third readings. You should begin writing now.

The last reading. Now, you have two minutes to check through your work.

(*a 2-minute interval*)

This is the end of the Dictation.

Part Ⅲ   Listening Comprehension

In Sections A, B and C you will hear everything once only. Listen carefully and then answer the questions that follow. Mark the correct answer to each question on your answer sheet.

Section A   Statement

In this section you will hear nine statements. At the end of each statement you will be given 10 seconds to answer the question.

1. I have to teach the same course books several times in the summer holiday camp, which is sometimes boring and not well-paid, but by and large, I'm quite delighted in being with young people.

2. The poor living conditions in such a large city have resulted from the unplanned real estate development, which is rarely seen in small cities.

3. At a recent seminar, many participants were worried about the fact that overpopulation may give rise to many social security problems.

4. May I have your attention, please? Flight 998 is leaving at 11:30 a. m. Please check in half an hour prior to the departure.

5. Having gone through your claims for fire damage, I don't think the policy you have provides protection against loss by fire.

6. Ian lost one eye in a childhood accident, but he nonetheless had a very successful athletic career.

7. Mr. and Mrs. Clark used to smoke. But now Mrs. Clark has stopped, and she's afraid her husband will fall ill if he doesn't get rid of his bad habit of smoking both at home and at work.

8. I heard from Mary that last semester Susan found it difficult to stay on good terms with her roommate, Jenny.

9. Jack says that he is up to his eyes in work at present, and really can't afford the time to have dinner with us.

Section B   Conversation

In this section, you will hear nine short conversations between two speakers. At the end of each conversation you will be given 10 seconds to answer the question.

10. WAN: I want to find a part-time job during the summer vacation and earn some money. How about you?

WOMAN: I'm going to take a few summer courses so that I can graduate earlier next year.

11. WOMAN: Excuse me, I want some dictionaries. Where can I find them?

WAN: The regular-priced ones are here. And on that table in the corner of the room, we have some on discount.

WOMAN: Thank you.

12. WAN: I wonder where I can take my girlfriend for dinner after work tonight.

WOMAN: Have you been to the Chinese restaurant near the school?

13. WOMAN: Hello, the pipe in my bathroom is leaking. Can you come to get it repaired right away?

WAN: Well, it depends on how soon I can finish the drains at the office building.

14. WOMAN: Do you think you could play the music tape another time, dear? I've got a slight headache.

WAN: Of course. Sorry, I didn't realize you could hear it. You want me to call the doctor?

WOMAN: No, thanks. I'll be OK in a minute.

15. WAN: Lisa, how are you getting along with your term paper?

WOMAN: I've been writing and rewriting it. I simply don't know if I'll ever get it finished.

16. WOMAN: I must go to the library, the one near the laboratory, because I have to finish my research project by tomorrow. But if I could, I'd prefer to go with you to the theater.

WAN: I wish you could come along.

17. WOMAN: Why did Jackson suddenly decide to quit his job?

WAN: He said he wouldn't break his back working for such a low pay.

WOMAN: I see.

18. WAN: Are you sure you can't remember the name of the film you saw last week?

WOMAN: It's just on the tip of my tongue.

Section C News Broadcast

Questions 19 and 20 are based on the following news. At the end of the news item, you will be given 20 seconds to answer the questions.

Now listen to the news.

Commonwealth leaders agree to lift Nigeria's three-and-a-half-year suspension on May 29, the day the military government hands over power to an elected president, the organization's Secretary General announced yesterday. Nigeria was suspended from the fifty-four-nation group of mainly former British colonies in 1995 after it executed nine minority rights activists, including writer Ken Saro-WiWa. But now that the country has embarked on a return to democracy, Commonwealth heads of government have agreed to end its estrangement. Secretary General

Chief Emecka Anyaoku said in a statement, "I'm delighted that an unfortunate episode in Nigeria-Commonwealth relations will now come to an end, and Nigeria is resuming its rightful place in the Commonwealth."

Questions 21 and 22 are based on the following news. At the end of the news item, you will be given 20 seconds to answer the questions.

Now listen to the news.

The space shuttle Discovery made a rare night landing at the Kennedy Space Center early on Thursday. The night landing, the eleventh in the Center's ninety-four shuttle missions, ended a ten-day mission to outfit the orbiting International Space Station.

Although the spacecraft created a sonic boom that could be heard along much of Florida's eastern seaboard, witnesses on the ground could not see the orbiter until it was directly over the runway lights.

Scattered showers off the Florida coast had threatened to postpone the shuttle's return, but forecasters gave the green light when they decided no rain would fall within forty-eight kilometers of the space center.

Questions 23 and 24 are based on the following news. At the end of the news item, you will be given 20 seconds to answer the questions.

Now listen to the news.

Five people died, two were missing, and at least eighteen were injured on Wednesday when an Italian patrol vessel collided with the dinghy filled with refugees crossing the Adriatic Sea from Albania, authorities said. The victims were believed to be Albanians from either Albania or Kosovo, said authorities from Italy's tax police division, which, along with the coast guard, patrols the nation's coast. The cause of the collision was not immediately known. Three Albanians, believed to have smuggled the refugees, were arrested a few hours after the accident.

Question 25 is based on the following news. At the end of the news item, you will be given 10 seconds to answer the question.

Now listen to the news.

Malaysian authorities are discussing possible salvage efforts with Sun Cruises, the Singapore owner of a luxury liner that sank off Malaysia last week, a news report said yesterday. Sun Cruise had received "some advice" from Malaysia on the matter, the Business Times newspaper quoted company's spokeswoman Judy Choo as saying. Choo and other Sun Cruises' officials could not immediately be reached for further comment, as they were away in Indonesia. The Sun Vista went down in international waters. But nearby Malaysia may have the right to order the wreck's removal, the newspaper said. Salvage experts said the wreck of the Sun Vista, which sunk in sixty meters of water, poses no threat to ships passing over it. But Malaysia may still want it removed.

2002 年英语专业四级考试听力理解

Part II   Dictation

Listen to the following passage. Altogether the passage will be read to you four times. During the first reading, which will be read at normal speed, listen and try to understand the meaning. For the second and third readings, the passage will be read sentence by sentence, or phrase by phrase, with intervals of 15 seconds. The last reading will be read at normal speed again and during this time you should check your work. You will then be given 2 minutes to check through your work once more.

Please write the whole passage on ANSWER SHEET TWO.

Disappearing Forests

The world's forests are disappearing. / As much as a third of the total tree cover has been lost/ since agriculture began some 10,000 years ago. / The remaining forests are home to half of the world's species, / thus becoming the chief resource for their survival.

Tropical rain forests once covered 12% of the land of the planet. As well as supporting at least half of the world's species of plants and animals, / these rain forests are home to millions of people. / But there are other demands on them. / For example, much has been cut for timber. / An increasing amount of forest land has been used for industrial purposes, / or for agricultural development such as crop-growing. / By the 1990's, less than half of the earth's original rain forests remained, / and they continued to disappear at an alarming rate every year. / As a result, the world's forests are now facing gradual extinction. /

The second and third readings. You should begin writing now.

The last reading. Now, you have two minutes to check through your work.

(*a 2-minute interval*)

This is the end of the Dictation.

Part III   Listening Comprehension

In Sections A, B and C you will hear everything once only. Listen carefully and then answer the questions that follow. Mark the correct answer to each question on your answer sheet.

Section A   Statement

In this section you will hear eight statements. At the end of each statement you will be given 10 seconds to answer the question.

1. Next, I'd like to show you a three-bedroom apartment on the second floor, which is a newly-built one we have for rent.

2. It used to take a fortnight to travel from London to Edinburgh by coach. However, you can now travel many times around the world in that time.

3. Jack, thank you for inviting us to dinner in your house tomorrow, but I am extremely sorry that my wife and I won't be able to make it.

4. Last time we discussed some patterns of animal behavior, and in today's lecture, we will

concentrate on the methods used in the study of animals.

5. In my opinion, motivation, rather than intelligence, often decides how far a person can go in his career.

6. In order to understand this writer thoroughly, you have to read between the lines.

7. Last week at the sale, Jane bought herself an overcoat for 30 pounds, which was one quarter of the regular price.

8. Due to the continual rain, the school sports meet has been postponed again till further notice from the principal's office.

Section B   Conversation

In this section, you will hear nine short conversations between two speakers. At the end of each conversation you will be given 10 seconds to answer the question.

9. WAN: I am really getting worried about Mary. She will sit in for an exam in two weeks' time, but all she is talking about now is nothing but the upcoming concert.

   WOMAN: She may fail along that line. Let's try to talk some sense into her.

10. WOMAN: Tony, do you ever believe in UFO?

    WAN: Me? Well, I have never seen it. But there are a lot of people who have— or who think they have—seen it.

11. WAN: You know, I started out in civil engineering. Then I switched to electronic engineering. But what really interests me is electronic music.

    WOMAN: Well, that's a long way away from civil engineering.

12. WOMAN: I bought a pint of milk for our breakfast, but it doesn't seem to look fresh now. Do you think it's still all right to drink?

    WAN: Let me smell it. Well, it has gone off. If I were you, I wouldn't even think of it.

13. WOMAN: It is true that all of them survived the fire last night?

    WAN: Yes, a miracle, isn't it? There was a couple on the second floor, and two women and three kids on the ground floor, but no one was badly hurt.

14. WOMAN: I'm going to take the blood test at 7:45 tomorrow morning.

    WAN: In that case you won't miss any courses tomorrow morning then.

15. WAN: I'm not really an expert on precious stones. But these are superb. Don't you like them?

    WOMAN: Have you looked at the price tag? It costs almost twice as much as the house we're now living in.

16. WOMAN: You seem to have been restless the whole day today. What's up?

    WAN: Later in the afternoon they will announce who will get permission for the study trip to Africa.

17. WOMAN: I will never go with Bill again. He could never remember where he parked his car.

WAN: That certainly sounds like Bill.

Section C   News Broadcast

Questions 18 and 19 are based on the following news. At the end of the news item, you will be given 20 seconds to answer the questions.

Now, listen to the news.

Britain has announced that it is to cancel about 200 million pounds' worth of debts owed to it by poorer Commonwealth countries. The International Development Secretary says the relief was being offered to countries committed to eliminating poverty and pursuing good government. This would include taking action against corruption. At the same time, Common Market Finance Ministers are meeting in Mauritius. Britain is expected to put forward a fresh initiative on reducing the debts of the poorest countries. The Chancellor of the Exchequer has indicated he plans to revive the scheme put forward last year by the International Monetary Fund which has not yet provided any relief.

Questions 20 and 21 are based on the following news. At the end of the news item, you will be given 20 seconds to answer the questions.

Now, listen to the news.

An underground train derailed at a station in central Paris yesterday, injuring 23 people and just missing another underground train standing on the opposite track.

French Emergency Services said the train was traveling at 35 kilometers per hour when it derailed as it entered the station. No one had been killed and no one was trapped in the train during the accident.

Ambulances rushed to the scene and doctors began treating casualties in the station and at a nearby cafe. Some people have broken limbs, and others have suffered bruising. No one was in critical condition.

Last night it was not known why the train came off the tracks.

Questions 22 and 23 are based on the following news. At the end of the news item, you will be given 20 seconds to answer the questions.

Now, listen to the news.

Argentine civil servants held a 24-hour strike yesterday to protest pay cuts of 12 to 15 percent for anyone earning more than US $ 1, 000 a month.

Public service unions planned to hold a protest rally in front of the government house.

The work stoppage comes after last Friday's general strike when many of Argentina's 12 million workers stayed home after the nation's powerful General Workers' Confederation, the nation's largest union group, called a one-day strike to protest spending cuts and free market reforms.

Questions 24 and 25 are based on the following news. At the end of the news item, you will be given 20 seconds to answer the questions.

Now, listen to the news.

Germany was due to strike a deal yesterday to close down its 19 nuclear power plants,

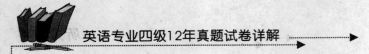

making it the first major industrial nation to commit to withdrawing from nuclear energy.

Talks between Chancellor Gehard Schroeder's Government and the chiefs of German energy industry were to begin at 8：30 pm.

Closure of Germany's 19 reactors, which provide around 1/3 of the country's electricity needs, was a key pledge of the Greens, the junior partner in Schroeder's coalition government.

2003 年英语专业四级考试听力理解

Part Ⅱ   Dictation

Listen to the following passage. Altogether the passage will be read to you four times. During the first reading, which will be read at normal speed, listen and try to understand the meaning. For the second and third readings, the passage will be read sentence by sentence, or phrase by phrase, with intervals of 15 seconds. The last reading will be read at normal speed again and during this time you should check your work. You will then be given 2 minutes to check through your work once more.

Please write the whole passage on ANSWER SHEET TWO.

Salmon

Every year millions of salmon swim from the ocean/ into the mouth of the rivers and steadily up the rivers. / Passing through waters, around rocks and waterfalls,/ the fish finally reach their original streams or lakes. / They dig up nests in the riverbed and lay their eggs. / Then exhausted by their journey, the parent salmon die. /They have finished their task that nature has given them. / Months or years later, the young fish start their trip to the ocean. / They live in the salt water from two to seven years/ until they too are ready to swim back to reproduce. / Their life cycle helps man provide himself with a basic food：fish. / When the adult salmon gather at the river mouth for the annual trip up the rivers,/ they are in the best possible condition. / And nearly every harbor has a salmon fishing fleet/ ready to catch thousands for the market. /

The second and third readings. You should begin writing now.

The last reading. Now, you have two minutes to check through your work.

(*a 2-minute interval*)

This is the end of the Dictation.

Part Ⅲ   Listening Comprehension

In Sections A, B and C you will hear everything ONCE ONLY. Listen carefully and then answer the questions that follow. Mark the correct answer to each question on your answer sheet.

Section A   Statement

In this section you will hear seven statements. At the end of each statement you will be given 10 seconds to answer the question.

1. You must relax. Don't work too hard and do watch your drinking and smoking.

2. We hadn't quite expected the committee to agree to rebuild the hospital. So we were taken aback when we got to know that it was finally agreed.

3. The coach leaves the station every 20 minutes. It's 9:15 now, and you have to wait for five minutes for the next one.

4. Perhaps Jane shouldn't have got the married in the first place. No one knows what she might be doing now, but not washing up. That's for sure.

5. I have to be working on the similar project at the moment. I'm only too pleased to help you.

6. The man arrived for the ceremony with patched jackets and faded jeans that the average person would save for mowing the lawn in his garden at the weekend.

7. Mark. Here you are. This is the last place in the world that I would have expected to find you.

Section B Conversation

In this section, you will hear ten short conversations between two speakers. At the end of each conversation you will be given 10 seconds to answer the question.

8. WOMAN: I couldn't stand this morning. My right leg went stiff.

MAN: I'm afraid it's probably a side-effect from the drugs I put you on.

9. WOMAN: How did your writing go this morning? Is the book coming along alright?

MAN: I am not sure. I think the rest of it would be difficult to write.

10. WOMAN: Is there anything you can do to make the cold go away more quickly?

MAN: No, there isn't. And the cold isn't really serious enough for a visit to your doctor.

11. WOMAN: Look, what I have got here.

MAN: Oh, So you did go to that bookstore.

12. MAN: Excuse me, has there been an emergency?

WOMAN: Oh. No, Sir. That's just a storm, so the plane will leave a little later this afternoon.

13. WOMAN: I wish I had not hurt Linda's feelings like that yesterday. You know I've never meant to.

MAN: The greatest thing about Linda is that she doesn't hold any grudges. By tomorrow she'll have forgotten all about it.

14. MAN: My grade is not bad, but not good enough. I know I didn't study at all this semester. Now I have to work very hard next semester to keep my scholarship.

WOMAN: I will see you in the library then.

15. WOMAN: I'll wear this blue jacket for the evening. I like the color on me. Don't you think?

MAN: I think it looks terrific on you, really!

16. WOMAN: Do you know that Sam turned down that job offered by a travel agency.

MAN: Yeah. The hours were convenient, but if he had accepted it, he wouldn't have been able to make ends meet.

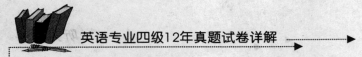

17. WOMAN: At the rate it has been used, the printer is not good to make it through the rest of the year.

　　MAN: 　　　The year? It is supposed to be good for four.

Section C　News Broadcast

Questions 18 and 19 are based on the following news. At the end of the news item, you will be given 20 seconds to answer the questions.

Now, listen to the news.

The UN resolution calls for greater international intelligence law enforcement co-operation and requires states to change their banking laws in order to police the global network of terrorism's financiers. It makes providing funds for terror activities a criminal offence and would freeze bank accounts of those who sponsor terrorism.

Questions 20 and 21 are based on the following news. At the end of the news item, you will be given 20 seconds to answer the questions.

Now, listen to the news.

A police spokesman said the devices were made safe by explosives experts in the Ardoyne district, where a woman was shot in the leg and 13 police officers were injured during a second successive night of violence. Northern Ireland's police chief had earlier called on community leaders to work to end the violence, which has erupted sporadically throughout a summer of sectarian tension in north Belfast.

Question 22 is based on the following news. At the end of the news item, you will be given 10 seconds to answer the question.

Now, listen to the news.

Airlines have been hit with huge increases to ensure their planes after the terrorist attacks the United States. Goshawk Insurance Holdings which ensures aircraft around the world said rates have soared as much as 10 foldl since the September 11th terror attacks. Airlines around the world have cut services and dismissed staff as their business has plunged in the week of the crisis. They are also struggling with increased security costs.

Questions 23 and 24 are based on the following news. At the end of the news item, you will be given 20 seconds to answer the questions.

Now, listen to the news.

A Pakistani lawyer said the resumption of the trial of 8 foreign aid workers accused of preaching Christianity in Afghanistan has been put off until Sunday. He had met earlier Saturday with the aid workers, two Americans, two Australians and four Germans. They insist they were in Afghanistan to help the poor, not to convert them. The penalty for these captured aid workers could range from the expulsion to jail term to death.

Question 25 is based on the following news. At the end of the news item, you will be given 10 seconds to answer the question.

Now, listen to the news.

On the 20th anniversary of the first official report on AIDS the head of the United Nations'

AIDS program warns the deadly disease only may be at its early stages in many parts of the world. Dr. Piot said the disease has already reached the staggering proportion since first being identified in 1981. 58 million people world-wide have contracted the HIV virus which causes AIDS while 22 million have died from related illnesses. The UN estimates the world HIV-positive population at 36 million, including 25 million in Sub-Saharan Africa. International officials warned the disease would have disastrous political, social and economic consequences in many developing countries.

2004 年英语专业四级考试听力理解

Part Ⅱ Dictation

Listen to the following passage. Altogether the passage will be read to you four times. During the first reading, which will be read at normal speed, listen and try to understand the meaning. For the second and third readings, the passage will be read sentence by sentence, or phrase by phrase, with intervals of 15 seconds. The last reading will be read at normal speed again and during this time you should check your work. You will then be given 2 minutes to check through your work once more.

Please write the whole passage on ANSWER SHEET TWO.

Money

Money is accepted across the world as payment for goods or services. / People use money to buy food, clothes and hundreds of other things. / In the past, many different things were used as money. / People on Pacific islands once exchanged shells for goods. / The Chinese used cloth and knives. / In Africa, elephant tusks or salt were used. / Even today, some people in Africa are still paid in salt. / Coins were first invented by the Chinese. / Originally, they were round pieces of metal with a hole in the center, / so that a piece of string could keep them together. / This made doing business much easier, / but people still found coins inconvenient to carry/ when they wanted to buy something expensive. / To solve this problem, / the Chinese again came up with the solution. / They began to use paper money for coins. / Now paper notes are used throughout the world. /

The second and third readings. You should begin writing now.

The last reading. Now, you have two minutes to check through your work.

(a 2-minute interval)

This is the end of the Dictation.

Part Ⅲ Listening Comprehension

In Sections A, B and C you will hear everything ONCE ONLY. Listen carefully and then answer the questions that follow. Mark the correct answer to each question on your answer sheet.

Section A　Statement

In this section you will hear eight statements. At the end of each statement you will be given 10 seconds to answer each question.

1. WOMAN: Lily studied drama at the university. But she used to work as a policewoman. Now she is a teacher, because she likes children.

2. MAN: May I have your attention, please? Flight 5125 scheduled to take off at 11:30 will be delayed for 20 minutes. Please check in half an hour prior to the departure.

3. MAN: There is a railway strike in the South Region and several trains have been cancelled. However, the strike doesn't seem to be spreading to other regions.

4. WOMAN: Latest reports from the northeast provinces say that at least sixteen people lost their lives in Sunday's floods. A further nine people, mostly children, are reported missing.

5. MAN: John, your paper must be revised over the weekend and handed in its final form on Monday. If you have any problem, call the office directly.

6. MAN: My discovery of Mary Jackson was, as a matter of fact, a gift from a friend. Years ago I was given a copy of *Tell Me a Riddle*, and I liked the stories.

7. WOMAN: Oh! Talking about money, it's terrible when you think how tiring the work is. It's only with tips and free meals that I manage to get by.

8. MAN: A lot of drugs are missing from the cupboard here in this room so I think we will have to look into the matter immediately.

Section B　Conversation

In this section, you will hear nine short conversations between two speakers. At the end of each conversation you will be given 10 seconds to answer each question.

9. MAN: Would you mind if we discuss tomorrow's agenda before dinner this evening?
   WOMAN: Not at all. I certainly don't want to talk about it during our meal.

10. MAN: Are you going home for the summer vacation?
    WOMAN: Well, Jane and I have decided to stay on here as research assistants.

11. WOMAN: It's so hot today, I can't work. I wish the air conditioning was on in this library.
    MAN: So do I, I'll fall asleep if I don't get out of this stuffy room soon.

12. WOMAN: I can't imagine what happened to Janet.
    MAN: Neither can I, but I'm sure she plans to come to the party.

13. MAN: Check in here?
    WOMAN: Yes, can I see your flight ticket, please?
    MAN: Here it is. I'm going to Lanzhou.

14. MAN: I heard that PICC is going to hold interviews on campus next week.
    WOMAN: Yeah, what day? I'd like to talk to them and drop my resume.

15. WOMAN: There must be a thunderstorm in some place because the picture isn't very sharp and the sound isn't very clear.

MAN: I think you're right, they said on the radio last night that a storm was coming in from the mountains and the morning paper forecast heavy rain.

16. WOMAN: The party will start at 6:30 but there are a lot of preparations to make and I need your help. Can I expect you at 5:00?

　　MAN: I'll be there around 5:30, all being well that is.

17. MAN: Excuse me, I'm enrolled to take Professor Lee's literature course 102 and I hear some changes have been made.

　　WOMAN: Yes, the class has been moved to the north building. Also it is now Tuesdays and Thursdays from 2:00 to 4:00 pm. Instead of being held on Monday and Friday from 2:00 to 3:00 pm.

　　MAN: What changes! Professor Lee will still be teaching the class, right?

Section C News Broadcast

Questions 18 and 19 are based on the following news. At the end of the news item, you will be given 20 seconds to answer the questions.

Now, listen to the news.

A court in Zimbabwe is due to deliver its verdict today in a trial of a journalist who works for the British newspaper The Guardian. The trial is seen as a test case for the country's strict new media laws. Andrew Meldrum, an American who's lived in Zimbabwe for over twenty years is accused of publishing an untrue story and faces up to two years in prison if found guilty. A dozen other journalists have also been charged with offenses relating to the new laws. In court Mr. Meldrum's defense argued that his story was published in Britain. It was beyond the jurisdiction of Zimbabwean laws.

Questions 20 and 21 are based on the following news. At the end of the news item, you will be given 20 seconds to answer the questions.

Now, listen to the news.

Kuala Lumpur—Afghanistan will play soccer at the Asian Games. Mongolia's withdrawal has given the war-torn nation a confidence boost. The Asian Football Confederation (AFC) announced in a statement yesterday that Afghanistan would play in the under-twenty-three tournament at the games in Bussan. Afghanistan's first match will be against Iran on September 28. The group's other teams are Qatar and Lebanon. Afghanistan was a founding member of the confederation in the 1950s, before entering long periods of war and factional fightings. The country's chaos was largely ended after US-led forces overthrew the Taliban regime last year in response to the September 11th terrorist attacks in the United States. During the Soccer World Cup in June, the President of Afghanistan's Football Association (AFA), Abdul Aleem-Kohistani said he hoped his country would be able to take part in the Asian Games.

Questions 22 and 23 are based on the following news. At the end of the news item, you will be given 20 seconds to answer the questions.

Now, listen to the news.

The expected life span of Beijing residents has gone up to 75.5 years old, compared with

74.4 years old, a decade earlier, while the death rate of middle-aged residents increases dramatically, according to a recent official report. The report made public by the Beijing Disease Control and Prevention Center said the past mortality of people aged between 35 to 54 years old had gone up 58.5% during the past ten years, from 158 people per 100,000 in 1991 to 251 people per 100,000 last year. Infant and maternal mortality rates went down 132% and 147% respectively. Health experts said chronic non-infectious diseases were the main causes of death covering 60% of the total number of death. The male mortality is higher than that of females and the death rate among rural residents is higher than that of the urban ones.

Questions 24 and 25 are based on the following news. At the end of the news item, you will be given 20 seconds to answer the questions.

Now, listen to the news.

Islamabad—Pakistani President, Pervez Musharraf said yesterday there was no danger of the country going to war with neighboring India but that Pakistani forces would be ready to repel any aggression. "There is no danger of war," Musharraf told reporters in the Pakistani capital of Islamabad, "We should have confidence in ourselves. We are not sitting idle. We are prepared for everything. There should not be any misunderstanding." Tensions were raised this week because the two accused each other of links to killings in the two countries. India says it suspects the two gunmen who killed twenty-eight people at an Indian temple on Tuesday have links to Pakistan-based Islamic militant groups. Pakistan has denied any involvement in the temple massacre and police in Karachi said there were indications of India intelligence agents behind the murder of seven Christian charity workers in the city, but India rejected the charges yesterday.

2005 年英语专业四级考试听力理解

Part Ⅰ   Dictation

Listen to the following passage. Altogether the passage will be read to you four times. During the first reading, which will be read at normal speed, listen and try to understand the meaning. For the second and third readings, the passage will be read sentence by sentence, or phrase by phrase, with intervals of 15 seconds. The last reading will be read at normal speed again and during this time you should check your work. You will then be given 2 minutes to check through your work once more.

Please write the whole passage on ANSWER SHEET ONE.

Now listen to the passage.

The Wrist Watch

It is generally believed that wrist watches are an exception/ to the normal sequence in the evolution of man's jewelry. / Reversing the usual order, they were first worn by women, / and then adopted by men. / In the old days, queens included wrist watches among their crown jewelry. / Later, they were worn by Swiss workers and farmers. / Until World War, Americans associated the watch with fortune hunters. / Then army officers discovered that the wrist watch was most practical for active combat. / Race car drivers also loved to wear wrist watches, / and pilots found them most useful while flying. / Soon men dared to wear wrist watches without feeling self-conscious. / By 1924, some 30 percent of men's watches were worn on the wrist. / Today, the figure is 90 percent. / And they are now worn by both men and women / for practical purposes rather than for decoration. /

The second and third readings. You should begin writing now.

The last reading. Now, you have two minutes to check through your work.

(a 2-minute interval)

This is the end of the Dictation.

Part Ⅱ Listening Comprehension

In Sections A, B and C you will hear everything ONCE ONLY. Listen carefully and then answer the questions that follow. Mark the correct answer to each question on your answer sheet.

Section A Conversation

In this section you will hear several conversations. Listen to the conversations carefully and then answer the questions that follow.

Questions 1 to 3 are based on the following conversation. At the end of the conversation, you will be given 15 seconds to answer the questions.

Now listen to the conversation.

WOMAN: Good morning, sit down please, Mr. Johnson.

MAN: Thank you, ma'am.

WOMAN: I have read your letter here. You seem to have done very well at school. Can you tell me something about your schoolwork?

MAN: As you can see, my strongest subjects were art subjects. My best subject was history, and my second best was geography. However, my favorite subject was math, and the results I got in the math paper were quite reasonable.

WOMAN: That's true. Now, can you tell me why you think these subjects will help you in this job?

MAN: Well, ma'am, I understand you manufacture computers, prepare software, and advise clients on how to use them. Is that right?

WOMAN: That's right.

MAN: And I've been told that working with computers needs a logical mind rather than great skills in mathematics. That's especially true, I believe, when it comes to writing programs. So I think my results show that I have some ability in logic and in mathematics, as well.

WOMAN: So, you would like to write material for computers, would you?

MAN: Yes, ma'am. That's what interests me most about computers, writing programs. But I think the computer industry itself is still expanding enormously. I'm sure that career prospects in the industry would be very good no matter what sort of job I

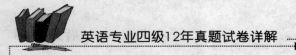

went into.

WOMAN： I see. Well, thank you. I've enjoyed our talk. We'll be writing to you.

MAN： Thank you, ma'am. Good morning.

Questions 4 to 7 are based on the following conversation. At the end of the conversation, you will be given 20 seconds to answer the questions.

Now listen to the conversation.

WOMAN： Excuse me, could I ask you some questions?

MAN： Of course.

WOMAN： I work for an advertising agency, and I'm doing some research. It's for a new magazine for people like you.

MAN： People like me? What do you mean?

WOMAN： People between 25 and 35 years old.

MAN： Okay.

WOMAN： Right. What do you do at the weekend?

MAN： Well, on Friday, my wife always goes to her exercise class, then she visits friends.

WOMAN： Don't you go out?

MAN： Not on Fridays. I never go out on Fridays. I stay at home and watch television.

WOMAN： And on Saturdays?

MAN： On Saturdays, my wife and I always go sailing together.

WOMAN： Really?

MAN： Mmm hmm. We love it! We never miss it. And then in the evening we go out.

WOMAN： Where to?

MAN： Different places. We sometimes go and see friends. We sometimes go to the cinema or a restaurant. But we always go out on Saturday evenings.

WOMAN： I see. And now, Sunday. What happens on Sunday?

MAN： Nothing special. We often go for a walk, and I always cook a big Sunday lunch.

WOMAN： Oh! How often do you do the cooking?

MAN： Mmm... Twice a week, three times a week.

WOMAN： Thank you very much. All I need now are your personal details: your name, job, and so on. What's your surname?

MAN： Robinson.

Questions 8 to 10 are based on the following conversation. At the end of the conversation, you will be given 15 seconds to answer the questions.

Now listen to the conversation.

MAN： Parcel Express. Good morning. How can I help you?

WOMAN： Good morning. I'm thinking of sending a parcel to New York next week. Can you tell me what the procedure is, please?

MAN： Certainly. When you ring us, we need the following information: The invoice address. That's probably your address, isn't it? And then the pickup address if that's different, and a contact phone number.

WOMAN: Just a moment. I'm taking notes. Phone number. Right.

MAN: Then we need the full name, address, and phone number of the person you're sending the parcel to.

WOMAN: Okay. Anything else?

MAN: Yes. The weight and dimensions of the parcel, that's height, width, and length, the value of the goods, and a full description.

WOMAN: Value, description.

MAN: Yes, but don't seal the parcel. You need to leave it open so that the driver can check the contents when he collects it. After the recent bombing, the airline said that we have to check all parcels. They told us we had to do it.

WOMAN: Fine. Now, last question. How long will the parcel take to get to New York.

MAN: One to two working days. There are daily flights at midday. And if we collect the parcel from you at 10:15, then your parcel catches that flight and it will arrive within 24 hours.

WOMAN: Right. Thank you very much. You've been very helpful.

MAN: Not at all. Goodbye.

WOMAN: Goodbye.

Section B   Passages

In this section, you will hear several passages. Listen to the passages carefully and then answer the questions that follow.

Questions 11 to 13 are based on the following announcement. At the end of the announcement, you will be given 15 seconds to answer the questions.

Now listen to the announcement.

Attention, all passengers. Platform change. This is a platform change. The train now standing at Platform 9 is the 10:48 train calling at all stations to Nanjing. Please note the train on Platform 9 is not the 10:52 train to Jinan. It's the 10:48 train calling at all stations to Nanjing. The 10:52 to Jinan will now leave from Platform 7. Train announcement. The 11:20 train to Zhengzhou from Platform 8 will be subject to a 15-minute delay. I repeat, there will be a 15-minute delay for the Zhengzhou train on Platform 8. It will now leave at 11:35, not 11:20. The 11:28 train to Hangzhou has been cancelled. We apologize to customers, but due to a signal problem, the 11:28 train to Hangzhou from Platform 15 has been cancelled. The 11:32 train to Tianjin is now standing at Platform 13. Please note there will be no restaurant car on this train. I repeat, there will be no restaurant car on the 11:32 to Tianjin now standing at Platform 13.

Questions 14 to 16 are based on the following passage. At the end of the passage, you will be given 15 seconds to answer the questions.

Now listen to the passage.

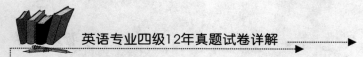

The International Red Cross and Red Crescent Museum was opened in Geneva in 1988. It tells the story of men and women who, in the course of the major events of the last 150 years, have given assistance to victims of war and natural disasters. The organization was established in 1863, and was based on an idea by a Swiss businessman called Henry Durant. He had witnessed the heavy casualties at the Battle of Solferino in Italy four years earlier, in which 40,000 people were killed, wounded, or missing. He had seen the lack of medical services and the great suffering of many of the wounded who simply died from lack of care. The International Red Cross or Red Crescent exists to help the victims of conflicts and disasters regardless of their nationalities. The symbol of the organization was originally just the Red Cross. It has no religious significance. The founders of the movement adopted it as a tribute to Switzerland. However, during the Russo-Turkish War, the Turks felt that the cross could be seen as offensive to Muslim soldiers and a second symbol, the Red Crescent, was adopted for use by national organizations in the Islamic world. Both are now official symbols.

Questions 17 to 20 are based on the following passage. At the end of the passage, you will be given 20 seconds to answer the questions.

Now listen to the passage.

At major college or high school sports events, cheerleaders, both male and female, jump and dance in front of the crowd and shout the name of their team, running around yelling, "Go, team, go." The first cheerleader ever was a man. In 1898, Johnny Campbell jumped in front of the crowd at the University of Minnesota and shouted for his team. He shouted, "Hurrah, Min-ne-so-ta!" This was the first organized shout or yell. For the next 32 years, cheerleaders were men only. Cheerleading is not just about cheering. They practice special shouts, dances, and athletic shows. The men throw the women high in the air and catch them. The team members climb on each other's shoulders to make a human pyramid. They yell and dance, too. It is like human fireworks. Of course, they may often suffer serious knee and wrist injuries and bloody noses. Cheerleaders have their own contests every year at local, state, and national levels. And the crowd shouts for them. It is not fair to think cheerleading is just being cheerful and lively and having a loud voice. Cheerleading is a sport in itself.

Section C   News Broadcast

In this section you will hear several news items. Listen to them carefully and then answer the questions that follow.

Questions 21 to 22 are based on the following news. At the end of the news item, you will be given 10 seconds to answer the questions.

Now listen to the news.

The bodies of dozens of African immigrants discovered off the Italian coast last week might have been thrown overboard, Italian officials said on Monday. A Coast Guard spokesman said 15 illegal immigrants, all believed to come from Somalia, survived being thrown into the Mediterranean Sea, but one of the survivors, a woman, was in a serious condition. They told the Coast Guard that their boat had left Libya 20 days before with around 100 immigrants aboard.

They said most had died during the trip. Last Friday, seven Africans, including three children, died before their boat could reach the island. A further 25 people survived.

Question 23 is based on the following news. At the end of the news item, you will be given 5 seconds to answer the question.

Now listen to the news.

China has set its sight on putting three people into space for a week, the China News Service said on Tuesday. The news agency reported an official as saying that preparations were underway for the next Shenzhou launch. The Shenzhou VI is expected to blast off within the next two years. Shenzhou V carried a Chinese astronaut aloft. He circled the earth 14 times during his 21-hour trip October 15 to 16, 2003, making China the third country to put a man into space.

Questions 24 and 25 are based on the following news. At the end of the news item, you will be given 10 seconds to answer the questions.

Now listen to the news.

Gigantic waves of flame that covered entire neighborhoods and filled the skies over Southern California with ash have killed at least 13 people. At least six separate wildfires were still burning on Monday morning all the way from the Mexican border to the suburbs of Los Angeles. They were reported to have destroyed 800 homes and consumed about 120,000 hectares of land. Authorities said they were seeking two men in connection with the fires, which they believe were started deliberately.

Questions 26 to 28 are based on the following news. At the end of the news item, you will be given 15 seconds to answer the question.

Now listen to the news.

There has been modest growth in tourism worldwide despite two years of terrorism, war, and disease, and China is the engine driving it, according to the World Tourism Organization. International tourist numbers hit a record 702 million last year, a rise of 2.7 percent over 2001, the year of the September 11 attacks. France remains the most popular destination, receiving more than 77 million visitors, followed by Spain, the United States, and Italy. China, however, marked 11 percent growth over that period, attracting 36.8 million international visitors. It ranked fifth among leading tourism nations. By 2020, it will be top, with predictions of 130 million visitors per year. Chinese themselves are also becoming a major force as travelers. According to a Xinhua report, over 16.6 million Chinese traveled abroad last year, up 37 percent from the previous year. Their numbers are expected to grow to 30 million by the end of the decade and a hundred million in 2020.

Questions 29 and 30 are based on the following news. At the end of the news item, you will be given 10 seconds to answer the questions.

Now listen to the news.

Around 40 former military officers in Argentina have been arrested for possible extradition to Spain on human rights charges. The arrests came as the Argentine government struck down

the decree prohibiting such extraditions, saying all Argentines should be equal before the law. Those detained include a former Navy captain and several other ex-officers suspected of torture or murder during the last period of military rule in Argentina, which ended in 1983.

2006 年英语专业四级考试听力理解

Part Ⅰ Dictation

Listen to the following passage. Altogether the passage will be read to you four times. During the first reading, which will be read at normal speed, listen and try to understand the meaning. For the second and third readings, the passage will be read sentence by sentence, or phrase by phrase, with intervals of 15 seconds. The last reading will be read at normal speed again and during this time you should check your work. You will then be given 2 minutes to check through your work once more.

Please write the whole passage on ANSWER SHEET ONE.

Now listen to the passage.

The Internet

The internet is the most significant progress in the field of communications. /Imagine a book that never ends, a library with a million floors. / Or imagine a research project with thousands of scientists/ working around the clock forever. / This is the magic of internet. / Yet the internet has the potential for good and bad. / One can find well-organized information-rich websites. / At the same time, one can also find wasteful websites. / Most websites are known as different internet applications. / These include online games chatrooms, and so on. / Sometimes the power can be so great/ that young people may easily become victims to their attraction. / So we need to recognize the seriousness of the problem. / We must work together to use its power for better ends. /

The second and third readings. You should begin writing now.

The last reading. Now, you have two minutes to check through your work.

(a 2-minute interval)

This is the end of the Dictation.

Part Ⅱ Listening Comprehension

In Sections A, B and C you will hear everything ONCE ONLY. Listen carefully and then answer the questions that follow. Mark the correct answer to each question on your answer sheet.

Section A Conversation

In this section you will hear several conversations. Listen to the conversations carefully and then answer the questions that follow.

Questions 1 to 3 are based on the following conversation. At the end of the conversation, you will be given 15 seconds to answer the questions.

Now listen to the conversation.

WOMAN: Oh, hello, you must be a new student. Did you find us OK?

MAN: Well... I got a bit lost and I had to ask a stranger, but I got here eventually.

WOMAN: Oh, dear! Have you come far today?

MAN: Only from Brighten—I was staying with my brother.

WOMAN: Oh, good! How did you get here?

MAN: My brother took me to the railway station, and I got a bus at this end.

WOMAN: Uh-huh. Well, you'd better tell me your name so I can find your form.

MAN: It's Mark Burn.

WOMAN: Burn... Burn... Ah, yes. Oh, you've changed since this photo! What happened to your beard and moustache? And you're not wearing glasses, either.

MAN: No, I thought I'd better look smarter!

WOMAN: Here's the key to your room. It's 501.

MAN: Thanks. How do I get there?

WOMAN: Go to the end of this corridor, turn left, and it's the third door on the right.

MAN: Thank you. Oh, there's a meeting for new students. What time is that?

WOMAN: Half past five in the Common Room on the ground floor at the other end of the corridor.

MAN: Thanks a lot. Bye!

Questions 4 to 6 are based on the following conversation. At the end of the conversation, you will be given 15 seconds to answer the questions.

Now listen to the conversation.

WOMAN: Hi, Steve. How are things?

MAN: Hi, Maggie. Good. Thanks. What's new with you?

WOMAN: Oh, I was just wondering if you want to go out tonight.

MAN: Well, I was thinking of going to the university library to do a bit of study. What've you got in mind?

WOMAN: I thought we could just go for walk, maybe down to the park near the beach.

MAN: Tonight, you must be joking! it's too cold.

WOMAN: Oh, yes. It's too cold. But I still want to go out somewhere. That new Tom Cruz's film is on in town. How about that?

MAN: Ok, What time does it start?

WOMAN: Oh, I think it's half past eight or something. I'll just get the paper and have a look. Just hang on for a minute. Look, the film got a fantastic review in the paper last week.

MAN: Ok, Ok. Where are we going to meet?

WOMAN: It'll be easier if we meet at the cinema.

MAN: Where is it?

WOMAN: Oh, you know. The Youyang.

MAN: Where is that?

English

WOMAN: Near the Town Hall. And opposite the bank.

MAN: Oh yea, I know where it is. Ok, look. I'll meet you there at fifteen past eight.

Questions 7 to 10 are based on the following conversation. At the end of the conversation, you will be given 20 seconds to answer the questions.

Now listen to the conversation.

WOMAN: What are you reading, Bill?

MAN: It's this week's *New Scientist*. Why?

WOMAN: I was just wondering—it looks interesting, but I've never actually read it myself. It's for real scientists. Erh... Can ordinary people like me understand it?

MAN: Oh, it's for anyone, really. It usually has articles and stories about current affairs about science as well as papers about new developments in research. I'm reading about a new telephone that allows you to see the person you're speaking to as well as hear him.

WOMAN: Oh, I've heard about it. Is it on the market yet? Can I buy one?

MAN: No, Not this one. But the company has made other models to try out on business. This one is special because its color and image is moving.

WOMAN: Oh, that's interesting.

MAN: You see the first video-phones, that's what they're called, were made in Japan. But they can only show a still black-and-white image. So, this video-phone is much better than that. Mind you, I'm not sure I want one. Would you?

WOMAN: Well, no, I don't think I would. I bet it costs a lot of money. Does it say how much it costs?

MAN: Yes. The early black-and-white ones cost several hundred pounds, but the one the story is about costs several thousand pounds.

WOMAN: Hmm, why does anybody want one, do you think?

MAN: Business organizations that need to frequently contact overseas organizations would want it. It's like a face-to-face conversation. So maybe a lot of overseas travels can be avoided.

WOMAN: Yes. I suppose so.

Section B Passages

In this section, you will hear several passages. Listen to the passages carefully and then answer the questions that follow.

Questions 11 to 13 are based on the following announcement. At the end of the announcement, you will be given 15 seconds to answer the questions.

Now listen to the announcement.

If you are in a Western country, you'll often see people walking their dogs. It is still true that a dog is the most useful animal in the world. However, the reason why people keep a dog has changed. Once upon a time, a man met a dog and wanted it to help him in the fight against other animals, and the dog listened to him and did what he told him to do. Later people used dogs for hunting other animals, and dogs did not eat what they got until their masters agreed. Dogs were also used for driving sheep and guarding chickens.

But now people in the towns and cities do not need dogs to fight other animals any more. Of course, they keep them to frighten thieves, but the most important reason for keeping dogs is that they feel lonely in the city. For a child, a dog is his best friend when he has no friends to play with. For a young wife, a dog is her child when she does not have her own. For old people, a dog is also a child when their real children have grown up and left. Now people do not have to use a dog, but they keep it as a friend, just like a member of the family.

Questions 14 to 17 are based on the following passage. At the end of the passage, you will be given 20 seconds to answer the questions.

Now listen to the passage.

I'm going to work in a totally new environment. How to get used to different working conditions. I am used to working in quite high-tech sort of industry that's got lots of machinery and everything. But now I'm going to a place that has no machinery as such, apart from a typewriter. The place has no electricity at all, no photocopiers, all the things that you just take for granted here. They just won't be there any more. I'll be staying near the school in quite small a village. And I'll be staying in a teacher's house living two or three other volunteer teachers. I'll have to get used to not having the variety of different foods that you have here, like twenty different varieties of breakfast cereal and the range of food is much smaller, not many choices. I'll also have to get used to getting water from a well, not having electricity, which means gas lamps in the evening, which means the difficulty of preparing for the next day's lessons in poor light, which means different ways of getting your clothes washed. There'll be all sorts of big differences like that that I'll have to get used to when I arrive there.

Questions 18 to 20 are based on the following passage. At the end of the passage, you will be given 20 seconds to answer the questions.

Now listen to the passage.

The most common type of child abuse, you know, is beating with their hands with the instrument, usually a cane in some places. Nearly a third of the abused children, we see, are in the age group between six and ten, and about 65 percent of them are boys. This is the age group when children are first expected to study hard and parents have great expectations of their progress in school. Boys, of course, attract more abuse such as beating because once again parental expectations are high, and boys tend to be more energetic and difficult to control than girls. Most experts seem to agree that child abuse is caused by a combination of social and psychological factors. Families sued to beat their children are not particularly different from other people. The only difference that exists between them is they lack skills in establishing good relationships with their children. These families, too, generally speaking, have other problems, such as marriage problems or financial problems. Some parents are hurting their children because they strongly believe in the use of traditional disciplinary methods, but many of them have emotional problems. They're often the victims of violence themselves. Sometimes they e-

ven bear an unreasonable hatred for a child, because they believe that the child has brought the family bad luck.

Section C   News Broadcast

In this section you will hear several news items. Listen to them carefully and then answer the questions that follow.

Questions 21 to 22 are based on the following news. At the end of the news item, you will be given 10 seconds to answer the questions.

Now listen to the news.

An American coast guard official in Florida says they have returned to Cuba a group of would-be migrants who tried to make their way to the United States in an unusual vessel, a floating truck. They said one of their planes spotted the Cubans more than half way through their journey, and the coast guards could not believe their eyes when they saw the vessel. The Cubans had attached floats and propellers to a 1951 shabby truck.

Question 23 is based on the following news. At the end of the news item, you will be given 5 seconds to answer the question.

Now listen to the news.

All large and medium-sized Chinese cities will have greater air quality monitoring by 2010, says a government official. The government has spent 150 million yuan on air quality monitoring systems across China since 2000, when officials began paying greater attention to air quality monitoring. More than 220 cities now have air quality monitoring systems and 42 others will have systems in place by the end of this year.

Questions 24 and 25 are based on the following news. At the end of the news item, you will be given 10 seconds to answer the questions.

Now listen to the news.

Storms sank two river ferries in southern Bangladesh on Sunday and some 90 passengers were reported missing while at least another 68 died. One of the packed ferries, carrying a-round 150 people, capsized early on Sunday on the Meghna river and fifty were rescued. A second ferry sank on the same river just one kilometer away, leaving forty passengers missing after six were rescued.

Question 26 are based on the following news. At the end of the news item, you will be given 5 seconds to answer the question.

Now listen to the news.

Indonesian government has given an official approval for an Australian consulate in Dili. The first Australian consulate officials will travel to the East Timor capital next week, as well as serving the consular needs of Australians in the region. The consulate will facilitate Australia's support to the United Nations' assistance mission in East Timor. The announcement follows in principle the agreement received on the opening of the consulate between Australian Prime Minister and Indonesian President in Bali last month.

Questions 27 and 28 are based on the following news. At the end of the news item, you will

be given 10 seconds to answer the questions.

Now listen to the news.

PepsiCo of the US and Unilever of the UK have become the latest foreign entrances in China's competitive bottle tea market. The two companies launched Lipton's iced tea in Guangzhou last week in a 50 − 50 venture. PepsiCo is contributing its bottling facilities and distribution networks to the allies while Unilever provides the famous tea brand and recipe, company executive said. China has a growing bottle tea market, estimated to be worth 10 billion yuan. It has been dominated in recent years by two Taiwanese brands: Master Kang and Uni-President. Three other big brands, Nestlé, Guangdong-based Jianlibao, and Lipton have just entered the market this year. Swiss company, Nestlé, is working in conjunction with Coca Cola.

Questions 29 and 30 are based on the following news. At the end of the news item, you will be given 10 seconds to answer the questions.

Now listen to the news.

The Israeli peace camp has launched the biggest protest in years with more than one hundred thousand people protesting on Saturday and demanding the country leave Gaza after Palestinian militants dealt Israel's army its deadliest blow since 2002. Crowds at Tel Aviv's main square added to the growing call for withdrawal from the war-torne territory. The killing of 13 soldiers by militants in the Gaza strip last week has deepened the already strong support in Israel for Prime Minister Sharon's Gaza pullout plan, which has been delayed by hardliners in his right-wing Likud Party.

2007 年英语专业四级考试听力理解

Part Ⅰ Dictation

Listen to the following passage. Altogether the passage will be read to you four times. During the first reading, which will be done at normal speed, listen and try to understand the meaning. For the second and third readings, the passage will be read sentence by sentence, or phrase by phrase, with intervals of 15 seconds. The last reading will be done at normal speed again and during this time you should check your work. You will then be given 2 minutes to check through your work once more.

Please write the whole passage on ANSWER SHEET ONE.

ADVERTISING

Advertising has already become a very specialized activity in modern times. / In today's business world supply is usually greater than demand. / There is a great competition between manufacturers of the same kind of product / because they want to persuade customers to buy their particular brand. / They always have to remind their customers/ of the name and qualities of their products by advertising. / The manufacturer advertises in newspapers and on the radio. / He sometimes employs sales girls to distribute samples of his products. / He sometimes advertises on the Internet as well. / In addition, he always has advertisements put into televi-

sion programs that will accept them. / Manufacturers often spend huge sums of money on advertisements. / We buy a particular product because we think that is the best. / We usually think so because the advertisements say so. / People often don't ask themselves if the advertisements are telling the truth/ when they buy advertised products from shops.

The second and third readings. You should begin writing now.

The last reading. Now, you have two minutes to check through your work.

(*a 2-minute interval*)

This is the end of the Dictation.

Part Ⅱ   Listening Comprehension

In Sections A, B and C you will hear everything once only. Listen carefully and then answer the questions that follow. Mark the correct answer to each question on your answer sheet.

Section A   Conversation

In this section you will hear several conversations. Listen to the conversations carefully and then answer the questions that follow.

Questions 1 to 3 are based on the following conversation. At the end of the conversation, you will be given 15 seconds to answer the questions.

Now listen to the conversation.

MAN A: Good evening, sir, can I help you?

MAN B: Yes, I think I left my digital camera on the train from London early today.

MAN A: Did you, sir! Oh, well, in that case, we'd better fill in a LOST PROPERTY FORM. Can you tell me your name?

MAN B: Yes, it's Mark Adams.

MAN A: Ok, your address...

MAN B: You mean in the UK or in the States?

MAN A: How long are you staying?

MAN B: Ah, I've still got a few months in Britain.

MAN A: Ok, then, can you give me your address here?

MAN B: Right. It's 18 Lyndon Drive, Layton, Essex. Do you want the phone number?

MAN A: Yes, I'd better have that, too.

MAN B: Ok, 080945233.

MAN A: Thanks. And you say it was a digital camera. What make and model?

MAN B: It's a Samsum J302.

MAN A: Ok, got that, you say it was a London train, what time did it arrive in Edinburgh?

MAN B: At 4:45 this afternoon.

MAN A: Well then. If we find it sir, shall we phone you or write to you?

MAN B: No, I think I will drop in the day after tomorrow to check up.

MAN A: Right you are, sir. We'll do our best.

Questions 4 to 7 are based on the following conversation. At the end of the conversation, you will be given 20 *seconds to answer the questions.*

    Now listen to the conversation.

MAN: Right, this is the tennis club reception area. As a member, you don't have to register when you arrive. But you must remember to register your guests, and you must be able to produce your membership card if a club official asks to see it.

WOMAN: How many guests can I bring with me?

MAN: You can bring up to three at any one time.

WOMAN: Hmm. that's good.

MAN: Yes, well, we want to attract people to our club. Now, here are changing rooms with showers and lockers for your clothes and things. Obviously, you don't have to leave your clothes in the lockers, but we strongly advise you to. It is much safer.

WOMAN: How much do the lockers cost?

MAN: Twenty cents. But you get the coin back when you take your things out. Right, and tennis courts are round here to the left.

WOMAN: Hmm, and we can play for an hour at a time?

MAN: You can book the courts for 30 minutes or an hour. But you can carry on playing until the next players arrive.

WOMAN: Of course. What about cafe or bar?

MAN: Yes, we have a club room which serves food and drink behind the reception. The club room is open until 11 o'clock, but all players must leave the courts by 10 o'clock.

WOMAN: Hmm, that seems very good. Thank you very much for showing us around.

MAN: Pleasure.

    Questions 8 to 10 are based on the following conversation. At the end of the conversation, you will be given 15 seconds to answer the questions.

    Now listen to the conversation.

WOMAN: Ah, good morning, it's Mr. Robinson, isn't it?

MAN: Yes.

WOMAN: Have a seat.

MAN: Thank you.

WOMAN: Ok, I've got your letter of application. Now, as you know, when you apply for a post with our company, we need to find out a few things about both your academic background and recent work experience.

MAN: Sure.

WOMAN: First of all, A-levels?

MAN: Yes, I've got three: geography, maths and physics.

WOMAN: Geography, maths and physics. Ok. And what about your degree?

MAN: I went to Manchester University and got an engineering degree with water man-

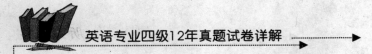

agement as my specialization.

WOMAN: En-ha-a, I see.

MAN: And as for work experience, I started out after graduating in 1996 in India, working for the Indian government.

WOMAN: Did you work as a volunteer?

MAN: No, it was a three-year water irrigation project.

WOMAN: That sounds fascinating. How did you organize that? You say it was a British company then.

MAN: No, no, my university had links with Indian Engineering University. So it was organized at that level.

WOMAN: And after that?

MAN: Then I came back, moved to Sheffield, and have been working with Lattema Engineering since then.

WOMAN: And what exactly are you doing for Lattema?

MAN: Ah, I'm working in water irrigation again. This time as the project research system.

WOMAN: Great, I've got your details. Now let's move on to more general discussion about what we are looking for here.

Section B   Passages

In this section, you will hear several passages. Listen to the passages carefully and then answer the questions that follow.

Questions 11 to 13 are based on the following talk. At the end of the talk, you will be given 15 seconds to answer the questions.

Now listen to the talk.

Hello, everybody, thank you very much for inviting me here. It's very pleasant to have a chance to talk to you about something that is obviously very much on everybody's mind. I want to talk about an area of security or safety: bicycles. I know a lot of you have bikes.

First, when you get your bike, whether it's new or second-hand, bring it as soon as possible to us. There we'll be able to stamp it with a serial number. We actually stamp it into the metal. We'll register the number, put it on our list. This can frighten criminals away if they realize there is a number stamped on it.

Second, make sure you buy a good lock. It can be expensive but it's never a waste of money. If you have an expensive bike, it's worth buying two locks. Do spend money on a good lock because the cheaper ones can be very very easy to cut. Also, make sure you lock the bike to something permanent. Though, do be considerate to pedestrians.

And if the worst happens, you lose your bike, you should immediately report it to the police station quoting the serial number that should have been stamped.

Questions 14 to 17 are based on the following talk. At the end of the talk, you will be given 20 seconds to answer the questions.

Now listen to the talk.

Good morning, everyone, and welcome to the English for Academic Purposes Center. I'd like to begin by briefly introducing services we offer here at our center.

First of all, we have a wide range of language courses. In the first semester we run an eight-week conversation class for students of non-English speaking background, which is to improve their fluency, grammar and pronunciation in English. The course is held on Tuesdays between 12:30 and 1:30. So there is one hour once a week. Please enrol with the secretary before Friday this week.

For those of you who are interested in developing your writing skills, we have a six-week course which runs for two hours between 4:00 and 6:00 on Wednesday afternoons beginning in Week One. It concentrates on the writing skills needed for assignments in the departments of economics and social sciences. Students must be enrolled in either of these departments.

You are probably not thinking about taking examinations yet, but later on towards the end of the term, you might like to enrol in an Examination Skills class. The course runs for five weeks and two hours in a week. The course deals with the skills you need in both written tests and oral examinations. It is not necessary to enrol before the course starts. Just turn up for the first class.

Questions 18 to 20 are based on the following passage. At the end of the passage, you will be given 15 seconds to answer the questions.

Now listen to the passage.

Leonardo da Vinci was born in 1452 in Tuscany. As early as 1466, he was working in a work shop. Then in 1482, he moved to Milan. After the plague swept the city of Milan in 1484 and 1485, he turned his attention to town planning and made several designs for churches and other buildings. He moved to Florence, another city in Italy, in 1500, where he painted the famous Mona Lisa in 1503. Then he returned to Milan. Between 1510 and 1515 after he had been working as an architect and engineer to the French king Louis XII, he devoted himself to painting again and produced two great works: St. Anne Mary and Child and St. John the Baptist. In 1515, the king of France invited Leonardo to live in France. He moved to a castle there, where he spent his last years carrying out his own research. He died in 1519.

Section C   News Broadcast

In this section you will hear several news items. Listen to them carefully and then answer the questions that follow.

Questions 21 and 22 are based on the following news. At the end of the news item, you will be given 10 seconds to answer the questions.

Now listen to the news.

Israel's army entered the West Bank area on Tuesday to evacuate the last two Jewish settlements there. This ended Israel's decades long occupation in the Gaza Strip and the West Bank. Conflicts between Israelis and Palestinians have been called the major stumbling block to Middle East Peace. Israel formally began the polite operation last Monday. Israeli Prime

Minister put forward the Disengagement Plan in 2003. It asked Israel to move all 21 settlements in the Gaza Strip and 4 in the West Bank.

Questions 23 and 24 are based on the following news. At the end of the news item, you will be given 10 seconds to answer the questions.

Now listen to the news.

Romania and Bulgaria on Monday signed an agreement to join the European Union on Jan. 1st 2007. That will bring the number of EU states to 27. The agreement has to be approved by Romania and Bulgaria as well as parliaments of all 25 EU states. The two states will join the 25 nation bloc provided they carry out reforms: they need to fight corruption, strengthen border controls, and improve justice, administration and state industrial support rules. If they do not, their membership could be delayed until 2008.

Questions 25 and 26 are based on the following news. At the end of the news item, you will be given 10 seconds to answer the questions.

Now listen to the news.

An economic forum on opportunities in China is expected to bring scholars, business leaders and government officials to Beijing next week. More than 800 delegates are expected to attend three-day Fortune global forum which opens on Monday. More than 250 foreign companies—including 76 of the Global 500—will be represented. The Forum is held annually by the US Fortune magazine. This will be the Forum's 10th year and the third in China. Shanghai hosted it in 1999 and Hong Kong in 2001.

Questions 27 and 28 are based on the following news. At the end of the news item, you will be given 10 seconds to answer the questions.

Now listen to the news.

Hong Kong Disneyland opened on Monday with a total of 15,000 visitors. Visitors from the mainland accounted for one third of the total. Most were from Guangdong. According to a survey, more than 55% of Guangzhou residents showed interest in visiting the theme park. Some 22% percent of Shanghai residents and 20% of Beijingers also said they planned to visit it. Disneyland is expected to receive at least 1.5 million visitors between September and December.

Questions 29 and 30 are based on the following news. At the end of the news item, you will be given 10 seconds to answer the questions.

Now listen to the news.

An Indonesian ferry packed with hundreds of refugees fleeing violence in the ravaged Spice Islands sank yesterday and it was not clear whether anyone had survived, rescue officials said. The official said she had a capacity of 200 passengers but around 500 were believed to have been aboard after hundreds of refugees fought their way onto the ferry on the island of Halmahera, scene of bloody religious violence this month. There were about 198 passengers and crew on top of around 290 refugees, Solaeman, head of the search and rescue team in the north Sulawesi capital of Manado told reporters.

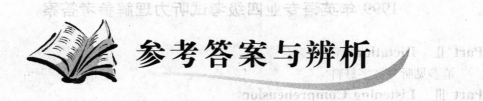

参考答案与辨析

1996 年英语专业四级考试听力理解参考答案

Part Ⅱ　Dictation
　　参见听力文字材料

Part Ⅲ　Listening Comprehension
　　1. A　2. D　3. B　4. C　5. D　6. B　7. C　8. A　9. D　10. D
　　11. A　12. C　13. C　14. A　15. B　16. D　17. B　18. D　19. A　20. C
　　21. A　22. D　23. A　24. C　25. B

1997 年英语专业四级考试听力理解参考答案

Part Ⅱ　Dictation
　　参见听力文字材料

Part Ⅲ　Listening Comprehension
　　1. D　2. C　3. A　4. A　5. B　6. D　7. D　8. C　9. B　10. C
　　11. C　12. B　13. D　14. D　15. C　16. A　17. B　18. B　19. C　20. B
　　21. C　22. D　23. D　24. C　25. B

1998 年英语专业四级考试听力理解参考答案

Part Ⅱ　Dictation
　　参见听力文字材料

Part Ⅲ　Listening Comprehension
　　1. B　2. B　3. D　4. C　5. B　6. A　7. A　8. B　9. C　10. D
　　11. B　12. D　13. C　14. B　15. B　16. A　17. A　18. C　19. A　20. C
　　21. B　22. D　23. C　24. A　25. D

1999 年英语专业四级考试听力理解参考答案

Part Ⅱ　Dictation
请参见听力文字材料

Part Ⅲ　Listening Comprehension
1. C　2. A　3. D　4. C　5. C　6. B　7. B　8. C　9. B　10. B
11. D　12. C　13. B　14. A　15. A　16. B　17. C　18. A　19. B　20. B
21. D　22. B　23. B　24. C　25. A

2000 年英语专业四级考试听力理解参考答案

Part Ⅱ　Dictation
参见听力文字材料

Part Ⅲ　Listening Comprehension
1. A　2. C　3. C　4. B　5. D　6. B　7. A　8. B　9. D　10. B
11. D　12. B　13. A　14. A　15. C　16. A　17. A　18. B　19. A　20. B
21. C　22. A　23. B　24. B　25. C

2001 年英语专业四级考试听力理解参考答案

Part Ⅱ　Dictation
参见听力文字材料

Part Ⅲ　Listening Comprehension
1. C　2. B　3. D　4. D　5. A　6. A　7. A　8. D　9. B　10. B
11. B　12. D　13. A　14. A　15. B　16. A　17. B　18. C　19. C　20. A
21. C　22. A　23. D　24. B　25. A

2002 年英语专业四级考试听力理解参考答案

Part Ⅱ　Dictation
参见听力文字材料

Part Ⅲ　Listening Comprehension
1. D　2. A　3. C　4. B　5. C　6. C　7. A　8. D　9. A　10. B
11. C　12. D　13. D　14. C　15. D　16. A　17. B　18. D　19. B　20. C
21. A　22. C　23. A　24. D　25. B

English

2003 年英语专业四级考试听力理解参考答案

Part Ⅱ   Dictation

参见听力文字材料

Part Ⅲ   Listening Comprehension

1. D   2. C   3. C   4. B   5. A   6. B   7. B   8. C   9. C   10. D

11. B   12. A   13. C   14. A   15. A   16. B   17. A   18. D   19. B   20. D

21. C   22. D   23. C   24. A   25. B

2004 年英语专业四级考试听力理解参考答案

Part Ⅱ   Dictation

请参见听力文字材料

Part Ⅲ   Listening Comprehension

1. D   2. B   3. C   4. B   5. B   6. C   7. A   8. D   9. A   10. B

11. B   12. C   13. D   14. D   15. C   16. D   17. D   18. B   19. C   20. C

21. A   22. D   23. D   24. B   25. C

2005 年英语专业四级考试听力理解参考答案

Part Ⅰ   Dictation

请参见听力文字材料

Part Ⅱ   Listening Comprehension

1. C   2. A   3. B   4. A   5. D   6. B   7. A   8. C   9. B   10. A

11. C   12. B   13. D   14. B   15. D   16. B   17. D   18. B   19. A   20. B

21. D   22. B   23. D   24. D   25. A   26. C   27. B   28. D   29. C   30. A

2006 年英语专业四级考试听力理解参考答案

Part Ⅰ   Dictation

请参见听力文字材料

Part Ⅱ   Listening Comprehension

1. C   2. A   3. B   4. D   5. B   6. D   7. C   8. C   9. C   10. A

11. D   12. A   13. D   14. B   15. B   16. A   17. C   18. B   19. A   20. B

21. D   22. B   23. D   24. B   25. D   26. C   27. A   28. C   29. B   30. D

2007 年英语专业四级考试听力理解参考答案

Part Ⅰ　Dictation

请参见听力文字材料

Part Ⅱ　Listening Comprehension

Section A　Conversation

1. B	2. D	3. A	4. C	5. A	6. D	7. B	8. C	9. A	10. C
11. A	12. A	13. B	14. A	15. C	16. B	17. C	18. B	19. D	20. A
21. B	22. D	23. C	24. A	25. C	26. A	27. B	28. A	29. C	30. B

1996 年英语专业四级考试语法与词汇参考答案与解析

41.　[C]　unless 意为"如果不,除非",例如:I will not go unless you compel me. 除非你强迫我,否则我不走。lest 作"以免"讲,例如:He went over the facts in his mind again and again lest the vital clues should elude him. 他反复思考那些事实,惟恐漏掉了关键性线索。in case 意为"以免",例如:Be strict with your children in case they feel superior to other children. 对你的孩子要严格,以免使他们觉得高别人一等。other than 作"除了"讲,例如:Other than mercury, all metals are solid. 除汞之外,所有的金属都是固体的。本题的句意为:"除非你作出某种担保,否则你不会得到贷款。"所以正确答案应是 C。

42.　[B]　请参见 1998 年第 51 题的解析。本题的句意为:"假以时日,他就会成为一名一流的网球手。"所以正确答案应是 B。

43.　[C]　虚拟语气用在条件句中表示对过去的假设,从句使用过去完成时,主句使用"would (should, could, might) + have done",例如:If I had been put in your position, I wouldn't have done that. 如果我处在你的位置,我是不会做那件事情的。/If you had come here yesterday, you would have met Professor Chomsky. 如果你昨天来这里的话,你就会见到乔姆斯基教授了。/If you had followed my advice, you would have passed the exam. 如果你听了我的劝告,你考试就会及格的。本题的句意为:"如果晚会上没有那么多人,我可能玩得更高兴。"所以正确答案应是 C。

44.　[B]　根据句子结构,从句"pay rises are related to performance at work"只可能是同位语从句或定语从句。如果是同位语从句,只有当先行词为 question, problem 时,才可用 which, where, whether 或 what。如果这个从句是定语从句,不可能使用 what, whether,因为这两个词不可引导定语从句。关系代词 which 也不可用在此处引导定语从句,因为该从句不缺乏名词性成分。那么只有关系副词 where 了,where 在引导定语从句时,在从句中作状语,相当于"介词 + which",例如:I will append a list of those institutions where (from which) you may get necessary information. 我附上一张你可以获得必要信息的机构的名单。但是在这里作者看不出 where 相当于哪个介词加 which。作者更倾向于认为[D]中的 what 是 that 的误拼。这样,根据句子结构,我们就不难看出 pay rises are related to performance at work 就是 policy 的同位语。本题的句意为:"这家公司已推出了一项新政策,加薪要与工作表现挂钩。"所以 B 为正确答案。

45. [D] 根据句子结构,我们可知这里不能使用谓语动词,由此可以排除[B]和[C]。由于 consider 和句子主语 He 是逻辑动宾关系,因此可以排除[A],而肯定[D]为正确选项。本句的意思是考虑到他在会员中不是很受欢迎,所以未请他出任主席一职。

46. [A] 并列介词短语"as well as"要连接平行结构,所以要选择 hunted,这样就成了 "the elephant from being wiped out as well as other animals (from being) hunted in Africa"。本题的意思为:"当初这也许能够使非洲大象以及其他动物免遭灭绝。"

47. [D] for lack of 意为"由于缺乏",例如:Pretty soon we were held up for lack of material. 不久,由于缺乏材料,我们进行不下去了。He dismissed the idea of travelling with her for lack of money. 因为缺钱他不再考虑和她旅游的事。He was compelled to suspend his experiment for lack of money. 因为缺钱,他不得不暂时中断实验。本题的句意为:"由于缺少资金,这个办事处不得不关闭了。"所以正确答案应是 D。

48. [B] avoid 后必须跟动名词作宾语,由于 beat 的逻辑宾语是 the only thing,因此这里只能选择[B],更多例句:He is wearing dark glasses to avoid being recognized. 他戴着墨镜以免被认出来。It was impossible to avoid being overtaken. 要避免被别人超过是不可能的。本句的意思是:在国际比赛中,保持名声是非常重要的,不被他人打败被认为是惟一重要的事情。

49. [A] need not have done sth. 意为"本来没有必要做某事",暗示已经做了,例如:I needn't have gone there yesterday. 昨天我本不必去那儿。must not do sth. 作"禁止做某事,不许做某事"讲,例如:Nations must not settle their differences by armed conflict. 国家之间不能以武装冲突来解决分歧。do not need to 意为"没有必要做某事",例如:You do not need to remind people of their mistakes all the time. 你不必老是提醒人们记住他们犯过的错误。英语中没有"must not have done sth."结构。本句的中文翻译为"那原本是一个小型家庭聚会,我们本不需要穿得这样正式。"所以正确答案应是 A。

50. [C] 在肯定句中,do 常用作助动词以避免重复前面已经用过的某个动词或动词短语,如:It's important to listen to people carefully, and I usually do. 仔细听取别人的意见是重要的,我通常也是这样做的。根据句子结构可以看出,该题中的 than 是从属连词,引导一个比较状语从句,than 前后是一个平列结构,因此在这里用 does 来代替前面使用过的动词短语 receives snow。本句的中文翻译为"内布拉斯加州西部的降雪量通常比东部少。"所以正确答案应是 C。

51. [D] 请参见 2000 年第 45 题精解。本句意思是"由于没有什么值得大惊小怪的,老人又回到卧室。"所以正确答案为 D。

52. [B] 请参见 1998 年第 50 题精解。本句意思是"他的讽刺文章充满睿智,连被讽刺对象也会大笑不止。"所以正确答案应是 B。

53. [A] carry on 意为"继续",例如:They carried on in spite of the extremely difficult conditions. 尽管条件极其困难,他们仍然继续坚持下去。carry off 意为"(轻而易举地或成功地)完成",如:It was really an embarrassing situation, but he carried it off well. 那场面确实很令人尴尬,但是他很轻松地应付过去了。carry away 作"冲昏某人的头脑"讲,例如:Don't be carried away by mere sentiment in this matter. 在这件事上不要感情用事。本句的翻译为"如果他再那样一意孤行,他就会被送上破产法庭。"所以正确答案应是 A。

54. [D] stand up to 意为"经得起",例如:My wife's health will not stand up to the cold damp weather. 我妻子的身体受不住寒冷潮湿的天气。look up to 作"尊敬,敬仰"讲,例如:Don't look up to him. He has gained every title by trick. 别把他当回事,他的所有头衔都是耍手腕搞到的。英语中没有短语动词 pay up to 和 keep up to。本句翻译为"尽管这些假币骗过了很多人,但是还是经不起细心的检测。"所以正确答案应是 D。

55. [B] otherwise 意为"要不然,否则",例如:Go and put on more clothes, otherwise you'll catch a cold. 快去加点衣服,不然你要着凉了。consequently 作"因而,所以"意思讲,例如:They ignored our warning; consequently, an accident happened. 他们对我们的警告置若罔闻,结果出事了。therefore 意为"因此,所以",例如:He has taken part in the movement; therefore, I presume this must be an eyewitness account. 他参加了这次运动,因此据我推测这一叙述一定是他亲眼目睹的事。英语中没有 doubtlessly,要表示"无疑地,毫无疑问地",使用 doubtless 就可以了。本句的意思是"他必须给我们更多的时间,否则我们就不能将这件事情做好。"所以正确答案应是 B。

56. [C] pause 意为"中止,暂停,停顿",例如:The teacher came to a pause and then went on lecturing. 老师顿了一下后,又继续讲下去。blank 作"空白"讲,例如:You are required to fill in the blanks with proper words. 要求你用适当的词填空。space 意为"场地,空地,余地,篇幅",例如:Between the two trees is space of ten feet. 两棵树之间有 10 英尺的空地。wait 作"等候"讲,例如:After a wait of perhaps three-quarters of an hour, she was called. 在等了大约 45 分钟后,她被叫了进去。本句翻译为"在谈话的间隙,我问谁想喝一杯。"所以正确答案应是 C。

57. [A] effort 意为"努力",例如:After many years' efforts, they have transferred wasteland into fertile fields. 经过多年的努力,他们已把荒地变成良田。strength 作"力;力量,力气;实力"讲,例如:The team is conserving its strength for the last match. 这个队正在为最后一场比赛保存实力。attempt 意为"尝试,企图",例如:My early attempts at learning to drive were unsuccessful. 我以前想学开车的企图都落空了。force 作"力;力量,力气"讲,例如:Some machines are used to gain force, speed and direction. 有些机器是用来获得力、速度和方向的。根据句意

“你们想做就做,不过我认为这件事太麻烦了,不值得做。”A 为正确答案。

58. ［A］ involve 意为“使……卷入,使……陷入”,例如:His remark involved him in the argument. 他的话使他卷入了争吵。include 作“包括,包含”讲,例如: Electricity and gas bills are not included in the rent. 电费和煤气费不包括在租金内。combine 意为“使……结合,使……联合”,例如:The two countries combined together against their enemy. 两个国家联合起来反对共同的敌人。contain 作“包含,容纳”讲,例如:There is nothing in the world that does not contain contradictions. 世上万物皆含矛盾。根据句意:“今天这条通过利脱伯里的大路被关闭了三个小时,原因是有两辆卡车出了车祸。”A 为正确答案。

59. ［D］ come up with 意为“想出”,例如:He claimed to have been the first to come up with that idea. 他声称他是第一个想出那个主意的人。come to 作“苏醒,复苏”讲,例如:The girl fainted and didn't come to until midnight. 那位女孩昏了过去,直到午夜才苏醒过来。come round 意为“顺便来访”,如:I hope to come round next time I'm in town. 希望下次进城时能去看看你们。come on 作“快点”讲,例如:Come on, it's your turn. 快点,轮到你了。本句意思为“很少有科学家能想出一些全新的答案,来解决一些世界性问题。”所以正确答案应是 D。

60. ［C］ vacate 意为“腾出,搬出;让出,空出”,例如:The landlady forced the poor tenant to vacate the room. 女房东强迫那个贫穷的房客搬出。depart 作“(人)离开,起程”讲,例如:The guests having departed, the old house again became quiet. 客人们都离去了,那座古老的住宅又安静了下来。abandon 意为“抛弃,放弃”,例如:Systems that have outlived their usefulness should be abandoned. 过时无用的体制应予以摒弃。displace 作“代替,取代”讲,例如:I don't want to be displaced in your heart by that young fool. 我不希望我在你心中的地位被那位年轻的傻小子而取代。根据本句翻译“宾馆的房间中午前必须腾空,行李可以存放在行李搬运工那儿。”所以正确答案应是 C。

61. ［B］ 短语动词“get away with”作“成功地行骗,侥幸地获取”,例如:Those who lie and cheat will never get away with it. 那些撒谎和欺骗别人的人决不会逃脱惩罚。根据句意“她给出的理由有一半是假的,但她却总是能不被人发觉。”所以正确答案应是 B。

62. ［A］ respectable 作“可敬的,值得尊敬的”讲,有被动意义,例如:The teacher is respectable for his love of teaching. 这位教师热爱教学,值得尊敬。respectful 意为“恭敬的,尊敬人的,尊重人的”,有主动含义,例如:The children are respectful to their grandparents. 孩子们对祖父母都很尊敬。respective 意为“各自的,各个的”,例如:The party ended and we came back to our respective rooms. 晚会结束了,我们都各自回到自己的房间。respecting 作“关于”讲,相当于一个介词,例如:The legislation respecting property is still being discussed. 关于财产的立法,仍在讨论之中。本句意思是“那位可敬的物理学家受到了来自本专业人士的挑战。”所以正确答案应是 A。

63. ［B］ productive 意为“丰饶的,多产的”,例如:He was worn-out from years of toiling on

a rocky unproductive farm. 由于多年在一个遍地砂石、产量不高的农场上劳作，他的身体非常虚弱。profound 作"很深的；深远的，深厚的"讲，例如：Einstein's theory of relativity is too profound for me to understand. 爱因斯坦的相对论对我来说太深奥了，理解不了。prosperous 意为"繁荣的，昌盛的"，例如：His business is becoming more prosperous than before. 他的生意比以前更加兴隆。plentiful 作"富裕的，丰富的，多的"讲，例如：The guests were treated to plentiful food and drink. 有丰富的食品和饮料招待来宾。本句翻译为"身后留了数百幅作品，毕加索被认为是一位非常多产的艺术家。"所以正确答案应是 B。

64. [C] considerable 意为"相当大（或多）的"，例如：He is a considerable man in local affairs. 他在地方事务中是个相当重要的人物。considered 意为"经过深思熟虑的"，例如：It's my considered opinion that you should resign. 经过再三考虑，我认为你应该辞职。considerate 用来形容人，意为"考虑周到的，体贴人的，体谅的"，例如：It's considerate of you not to play the guitar while she is having a nap. 她午睡时你不弹吉他，真是会体贴人。considering 的作用有时相当于介词或连词，表示"考虑到，鉴于"之意，例如：Considering the signs she showed of her hearty friendship, I accepted her invitation. 考虑到她所表现出的真诚的友谊，我接受了她的邀请。本句意思是"由于地震，这座城市损失惨重。"所以正确答案应是 C。

65. [A] have access to 意为"有机会或权利（接近某人或使用某物）"，例如：Only high officials have access to the president. 只有高级官员才可以接近总统。entrance 作"入口，进口"讲，例如：The entrance examination to high school will begin next Monday. 中学入学考试将在下周一开始。way 意为"道路，途径"，例如：We made our way with difficulty through dense forest. 我们艰难地穿过了茂密的森林。path 作"小径，小路"讲，例如：She peered through the mist, trying to find the right path home. 她透过薄雾，想找到回家的那条路。根据本句意思为"本科生没有资格借阅图书馆中的珍藏图书。"所以正确答案应是 A。

1997 年英语专业四级考试语法与词汇参考答案与解析

41. [C] "are... interrupting"动词用在进行时中可以表示重复不断的动作，传达说话人的情绪，如厌烦、不满、愉悦等，例如：The wife is being friendly to her husband today. 今天妻子对丈夫特别好。（暗示平时不是这样）本句意思是"你总是这样不停地问我一些愚蠢问题，我又怎么能集中注意力呢？"所以正确答案应是 C。

42. [B] 祈使句的附加疑问句的谓语通常使用 will you，而且通常用肯定形式，例如：Have a little more coffee, will you? 再喝点咖啡，怎么样？Let us know what has become of you, will you? 请你告诉我们你出什么事了，好吗？本句意思是"看完那盘录像带后，别忘了放到我的抽屉里，好吗？"所以正确答案应是 B。

43. [A] 在与 motion, order, plan, recommendation, proposal, idea, request, suggestion

等名词相关的名词性从句中,谓语要使用动词原形或"should + 动词原形",例如:The order soon came that all civilians evacuate the village. 不久命令下来了,所有居民都必须撤出村子。An order has come from Berlin that no language but German be taught in schools of Alsace and Lorraine. 柏林已下令,阿尔萨斯和洛林地区的学校里只许教德语。本句意思是"他命令在警方到来之前什么都不要动。"所以正确答案应是 A。

44. [D] 在这里,现在进行时表示在目前短时间内正在进行的动作,例如:Half the houses in the street are being pulled down to make room for the new post office. 为建新邮局,街上一半的房子正在拆除。本句意思是"怀特先生在一家化工产品进出口公司工作,但他目前在休假,正在为此次工业展览会工作。"所以正确答案应是 D。

45. [C] 我们可以将 I think 看作插入语,将其去掉也不会影响句子的完整,例如:Do what you believe is right. 你认为什么对就做什么。本句意思是"那位物理学家有个发现,我认为这项发现对科学和技术的进步都非常重要。"所以正确答案应是 C。

46. [B] for (all) 意为"尽管",后跟名词,相当于 in spite of,例如:For all his efforts, he didn't succeed. 虽然他尽了力,但还是没有成功。For all his knowledge and academic background, he is basically stupid. 尽管他知识丰富而且理论非常好,但是总的来说他很愚蠢。本句意思是"尽管他贡献非常突出,但是他还是愿意接受来自各个方面的建议。"所以正确答案应是 B。

47. [D] whatever 是关系代词,可以引导名词性从句,同时又可在从句中作主语、宾语等成分。whatever 在这里的从句中作 needs 的主语,再例如:Sin is whatever obscures the soul. 罪恶都是昧着良心干的。Whatever is worth doing at all is worth doing well. 无论什么事情,既值得做,就值得做好。To do whatever needs to be done to preserve this last and greatest bastion of freedom. 为了保住这最后的、最伟大的自由堡垒,我们必须尽我们所能。有些人误选了[C],他们认为可以让 whatever 在从句中作动名词 handling 的宾语,但是他们或许忘记了 need 和 want 等动词后的动名词有被动含义,其逻辑宾语应该是句子的主语,例如:The building needs restoring. 这座大楼需要维修。本句意思是"这个团队能够处理一切需要处理的事情。"所以正确答案应是 D。

48. [C] convenient 意为"便利的,方便的,合适的",该词的主语一般意为时机、位置等,通常不能用人作主语,例如:When would it be convenient for you to go? 你什么时候去方便?I'd like to see you whenever (it is) convenient. 什么时候方便,我想去看一看你。另外,由于这里用的是状语从句,因此从句谓语不能使用将来时。本句意思是"你什么时候方便,就什么时候来看我。"所以正确答案应是 C。

49. [A] as such 意为"像这样的人或物;作为这样的人或物;以……资格或身份",例如:He considered this matter as unimportant and treated it as such. 他认为这件事无关紧要,因此把它当成无关紧要的事来对待。She is a teacher, and should

be respected as such. 她是教师,该受到教师般的尊重。本句意思是"他是作为一名医生出现在人们面前的,并且是一位颇受欢迎的医生。"所以正确答案应是 A。

50. [B] 请参见 1999 年第 47 题详解。本句意思是"我从来未去过伦敦,但那却是我最想参观的城市。"所以正确答案应是 A。

51. [C] 根据句意,我们可以看出这里表示的是对一般过去的虚拟,例如:The instructions would have been clear enough if she had spoken in a more distinct voice. 如果当时她用清晰的声音说出来,训令就不至于含糊不清。本句意思是"若不是被人叫走,我本来是要发言的。"所以正确答案应是 C。

52. [B] enough 用来修饰形容词或副词时,一般要后置,例如:It is man's duty to be courageous enough to seek for truth. 勇于追求真理是人的天职。Advertising may be described as the science of arresting human intelligence long enough to get money from it. 广告可被视作一种长久蒙蔽人类智慧以期从中赚钱的技巧。本句意思是"我觉得自己身体还不够好,不能出国旅游。"所以正确答案应是 B。

53. [C] verify 意为"核实,查证",例如:The prediction of a severe storm was verified in every detail. 强暴风雨的预报被一一证实了。而 ensure 意为"担保,保证(获得),使……必然发生",例如:They spared no effort to ensure our comfort and safety. 他们不遗余力地确保我们的舒适和安全。testify 意为"作证,证实;表明,证明",例如:Her tears testified her grief. 她的眼泪证实了她的悲伤。本句意思为"这架飞机发现了那个点,就尽可能地接近它,在其上空盘旋,终于查明那是一辆汽车。"所以正确答案应是 C。

54. [B] vast 意为"巨大的,庞大的",例如:They comprise the vast majority of the white people. 他们构成了白人中的绝大多数。numerous 作"许多的,大量存在的"讲,例如:When the tide was out, numerous pretty pebbles were left on the beach. 海潮退去了,很多美丽的鹅卵石便留在了海滩上。most 意为"很多的",例如:Calm has returned to most areas following the recent disturbances. 最近的骚乱过后,大部分地区恢复了平静。massive 作"大而沉重的,笨重的"讲,例如:The strain on these massive cables supporting the bridge is enormous. 这些拉起大桥的巨型缆索所承受的拉力是非常大的。根据本句意思是"令人鼓舞的是,绝大多数人都认为变革的想法是可以接受的。"所以正确答案应是 B。

55. [D] pose 意为"提出,造成,形成",例如:The delegate posed a question for discussion at the meeting. 这位代表提出了一个问题供大会讨论。force 作"强迫,迫使,逼"讲,例如:The aggressors will be forced to leave their occupied areas in the end. 侵略者将最终被迫离开被他们占领的地区。press 意为"压,扳;强迫",例如:The police pressed the students back behind the barriers. 警察迫使学生退到栅栏后面。provide 作"提供"讲,例如:We also provided relief for victims of famine. 我们还救济了饥民。本句意思是"学生数量的增加会给大学带来很多问题。"所以正确答案应是 D。

56. [A] refrain 是不及物动词,是正式用语,意为"克制,抑制,避免",经常与介词 from

搭配,例如:He could not refrain from tears at the sight of the old photos. 看到这些老照片时,他不禁泪流满面。restrain 是及物动词,意为"阻止,管制,约束",其惯用搭配是 restrain sb. (sth.) from sth. (doing sth.),例如:Who can restrain them from going their own way? 谁能阻止他们自行其是? prevent 意为"阻止,阻挡,制止,妨碍",例如:I regret that a prior engagement prevents me from accepting your kind invitation. 我有约在先,故不能接受你好意的邀请,实在很遗憾。resist 作"抵抗,反抗,对抗"讲,例如:There is not a conductor but resists the flow of the electrical charges. 没有一种对电荷的流动没有阻力的导体。本句意思是"飞机升到空中前,请不要抽烟。"所以正确答案应是 A。

57. [B] 固定搭配"take offence at"作"对……生气,因……见怪"讲,例如:She takes offence at the slightest thing. 她动不动就生气。本句意思是"新闻记者和摄影记者对那名演员在采访中的粗鲁表现都感到很不满。"所以正确答案应是 B。

58. [D] relevant 意为"有关的,贴切的,恰当的",例如:His remarks are not relevant to our discussion. 他的话和我们的议题不相关。concerned 作"和……有关的,和……有牵连的"讲,例如:He declared he was not concerned with that matter. 他声称他与那事无关。dependent 意为"依靠的,依赖的;从属的,隶属的",例如:The widow with several dependent children lived a hard life. 这个寡妇带着几个要靠人照顾的孩子,生活的很艰苦。connect 作"连接,连结"讲,例如:This flight connects with a flight for Hong Kong at Shanghai. 这班飞机在上海可接上另一飞往香港的班机。本句意思为"作文题目应该符合学生的经历和兴趣。"所以正确答案应是 D。

59. [B] glimpse 意为"一瞥,一看",例如:I caught a glimpse of the falls as our train went by. 我们所乘的火车经过时,我瞥见了瀑布。glance 作"看一下,一瞥,扫视"讲,例如:He saw at a glance that she had been crying. 他一眼就看出她一直在哭。glare 意为"令人目眩的光,强烈的阳光",例如:I can't see it clearly due to the reflective glare of the beach. 由于海滩反射的强光,我看不清楚。gleam 作"微光,闪光,一线光明;(希望、机智等的)闪现"讲,例如:We saw a single gleam of light from the signal tower. 我们看到了信号塔上的一道闪光。本句意思是"这部小说里有一些非常有见地的关于 19 世纪乡村生活的描述。"所以正确答案应是 B。

60. [A] reaction 意为"(to)反应,感应",例如:The secret of happiness is this: let your interests be as wide as possible, and let your reactions to the things and persons that interest you be as far as possible friendly rather than hostile. 幸福的秘密在于:让你自己的兴趣尽可能广泛,对你所感兴趣的人和事物尽可能友好而不是充满敌意。comment 作"(on)批评,评论"讲,例如:Newspapers often give comment on the news in the editorials. 报纸常在社论里对新闻发表评论。impression 意为"印象,感想",例如:You should take advantage of the opportunity and try to make a good impression on her. 你应该利用这次机会,给她留个好印象。comprehension 作"理解"讲,例如:Skimming helps double your reading speed and im-

prove your comprehension as well. 浏览不仅使你的阅读速度提高一倍,而且还有助于提高你的阅读能力。本句意思是"有时学生会被要求在看了一本与正在学习科目相关的书或一篇文章之后写一些感想。"所以正确答案应是 A。

61. [B] prohibit 意为"禁止,阻止",例如:Many firms prohibit smoking in their stores. 许多商号都禁止在其商店里抽烟。avoid 作"避免,回避,躲开"讲,例如:He is wearing dark glasses to avoid being recognized. 他戴着墨镜以免被认出来。reject 意为"拒绝,抵制,丢掉,抛弃",例如:We were angry that our request had been rejected. 我们的请求遭到了拒绝,我们感到忿忿不平。repel 作"击退,抵制"讲,例如:If one can't repel the temptation of money, he will make a great mistake. 如果一个人抵挡不住金钱的诱惑,那么他就要犯大错。本句意思是"严禁在公园里摘花。"所以正确答案应是 B。

62. [A] intention 意为"意图,打算,目的",例如:He went to see the boss with the intention of asking for a pay rise. 他去见老板,想要求增加工资。interest 作"兴趣,趣味"讲,例如:My job corresponds with my interests. 我的工作与我的兴趣相符。wish 意为"希望,盼望,想要",例如:She could not speak, but made her wishes known by means of gesture. 她不会说话,但她用手势让人知道她的愿望。desire 作"愿望,欲望,要求"讲,例如:The speaker inspired all of us with an ardent desire to do our best for the old people. 发言人大大鼓舞了我们,我们人人都渴望尽最大努力为老年人做些事情。本句意思是"托尼一点也没想放弃他的研究工作。"所以正确答案应是 A。

63. [D] separate 意为"分离的,分开的;各自的,单独的",例如:We went our separate ways home from the cinema. 从影院出来,我们各自回家。本句意思是"有两个孩子不得不在同一张床上睡觉,其他三个孩子可以各自睡一张床。"所以正确答案应是 D。

64. [C] carry 意为"运送,搬运;携带,怀有",例如:Speak softly, and carry a big stick. 说话要温和,但是手里要拿着一根大棒。Beware of people carrying ideas. Beware of ideas carrying people. 当心带有思想的人,当心思想控制人。本句意思是"我是不是可以这样理解,他的新岗位毫无责任可言?"所以正确答案应是 C。

65. [B] adapt 意为"使适应,适合",例如:This machine has been specially adapted for use in cold area. 这台机器被改动以适应寒冷地区的使用。change 作"改变"讲,例如:Having listened to the report, he changed his negative attitude toward his work. 听完报告后,他改变了对工作的消极态度。modify 意为"更改,修改",例如:He'll have to modify his views if he wants to be elected. 他想当选就得把观点变得温和些。conform 作"遵守,依照,符合,顺应"讲,例如:The results which we have obtained conform to theirs. 我们得到的结果和他们的一致。本句意思是"那些不能够适用改变了的环境的动物都死掉了,而那些能够适应的动物都存活了下来。"所以正确答案应是 B。

1998 年英语专业四级考试语法与词汇参考答案与解析

41. ［A］ no less... than 表示前后两者都肯定,例如:Peace hath her victories No less renowned than war. 和平的胜利与战争的胜利一样辉煌。no more... than 表示前后两者都否定,例如:The lion is no more merciful than the tiger. 狮子与老虎一样残忍。本句意思是"约翰和他的姐姐一样都很刻苦,但是他却没考及格。"所以正确答案应是 A。

42. ［C］和［D］ that/when 可以作关系副词引导定语从句,在从句作状语,此时 that/when 相当于"介词 + which",例如:The summer of 1969, the year (when, that, in which) men first set foot on the moon, will never be forgotten. 1969 年夏是人们永远不会忘记的,这一年人类第一次登上月球。本句意思是"她记得过去有好几次,她都有同样的感觉。"所以 C 与 D 均为正确答案。

43. ［B］ should 用在条件句中,可表示虚拟语气,意为"万一",强调该条件不太可能,例如:Should the leading pilot have a heart attack, the backup could take over. 万一机长突发心脏病,可由副驾驶接替。本句意思是"如果你购买的汽车在最初的 12 个月中万一出现什么问题,请与我们授权的经销商交涉。"所以正确答案应是 B。

44. ［A］ 请参见 2002 年第 49 题详解。本句意思是"这个室内游泳池看起来没有必要这么豪华。"所以正确答案应是 A。

45. ［C］ 由于非谓语动词 obtain 和句子主语 he 是逻辑主谓关系,因此这里要使用现在分词作状语,另外由于 obtain 的动作发生在句子谓语动词 watch it on TV 之前,再看本句的句意为:由于没有买到比赛的票,他只能在家通过电视开看比赛了。由此可以断定［C］为正确答案。例如:Looking up, she saw a bright moon hanging in the sky. 抬头仰望,她看到一轮明月悬挂在天空。Returning to my apartment, I found my watch missing. Whistling the merry tune, Jack fixed the tire. 吹着欢快的口哨,杰克把轮胎修好了。

46. ［A］ "prefer A to B"相当于"like A better than B",例如:Who are happy in marriage? Those with so little imagination that they cannot picture a better state, and those so shrewd that they prefer quiet slavery to hopeless rebellion. 婚姻中什么样的人是幸福? 是那些缺乏想像力无法想出更佳状况的人;还是那些精明透顶,选择了安详顺从而不是无望叛逆的人。本句意思是"孩子宁愿到山里宿营,也不愿意进行室内活动。"所以正确答案应是 A。

47. ［C］ as much as 作"同样地"讲,例如:John, as much as his brothers, was responsible for the failure. 约翰和他的兄弟们一样要对这次失败负责。as far as 相当于从属连词,引导一个状语从句,对主语的行为或状态作出范围上的限制,意为"就……而言,就……而论,根据……",例如:As far as the quality of tone is concerned, this radio set is quite up to the standard. 就音质而言,这台收音机已经很合乎标准了。the same as 作表语时,表示"是和……一样的",引导状语从句

时,相当于 just as,例如:The relation of genius to talent is the same as that of instinct to reason. 天资之于才华一如本能之于理智。The brain can be developed just the same as the muscles can be developed, if one will only take the pains to train the mind to think. 头脑可以像肌肉一样得到发展,只要你肯不辞辛苦地训练心智去思想。as long as 可以引导条件状语从句,表示"只要……",例如:As long as the world shall last there will be wrongs, and if no man rebelled, those wrongs would last forever. 只要世界还存在,就会有错误,如果没有人反叛,这些错误将永远存在下去。本句意思是"语言属于社会中的每一个人,对于清洁工和教授而言没有什么两样。"所以正确答案应是 C。

48. [A]和[B]　as 和 though 作"即使"讲,可以引导让步状语从句。as 引导让步状语从句时,从句主谓要倒装;though 引导让步状语从句时,从句主谓可倒装,也可以不倒装。例如:Much as /though we admire Shakespeare's comedies (Though we admire Shakespeare's comedies very much), we cannot agree that they are superior to his tragedies. 虽然我们推崇莎士比亚的喜剧,但对其喜剧胜于悲剧的说法却不敢苟同。Much as though he likes her (Though he likes her very much), he does get irritated with her sometimes. 尽管他喜欢她,可有时他确实也对她发火。本句意思是"尽管他非常需要钱买一辆新车,但是他仍决定不从银行贷款。"A和B均为正确答案。

49. [C]　在这里 which hotel to stay at 作动词 decide 的宾语,由于 which 要在该不定式中作成分,因此不及物动词 stay 后必须跟介词 at,更多类似例句:I have got a loaf of bread; now I'm looking for a knife to cut it with. 我有一块面包,我在找一把小刀将它切开。He is the best man to consult with. 他是可以与之商量的最合适的人。本句意思是"克拉克夫妇还没有决定住在哪家宾馆。"所以正确答案应是 C。

50. [B]　"such as to"后跟不定式,引出结果状语,作"如此……以至……"讲,例如:The problem is such as to interest only a few people. 这样的问题只能使少数人感兴趣。本句意思是"他非常有幽默感,使房间的每个人都朗声大笑。"所以正确答案应是 B。

51. [C]　过去分词 given 有时可以作介词,后跟名词,作"如果有"讲,相当于"with",例如:Given much more time, he would have done it much better. 如果给他更多的时间,他会做得更好。Given good weather, our ship will reach Bombay Friday. 假如天气好,我们的船星期五就会到达孟买。Given the opportunity, he might well have become an outstanding painter. 如果有机会,他也能成为一位杰出的画家。本句意思是"如果当时给予了足够的时间和资金支持,研究人员就可以在这个领域有更多发现。"所以正确答案应是 C。

52. [A]　needn't have done sth. 意为"你本没有必要做某事",暗示已经做过了该事情,例如:I needn't have gone there yesterday. 昨天我本不必去那儿。needn't do sth. 作"没有必要做某事"讲,例如:As for (As to) the tuition, you needn't worry about it. 至于学费,你就不必担心了。mustn't do sth. 意为"不许做某事",例如:

You mustn't tell or we'll get into trouble. 你不得说出去,否则我们就要倒霉了。英语中没有 mustn't have done sth. 结构。本句意思是"你本来没有必要告诉马克,这与他没有什么关系。"所以正确答案应是 A。

53. [D] be entitled to sth. / to do sth. 意为"有权享受……",例如:If you fail again, you'll not be entitled to any requirement. 如果你再失败,就无权提任何要求。These retired officers are entitled to enter the special military zone freely. 这些退役军官被授予特权,可以自由进入这一军事特区。本句意思是"因为有了会员证,他可以在俱乐部享受一些特权。"所以正确答案应是 D。

54. [B] spontaneous 意为"自发的,自然的,自动的",例如:Poetry is the spontaneous overflow of powerful feelings: it takes its origin from emotion recollected in tranquillity. 诗歌是强烈的感情的自发流溢:它渊源于平静中重新积聚起来的情感。simultaneous 意为"同时发生的,同时做出的,同时的",例如:Simultaneous interpretation in the United Nations is a demanding job. 联合国里的同声翻译工作是要求很高的。synthetic 意为"综合的,综合性的;(化学)合成的,人造的",例如:This synthetic dress material does not crush. 这种合成纤维衣料不会皱。本句意思是"显然,主席在会议上的讲话是未加思索的、事先未做准备的。"所以正确答案应是 B。

55. [D] 短语 make the most of 作"充分利用"讲,例如:Those that make the most of their time have none to spare. 最充分利用时间的人腾不出多余的时间。本句意思是"为了使项目成功,公司应该充分利用手头的机会。"所以正确答案应是 D。

56. [C] disqualify 意为"使不能,使不合格,吊销资格",例如:As he was a professional, he was disqualified from taking part in the Olympic Games. 由于他是个职业运动员,因此没资格参加奥运会。disfavour 意为"不喜欢,不赞成,反感",例如:We disfavoured their unethical actions. 我们不赞成他们的不道德行为。dispel 意为"驱散,消除",例如:The only true love is love at first sight; second sight dispels it. 真爱仅是第一眼所生的爱慕。第二眼便荡然无存了。dismiss 意为"免……之职,解雇;让……离开,遣散",例如:The man was dismissed for culpable negligence. 这人因玩忽职守而被革职。本句意思是"由于未能遵守俱乐部条例,他被取消了排球队员资格。"所以正确答案应是 C。

57. [B] infinite 意为"无限的,无穷的,无际的;巨大的,无数的",例如:We must accept finite disappointment, but we must never lose infinite hope. 我们必须接受有限的失望,但是千万不可失去无限的希望。eternal 意为"永远(不变)的,永恒的",例如:Honesty and diligence should be your eternal mates. 诚实和勤勉应该成为你永久的伴侣。ceaseless 意为"不停的,不断的",例如:The ceaseless dripping of water will hollow out a stone. 水滴石穿。everlasting 意为"持续不断的,永久的",例如:The interests to be considered should be the interests of all; the fame to be sought should be an everlasting fame. 计利当计天下利,求名应求万世名。本句意思是"在全国各地都发现了新油田,这使政府充满了无限希望。"所以正确答案应是 B。

58. [A] subsequently 作"随后地,后来地"讲,例如:We rarely fathom another person's thoughts, and if a similar reflection subsequently occurs to us it presents so many aspects which have escaped us that we are easily persuaded it is new. 我们很少揣摩他人的思想,如果一种类似的想法产生,这想法会呈现那么多被我们忽略的侧面,以至于我们很容易相信它是一种全新的思想。successively 作"先后地"讲,例如:Friction can be conceived as a series of small impacts occurring successively and side by side, impact as friction concentrated at one spot and in a single moment of time. 摩擦可以看作一个跟着一个和一个挨着一个的一连串的小碰撞;碰撞可以看作集中于一个瞬间和一个地方的摩擦。predominantly 意为"主要地,在数量上占优势地",例如:More and more Chinese are learning foreign languages, predominantly English. 越来越多的中国人学习外语,主要是英语。preliminarily 的形容词 preliminary 意为"预备的,初步的",例如:A preliminary exam is one which is in preparation for something. 初试就是在事前进行的测试。本句意思是"起初该公司拒绝购买这种设备,但后来修正了这一决定。"所以正确答案应是 A。

59. [B] halt 意为"停止前进,停止,停住",例如:No one can halt the advance of history. 谁也阻挡不了历史的前进。repel 意为"逐退,驱逐;使厌恶,使反感",例如:Two positive charges repel each other, and so do two negative charges. 两个正极相互排斥,两个负极同样也相互排斥。本句意思是"当地警方得到授权,只要他们认为合适,就可阻止任何人的行动。"所以正确答案应是 C。

60. [C] word 用单数,可以表示"消息,谣言",例如:Any word on your promotion? 有你升迁的消息吗? Word has it they're divorcing. 有传言说他们在办离婚。本句意思是"你有没有听说过有关于她的一些传闻?"所以正确答案应是 C。

61. [A]和[B] 请参见 2001 年第 45 题之精解。
12 之于 3 同 4 之于 1。

62. [B] luck 意为"运气,命运,幸运",例如:Luck is a matter of preparation meeting opportunity. 幸运是准备与机会的遇合。chance 意为"机会;可能性",更强调可能性,例如:Chance favours the minds that are prepared. 机会只惠顾那些时刻做好准备的人。本句意思是"她的早年生活还比较顺利,但中年时期命运好像变了。"所以正确答案应是 B。

63. [C] take notice of 意为"注意",例如:She always took particular notice of me. 她总是特别注意我。He didn't take notice of Tom's proposals at the meeting. 在会上他不理会汤姆的建议。Don't take notice of what he said. 别理会他说的话。本句意思是"尽管我将此事告诉过她好几次,但是她对我的话毫不在乎。"所以正确答案应是 C。

64. [D] abandon 意为"抛弃,放弃",例如:He abandoned the intention of becoming a lawyer. 他放弃了当律师的打算。resign 作"放弃,辞去"讲,例如:Would it surprise you to know that I'm thinking of resigning? 当你得知我打算辞职时,是不是有点惊讶? surrender 意为"使……投降,使……自首",例如:They would rather to die

fighting rather than surrender. 他们宁愿战死,也不投降。release 作"释放,解放" 讲,例如:Automation is beginning to release workers from the bondage of mindless and repetitive toil. 自动化正逐步把工人从刻板而重复的苦役中解放出来。本句 意思是"人们发现这项计划要花费大量资金后就将其放弃了。"所以正确答案 应是 D。

65. [A] furniture 是不可数名词,例如:Will you please help me to shift the furniture round please? 请帮我移下家具好吗? They had stored their furniture when they went a-broad. 他们出国时把家具保存在仓库里。possession 作"占有"讲时,是不可数 名词,例如:The keys are in the hostess's possession. 钥匙在女主人手中。The soldiers took possession of the enemy's fort. 士兵们攻占了敌人的堡垒。posses-sion 作"所有物"讲时,是可数名词,要用复数,例如:The flood destroyed all of his possessions. 洪水使他所有的财物化为乌有。He lost most of his possessions during the war. 他大半财产都在战争期间丢了。本句意思是"昨天我姨妈买了 一些新家具,来布置她那座位于海滨的公寓。"所以正确答案应是 A。

1999 年英语专业四级考试语法与词汇参考答案与解析

41. [C] 关系代词 what 在这里引导名词性从句,作介词 after 的宾语,又如:After what had happened he could not continue to work there. 发生了这一切之后,他不能再 在那里工作了。本句意思是"在无休止的等待后,终于轮到她进入人事经理的 办公室。"所以正确答案应是 C。

42. [C] 在这里 only 跟不定式放在句末,表示结果,例如:At sports meet, if white and black are present, they support opposing sides, only to result in friction. 在体育项 目上,如果黑人和白人都在场,他们分别支持对立方,结果就会产生摩擦。本 句意思是"那三个人多次企图偷越边境进入邻国,结果每次都被警察逮住了。" 所以正确答案应是 C。

43. [C] be said to have done sth. 表示"据说已经……",此处不定式表示的动作发生在 主句动作之前,因此要使用完成体,再例如:Cesar Frank is said to have walked around with a dreamlike gaze while composing, seemingly totally unaware of his surroundings. 据说塞撒尔·弗兰克创作时到处走动,目光梦幻般凝视前方,似 乎对周围的环境全然不知。本句意思是"据说在过去一年里约翰逊教授的研 究工作取得了重大进步。"所以正确答案应是 C。

44. [A] "A not ... any more than B" 表示"正如 A 不能……,B 也不能……",该结构另 一个变体是"A no more than B",例如:A great memory is never made synony-mous with wisdom, any more than a dictionary could be called a treatise. 好的记 性从来不是智慧的同义词,犹如字典不能称为论文一样。Creativity is no more teachable than heritable. No more than the most detail-perfect doll can transubstan-tiate into a living, breathing baby. 创造能力既不是遗传的,也不是教得会的。 正如再怎样完美制作的洋娃娃,也不能够变成一个会呼吸的活的婴儿。本句

意思是"脂肪不能变成肌肉,就如同肌肉不会变成脂肪一样。"所以正确答案应是 A。

45. [C] "not so much A as B"结构表示"与其说 A,不如说 B",例如:Human felicity is produced not so much by great pieces of good fortune that seldom happen, as by little advantages that occur every day. 与其说人类的幸福来自偶尔发生的鸿运,不如说来自每天都有的小实惠。本句意思是"与其说是语言,还不如说是文化背景使得此书晦涩难懂。"所以正确答案应是 C。

46. [A] 请参见 2002 年第49 题详解。本句意为:"由于感到登山存在危险而产生的焦虑不像如今公众心里所想像的那么多。"故正确答案为 A。

47. [A] 这里需要一个关系代词引导定语从句,而且该关系代词还要在从句中作及物动词 visit 的宾语,所以[C]错误。[B]中 mostly 用词不当,意为"多半,主要地",可改为 most。[D]中 much 位置不对,可放在动词 like 前。本句意思是"我从未去过拉萨,但这座城市是我最想参观的。"所以正确答案应是 A。

48. [A] may have done 表示对过去可能性的推测,例如:Science may have found a cure for most evils; but it has found no remedy for the worst of them all—the apathy of human beings. 科学或许已经为大多数的病症找到了药方,但是它对于最坏的一个病症却束手无策,那就是人类的冷漠。而 must have acted 则表示对过去的肯定推测,例如:A man of noble mind cannot owe his culture to a narrow circle. His country and the world must have influenced him too. 一个心灵高尚的人不可能是从一个狭小的圈子当中得到教养的,他一定也受到了国家和世界的影响。本句意思是"他也许做得不十分明智,但至少他在努力帮忙。"所以正确答案应是 A。

49. [B] 请参见 2002 年第51 题之解析。本句意思是"如果你真的学了这么长时间英语了,你现在应该差不多能够用英语写信了。"所以正确答案应是 B。

50. [C] "what is called...","what we call...","what is known as..."等结构可放在名词或名词性词组之前,表示"所谓的……",例如:What we call the weight of a body is really the attractive force. 我们称之为物体重量的,实质上是一种吸引力。What were called radicals were involved in leading the general strike. 所谓的激进分子们参与领导了大罢工。本句意思是"他就是那种所谓的嘀嘀咕咕爱抱怨的人——总是怨这怨那。"所以正确答案应是 C。

51. [B] however 作关系副词引导让步状语从句时,该词修饰的形容词或副词要和 however 一起移到从句句首,例如:However hard the task may be, we must fulfil it on time. 不管任务多么艰巨,我们都必须按时完成。However hard she tries, she can not understand what you mean. 无论她怎么努力,她也弄不明白你的意思。though 在引导让步状语从句时,从句内容可以倒装也可以不倒装,倒装时,必须将需倒装成分置于从句句首,例如:Though they were going to part, they trusted each other. 尽管他们就要分离,但他们都彼此信任。Much though I like ice-cream, I never eat too much at once. 尽管我很喜欢吃冰淇淋,但是我从不一次吃得太多。本句意思是"无论这项工作多么艰苦,他总会尽最大努力按时完成。"所以正确答案应是 B。

52. [A] "Much as I would have liked to" 表示"尽管我是会非常乐意",例如：Much as he would have like to pay a visit to Beijing, he did not have enough money. 尽管他非常想参观北京,但是他没有足够的钱。本句意思是"尽管我是会非常乐意借钱给他的,但是我确实没有那么多的多余的现金,所以还是不能借给他那笔钱。"所以正确答案应是 A。

53. [C] particular 意为"讲究的,苛求的,挑剔的",例如：A good writer should be very particular about the use of words. 好作家应该很讲究遣词造句。special 作"特殊的,特别的"讲,例如：The manager assembled the staff for a special announcement. 经理把职工召集在一起,宣布一个特别声明。peculiar 意为"特有的,独具的",例如：These are the customs peculiar to the inhabitants of this area. 这些都是这一地区居民所特有的习俗。specific 作"具体的,明确的"讲,例如：Be more specific on what you want to know. 你想知道什么请讲具体点。本句意思是"我的表哥胃口很大,但是对吃的食物却不怎么挑剔。"所以正确答案应是 C。

54. [A] exceedingly 意为"极度地,非常",例如：I'm exceedingly pleased to meet you. 见到你,我特别高兴。excessively 意为"过度,过分地",常含有贬义,如：Don't drink excessively. 不要酗酒。extensively 作"广泛地,广阔地"讲,如：You should read extensively in order to enlarge your vocabulary. 你应该广泛阅读以便扩大词汇量。exclusively 意为"惟一地,只",如：He's exclusively employed on repairing cars. 他是专雇来修理汽车的。本句意思是"你的建议对他会非常有用,他现在正不知所措呢。"所以正确答案应是 A。

55. [C] convey 意为"传达,传递",例如：This picture will convey to you some idea of the beauty of the scenery. 这幅画将把那里秀丽的风景向你传达一二。exchange 作"交换,调换;互换,交流"讲,例如：Mary exchanged seats with Anne. 玛丽和安妮交换了座位。transfer 意为"转移,传递,传输",例如：The head office of the company has been transferred to New York. 该公司总部已迁至纽约。convert 作"改变,转变"讲,例如：The room was converted from a kitchen to a drawing room. 这间房由厨房改成了客厅。本句意思是"用英语将汉语成语表达出来往往是非常困难的。"所以正确答案应是 C。

56. [D] hand over 意为"移交,交出",如：The captain was unwilling to hand over the command of his ship to a young man. 船长不愿把船的指挥权移交给年轻人。而 hand in 作"交上,上缴"讲,如：Please hand in your homework on time. 请按时交作业。hand out 意为"分给(每个人)",如：Hand out the pencils. 把铅笔分给每个人。hand down 意为"传给",常用被动形式,如：This custom has been handed down since the 18th century. 这风俗从 18 世纪一直流传至今。本句意思是"她拒绝将大门钥匙交给女房东,直到她领回押金。"所以正确答案应是 D。

57. [D] pursue 意为"从事(工作、研究等)",例如：Students showed great enthusiasm in

pursuing the new learning. 学生们学习这一新知识时表现出了极大的热情。engage 作"(使……)从事于"讲,例如:The children are engaged in extracurricular dramatics. 这些孩子正从事课外戏剧表演。devote 意为"把……专用(于),将……奉献(给)",例如:His mother died when he was young; thereafter he devoted himself to medicine study. 他年轻时,母亲就去世了,这以后他便致力于医学研究。seek 作"寻求,探索,追求"讲,例如:You should seek relaxation after a day's hard work. 辛勤劳动一天之后你应寻求娱乐。本句意思是"科学家有绝对的自由,来从事他们认为最好的研究。"所以正确答案应是 D。

58. [A] originate 意为"发源,创始,开始",后可跟 from 或 in 引导出介词宾语,例如:The two brothers' quarrel originated in a misunderstanding. 这两兄弟的争吵源于一场误会。stem 作不及物动词,意为"起源,发生",后常跟介词 from,例如:Correct decisions stem from correct judgements. 正确的决心来源于正确的判断。derive 意为"取得,得到;追溯……的起源(由来),衍生",是及物动词,例如:Life is the enjoyment of emotion, derived from the past and aimed at the future. 人生是起源于过去又着眼于未来的情感享受。descend 意为"下降,下跌,落下;祖传,起源于,是……的后裔",例如:He descended from the platform amidst applause. 在掌声中他从舞台上走下来。本句意思是"奥运会起源于公元前776年希腊一个叫奥林匹亚的小城。"所以正确答案应是 A。

59. [D] hasty 意为"草率的,仓促的",如:She is too hasty; if she would only think before speaking she wouldn't have so much trouble. 她太草率了,只要她说话前考虑一下就不会惹这么多的麻烦了。urgent 作"紧急的,迫切的"讲,如:The earthquake victims were in urgent need of medical supplies. 地震灾民急需医疗援助。instant 意为"立刻的",如:He wants an instant answer to all his questions. 他要求即刻答复他所有的问题。prompt 则作"迅速的"讲,如:Prompt payment of bills greatly helps the account in shops. 即刻付款对商店的银根大有帮助。本句意思是"我们要永远牢记,匆匆拍板常常会导致严重后果。"所以正确答案应是 D。

60. [D] agreement with 表示"与……达成一致,取得一致意见",例如:They reached an agreement with the enemy and soon made peace. 他们与敌方订立了协定,很快就休战了。本句意思是"资方正在努力与五个不同的工会达成一致意见,这一事实引发了漫长的谈判。"所以正确答案应是 D。

61. [D] radically 作"根本上,以激进的方式"讲,例如:The profligate heir radically decreased his trust fund. 这位恣意挥霍的继承人急剧减少了信托基金。而 violently 意为"猛烈地,激烈地",如:The robbers attacked the innocents violently. 抢劫犯猛烈地袭击无辜的人。severely 作"严重地,严厉地"讲,例如:He commits this kind of error again and again. It is difficult for you to criticize him too severely. 他一次又一次地犯这种错误,你无论多么严厉地批评他也不会过分。extremely 意为"非常,极其,极端",例如:There are three things extremely hard: Steel, Diamond, and To know oneself. 有三样东西是非常坚硬/艰难的:钢、钻

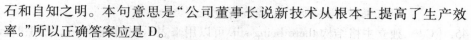

石和自知之明。本句意思是"公司董事长说新技术从根本上提高了生产效率。"所以正确答案应是 D。

62. [D]　provision 意为"准备,预备",强调"未雨绸缪",例如:They spent all their money and made no provision for the future. 他们把钱都用光了,未留日后需用。preparation 意为"准备,筹备,安排",例如:Luck is a matter of preparation meeting opportunity. 幸运是准备与机遇的会合。根据本句意:"地方当局意识到有必要在住房规划上为老年人预做安排。"得知 D 为正确答案。

63. [C]　介词 to 可以用来表示比分,例如:The score was 9 to 6. 比分是九比六。本句意为:"客队在去年的亚俱杯决赛中以 2:4 不敌主队。"得知 C 为正确答案。

64. [A]　be guilty of 作"犯……罪"讲,例如:He confessed himself guilty of theft. 他承认自己犯了盗窃罪。It was difficult to decide which country was guilty of aggression. 很难断定哪个国家犯了侵略罪。本句意思是"警察将他释放了,原因是警方没有发现他犯有谋杀罪。"所以正确答案应是 A。

65. [D]　keep pace with 作"跟上,与……同步"讲,相当于 keep up with,例如:She works so fast that I can't keep pace with her. 她干得太快,我赶不上她。You are thinking much too fast for me; I can't keep pace with you. 对我来说你的思维太快了,我跟不上。The children ran along, trying to keep pace with the adults. 孩子们跑着,试图跟上大人的步伐。本句意思是"作为一个发展中国家,我们必须与世界经济的快速发展保持一致。"所以正确答案应是 D。

2000 年英语专业四级考试语法与词汇参考答案与解析

41. [A]　do 作为代动词,可以代替前文出现的动词,此处代替了 sense the approach of thunderstorms,例如:Two positive charges repel each other, and so do two negative charges. 两个正极相互排斥,两个负极同样也相互排斥。本句意思是"敏锐的听觉可以帮助大多数动物在人还未感觉之前就可感觉到雷暴的来临。"所以正确答案应是 A。

42. [B]　if 在引导条件状语从句时,且当从句主语和主句中的主语是一致的,而且从句谓语又包含 be 时,常用省略结构,例如:I will not accept if nominated, and will serve if elected. 如果被任命,我不愿接受,但是如果被选上,我将效力。本句意思是"这种疾病如果不予治疗会导致完全失明。"所以正确答案应是 B。

43. [A]　连词 and 在此引导平行结构,可省略其后与前面相同的成分,补充完整后就是"The central provinces have drought in other years"。本句中文翻译为:"这些中部省份有有些年份发洪水,有些年份遭旱灾。"所以正确答案为 A。

44. [D]　祈使句的附加疑问句的谓语通常使用 shall 或 will,而且通常用肯定形式,例如:Have a little more coffee, will you? 再喝点咖啡,怎么样? Let's meet at the station, shall we? 咱们车站见,好不好? 需要注意的是,当第一部分为第二人称肯定的祈使句,而且第二部分使用否定附加疑问句时,这种情况一般用在请客的场合,例如:Have a cigarette, won't you? 请抽烟。本句的中文翻译为"吃点水果,好吗?"所以正确答案应是 D。

45. [C] 独立主格结构 there being sth. 可以用来表示原因、条件等,例如:There being no work, they decided to go to the movies. 由于无事可做,他们决定去看电影。There being no bus, they had to set out on foot. 由于没有公共汽车,他们只好步行前往。本句意思是"由于没有更多的事情需要讨论,因此会议提前半个小时就结束了。"所以正确答案应是 C。

46. [A] get about 指"(病愈后)下床走动"。get in 则作"进去;收获(庄稼等)"讲,get on 意为"过活,生活,相处融洽(with);上车;继续进展",get through 表示"通过(考试等);度过,用完;接通(电话等)"。本句意思是"我母亲患有风湿病,不能下床走动。"所以正确答案应是 A。

47. [B] put off 除了作"推迟,延误"讲,还可作"使……厌恶"解,例如:I'm put off by my husband taking me for granted! 我干什么我丈夫都以为是理所当然的,这真叫我厌恶极了! 本句意思是"我对马克的粗鲁行为很反感,他让太我生气了。"所以正确答案应是 B。

48. [A] needn't have done 表示"本来没有必要做某事",暗示实际上已经做了,例如:The Ericksons needn't have worried. 埃里克森一家本不必担心。本句意思是"你本来没有必要将这件事情告诉吉姆,这事与他毫不相干。"所以正确答案应是 A。

49. [C] 虚拟语气用在条件句中表示对过去的假设,从句使用过去完成时,主句使用 would (should, could, might) + have done,例如:If the facts had been collected earlier, we would have had more time to study them. 如果这些材料早些时候就搜集到,我们就会有更多的时间对其进行研究了。If I had answered the policemen seriously, I would not have been arrested. 如果我认真地回答了警察的问题,我就不会被逮捕了。本文中文翻译为:如果当时那里没有那么多人的话,我们大家本可以玩得更高兴些。

50. [D] that 可以引导定语从句,例如:It's difficult to select from his voluminous works short passages that are really representative. 在他卷帙浩瀚的著作中要选出真正有代表性的片段相当困难。[B]as 也可引导定语从句,但是一般要与 such, the same 等连用,例如:It turned out not to be such a good banquet as she had promised us. 那次宴会不像她许诺的那样好。[A]whose 引导定语从句时,要在从句中作定语修饰一个名词,例如:She courageously married a young man whose social position is beneath her. 她勇敢地和一个社会地位低于自己的小伙子结了婚。[C]what 不可以引导定语从句,只可引导名词性从句,例如:I am gratified that they appreciated what I had done for them. 我很满意,因为他们很感激我对他们做的事。本句意思是"使用计算机的公司发现,用来监督质量的员工人数大大减少了。"所以正确答案应是 D。

51. [B] 非谓语动词 look at,与句子主语 the present economic situation 是逻辑动宾关系,因此这里要使用过去分词来作状语,例如:Written in a terse, lucid style, the book describes the author's childhood experiences in Louisiana just before the out-

break of the Civil War. 这本书以简明、透彻的文体，描述了南北战争前作者在路易斯安娜州的童年生活。本句意思是"这样看来，目前的经济形势并不很令人悲观。"所以正确答案应是 B。

52. [B] allergic 意为"过敏性的"，例如：An allergic skin is easily hurt by too much sunshine. 过敏性的皮肤晒太阳过多易受伤害。[A]insensitive 作"不敏感的，不容易感受的"讲，例如：She's insensitive to other people's feelings. 她对别人的感情毫无感觉。[C]sensible 意为"明白事理的，明智的"，例如：It was sensible of you not to tell him about it. 你没有将此事告诉他，实属明智之举。[D]infected 作"受传染的，被感染了的"讲，例如：The nurse wept as she dressed the infected wound. 那位护士一边包扎感染了的伤口，一边抽泣。本句意思是"很多人对昆虫叮咬非常敏感，有的人甚至不得不去看医生。"所以正确答案应是 B。

53. [D] lane 意为"车道，行车线；（船或飞机的）航道"，例如：They decided to widen a highway by adding two lanes. 他们决定加宽公路增添两条车道。track 则意为"小径，小道；跑道，田径运动；铁轨，轨道"，例如：The track leads direct to the farm. 小路直接通向农场。本句意思是"在高速公路上开车的时候，你必须遵循车道标志行车。"所以正确答案应是 D。

54. [A] swerve 意为"突然转向，转弯"，例如：The car swerved to avoid the dog. 小汽车为了避开这只狗急忙转向。而[C]depart 意为"起程，离开，辞世"，例如：Nothing that was worthy in the past departs; no truth or goodness realized by man ever dies, or can die. 过去的一切有价值的东西都不会消逝；任何被人类认知的真与善都不会死亡，也不能死亡。[D]swing 意为"（使）来回摆动，摇荡（使）旋转，（使）回旋"，例如：A pendulum swings. 钟摆来回摆动。[B]twist 意为"搓，捻，绞；转动，拧，扭；曲解；盘旋，迂回"，例如：The path twists up on the mountainside. 这条山路在山腰盘旋而上。本句意思是"为了避免撞着那位走在路中央的老太太，这位驾驶员不得不突然将车转向一边。"所以正确答案应是 A。

55. [B] skid 意为"打滑，滑向一侧"，例如：Even as I gave the warning, the car skidded. 正当我提出警告时，那轿车就滑向一边。而skate 则意为"滑冰，溜冰；滑过，掠过"；slide 意为"滑动，滑行；溜进，潜行"，例如：The drawer of this desk slides in and out easily. 这张桌子的抽屉容易拉进拉出。slip 意为"失足，滑倒，溜走，潜行；滑落，滑脱"，例如：In the act of picking up the ball, he slipped and fell. 他在接球时滑了一跤。本句意思是"在冬天，避免汽车在结了冰的路上打滑对司机来说很不容易。"所以正确答案应是 B。

56. [C] entail 意为"必需，使……承担"，例如：Building the new road has entailed pulling down a lot of houses. 修建新公路必需拆毁许多房屋。短语 result in 作"结果，导致"讲，例如：The accident resulted in the death of two passengers. 这起事故导致两名乘客死亡。assure 意为"使确信，使放心，向……保证"，例如：The doctor assured the parents that he could cure their child. 医生向孩子父母保证能治愈这个孩子。accomplish 作"完成，实现，达到"讲，例如：The spy has accomplished his mission in Japan. 那个间谍已完成了他在日本的使命。本句意思为"这个

项目意味着要大量增加国防开支。"所以正确答案应是 C。

57. [B]　slim 意为"微小的,纤细的",例如:There's still a slim chance that we'll find the child alive. 我们还有一线希望能够活着找到这个孩子。distant 作"远的,久远的,远隔的"讲,例如:Focus the telescope on that distant lighthouse please. 请把望远镜对准远处那座灯塔。unlikely 意为"不可能的",例如:He is only too credulous to believe such an unlikely story about flying saucers. 他太容易上当了,居然相信有关飞碟的传闻。narrow 作"窄的,狭窄的"讲,例如:It was a hard narrow chair and not made for comfort. 这把椅子又硬又窄,并不是为让人坐着舒适而制作的。本句意思是"实际上,再次发生这些不幸事件的可能性微乎其微。"所以正确答案应是 B。

58. [C]　distinction 意为"区分,区别,差别",例如:A distinction should be made between the primary and secondary contradictions. 要区分主要矛盾和次要矛盾。separation 作"分离,分开"讲,例如:I have wept over our separation. 我们分离后,我经常为此而啜泣。division 意为"分,分开,分割",例如:An element is a substance, the nature of which cannot be changed by any ordinary method of division. 元素是一种物质,其性质不能被一般的分裂而改变。difference 作"差异,区别"讲,例如:I can hardly see the slight difference between the two. 我几乎看不出两者的微小差别。本句意思是"为了讨论的方便,我们应该清楚地区别"胜任的"和"精通的"。"所以正确答案应是 C。

59. [D]　climate 意为"一般(社会)趋势,(社会)风气",例如:The academic climate here doesn't agree with me. 这里的学术氛围对我不适宜。air 作"空气,大气"讲,例如:The State Council has decided to carry on nation-wide investigations of air pollution. 国务院已经决定进行全国性的空气污染调查。mood 意为"心境,心情,情绪",例如:He is swayed by fashion, by suggestion, by transient moods. 他被流行式样、建议、无常的情绪所打动。area 作"地区"讲,例如:This weather chart clearly indicates that there was little rain in this area last year. 这张气象表清楚地表明了去年这个地区几乎没有什么降水。本句意思是"在现如今的经济条件下,我们可以作出比以前更大的进步。"所以正确答案应是 D。

60. [B]　consequently 意为"因而,所以",例如:If you wage war, do it energetically and with severity. This is the only way to make it shorter, and consequently less inhuman. 如果打仗,就要毫不留情地全力去打。这是缩短战争的惟一方法,因为也可以减少战争的残酷。而 consistently 则意为"认真地,诚心诚意地",例如:We have consistently pursued a friendly policy towards them. 我们对他们一贯奉行友好政策。invariably 则意为"一直地,总是",例如:Differences—both real and imagined—are invariably exaggerated in the media and in society as a whole. 差别——不管是真实的还是主观想像的——总是被传媒和社会夸大。本句意思是"无论根据什么标准,《生命仪式》都一部好小说,因此,这本书应该在任何科幻小说名录上名列前茅。"所以正确答案应是 B。

61. [C]　inexhaustible 意为"无穷尽的,用不完的",例如:He is immortal, not because he

alone among creatures has an inexhaustible voice, but because he has a soul, a spirit capable of compassion and sacrifice and endurance. 人之不朽不是因为在动物中惟独他永远能发言,而是因为他有灵魂、有同情心、有牺牲和忍耐精神。controversial 意为"引起争论的,有争议的",例如:He refused to commit himself on a controversial subject before making due investigation. 在做必要的调查研究之前,他拒绝对争论的问题表态。remarkable 意为"不平常的,杰出的,值得注意的,显著的",例如:Edison had a remarkable aptitude for inventing new things. 爱迪生具有发明新事物的非凡天资。本句意思是"这个地区热带植物多种多样,这表明那是一个有着似乎取之不尽的原料的地方,而这些原料才被利用了一小部分。"所以正确答案应是 C。

62. [A] visit 意为"访问,访晤(某人),参观,游览",例如:His nephew used not to visit him at Christmas. 以前过圣诞节他侄子不经常来看他。travel 作"旅行"讲,例如:It usually takes much less time to fly from one country to another than to travel by train. 出国旅行坐飞机比坐火车花费的时间要少得多。watch 意为"注视,观看",例如:He was profoundly conscious that he was being watched. 他深知自己正在受到监视。tour 作"旅行,游历,观光"讲,例如:She toured a great deal as did most of her friends. 她和大多数朋友一样,周游过好多地方。本句意思是"在北京期间,他把所有的时间都用来参观重要的博物馆和建筑物。"所以正确答案应是 A。

63. [D] 习惯搭配 without fail 作"务必,必定,必须"讲,例如:Resolve to perform what you ought; perform without fail what you resolve. 应该做的就决心去做,决心做的就务必去做。without hesitation 作"毫不犹豫的",例如:Do as I tell you without hesitation. 不要犹豫,按照我说的去做。本句意思是"你明天十点前务必将年报送到我手上。"所以正确答案应是 D。

64. [B] on sb.'s behalf 意为"代表某人",例如:I requested that he (should) use his influence on my behalf. 我请求他为我施用他的影响力。英语中有 on no account 短语,作"无论如何都不"讲,例如:We must on no account view problems superficially and in isolation. 我们决不能仅从表面上孤立地看待问题。for sb.'s part 意为"至于某人,对某人来说",例如:The physician dismissed the matter as worthy of no further discussion on his part. 这件事情在这位医生看来不值得进一步讨论。in sb.'s interest/in the interest of sb. 作"为了……的利益"讲,例如:The Prime Minister resigned for the interest of the state. 首相为了国家的利益辞职了。本句意思是"由于主任不能参加接待会,我就以他的名义代表公司出席。"所以正确答案应是 B。

65. [A] uninformative 作"不提供信息(或资料)的,不增进知识的,不增长见闻的",例如:Because all the witnesses were uninformative, the case came to no end. 由于所有的证人都不能提供信息,因此案件不了了之。本句意思是"梦本身并不提供什么信息,但若结合其他数据,却能大大地帮助我们了解做梦的人。"所以正确答案应是 B。

2001 年英语专业四级考试语法与词汇参考答案与解析

41. [C] for one thing ... for another... 作"一方面……,另一方面……"讲,例如:For one thing I know that this job of mine isn't much, for another I don't feel tied down. 一方面我知道我的工作并不重要,但另一方面我感到不会受到束缚。本句意思是"我不能去——一方面我没有钱,另一方面我有太多的工作要做。"所以正确答案应是 C。

42. [D] 当介词短语作状语时,其逻辑主语应为句子的主语,否则该介词结构就成为悬垂结构,例如:Without a friend to counsel him, the temptation proved irresistible. (介词短语 without a friend to counsel him 与句子主语 the temptation 无逻辑关系,可将本句改为 Because he hadn't a friend to counsel him, the temptation proved irresistible.) 没有一个朋友给他出主意,结果他没有能抵制住诱惑。本句意思是"即使在她还是一个小姑娘的时候,美丽莎就知道表演将成为她的生活,戏剧观众将成为她最好的老师。"所以正确答案应是 D。

43. [D] why not do sth. 是习惯用法,表示"为什么不……",例如:Why not seize the pleasure at once? How often is happiness destroyed by preparation, foolish preparation! 为何不当机立断地留住欢乐? 君不见,快乐经常是毁在充分而愚蠢的准备里的。本句意思是"为什么不明天去看他?"所以正确答案应是 D。

44. [B] doubt 用在否定句中,后面要用 that 引导名词性从句,例如:I don't doubt that he will come. 我相信他会来。There is no doubt that the whole story was invented. 毫无疑问整篇故事全是虚构的。本句意思是"毫无疑问,这家公司在销售计划上作出了正确的决定。"所以正确答案应是 B。

45. [A]和[B] what 和 as 可作连词用,引导方式状语从句,例如:The people is to the people's army what (as) water to fish. 人民的军队离不开人民,就像鱼离不开水一样。Reading is to the mind what (as) exercise is to the body. 读书对于思想,好比运动对于身体一样。Leaves do for plants what (as) lungs do for animals. 叶子对于植物的作用,正如肺对于动物的作用一样。The blueprint is to the builder what (as) the outline is to the writer. 蓝图对于建筑师就像提纲对于作家一样。本句意思是"智力之于大脑,犹如视力之于躯体。"所以 A 与 B 均为正确答案。

46. [C] while 意为"当……的时候;然而",引导让步状语从句,表示对比,例如:A bad woman raises hell with a good many men while a good woman raises hell with only one. 坏女人会生很多男人的气,好女人只会生一个男人的气。尽管 as 也可引导让步状语从句,但是该从句必须倒装,例如:Tired as he was, he kept on. 尽管他很累了,他还是继续下去。as long as 引导条件状语从句,表示"只要",例如:A man may destroy everything within himself, love and hate and belief, and even doubt, but as long as he clings to life he cannot destroy fear. 一个人可以摧毁自己心中的一切:爱、恨、信仰,甚至怀疑。但是只要他仍然活着,他就无法摧毁恐惧。even 一般作副词,意为"甚至……(也),甚至(比)……更,还",例

如：Although planning involves material investment, even more important is the investment in man. 虽然计划中包括物质投资,但更重要的是对人的投资。本句意思是"尽管我很同情他们,但是我确实做不了很多事情来帮助他们摆脱困境。"所以正确答案应是 C。

47. [A] nearly 意为"几乎",如用在此处则表示否定意义,例如：Nearly all the people believed Ali because he was a very good man. 阿里是个大好人,因此几乎所有的人都信任他。barely 作"勉强,好容易才"讲,例如：They have barely enough time to catch the train. 他们的时间刚好能赶上火车。hardly 作"几乎不,简直不"讲,例如：She had changed so much that I could hardly recognize her. 她变化这么大,我简直认不出她了。merely 意为"仅仅,只不过",例如：We can't go into all the details of that case now, I merely mention it by the way. 我们现在不能详述那个案件,我只是附带提一提。本句意思是"病人的恢复非常令人鼓舞,他现在勉强可以在没人帮助的情况下自己下床了。"所以正确答案应是 A。

48. [A] much of a 作"非常的"讲,后跟名词,例如：I am afraid I'm not much of a dancer. 恐怕我的舞跳得不是很好。To travel a long way would be too much of a tax on my father's strength. 我父亲的体力经不起长途旅行。本句意思是"他胆子很小,不敢将事实告诉他最亲密的朋友。"所以正确答案应是 A。

49. [B] in that 作"由于,因为"讲,例如：The machine has an enormous advantage in that it is equipped with an automatic control system. 这台机器因装有自动控制装置而具有很大的优越性。I like the city, but I like the country better in that I have more friends in the country. 我喜欢城市,但我更爱乡下,因为在乡下我有很多朋友。Human beings are superior to animals in that they can use language as a tool to communicate. 人比动物优越在于人可以把语言作为交流的工具。本句意思是"巴力比他的母亲更有优势,因为他会说法语。"所以正确答案应是 B。

50. [C] as regards 相当于复合介词 with regard to 或 with reference to,多用于书面语,意为"对……来说",例如：As regards world peace, we Chinese people will staunchly defend it. 至于世界和平,我们中国人民一定要坚决保卫。With respect to your other proposals, I am not able to tell you our decision. 至于你提出的其他建议,我现在还不能把我们的决定告诉你。As regards the question how we should proceed in our work, there are still different opinions. 至于我们应如何进行工作,意见尚未一致。本句意思是"你不必担心手术费用。"所以正确答案应是 C。

51. [D] 动名词短语可以作主语,例如：Looking after children requires patience. 照看孩子需要有耐心。Setting fires to public facilities is highly dangerous and punishable by law. 放火焚烧公共设施是非常危险的,而且要受到法律的制裁。另外,非谓语动词的否定式只需要将 not 置于非谓语动词前面,不可采用否定谓语的办法来否定非谓语动词,例如：He apologized for his not being able to come. 他因未能前来而表示歉意。His mother never having been here before, he has to meet her at the station. 由于他母亲从未来过这儿,因此他不得不到车站接她。For a long time air was thought of as not being a kind of matter, that is, not having

weight or occupying space. 在很长的一段时间里,空气未被认为是一种物质,也就是说,空气没有重量,也不占空间。本句意思是"个头矮并不是人生的一个多么严重的劣势。"所以正确答案应是 D。

52. [B] be reduced to doing sth./sth. 作"不得不"讲,例如:He was reduced to begging in the streets. 他沦为街头乞丐。Its people were thus reduced to slavery. 这样它的人民沦为奴隶。He was reduced to despair. 他陷入绝望。本句意思是"由于饥荒,很多人不得不一连数天无饭可吃。"所以正确答案应是 B。

53. [B] tackle 意为"着手处理,对付",例如:Everyone has his problems to tackle. 每人都有一些问题要去解决。assign 意为"委派,指派",例如:The director assigned parts among the actors. 导演给演员们分配了角色。realize 作"认识到,认清,了解"讲,例如:He did not realize the danger of driving on an icy road. 他并未认识到在结冰的路面上开车是危险的。solve 意为"解释,解答,解决",例如:We were amazed at the ingenuity with which they solved their difficulties. 他们在解决困难时所表现出的聪明才智令我们惊叹。本句意思是"可以给计算机编写程序让它来完成很多不同的任务。"所以正确答案应是 B。

54. [A] frustrate 作"挫败,阻挠,使感到灰心"讲,例如:The young artist was often frustrated in his ambition to paint. 这位年轻艺术家的绘画抱负时常遭到挫折。prevent 意为"阻止,阻挡,制止,妨碍",例如:I regret that a prior engagement prevents me from accepting your kind invitation. 我有约在先,故不能接受你好意的邀请,实在很遗憾。discourage 作"使……泄气,使……失去信心,使……沮丧"讲,例如:We must not get discouraged because of such a minor setback. 我们决不可因这样一个小小的挫折而灰心丧气。accomplish 意为"完成,实现,达到",例如:The spy has accomplished his mission in Japan. 那个间谍已完成了他在日本的使命。本句意思是"这个球队的进球努力一次次被对方守门员化解。"所以正确答案应是 A。

55. [C] sight 作"望见,瞥见"讲,例如:Their first sight of land came after three days at sea. 他们在海上漂泊了三天后才看到陆地。chance 意为"机会",例如:John seized the chance and poured out his complaints about the poor working conditions in the factory. 约翰立即抓住那个机会,发泄了他对工厂简陋的工作条件的不满。heart 作"心情,心肠"讲,例如:She must be a nurse beloved by patients because she has a mild disposition and warm heart. 她一定是位病人喜欢的护士,因为她性情温柔,待人热情。experience 意为"经验,体验",例如:The job needs courage and experience as well. 做这项工作,不但需要勇气,而且更需要经验。本句意思是"我只是见过那个人一面,却从未和他说过话。"所以正确答案应是 C。

56. [B] distinction 作"区分,区别,差别"讲,make a distinction between 作"区分,找出……和……的区别",例如:A distinction should be made between the primary and secondary contradictions. 要区分主要矛盾和次要矛盾。difference 意为"差异,区别",例如:It won't make much difference whether you go today or tomorrow. 你

今天去或明天去没有多大关系。comparison 作"比较,对照"讲,例如:It is often useful to make a comparison between two things. 经常比较两件事物是有用的。division 意为"分,分开,分割",例如:An element is a substance, the nature of which cannot be changed by any ordinary method of division. 元素是一种物质,其性质不能被一般的分裂所改变。本句意思是"由于色盲,萨莉区分不出红色和黄色。"所以正确答案应是 B。

57. [C] consistent 作"一致的,连贯的,始终如一的"讲,例如:His actions are always consistent with his words. 他始终言行如一。relevant 意为"有关的,贴切的,恰当的",例如:With such knowledge he can determine which properties are relevant to his problems. 有了这些知识,他就可以决定哪些性质与自己的问题有关。simultaneous 作"同时发生的,同时存在的,同时的"讲,例如:Simultaneous interpretation in the United Nations is a demanding job. 联合国里的同声传译工作是很难做的。practical 意为"可行的,有实效的,实用的",例如:He took a reasonable view of the dispute and offered a solution that was fair, sensible and practical. 他对这一争端持通情达理的态度,提出了一个公平、明智、切实可行的解决办法。本句意思是"你应该坚持,学生应该找出真实的与现实一致的答案。"所以正确答案应是 C。

58. [C] part 是不及物动词,作"分别,离别"讲,例如:Scarcely an hour has passed since we parted. 我们分开才一个小时。divide 意为"分,划分",例如:Is the land to be divided up or sold as a whole? 那块土地是分割,还是整块出售? separate 作"使……分离,使……分开,把……分离"讲,例如:England is separated from France by the English Channel. 英吉利海峡将英国和法国分开。abandon 意为"抛弃,放弃",例如:The order was given to abandon ship. 弃船的命令已经下达。本句意思是"为了集资,尼克拉婶婶不得不忍痛舍弃她的一些至爱物件。"所以正确答案应是 C。

59. [A] order 作"状态"讲,例如:Not that the machine is out of order, but that I have not learned how to operate it. 不是机器出了故障,而是我还没学会如何操作它。form 意为"形状,形态;外形,体型;形式,方式",例如:Which literary form do you like best? 你最喜欢哪种文学形式? state 作"状态,状况,情形"讲,例如:The child was in a state of neglect. 这个孩子没人管。circumstance 意为"情况,情形,环境",例如:Circumstances will force us finally to adopt this policy. 环境会迫使我们最终采纳这项政策。本句意思是"几个月前我买这辆车时,车的状况非常好。"所以正确答案应是 C。

60. [B] distaste 意为"(for)不喜欢,厌恶",例如:He has distaste for hard work. 他厌恶干重活。disapproval 意为"(of)不赞成,否决,不喜欢",例如:The roar of praise and disapproval swelled through the theater. 赞赏声及喝倒彩声震撼着整个剧院。She spoke with disapproval of his behaviour. 她不赞成他的行为。dissatisfaction 意为"(with)不满意,不高兴",例如:The government would be unwise to ignore the growing dissatisfaction with its economic policies. 政府忽视人民对其经

济政策的日益不满是不明智的。dismay 作"(over, at)惊慌,沮丧"讲,例如:I couldn't hide my dismay over (at) her poor grades. 看到她如此低的分数我掩饰不住我的惊愕和沮丧。本句意思是"那位顾客表示不喜欢那顶宽边帽。"所以正确答案应是 B。

61. [D]　versatile 意为"多方面的,多才多艺的",例如:He is a versatile athlete. 他是一位多才多艺的运动员。restless 作"安定的,焦虑的,烦躁的"讲,例如:Americans are historically a restless and mobile people. 美国人历来是爱动不爱静的民族。skilled 意为"熟练的,有技术的",例如:We need skilled workers who can assemble cars very quickly. 我们需要会迅速装配汽车的熟练工人。strong 作"强壮的,沉重的"讲,例如:Is this bridge strong enough to sustain heavy lorries? 这座桥经得起重型卡车通行吗? 为了修谷仓、扎篱笆、种庄稼、养牲畜,实际上农民必须无所不能。

62. [A]　in comparison with 意为"和……比较起来",既可以比较相同点也可以比较不同点,如:The tallest buildings in London are small in comparison with those of New York. 伦敦最高的楼房同纽约的比起来仍然很低。in proportion to 表示"与……成比例",例如:The insolence of the vulgar is in proportion to their ignorance: they treat everything with contempt which they do not understand. 庸人的傲慢与他们的无知成正比:他们轻视一切自己不懂的事物。in association with 作"与……联合,与……共同"讲,例如:They finished the work in association with their friends. 他们与朋友一起合作完成了这项工作。calculation 意为"计算",例如:Farad is too large a unit to be used in radio calculation. 法拉这个单位太大,在无线电计算中不便使用。本句意思是"和他的收入比较起来,他花在度假、过奢侈生活上的钱太多了。"所以正确答案应是 A。

63. [C]　frugal 意为"节俭的,节约的,廉价的",一般修饰人,例如:The more frugal and honest you are, the less power you need. 越节俭、越诚实的人越不需要权力。thrifty 意为"节俭的,俭约的",一般用来修饰动作,例如:It is thrifty to prepare today for the wants of tomorrow. 今天为明天打算就是节俭。economic 意为"经济(上)的,经济学的",要和 economical 区别开,后者意为"节俭的,经济的,精打细算的",例如:We talk of freedom, but today political freedom does not take us far unless there is economic freedom. 我们谈论自由,但今天除非有经济上的自由,否则政治自由对我们也是有限的。The new technique is economical of time and energy. 这项新技术既省时又节能。careful 意为"小心的,注意的,谨慎的",例如:Be careful of your thoughts; they may become words at any moment. 小心你的思想,它随时都可能变成言辞。本句意思是"他尽管很富有,但是仍然很节约钱。"所以正确答案应是 C。

64. [C]　chair 作"主持(会议)"讲,是及物动词,例如:He should learn how to chair a meeting. 他应学会如何主持会议。preside 是不及物动词,后跟介词 at 或 over,意为"作工作会议的主席,主持(会议)",例如:He was invited to preside over/at the opening ceremony of the trade fair. 他应邀主持了交易会的开幕式。introduce 作"介绍"讲,例如:Allow me to introduce you to the head of our department.

请允许我把你介绍给我们系主任。dominate 意为"统治,支配",例如:These is-sues dominated the election. 这些问题成为这次选举的主要话题。本句意思是"经理由于出差,要求我主持每周一次的员工会议。"所以正确答案应是 C。

65. [A] origin 作"来源,根源"讲,例如:Do you know the origin of the custom of giving presents at Christmas? 你知道在圣诞节互赠礼品这一风俗的来源吗? genera-tion 意为"代,一代,世代,一代人",例如:This farm has been transferred from fa-ther to son for generations. 这个农场父子相传已有好几代了。descent 作"下降"讲,例如:The company has gone into a descent because of falling demand. 由于市场需求下降,这家公司的生意每况愈下。cause 意为"原因,起因;理由,缘故",例如:They are doing research into the cause of cancer. 他们正在研究癌症的起因。本句意思是"目前还不清楚这个词的来源,但可以肯定的是,它不是源于希腊语。"所以正确答案应是 A。

2002 年英语专业四级考试语法与词汇参考答案与解析

41. [A] as 作连词,引导方式状语从句,作"像……的那样"讲,例如:Money is not the root of all evils as is usually claimed. 金钱并非像平常说的那样是万恶之源。本句意思是"她按经理的指示工作。"所以正确答案应是 A。

42. [C] neither 表示"两者都不",例如:Neither of the twins has finished their homework. 双胞胎中哪一个也没完成作业。本句意思是"那对双胞胎谁也没有被捕,因为我昨天晚上还在一个宴会上见到了他们俩。"所以正确答案应是 C。

43. [B] 根据 for some time now 就可知,这里需要使用现在完成进行时,例如:I'm in-debted to all the staff who have been working so hard. 我十分感激一直如此努力工作的全体员工。本句意思是"一段时间以来,世界各国的领袖都一直指出有必要就裁军问题达成共识。"所以正确答案应是 B。

44. [B]或[D] 关系副词 that 和 where 都可用来引导定语从句,用来修饰表示地点的先行词,这两个副词在从句中作状语,相当于"介词 + which",例如:The place where optimism most flourishes is the lunatic asylum. 乐观主义最盛行的地方是疯人院。Work is measured by the product of the force and the distance that the force acts. 功是以力和力的作用所通过的距离的乘积来测定的。本句意思是"你是否经历过这样的场合,你明知对方是对的,但你又不愿意同意其观点?"所以答案 B 和 D 均可。

45. [A] 关系代词 which 可以用来引导非限制性定语从句,表示对主句的解释说明,which 指代整个主句,例如:The camera has a lot of small buttons, which makes it rather awkward to use. 这架照相机有许多小按钮,用起来很不方便。本句意思是"我们刚在公寓里装了两台空调,这样会使明(今)年夏天的生活大不一样。"所以正确答案应是 A。

46. [C] 当不定式表示的动作发生在主句谓语动词前,可以根据具体情况使用完成时,例如:The liner is reported to have been in collision with an oil tanker. 据报道,这

艘客轮与一艘油轮相撞。本句意思是"据说爱滋病在过去的几年中对于那个地区的男女来说都是头号杀手。"所以正确答案应是 C。

47. [D] what little + 名词,含有"所仅有的"之意,例如:She saved what little money she could out of her slim salary to help her brother go to school. 她尽可能从她微薄的工资中留出钱来送她弟弟上学。本句意思是"她设法将从自己工资中节省出的仅有的钱来帮助她的兄弟。"所以正确答案应是 D。

48. [B] as 在此作连词,引导让步状语从句,从句内容要倒装,需要注意的是,在这里,名词前不能用冠词,例如:Tall man as Michael is, he is admired by few people. 虽然迈克尔是个大个子,但是很少有人尊敬他。本句意思是"尽管简有些傻,但是她也不可能作出这种事来。"所以正确答案应是 B。

49. [C] than 在语法上既是连词,和 more 一起引导比较状语从句,在语法上相当于关系代词,引导定语从句,修饰先行词 money,并在从句中作主语,再例如:She gave me the impression of having more teeth than were necessary for any practical purpose. 她给我的印象是,她长着比实际需要更多的牙齿。本句意思是"这次实验需要更多的资金投入。"所以正确答案应是 C。

50. [A] had it not been for 引导条件句,表示对一般过去的虚拟,例如:Had it not been for your advice, I would have got into trouble. 如果不是你的建议,我就会遇到麻烦。本句意思是"她要不是摔断了腿,就会通过考试了。"所以正确答案应是 A。

51. [B] 在 it is (high) time that 结构中,从句使用一般过去式,表示虚拟语气,意为"早该……了",暗示实际上还没有做,例如:It is high time that a doctor were sent for. 早就该让人去请医生了。It is high time that you got a wife and settled down. 你早该娶个妻子安个家了。本句意思是"你打算下学期学些什么课程?"本句意为"不知道,不过现在是作出决定的时候了。"所以正确答案应是 B。

52. [D] reward 在这里作"奖励,奖赏"讲,例如:The only reward of virtue is virtue; the only way to have a friend is to be one. 报答美德的惟一办法是还报以美德;找朋友的惟一办法是自己成为别人的朋友。本句意思是"警方已经提供大笔悬赏金,以奖励提供有助于抓捕抢劫犯信息的人。"所以正确答案应是 D。

53. [C] narrowly 作"仅仅,勉强,差点"讲,例如:One car narrowly missed hitting the other one. 一辆车差点儿和另一辆相撞。The boy narrowly escaped being drowned. 那个男孩差一点被淹死。本句意思是"我很晚才到机场,差点误了飞机。"所以正确答案应是 C。

54. [A] justified 作"有根据的,正确的"讲,例如:If the subject matter is difficult, careful reading is justified; when it is easy, one should zip through it. 如果材料很难,就该认真仔细地阅读;如果不难,则应快速浏览。本句意思是"这部电影很受欢迎,表明评论家们的担忧是没有根据的。"所以正确答案应是 A。

55. [D] obliging 意为"乐于助人的,有礼貌的",例如:The United States and Australia were not so obliging. The two countries banned the import of British beef as early

as 1988. 美国和澳大利亚就没有那么乐于助人了,这两个国家早在 1988 年就开始禁止进口英国牛肉了。本句意思是"博物馆馆长非常热心,同意我们慢慢观看这些古籍手稿。"所以正确答案应是 D。

56. [B] bid 意为"(拍卖时)喊(价),出(价)",例如:Bids for building the bridge were invited. 应邀参加建造那座桥梁的投标。本句意思是"这家跨国公司正在投标一家不动产公司。"所以正确答案应是 B。

57. [A] indicative 作"标示的,指示的,陈述的"讲,例如:His presence is indicative of his interest in our plan. 他的到来表明他对我们的计划有兴趣。本句意思是"该党得票减少表明其政策缺少支持。"所以正确答案应是 A。

58. [B] regrettable 作"可叹的,可惜的"讲,例如:What is the fastest while the slowest, the longest while the shortest, the most ordinary while the most valuable, ignored most easily while most regrettable in the world is time. 世界上最快而又最慢、最长而又最短、最平凡而又最珍贵、最容易被人忽视而又最令人后悔的就是时间。本句意思是"令人遗憾的是,工会和资方之间缺乏交流。"所以正确答案应是 B。

59. [D] confidently 意为"充满信心地",例如:If one advances confidently in the direction of his dreams and endeavours to live the life he imagined, he will meet with a success unexpected in common hours. 如果他信心百倍地朝着自己的梦想前进,并且努力去创造自己所想像的那种生活,那么他便会取得平常意想不到的成功。而 assuredly 意为"确定地,无疑地",例如:We must indeed all hang together, or most assuredly, we shall all hang separately. 我们必须拧成一股绳,不然,可以肯定,我们将逐个被拧断。另外,confidentially 则作"秘密地,机密地"讲。本句意思是"这位老师信心十足,希望他的学生都能通过大学入学考试。"所以正确答案应是 D。

60. [B] average 意为"普通的,平常的,平均的",例如:The average man, who does not know what to do with his life, wants another one which will last forever. 不知道如何度过一生的普通人,总想获得另一种永恒的生命。而 normal 作"正常的,标准的,常态的"讲,例如:The perfectly normal person is rare in our civilization. 在我们这个文明世界中,几乎找不到完全正常的人。usual 作"通常的,惯常的"讲,例如:All that happens is as usual and familiar as the rose in spring and the crop in summer. 世间发生的一切,如春天的玫瑰和夏日的庄稼一样,都是既平常又熟悉的事。general 作"一般的,普遍的,综合的"讲,例如:Liberty cannot be preserved without a general knowledge among the people. 人民没有普遍理解自由,自由便不能保持。本句意思是"在中国,普通城市家庭花在住房上的钱比以前的要多。"所以正确答案应是 B。

61. [C] claim 意为"声称,主张",例如:A man claiming to represent every minority group in the city won the election for mayor. 一个声称能够代表城市里每一个少数民族的人赢得了市长选举。confess to 中 to 是介词,后可跟名词或动名词,例如:The man confessed to robbing a woman of her purse. 那人供认曾抢过一位妇女的钱包。confirm 意为"证实,认可;使坚定,加强",例如:The news has not been

confirmed officially. 消息尚未得到官方证实。本句意思是"这位新同事声称，在他加入我公司前曾在几家大公司工作过。"所以正确答案应是 C。

62. [D]　extract 作"节录，引文，选段"讲，例如：He applied to the publisher for permission to reprint an extract. 他向出版者请求准予转印节录。而 fragment 作"碎片，断片；(文艺作品等)残存部分"讲，例如：Liberty and civilization are only fragments of rights wrung from the strong hands of wealth and book learning. 自由和文明不过是从有钱人和读书人有力的手中强夺过来的一些权利的碎片。本句意思是"在阅读课上，老师要求学生看这部小说的选段。"所以正确答案应是 D。

63. [B]　vacant 作"空的；空缺的，悬空的"讲，例如：The vacant post was advertised in today's paper. 今天报纸上刊登了那个空缺职位的招聘广告。本句意思是"暑假里要在这个地方的旅馆找一间空房很难。"所以正确答案应是 B。

64. [A]　get over 则作"痊愈，恢复，淡忘"讲，如：Sooner or later you will get over the shock. 迟早你会从惊恐中恢复过来的。本句意思是"这对老夫妻将永远不能从丧子之痛中恢复过来。"所以正确答案应是 A。

65. [B]　apply 意为"应用，施用，运用"，例如：Apply yourself to true riches; it is shameful to depend upon silver and gold for a happy life. 要争取真正的财富，靠金银谋取幸福是不光彩的。本句意思是"现在科研成果很快就能应用于工厂生产。"所以正确答案应是 B。

2003 年英语专业四级考试语法与词汇参考答案与解析

41. [D]　在这里 wheat being by far the biggest cereal crop 是独立主格结构，用来表示解释说明，再例如：Almost all the metals are good conductors, with silver being the best. 几乎所有的金属都是好导体，银是最好的导体。本句意思是"农业是该国的主要收入来源，小麦是最重要的谷类作物。"所以正确答案应是 D。

42. [A]　根据句中的时间状语 for two days now，就可知这里需要使用完成时，例如：They have been peddling around the corner for weeks. 他们在附近已经叫卖了好几个星期了。另外，需要注意的是，表示"丢失，遗失"时，要用 missing 或 lost，例如：The power of love itself weakens and gradually becomes lost with age, like all the other energies of man. 爱情的力量，也像人的其他活力一样，会随着年龄而减弱，并逐渐消失。Ten passengers are missing, presumed dead. 10 名乘客失踪，据信已经死亡。本句意思是"杰克离家已经两天了，我真开始为他的安全担心。"所以正确答案应是 A。

43. [C]　在这里 whose 作关系代词，引导定语从句，在从句中作定语，修饰名词 magnificence，并和该名词一起作动词 reflects 的宾语。例如：Time, whose tooth gnaws away everything else, is powerless against truth. 时间的利齿可以吞噬一切别的东西，而对真理却无能为力。本句意思是"群山位于树林之颠，一条小河在河面上清楚地映出群山之雄伟壮丽。"所以正确答案应是 C。

44. [B]　这是一个复杂的疑问句。主句主语是 you，谓语动词是 said，因此发生倒装的是 you said。而 who was coming to see me in my office this afternoon 相当于 said 的宾语从句。虽然 who 放在句首,从句的主谓语并不倒装,这一点通过分解就可以知道,肯定句: you said who was coming to see me in my office this afternoon. 而疑问句则为 who did you say was coming to see me in my office this afternoon? 再例如: What do you suppose would happen if the director knew you felt that way? 要是主任知道你是那么想的话,你认为会怎样? Which bus do they say they would take? 他们说要乘坐哪趟车? How long did he tell you he waited? 他告诉你他等了多长时间? 本句意思是“你告诉过我谁今天下午要到我的办公室来看我。”所以正确答案应是 B。

45. [D] so much so that 作“如此以至于”讲,例如:At sports meet, if white and black are present, they support opposing sides and the result is friction—so much so that in many grounds only whites are allowed. 在体育项目上,如果黑人和白人都在场,他们分别支持对立方,结果就会产生摩擦,摩擦的结果是只有白人才能上运动场。He could see that she had been patient all her life, so much so that now, after years of it, her lips were set in a gentle and saintly smile. 他看得出,她一生都很有耐心,经过多年的忍耐以后,现在她的嘴边总挂着一丝温柔、圣洁的微笑。本句意思是“——阿兰喜欢吃汉堡吗?

——对,他非常喜欢,以至于他几乎每天都吃。”所以正确答案应是 D。

46. [B] 根据句子结构,这里要使用名词性物主代词 hers,来指代 her ideas。再例如: Woman's dearest delight is to wound Man's self-conceit, though Man's dearest delight is to gratify hers. 女人最大的乐事是伤害男人的自负心理,男人最大的乐事却是满足女人的自负心理。本句意思是“在我看来,你的看法和她的一样不同寻常。”所以正确答案应是 B。

47. [A] 由于 it is essential that 句型中谓语动词要使用虚拟语气,例如:It is essential that he (should) be prepared for this. 重要的是他要为此作好准备。由此我们可以将 [B] 排除。介词 of 和 for 都可以引导出不定式的逻辑主语,其区别为: of 后面的名词或代词与句子表语是逻辑主表关系,而 for 后面的名词或代词却与句子表语没有任何关系,例如:It is kind of you to help me out. 你真好,帮助我度过了难关。It is easy for one to propose a plan. 提出一个计划是很容易的。本句意思是“开幕式是一个重要场合,我们必须做好准备。”所以正确答案应是 A。

48. [B] 除在极个别的情况下,分词作状语时,应与句子的主语存在一定的逻辑关系(主谓或动宾关系),否则该分词就应该有自己的逻辑主语或逻辑宾语,来构成“名词或代词 + 分词”结构,即独立分词结构,独立分词结构一般可置于句首,也可置于句末,用来表示原因、时间、条件、方式或伴随情况等。值得一提的是,使用独立分词结构是避免出现悬垂结构的重要方法之一,例如:The experiment being over, the students began their discussion. 做完实验,学生们开始讨论。Other things being equal, iron heats faster than aluminium. 其他条件相同的条件下,铁比铝加热快。Nobody having any more to say, the meeting was

closed. 大家都没有什么可说的了，会议也就结束了。本句意思是"时间允许的话,庆祝活动将如期举行。"所以正确答案应是 B。

49. [D] 连词 as 作"即使"讲,可以引导让步状语从句,此时从句不能使用正装语序,例如:Much as we admire Shakespeare's comedies, we cannot agree that they are superior to his tragedies. 虽然我们推崇莎士比亚的喜剧,但对其喜剧胜于悲剧的说法却不敢苟同。Much as he likes her, he does get irritated with her sometimes. 尽管他喜欢她,可有时他确实也对她发火。本句意思是"尽管我非常喜欢经济学,但是我更喜欢社会学。"所以正确答案应是 D。

50. [C] 由 neither ... nor 连接的两个名词或代词共同作主语时,谓语动词应与后一个主语的人称和数一致,例如:If law and order is not preserved, neither the citizen nor his property is safe. 如果法律和秩序得不到维护,公民的人身和财产就得不到安全。Neither Russia nor the United States has been able to discover a mutually satisfactory program for gradual disarmament. 俄国和美国双方都没能找到一个能使双方都满意的分阶段裁军方案。Time cures sorrows and squabbles because we all change, and are no longer the same persons. Neither the offender nor the offended is the same. 时间可以治愈忧伤,消除争吵,因为我们都在改变,都不再与从前一样了。不管是触犯者和被触犯者也已不是从前的那个人了。本句意思是"进一步讨论这个问题也没有什么用处了,因为你和我今天不会达成任何共识。"所以正确答案应是 C。

51. [A] which 引导的修饰整个主句的非限制性定语从句,一般对主句的内容作进一步的说明,相当于一个并列分句,此时 which 可用 and this 代替,例如:She married Joe, which surprised everyone. 她嫁给了乔治,这使大家都感到意外。Liquid water changes to vapour, which is called evaporation. 液态水变为蒸汽,这个过程就叫作蒸发。Friction wears away metal of the moving parts, which shortens their effective working life. 摩擦会使运动部件的金属磨损,这就会缩短其有效的使用期限。本句意思是"他们克服了重重困难,提前两个月完成了这项工程,这是我们原先无论如何也想不到的。"所以正确答案应是 A。

52. [B] 在这里关系代词 that 引导定语从句,该代词在从句中作表语,例如:A young man married is a man that's marred. 年少成婚,毁人前程。Any woman will love any man that bothers her enough. 女人终会爱上死缠着她的男人。本句意思是"多年来的辛苦劳作使得他看上去非常疲倦,他现在一点也不像他 20 年前的样子。"所以正确答案应是 B。

53. [C] 当陈述句是一个主从复合句时,附加疑问部分一般要根据主句的谓语形式而定,例如:Frank is working late again. For this is the fifth time this week he's had to study late, isn't it? 弗兰克又开夜车了,这是他本周第五次学得很晚了,不是吗? It isn't colder today than it was yesterday, is it? 今天不如昨天冷,不是吗? 本句意思是"如果她稍微改变一下,她就会变得更和蔼可亲。"所以正确答案应是 C。

54. [D] 短语 in sight 是"能够被看见的"的意思,有被动含意,例如:The rocky point was

in sight, broad on the lee bow. 可以在背风的船头清楚地看见岩石的尖角。He conceded to newsmen that an immediate agreement was nowhere in sight. 他向记者们承认近期内没有希望达成协议。本句意思是"在海拔 3 000 英尺的地方，宽阔的平原慢慢展示在人们面前，远处的群山无时无刻不映入你的眼帘。"所以正确答案应是 C。

55. ［A］ latter 意为"（两者中的）后者"，例如：In science, as in life learning and knowledge are distinct, and the study to things, and not of books, is the source of the latter. 就像在现实生活中那样，就科学而言，学问和知识是截然不同的，后者来源于对具体事物的学习而不是对书本的学习。latest 作"最后的，最新的"讲，例如：The latest research findings of the institute took the world by storm. 该研究所的最新研究成果在世界上引起轰动。later 意为"后来，较迟"，例如：For evil news rides fast, while good news baits later. 好事不出门，坏事传千里。last 意为"上一个；最后的人或东西"，例如：A good husband is never the first to go to sleep at night or the last to awake in the morning. 好丈夫在夜晚决不会第一个睡着，在早上也不会最后一个醒来。本句意思是"文明人发展的过程中两个最重要的初级阶段是武器的发明和火的发现，尽管没有人确切知道人是何时掌握火的使用的。"所以正确答案应是 A。

56. ［C］ allowing for 作"考虑，酌情留出"讲，例如：Allowing for extras, the tour will cost $150. 把额外费用都算在内，这次旅行将花费 150 美元。It takes about two hours to get to their office building, allowing for possible traffic delays. 考虑到路上可能遇到的交通耽搁，到他们的办公大楼大约要花费两小时。acknowledge 意为"承认"，例如：None but the well-bred man knows how to confess a fault, or acknowledge himself in an error. 惟有良好教养的人才知道如何承认缺点和错误。afford 意为"有（能找到）足够的时间（金钱）去（做某事）"，例如：There is no comfort in adversity sweeter than art affords. 世上没有任何一种东西比艺术会给身处逆境的人带来更多的安慰和甜蜜。account for 意为"说明……的原因或理由"，例如：In war, moral considerations account for three-quarters, the balance of actual forces only for the other quarter. 在战争中，三分靠士气，一分靠兵力。本句意思是"考虑到交通耽搁，我们到火车站需要 20 分钟。"所以正确答案应是 C。

57. ［B］ 短语动词 answer for 意为"承受……的后果"，如：You will have to answer for your violent behavior in court. 你行为粗暴，你会在法庭上承担其后果的。The bus driver should answer for the safety of the passengers. 公共汽车司机应对旅客的安全负责。本句意思是"有朝一日他将不得不为他的下流行为负责。"所以正确答案应是 B。

58. ［A］ rare 意为"罕见的，稀罕"，例如：One can find women who have never had one love affair, but it is rare indeed to find any who have only had one. 一次风流韵事也没有的女子不难找到，难的是找到只有过一次风流韵事的女人。unusual 意为"与众不同的，独特的"，例如：It requires a very unusual mind to undertake the a-

nalysis of the obvious. 分析显而易见的事物需要极不寻常的头脑。extraordinary 意为"非常的,特别的,破例的;离奇的,使人惊奇的,非凡的",例如:The most absurd and the most rash hopes have sometimes been the cause of extraordinary success. 最荒唐、最轻率的希望有时会导致非凡的成功。unique 意为"独特的,无可匹敌的;惟一的,(书籍)孤本的",例如:A genius is a man who does unique things of which nobody would expect him to be capable. 天才能够完成别人都觉得他无法完成的事。本句意思是"除极例外的情况下,这位前总统现在不在公共场合露面。"所以正确答案应是 A。

59. [B] favourable 意为"有利的,顺利的,适宜的",例如:Heaven's favourable weather is less important than Earth's advantageous terrain, and Earth's advantageous terrain is less important than human unity. 天时不如地利,地利不如人和。favourite 意为"特别喜爱的",例如:Fishing is his favourite relaxation. 垂钓是他最喜爱的消遣。本句意思是"我们听到的一直都是对你工作有利的评论。"所以正确答案应是 B。

60. [D] vacant 意为"空的;空缺的,悬空的",例如:I was despairing when I saw a vacant cab. 正在绝望之际,我看到了一辆没有载客的出租车。empty 意为"空的,未占用的;空洞的,空虚的,不真实的",例如:It is hard for an empty sack to stand upright. 空囊难直立。blank 意为"空白的;茫然的",例如:Take a blank sheet of paper and write your name at the top. 拿出一张空白纸,把你的名字写在顶端。deserted 作"被遗弃的"讲,例如:Declining population in the centres of American cities has resulted in a large number of deserted buildings. 美国一些城市市中人口的下降,已经造成了大批住房被遗弃。本句意思是"在这个海滨旅馆暑假没有空闲房间。"所以正确答案应是 D。

61. [A] sign 的意思较广,既可指符号、记号,又可指以身体的某部位,如手、头等作出的动作来示意出内心想要表达的思想,例如:There are lots of signs in staves. 在乐谱中有很多符号。As I rushed into the house, my sister put her finger to her lips as a sign to be quiet. 我冲进屋子时,姐姐把手指放在嘴唇上示意我别出声。signal 意为"信号,暗号",指传达某种信息所用的、人人皆知的或约定俗成的信号,例如:Soldiers in ancient China used to use smoke signals on the Great Wall. 中国古代士兵曾在长城上用烽火作信号。mark 既可指具体的"标记,记号,印号,符号",又可指抽象的"标志,标识",例如:His feet left dirty marks on the floor. 他的双脚在地板上留下了很脏的脚印。board 意为"木板,板",例如:The warning boards pull out their own old nails. 木板翘曲,它上面的旧钉子就会掉落。本句意思是"一直往前开,然后你就会看到上海—南京高速公路的标志。"所以正确答案应是 A。

62. [C] show off 作"炫耀,卖弄,使……显眼,使……夺目"讲,例如:He wanted to show off before me. 他想在我面前炫耀。show up 意为"使……显现,显出,露出",例如:The fraud was shown up. 这个欺诈案被人揭露出了。show... around (round) "带领……参观(某地)",例如:Please show the students round the

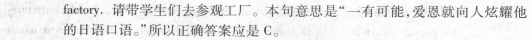

factory. 请带学生们去参观工厂。本句意思是"一有可能,爱恩就向人炫耀他的日语口语。"所以正确答案应是 C。

63. ［B］ scrap 意为"小片,碎屑;废料,废物",例如:A man comes round regularly collecting scraps. 有个人定时来收破烂儿。sheet 意为"被单,褥单;平板,薄片",例如:Lead sheet, if very thin, could completely stop X-rays. 即使铅板非常薄,也能完全阻断 X 射线的穿透。page 意为"页,一页",例如:The world is a book, and those who do not travel read only a page. 世界是一本书,没有旅行过的人只读了一页。slice 意为"薄片,切片,一片",例如:She spread the slice of bread with jelly. 她把果子冻敷在面包片上。本句意思是"房客除了一些破布片破纸片外,什么也没留下。"所以正确答案应是 B。

64. ［D］ fluctuate 意为"波动,变动,涨落",例如:There is something queer about the way his temperature fluctuates these days. 近些日子他的体温时高时低,这事有点奇怪。float 意为"漂浮,浮动,漂",例如:Writing should resemble floating clouds and flowing water, going whither it wants to go and stopping whenever it is right to stop. 作文应如行云流水,行于所当行,止于所不可不止。本句意思是"由于世界范围的经济低迷,股票市场上的分额出现了波动。"所以正确答案应是 D。

65. ［A］ intermediate 意为"中间的,居中的中级的,中等程度的",例如:Gray is intermediate between black and white. 灰色介于黑色和白色之间。medium 意为"中等的,适中的",例如:He is of medium height. 他是中等身材。本句意思是"我认为你可以选一门中级语言课,提高你的英语。"所以正确答案应是 A。

2004 年英语专业四级考试语法与词汇参考答案与解析

51. ［A］ so much as 用在否定句中,在该句型中,一般肯定前者,而否定后者。当然在否定句中也可以用 as much as。如果我们将该句的句子顺序调整为正常顺序,那么答案就更加显而易见了:I wasn't so much bothered by his loudness as by his lack of talent. 例如:Nothing spoils a romance so much as a sense of humour in the woman. 没有什么能比女人的幽默感更容易毁掉浪漫的爱情。Love, friendship, respect, do not unite people as much as a common hatred for something. 爱情、友谊和尊敬都不及对某种事物共同的憎恨那样能使人们联合起来。rather than 一般用在肯定句中,肯定前者,而否定后者,例如:Judge a man by his questions rather than his answers. 要判断一个人,看他的回答不如看他的问题。Few things are impossible in themselves; and it is often for want of will, rather than of means, that man fails to succeed. 几乎没有什么事情是根本做不成的;人们之所以失败,与其说是条件不够,不如说是缺乏意志。本句意思是"当然,那位唢呐手吹得够响亮的。但使我感到不安的,与其说他的音量太高,倒不如说他缺乏天分。"所以正确答案应是 A。

52. ［D］ be he rich or poor 是让步状语从句,相当于 whether he is rich or poor,如:He is the happiest, be he King or peasant, who finds peace in his home. 无论是国王还

是农夫,家庭和睦是最幸福的。In an urban society in which highly structured, fast-paced and stressful work looms large in life, experiences of a different nature, be it television watching or bird-watching, can lead to a self-renewal and a more "balanced" way of life. 在城市社会里中,层次严谨、节奏紧张、充满压力的工作占据着人们生活的很大一部分,所以一些与工作全然不同的体验,不管是看电视还是看鸟,都能使人们实现自我更新,使他们获得一种更趋"平衡"的生活方式。本句意思是"无论他是富还是穷,我都会嫁给他。"所以正确答案应是 D。

53. [C] 根据句子结构,我们可以看出,这里需要一个关系代词来引导动词 do 的宾语从句,而且该关系代词还必须在从句中作动词 lies 的主语,显然这个词只能是 whatever,例如:Liberty is the right to do whatever the law permits. 自由是在法律许可的范围内任意行事的权利。Books which teach and speak of whatever is highest and best are equally sacred, whatever be the tongue in which they are written, or the nation to which they belong. 那些能够教授和讲述任何最高、最好事物的书籍都是同样神圣的,不论它们是用什么语言写成的或者是属于哪个民族的。whichever 也可以起类似与 whatever 的上述作用,但是使用该词时,会暗示出一个选择范围,例如:You may choose whichever you want. 你想要哪一个,就挑选哪一个。本句意思是"政府已经承诺,将在职权范围内尽一切可能减轻洪灾地区受害者的苦难。"所以正确答案应是 C。

54. [D] 本题考查虚拟语气,从句使用过去完成时,主句要使用 would have done。例如:I don't know what would have happened if Jane hadn't been able to speak Greek. 要是珍妮不会说希腊语,我就不知道会发生什么事了。The instructions would have been clear enough if only she had spoken in a more distinct voice. 如果当时她用清晰的声音说出来,训令就不至于含糊不清。本句意思是"如果我不提前通知你,昨天就到达这里,那样你会不会感到惊讶?"所以正确答案应是 D。

55. [B] 在引导让步状语从句、条件状语从句和时间状语从句中,当从句的主语和主句的主语是一致的,而且从句的谓语动词是 be 的形式时,可将从句的主语和 be 的形式省略,如:When angry, count ten before you speak; if very angry, count a hundred. 愤怒的时候,开口说话之前先数到十;如果非常愤怒,就先数到一百。I have called this principle, by which each slight variation, if useful, is preserved, by the term Natural Selection. 每一个微小的变种,如果有用,就会保留下来,我把这个原则称为"自然选择"。本句意思是"如果得不到他认为应该得到的尊重,杰克就会勃然大怒,牢骚满腹。"所以正确答案应是 B。

56. [A] 与形容词 imperative 相关的名词性从句中要使用虚拟语气,也就是说,从句动词要使用原形或"should + 原形",例如:It is imperative that every one of us re-mould his world outlook. 我们每个人都必须改造自己的世界观。War is a matter of vital importance to the state; a matter of life or death, the road either to survival or to ruin. Hence, it is imperative that it be studied thoroughly. 兵者,国之

大事,死生之地,存亡之道,不可不察也。本句意思是"学生们都必须准时上交学期论文。"所以正确答案应是 A。

57. [A] the more... the more 结构表示"越……,越……",例如:The more things a man is ashamed of, the more respectable he is. 一个人感到羞愧的事情越多,越受人尊敬。The greater a man is, the more distasteful is praise and flattery to him. 一个人越伟大,对表扬和奉承就越反感。The more a man knows, the more he is inclined to be modest. 懂得越多的人就会越谦虚。本句意思是"承受满载卡车的地面面积越小,对卡车的压力就越大。"所以正确答案应是 A。

58. [B] sb. is believed to do sth. 作"某人被认为做某事"解,例如:The Vikings are believed to have discovered America. 人们相信是威金人发现了美洲。He is believed to be one of the best living composers. 他被认为是在世的最好的作曲家之一。本句意思是"据信财政部长正在考虑增加新税种,以增加额外税收。"所以正确答案应是 B。

59. [C] among 表示"是……之一","是……中之……",例如:Do not choose your wife at the dance, but in a field of grain among the harvestors. 别在舞会上物色你的妻子,要到谷地里去,在那些收割者中寻找。If well used, books are the best of all things; if abused, among the worst. 如果使用得当,书是最好的东西;如果滥用,书就是最坏的东西。本句意思是"价格、位置、促销和产品问题是人们制定市场战略时的传统关切。"所以正确答案应是 C。

60. [A] only if 在此为"只要,只有"意思,相当于 on condition that。当其置于句首时,主句要用倒装结构,例如:Only if a teacher has given permission, is a student allowed to enter this classroom. 只有得到老师的允许,学生才可以进这间教室。Only if the red light comes on, is there any danger to workers. 只要红灯一亮,就表示有危及工人的险情。if only 用来表示对现在或未来的愿望或用来表示与过去事实相反的愿望,句子用虚拟语气,例如:If only I were rich. 但愿我很富有。If only it would stop raining. 真希望雨能停。If only he had remembered to buy some apples. 他当时要是记得买些苹果来该多好。本句意思是"只要双方都接受这个协议,就可在这一地区建立持久的和平。"所以正确答案应是 A。

61. [C] 需要注意的是本句的主语 Mr. Wells,是单数,因此谓语动词要使用单数。例如:The hostess dressed in her Sunday best together with the guests of honour was seated comfortably in the drawing room. 女主人穿着她最好的礼服,和贵宾们一起舒适地坐在客厅里。begin, come, go, leave, start 等动词的现在进行时可以表示将来时意义,例如:They are coming to dinner tonight. 今晚他们要来吃晚饭。We're leaving for Rome next week. 我们下星期要到罗马去。本句意思是"威尔斯先生将在今天下午和他所有的家人一起动身去欧洲。"所以正确答案应是 C。

62. [D] disclose 作"(使)显露,揭露,泄露;公开,表明,说出"讲,例如:A man never discloses his own character so clearly as when he describes another's. 一个人在描述别人的性格时,最能暴露出自己的性格。discover 意为"发现,找到,使被知

晓",例如:When you aim for perfection, you discover it's a moving target. 当你把完美作为你的目标,你将发现完美是一个活动靶。uncover 作"移去(某物)的遮盖物,揭开(某物)的盖子;揭露,发现"讲,例如:What counts is to uncover the essence of a thing. 重要的是揭露事物的本质。本句意思是"有暗示表明,政府所有部长都应该将有关他们的财务权益的信息进行公开。"所以正确答案应是 D。

63. [D] pick up on 可作"拣起;自然学会"讲,例如:Where did you pick up your excellent English? 你在哪儿学到那么好的英语?Astronomers no longer regarded as fanciful the idea that man may one day pick up signals, which have been sent by intelligent beings on other planets. 人们能够接收到其他星球上有智慧的生命发来的信号,天文学家不再把这个想法看作胡思乱想了。clear up 作"(天)放晴;澄清"讲,例如:The teacher cleared up the harder parts of the story. 老师解释了故事中比较难懂的部分。catch up 意为"赶上",例如:Backwardness must be perceived before it can be changed. A person must learn from the advanced before he can catch up and surpass them. 认识落后,才能去改变落后;学习先进,才有可能赶超先进。make up 作"编造;化妆;组成"讲,例如:Historic responsibility has to make up for the want of legal responsibility. 历史责任一定要弥补法律责任的不足。本句意思是"下个星期我就要开始考试了,我要利用周末看点书。"所以正确答案应是 D。

64. [C] grudge 作"妒忌,怨恨,恶意"讲,例如:The high-minded man does not bear grudges, for it is not the mark of a great soul to remember injuries, but to forget them. 品格高尚的人不怀恨,因为一个伟大灵魂的标志不是牢记自己所受的屈辱,而是忘记它们。disgust 作"厌恶,恶心,作呕"讲,例如:Racial discrimination aroused popular indignation and disgust. 种族歧视引起了民众的愤慨和憎恶。curse 作"诅咒,咒骂,骂人话"讲,例如:Labour is the curse of the world, and nobody can meddle with it without becoming proportionately brutified. 劳累是这个世界发出的诅咒,谁倒行逆施,谁就会相应地受到惩罚。hatred 作"仇恨,憎恶,敌意"讲,例如:Physical deformity calls forth our charity. But the infinite misfortune of moral deformity calls forth nothing but hatred and vengeance. 身体畸形唤起我们的恻隐之心;而心灵畸形所造成的无穷灾祸则激起我们的厌恶和仇视。本句意思是"我很惊讶他们已经不再说话,但是他们之间好像都没有什么怨言。"所以正确答案应是 C。

65. [B] discharge 作"允许……离开,让……出院,开除"讲,例如:The prisoners were glad to get discharged. 犯人们获释都很高兴。dismiss 作"免……之职,解雇"讲,例如:The man was dismissed for culpable negligence. 这人因玩忽职守而被革职。expel 作"驱逐,开除,排出(气等)"讲,例如:One love expels another. 爱情相互排斥。resign 作"放弃,辞去;使听任,使顺从"讲,例如:The Prime Minister resigned for the good of the state. 首相为了国家的利益辞职了。本句意思是"玛丽希望下星期出院。"所以正确答案应是 B。

66. ［D］ worthless 作"无价值的，无用的"讲，例如：No matter how dry a desert may be，it is not necessarily worthless. 沙漠无论多么干旱，也未必没有价值。invaluable 作"无价的，非常宝贵的，极贵重的"讲，例如：Many invaluable documents relating to the early period of the revolution are preserved in the museum. 博物馆里收藏着许多有关革命初期的珍贵文献。priceless 作"无价的，昂贵的"讲，例如：The colleges of this country have been a priceless element in the making of the freedom and might of the nation. 该国的高等院校是构成该民族自由和力量的无法估价的要素。unworthy 作"不值得的，不足取的"讲，例如：Along with thoughts which are unworthy of us，we have ones of which we are not worthy. 我们既有比我们自身高贵的思想，也有比我们自身卑贱的思想。本句意思是"一幅画一旦被证明是赝品，那就一钱不值了。"所以正确答案应是 D。

67. ［C］ restore 可作"恢复，复兴；修复，重建"讲，例如：True revolutions in art restore more than they destroy. 真正的艺术革命是重建多于毁灭。All of us bear witness to the dissolution of our piece of creation. Only the novelist can restore to us，in the miracle of ink that pours itself like blood onto paper，the lineaments of our lost worlds，alive. 我们都眼见自己创造物的变化消亡，惟有小说家能凭借墨水拥有像血一样自行流注纸上的奇迹，为我们恢复失去的世界，使它的面貌活灵活现。renew 作"更新，使恢复"讲，例如：We must always change，renew，rejuvenate ourselves；otherwise we harden. 我们必须不断地改变、更新自己，使自己富有朝气；否则我们会变得僵硬。recover 作"挽回，弥补"讲，例如：Trees，when they are lopped and cut，grow up again in a short time，but men，being once lost，cannot easily be recovered. 树木经过修剪后，可以在短时期内再长好，但是人的品性一旦败坏了，就不容易修复了。revive 作"（使）苏醒，（使）恢复知觉；（使）复用，（使）复兴"讲，例如：The success revived his spirits and hopes. 成功使他精神振奋，重燃希望之火。本句意思是"吉米在博物馆修复艺术品，以此谋生。"所以正确答案应是 C。

68. ［D］ drip 作"滴下，滴水"讲，例如：The rain was dripping from the trees. 雨水正从树上滴下。The tap was dripping. 水龙头在滴水。drain 作"慢慢流走，排出"讲，例如：An unfulfilled vocation drains the colour from a man's entire existence. 一种未完成的使命会使整个人生黯然失色。drop 作"使……落下"讲，例如：Drop the hammer down to me. 把榔头扔下来给我。spill 作"（使）溢出，（使）溅出"讲，例如：The wrecked truck spilled its freight over the road. 出事的卡车把货物摔落在路上。本句意思是"因为浴室的水龙头一直在滴水，我昨晚没睡着。"所以正确答案应是 D。

69. ［A］ outline 作"提纲，要点，概括"讲，例如：The blueprint is to the builder what（as）the outline is to the writer. 蓝图对于建筑师就像提纲对于作家一样。reference 作"谈到，提及；参照，参考"讲，例如：In science，read，by preference，the newest books；in literature，the oldest. 在科学著作中，你最好参考最新的书；在文学著作中，你最好读最旧的书的。frame 作"构架，骨架，结构；框架，框子；体

格,身体"讲,例如:All thoughts, all passions, all delights, /Whatever stirs this mortal frame, /All are but ministers of Love,/ And feed his sacred flame. 一切思想、激情和欢乐,凡是肉身的一切都只不过是爱神的使者,使他的圣火烧得更旺。outlook 作"景色;前景,前途;观点,看法"讲,例如:The employment outlook for the next year is based on in part contracts signed this year. 今年签订合同的多少部分上决定明年的就业前景。本句意思是"这本书概括地介绍了他截止目前的研究的方向。"所以正确答案应是 A。

70. [B]　shiver 作"颤抖,发抖"讲,例如:She is shivering with cold so that her teeth are chattering. 她冷得直哆嗦,牙齿轧轧作响。spin 作"旋转"讲,例如:Ballet dancers must practice spinning on their toe. 芭蕾舞演员必须练习用脚尖旋转跳舞。shake 作"(使)摇动,(使)挥动,(使)震动;动摇,减弱"讲,例如:He stretched out to shake hands with the guests. 他伸出手去和客人们握手。stagger 作"摇晃,蹒跚蹒跚,踉跄"讲,例如:The wounded man staggered along. 受伤的人摇摇晃晃地走路。本句意思是"她站在外面的雪地里,冻得浑身发抖。"所以正确答案应是 B。

71. [D]　fit 作"使适合,使符合,合身"讲,该词的过去分词可表"合适的,适合的"之意,例如:Language happily restrict the mind to what is of its own native growth and fitted for it, as rivers and mountains bound countries. 语言得意洋洋地把思想限定在适合自己自然发展的范围内,就像河流与山脉限定着国家的疆界。adapt 作"使适应,适合;改编,改写"讲,例如:The reasonable man adapts himself to the world; the unreasonable one persists in trying to adapt the world to himself. 明白事理的人使自己适应世界;不明事理的人硬想使世界适应自己。equip 作"配备,装备,使有准备"讲,例如:This laboratory ought to be equipped again with modern apparatuses. 这个实验室应该用现代化的设备重新装备。suit 作"适合,使满意,中……的意"讲,例如:The same measures will not suit all circumstances, and we may play the same trick once too often. 同一措施不能适合所有的环境。同一把戏不能玩个不停。本句意思是"二楼的所有房间都铺有很得体的地毯,费用都包括在房价里了。"所以正确答案应是 B。

72. [B]　短语 to the exclusion of 作"把……除外,排斥"讲,例如:A leading member should never concentrate all his attention on one or two problems, to the exclusion of others. 一个领导人不能把全部注意力只集中在一两个问题上而不顾其他。本句意思是"他只打网球,不做其他任何体育活动。"所以正确答案应是 B。

73. [D]　emphatic 作"强调的,着重的,加强语气的"讲,例如:He answered the question with an emphatic "No." 他用一个加强语气的"不"字回答了这个问题。eloquent 作"雄辩的,有说服力的,口才好的"讲,例如:Silence is more eloquent than words. 沉默是更有说服力的言词。Eyes are as eloquent as lips. 眼睛像嘴一样会说话。effective 作"有效的,生效的"讲,例如:To be prepared for war is one of the most effective means of preserving peace. 作好战争的准备,是保持和平最有效的办法。emotional 作"感情(上)的,情绪(上)的;(易)激动

· 234 ·

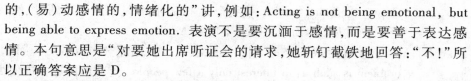

的，（易）动感情的，情绪化的"讲，例如：Acting is not being emotional，but being able to express emotion. 表演不是要沉湎于感情，而是要善于表达感情。本句意思是"对要她出席听证会的请求，她斩钉截铁地回答："不！"所以正确答案应是 D。

74. ［A］ vibrant 作"充满生气的，兴奋的"讲，例如：The new socialist world，on the other hand，is vibrant and alive. 而在另一方面，新兴的社会主义世界却生机勃勃，充满活力。violent 作"剧烈的，猛烈的；厉害的，极端的；（死伤等）暴力造成的"讲，例如：Hatred is something peculiar. You will always find it strongest and most violent where there is the lowest degree of culture. 仇恨是一种奇特的东西。文化程度最低，仇恨情绪往往最强烈。energetic 作"有力的，精力旺盛的，精神饱满的"讲，例如：An energetic middle life is，I think，the only safe precursor of a vitally happy old age. 我认为，精力旺盛的中年生活是生气勃勃的幸福晚年的惟一可靠预兆。本句意思是"每个参观过这座城市的人都认为，这是一个充满了生机与活力的城市。"所以正确答案应是 A。

75. ［C］ thereafter 作"此后，其后"讲，例如：His mother died when he was young；thereafter he devoted himself to medicine study. 他年轻时，母亲就去世了，这以后他便致力于医学研究。thereof 作"由此，其"讲，例如：They have discussed the evil and the remedy thereof. 他们讨论了这项弊端及其补救办法。thereby 作"因此，从而"讲，例如：And so from hour to hour，we ripe and ripe，and then from hour to hour，we rot and rot；and thereby hangs a tale. 就这样，随着时间的推移，我们不断成熟，随着时间的推移，我们变得老朽，于是就有了一段故事。thereabouts 作"在附近的某地；近于（某数目、数量、时间），大约"讲，例如：The factory is in Leeds，or somewhere thereabouts. 那家工厂在利兹，也许在利兹附近。I'll be home at 8 o'clock or thereabouts. 我 8 点钟回家，或 8 点左右。本句意思是"两个月前，我们在一次晚会上碰上了玛丽和他的丈夫，从此以后我们再没有任何联系。"所以正确答案应是 C。

2005 年英语专业四级考试语法与词汇参考答案与解析

51. ［A］ 本题考查的是虚拟语气的用法：条件从句中使用一般过去时，主句要使用 would do 来表示对一般现在的虚拟，例如：If there were no bad people，there would be no good lawyer. 假如没有坏人，就不会有好律师。Many would be wise if they did not think themselves wise. 许多人原本会成为聪明人——如果他们不自以为聪明。本句意思是"如果你将形势向律师解释一下，他能给你提供比我的要好的建议。"所以正确答案应是 A。

52. ［A］ 根据句意，尽管威尔斯先生是一位社会党人，但是他不同情劳动阶级。我们看出在这里主从句是转折关系，因此要使用连词 although，例如：Although the world is full of suffering，it is full also of the overcoming of it. 虽然世界多苦难，但是苦难总是能战胜的。Personally I'm always ready to learn，although I do not

always like being taught. 就我个人来说，我总是愿意学习的，虽然我并不总是愿意被别人教。所以正确答案应是 A。

53. [B] such as to 后跟不定式，引出结果状语，作"如此……以致……"讲，例如：The problem is such as to interest only a few people. 这样的问题只能使少数人感兴趣。本句意思是"他的讲话只会使出席会议的每个人都感到厌烦。"所以正确答案应是 B。

54. [B] come, go, leave, arrive 等动词的进行时，可表示将来概念，在这里 was coming 表示过去将来概念，例如：He said that he was arriving in ten minutes. 他说10分钟后就会赶到的。It amazed me to hear that you were leaving. 听说你要走，我感到十分惊愕。本句意思是"詹姆士刚刚到，我是昨天才知道他要来的。"所以正确答案应是 B。

55. [D] 在这里现在完成时表示过去开始一直持续到现在的动作；will be 表示现在将来的动作，例如：Women who have been happy in a first marriage, are the most apt to venture upon a second. 初次婚姻很幸福的女人最易于冒险尝试第二次婚姻。As to marriage or celibacy, let a man take which course he will, he will be sure to repent. 至于单身还是结婚，让男人自愿选择吧，但不管他怎么做，他肯定都要后悔。本句意思是"我一直明白，而且将永远明了自己作为一个公民的道德义务。"所以正确答案应是 D。

56. [A] some 在这里作"某个，某种"讲，相当于 certain，例如：The offhand decision of some commonplace mind high in office at a critical moment influences the course of events for a hundred years. 身居要职的平庸者随便作出的决定，在某个关键时刻竟会影响事态发展达百年之久。另外，type of 后跟可数名词单数时不需要用不定冠词，例如：A barograph is essentially an aneroid barometer with a type of fountain pen attached to the point. 自记气压计实际就是指针上装有一种自来水笔的无液气压表。本句意思是"因为燃料供给有限，而且很多人非常浪费，我们将不得不在我们家里安装一种太阳能设备。"所以正确答案应是 A。

57. [C] 显然这里要使用过去时，"was able to do sth." 表示过去通过努力设法做成某事，例如：After the police caught the murderer, the villagers were able to live in security once more. 警方抓获杀人犯后，村民们又可平安度日了。本句意思是"我1984年到过那里，那是我惟一一次能够在整整两天里完成这次旅程。"所以正确答案应是 C。

58. [B] anything but 作"根本不是"讲，相当于 not at all，例如：That support is anything but safe. 那个支柱一点也不安全。而 nothing but 则作"正是，只是"讲，例如：Nowadays nothing but money counts: fortune brings honours, friendships, the poor man everywhere lies low. 如今只有金钱才具有价值：财富带来荣耀、友谊，而贫穷的人总是在最底层的。本句意思是"尽管我知道他最后一次考试没及格，但他一点也不傻。"所以正确答案应是 B。

59. [B] much of a 表示"很好的……"之意，相当于 a very good，例如：He is much of a scholar. 他一个很好的学者。该短语的比较级则为 more of a，例如：He is

English

英语专业四级12年真题试卷详解

236

much more of a dancer than I. 他舞跳得比我好的多。本句意思是"你认识蒂姆的哥哥吗？他比蒂姆更像一位运动员。"所以正确答案应是 B。

60. [B] 在 It was the first time that 句型的从句一般要使用过去完成时,例如:It was the first time that Hurstwood had had a chance to see her facing the audience quite alone. 这是赫斯特伍德第一次有机会看到她独自一人面对观众。it is high time that 从句中要使用一般过去时构成虚拟语气,表示早就该做而尚未做的事,例如:It is high time that they were taught a lesson. 早就该教训他们一顿了。本句意思是"那不是他第一次背叛我们,我认为早就该对他采取行动了。"所以正确答案应是 B。

61. [A] there being 构成动名词的复合结构作介词 of 的宾语,再例如:I had no idea of there being so many wonderful flower in the country. 我过去根本就没想到这个国家有这么多漂亮的花卉。而 for there to be 则为不定式的复合结构,可作动词宾语,例如:It isn't cold enough for there to be a frost tonight, so I can leave Jim's car out quite safely. 今晚天不太冷,不会下霜,因此我可把吉姆的小汽车放在户外,而不必担心安全问题。本句意思是"今年举行大选的可能性如何?"所以正确答案应是 A。

62. [D] object to doing 是固定搭配,相当于 be opposed to doing,表示"反对"之意,例如:I object to being treated like a child. 我不喜欢被当成一个孩子。I am much opposed to your going abroad. 我非常反对你出国。本句意思是"会议延期召开是因为我们都反对在约翰缺席的情况下召开。"所以正确答案应是 D。

63. [C] 倒装结构 should sb. do 表示"万一"之意,例如:Should he misbehave like that again, he would be punished. 如果他再像那样胡来的话,他就会受到惩罚。if sb. had 表示虚拟语气,例如:If we had time, we could visit more places. 如果我们有时间,就能参观更多的地方了。in case 引导的从句中要使用动词原形或"should + 动词原形",表示"以免"之意,例如:Be strict with your children in case they feel superior to other children. 对你的孩子要严格,以免使他们觉得高别人一等。本句意思是"你的打印机万一还有什么问题,请联系经销商以获取建议。"所以正确答案应是 C。

64. [C] on condition that 引导从句,表示"只要,以……为条件",例如:I'll lend you this book on condition that you return it within ten days. 我可以借给你这本书,条件是 10 天内归还。only if 作"只要,只有"讲,相当于 on condition that,但是该短语后不可再跟 that,例如:Only if a teacher has given permission, is a student allowed to enter this classroom. 只有得到老师的允许,学生才可以进这间教室。on occasion 意为"有时,不时地",在句子中作状语,如:He goes to the cinema on occasion. 他有时去看电影。on purpose 作"故意地"讲,例如:Do you think that the cruel act was done on purpose? 你认为这残暴的行为是蓄意进行的吗?本句意思是"他要我借给他些钱,我同意了,但条件是他下星期还我。"所以正确答案应是 C。

65. [C] it 指代上文动词短语 stay away from school,例如:He who would do good to anoth-

er must do it in minute particulars; general good is the plea of the scoundrel, hypocrite and flatterer. 行善总是具体的、特定的;抽象的、笼统的行善是恶棍、伪君子和献媚者的托辞。If you wage war, do it energetically and with severity. This is the only way to make it shorter, and consequently less inhuman. 如果打仗,就要毫不留情地全力去打。这是缩短战争的惟一方法,因此也可以减少战争的残酷。本句意思是"孩子们不去上学,各有各的原因。"所以正确答案应是 C。

66. [B] 请参见第 56 题解析,同时请参见更多例句:He refused to put up with that kind of treatment. 他拒绝忍受那种待遇。Surely he didn't steal it; he is not that kind of person. 他肯定不会偷,他不是那种人。本句意思是"——你眼睛盯着看什么呢?

——我过去从未见过这种树。"所以正确答案应是 B。

67. [D] light at the end of the tunnel 表示不愉快的事情就将结束,黑暗即将过去,光明就要来临。本句意思是"虽然我们前面仍然还有很多问题,但是到明年这个时候,黑暗就将过去,光明就会到来。"所以正确答案应是 D。

68. [B] 短语 be under stress 表示"在承受压力之下",例如:Worry over his job and his son's health put him under a great stress. 担心自己的工作,又担心儿子的身体,他陷入了极度紧张状态。本句意思是"我们都知道到他正承受着巨大的压力,所以我们对他的坏脾气都装作没看到。"所以正确答案应是 B。

69. [A] move on to 表示"转移(到新事物上)",例如:I think we've talked enough about that; let's move on to the next. 我想那一点我们已谈得够多了,谈下一个话题吧。而 move out 则意为"迁出",move off 作"离开,出发"讲,move along 意为"向前(后)移动"。本句意思是"导演打手势让演员上下一场。"所以正确答案应是 A。

70. [C] impractical 作"不切实际的"讲,例如:He is not the impractical bookworm that he used to be. 他不再像从前那样是一个不切实际的书生了。imaginative 作"想像力丰富的"讲,例如:The tragedy of the world is that those who are imaginative have but slight experience, and those who are experienced have feeble imaginations. 世界的悲剧就在于有想像力的人缺乏经验,而有经验的人又缺乏想像力。ingenious 作"灵巧的,巧妙的"讲,例如:Can you detect any flaw in his ingenious theory? 你能在他的精妙理论中找出什么漏洞吗? theoretical 作"理论(上)的"讲,例如:Wisdom which is only theoretical and never put into practice, is like a double rose; its colour and perfume are delightful, but withers away and leaves no seed. 智慧只是理论而不能付诸实践,诸如一朵重瓣的玫瑰,虽然花色艳丽,香味馥郁,凋谢了却没有种子。本句意思是"他的同事总是指责他的观点不切实际。"所以正确答案应是 C。

71. [D] protest against 作"抗议,反对"讲,例如:The group protested against the country's foreign policy. 这一团体反对该国的对外政策。contradict 是及物动词,意为"反驳,抗辩",例如:You are a woman; you must never speak what you think; you words must contradict your thought, but your actions may contradict your words. 你

是女人:你千万别讲你想的事情;你的话一定会跟你的思想矛盾,而你的行动又可能跟你的话矛盾。counter 也是及物动词,意为"应对,反击,对付",如:They countered our proposal with one of their own. 他们用自己的建议来反对我们的。本句意思是"成千上万人走出家门走上大街,抗议地方当局决定修一条横穿田野的公路。"所以正确答案应是 D。

72. [A] minority 和上文中的 majority 构成对比,作"少数,少数派"讲,例如:Though the will of the majority is in all cases to prevail, that will, to be rightful, must be reasonable; the minority posses their equal right, which equal laws must protect, and to violate would be oppression. 大多数人的意志总是占优势的,但是公正地说,这种意志必须是合理的;少数人拥有同等法律必须加以保护的同等权利,破坏该权利就是压迫。本句意思是"尽管大多数护士都是女性,但是在医疗界高级人员中女性处少数。"所以正确答案应是 A。

73. [B] take effect 意为"生效,奏效",如:The new system of taxation will take effect next year. 新税制将于明年生效。而 carry into effect 和 put into effect 为及物短语,作"实行,实施,使生效,实现"讲,例如:When the time is ripe, the scheme will be put (carried) into effect. 时机一成熟这个计划就会被付诸实施。本句意思是"约翰逊教授退休决定从明年一月开始。"所以正确答案应是 B。

74. [A] finance 作动词时,表示"为……提供资金",例如:Unlike commercial motion pictures, educational films are not financed by paid admission. 教学片和商业片不同,教学片没有票房收入。动词 budget 作"事先编列预算"讲,例如:We needed help budgeting our income. 我们必需帮助计划我们的收入。本句意思是"总统解释说,税收的目的是为政府支出提供更多的资金。"所以正确答案应是 A。

75. [C] intense 作"强烈的,剧烈的"讲,intense heat 意为"酷暑",例如:Many people couldn't stand intense heat. 许多人不堪酷热。I can hardly stand such intense heat in summer. 夏季的酷热简直使我难以忍受。本句意思是"这个山区夏天一点也不热。"所以正确答案应是 C。

76. [A] forbid 作"(通过法律、规章等)禁止,不允许"讲,例如:The students in the dormitories were forbidden, unless they had special passes, to stay out after 11 pm. 除非有特别的证件,住在宿舍的学生晚上 11 点以后不准在外面逗留。本句意思是"由于可能损毁这些珍贵壁画,此处严禁拍照。"所以正确答案应是 A。

77. [C] pull through 作"度过难关,恢复健康"讲,例如:An announcement has been made by the Government that our country has pulled through the most difficult period. 政府已宣布我们国家已度过最困难的时期。What through good medical care and what through his natural strength, he pulled through very quickly. 一方面因为有良好的医疗措施,一方面因为他自己有很强的体力,所以他很快便恢复了健康。本句意思是"看起来布朗先生的病情很严重,他能否挺得过来值得怀疑。"所以正确答案应是 C。

78. [D] convenience 意为"便利,方便",例如:The telephone is the greatest nuisance a-

mong conveniences, the greatest convenience among nuisances. 电话是使人方便之物中的最大烦恼之物,使人烦恼之物中的最大方便之物。The reason for having diplomatic relations is not to confer a compliment, but to secure a convenience. 建立外交关系不是为了表达敬意,而是为了得到方便。本句意思是"自90年代初期以来,大多数企业倾向于提供按需生产、随时供应的商品和服务,以方便顾客而不是公司。"所以正确答案应是D。

79. [C] sign 可指符号、记号,又可指以身体的某部位,如手、头等作出的动作来示意出内心想要表达的思想,例如:As I rushed into the house, my sister put her finger to her lips as a sign to be quiet. 我冲进屋子时,姐姐把手指放在嘴唇上示意我别出声。signal 意为"信号,暗号",指传达某种信息所用的、人人皆知的或约定俗成的信号,例如:A red light is a signal of danger. 红灯是危险的信号。gesture 作"姿势,手势,姿态,表示"讲,例如:We sent her flowers as a gesture of sympathy. 我们给她送花以表同情。本句意思是"在进教堂时,牧师用手指划了一个十字。"所以正确答案应是C。

80. [B] sparsely 作"稀疏地,稀少地"讲,例如:Relative to its size, the city is sparsely populated. 与其面积相比,这个城市人口稀少。本句意思是"这间宽敞的房间里零零星星摆放着几件家具。"所以正确答案应是B。

2006 年英语专业四级考试语法与词汇参考答案与解析

51. [D] 根据句子结构,可以看出这里需要一个既能引导让步状语从句又能修饰形容词 dull 的关系副词,正确答案应为 However,例如:No country, however rich, can afford the waste of its human resources. 任何一个国家,不管它多么富裕,都浪费不起人力资源。本句意思是"无论他有多愚钝,他的确是一位非常成功的高层管理人员。"所以正确答案应是D。

52. [B] if only 后跟虚拟语气的动词,可以表示愿望、惋惜等情感色彩。谓语根据具体情况选择一般过去时、过去完成时、could 或 would 或 might 根据动词原形,根据句意,这里要使用"could + 原形",例如:If only I could know what you are thinking! 我要是能知道你想什么就好了! 本句意思是"我的吉他要是能弹得和你一样棒就好了!"所以正确答案应是B。

53. [D] "在……晚会上",要用 at ... party 来表达,例如:We don't usually get on well together but she was quite amicable at the party last night. 我们通常不怎么合得来,但她在昨天的晚会上表现得很友好。本句意思是"我以嘉宾身份出席那次晚会极其有趣。"所以正确答案应是D。

54. [A] 在 it is (high) time that 结构中,从句使用一般过去式,表示虚拟语气,意为"早该……了",例如:It is high time that they were taught a lesson. 早就该教训他们一顿了。本句意思是"早就该停止砍伐雨林了。"所以正确答案应是A。

55. [C] 根据句子结构,可以看出"he _____ impossible to comprehend"是定语从句,修饰先行词 a few points in the essay,根据句子结构,可以看出这里需要使用过去

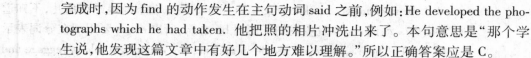

完成时,因为 find 的动作发生在主句动词 said 之前,例如:He developed the photographs which he had taken. 他把照的相片冲洗出来了。本句意思是"那个学生说,他发现这篇文章中有好几个地方难以理解。"所以正确答案应是 C。

56. [C] so that 引导结果状语从句,表示"如此……以致……",从句中一般使用 may/might 或 can 跟动词原形,例如:We must emancipate our thought so that we may speak and act boldly. 我们必须解放思想,以使我们言行果敢起来。These men risked their lives so that we may live more safely. 这些人冒着生命危险为的是让我们更安全地生活。本句意思是"大厅里安装了扬声器,这样每个人就都有机会听到演讲。"所以正确答案应是 C。

57. [A] 在 sb. is surprised that 或 it is strange ... that 等句型中,从句动词要用 should + 原形,表示"居然,竟然"意义,主要特别注意的是,在这里 should 不可省略,例如:I'm surprised that you should think this way. 你居然这样想,我实在想不到。本句意思是"我很惊讶,你竟然认为生活在这座城市里很没意思。"所以正确答案应是 A。

58. [B] 在这里 be good enough for 表示"对……来说足够了",例如:The cliché "good enough for government work" implies that people do not expect more of the government. 像"政府已经做的够多了"这样的陈词滥调表明人们并没有指望从政府那里得到更多的东西。本句意思是"苏珊非常勤劳,但是她的报酬和工作比起来就显得不多了。"所以正确答案应是 B。

59. [C] 与 imperative 等词相关的名词性从句中要使用虚拟语气,从句动词要用原形或"should + 原形",例如:It is imperative that we should strengthen the forecast and monitoring system if we fail to prevent earthquake. 既然不能防止地震发生,就必须加强预测和监测。本句意思是"政府必须为造船业吸引更多的投资。"所以正确答案应是 C。

60. [C]和[D] not such a + n. + as 和 no such + n. + as 都可以表示"没有……这回事",例如:There's no such thing as (not such a thing as) free speech. 根本就没有所谓什么言论自由。本句意思是"土地属于整个城市,根本就没有所谓的土地私有这么回事。"所以正确答案应是 C。

61. [C] that 可以作副词,用来修饰形容词和副词,表示"那么,如此"之意,例如:If all the tools are that bad, we can't fulfil the task on schedule. 如果所有的工具都那么差,我们就不能按期完成任务了。本句意思是"今天我的女儿步行了八英里,我们没想到她能够走那么远。"所以正确答案应是 C。

62. [D] prove 一般很少用于进行时,另外,statistics 在这里作"统计数据"讲,为复数,本句意为:"统计数据表明,最近本地区的生活水平得到了大幅度提高。"所以[D]为正确答案,例如:The statistics in that report are not so accurate. 这份报告中的一些数据不精确。

63. [A] 首先,不定式的否定形式是在 to 前加 not,现在分词的否定形式则是该分词前加 not,例如:It's far too late for you to go out and play football, not to mention the fact that it's raining. 你们现在出去踢球实在太晚了,更不要说还在下雨。I

stood there motionless, not knowing what to do. 我一动不动地站在那儿,不知道该怎么办。动词 count 发生在句子谓语 be 之前,所以 count 要用现在分词表示完成,例如:There were seven people in the car, not counting a pile of luggage and three dogs. 那辆汽车载了 7 个人,更不必说还有一堆行李和三条狗。本句意思是"除去几个坏了的苹果,篮子里只有 10 个了。"所以正确答案应是 A。

64. [C] much of a 表示"相当好的……"之意,相当于 a fairly good,例如:To travel a long way would be too much of a tax on my father's strength. 我父亲的体力经不起长途旅行。在这里 as much of a success as 表示同级比较,第一个 as 为副词,第二个 as 是关系代词,引导可表示比较意义的定语从句,例如:Her work was as good as we had imagined. 她的工作和我们原先想像的一样好。本句意思是"这件事没有我们原来希望的那样成功。"所以正确答案应是 C。

65. [D] 以 used 作谓语动词的句子的附加疑问句,可以用 usedn't 或 didn't 来反问,同时 there be 句型的附加疑问句要用 there 来反问,例如:There used to be a lot of trees around the place, usedn't(didn't)there? 这一带过去树很多,是吗? 本句意思是"公园附近有一家加油站,不是吗?"所以正确答案应是 D。

66. [D] discrimination 可以作"种族歧视"讲,例如:Racial discrimination aroused popular indignation and disgust. 种族歧视引起了民众的愤慨和憎恶。本句意思是"歧视别的种族是一种犯罪。"所以正确答案应是 D。

67. [B]和[C] restore 和 renovate 均可作"修复,重建"讲,例如:The local government restored/renovated the old building to its original form. 当地政府将修复那座古建筑,以使其恢复原貌。而 renew 则作"更新,更换"讲,例如:His project this year is to renew some of his household appliances. 他今年的计划是更新一些家用器具。refresh 意为"使精神振作,使精力恢复",例如:The tree of liberty must be refreshed from time to time with the blood of patriots and tyrants. It is its natural manure. 自由之树必须时时用爱国志士和暴君的血来浇灌,这是它的天然肥料。本句意思是"人们做了大量工作维修大教堂以恢复其往日的辉煌。"所以正确答案应是 B 和 C。

68. [D] 短语 on/at one's heels 表示"紧跟……后面",例如:The father walked steadily, with his little daughter at/on his heels. 父亲不紧不慢地走在前面,小女儿紧随其后。本句意思是"小偷逃跑了,警察紧追其后。"所以正确答案应是 D。

69. [A]和[B] "稳定就业"可以用 job security,也可以用 job safety 表示,请看摘自 U. S. News & World Report《美国新闻和世界报道》的两个例子:President Bush said, "This is about national security, not job security." 布什总统说:"这不是稳定就业问题,而是国家安全问题。"President Nixon's environmental, job safety, and Indian policies have been mostly followed by later administrations, with impressive reductions in pollution. 尼克松总统的环境政策、稳定就业政策和印第安政策得到了历届政府的遵从,结果是污染大大降低。本句意思是"经济衰退意味着鲜见稳定就业。"所以正确答案应是 A。

70. [C] provide 作"提供,预防"讲,例如:For years, successive governments have sought

to attack the state pensions and insisted that it is up to each person to provide for their own old age. 历届政府都不懈地攻击国家养老金制度,并一再声称养老是每个人自己的事情。而 cater for 则作"满足……需要"讲,例如:The store tried to cater for the need of the customers of various kinds. 这家商店设法迎合各种顾客的需求。本句意思是"当今很多人都存钱以备年老之需。"所以正确答案应是 C。

71. [B] reflect 意为"反映,影射",例如:What I saw and what I heard were fairly reflected in the paper. 我的所见所闻,都在我的论文里表达出来了。Words are chameleons, which reflect the colour of their environment. 词语是变色龙,它们随着周围的变化而变化。本句意思是"这篇文章的基调反映出了作者当时的心境。"所以正确答案应是 B。

72. [A] "the moment for sb. to do sth." 表示"做某事的时刻、时间、场合",例如:Now was the moment for her resolution to be executed. 现在是她将决心付诸实施的时候了。本句意思是"你现在不应该求我帮忙,我很忙,甚至没工夫听你讲。"所以正确答案应是 A。

73. [D] involve 意为"牵涉,卷入",例如:The test of a vocation is the love of the drudgery it involves. 检验一个人是否具备某种职业才能,就是看他能否热爱其中包含的枯燥劳动。Although planning involves material investment, even more important is the investment in man. 虽然做计划应包括物资投资,但最重要的是对人的投资。本句意思是"学生膳食官的工作包括多次拜访房东。"所以正确答案应是 D。

74. [B] 动词 stand 可以作"处立在,坐落于",表示某建筑、某单位的位置,例如:Notre Dame stands in the very heart of Paris. 巴黎圣母院位于巴黎的正中心。本句意思是"我们的家庭医生的诊所在两条交通繁忙道路的交叉口。"所以正确答案应是 B。

75. [C] squeeze through 意思为"勉强挤过去;勉强通过,险胜",例如:He squeezed through a crowd with great difficulty. 他费力地在人群中穿梭。The measure squeezed through the parliament. 议案在议会上勉强通过。本句意思是"她太胖了,勉强挤过这道门。"所以正确答案应是 C。

76. [A] leak 意为"(房屋)漏雨",例如:The roof leaks; it lets the rain comes in. 房顶漏了,雨漏进来了。而 drip 则指(水、雨)滴下来,例如:The rain was dripping from the trees. 雨水正从树上滴下。trickle 意为"一滴一滴地流,细流",例如:Blood trickled from the wound. 血从伤口一滴滴流出。本句意思是"大雨过后,一名建筑工人被叫来维修漏雨的房顶。"所以正确答案应是 A。

77. [C] prominent 作"杰出的,著名的"讲,例如:Several prominent scientists who participated in the space program are to appear before the welcome reception. 几位参与这次太空计划的杰出的科学家要出席今晚的欢迎会。而 excellent 则表示在某一个方面"优秀的,优异的";conspicuous 和 noticeable 同义,都可作"突出的,易被人看到的"。本句意思是"一些社区名流出席了招待会。"所以正确答案应是 C。

78. [A] regain 意为"取回,夺回;复(失物、失地)",例如：The company's stock has recently regained some lost ground to reach ＄20 a share, from ＄17, in early May. 最近公司的股票已经收复了部分失地,从五月初的每股 17 美元,上升到 20 美元。本句意思是"早晨交易所的股票价格急剧跳水,不过下午略有回升。"所以正确答案应是 A。

79. [C] productive 在这里作"生产性的,多产的"讲,例如：They work hard, but their efforts are not very productive. 他们很努力,但效率不太高。本句意思是"他大脑思维活跃,不停思考着,以期找出一个通用的治疗方案。"所以正确答案应是 C。

80. [A] inconsiderable 在这里意为"不足道的,不值得考虑的,无足轻重的,微小的",例如：An inconsiderable amount of money could help a children from the countryside to finish one-year schooling. 这笔微不足道的款项能够使一个来自农村的孩子完成一年的学业。本句意思是"这对夫妇向基金会捐献了一笔数目不小的资金。"所以正确答案应是 A。

2007 年英语专业四级考试语法与词汇参考答案与解析

51. [C] 在 as + adj. + a/an + n. + as 结构中,第二个 as 作关系代词,引导定语从句,as 在定语从句中可以作主语等,例如：He is as brave a man as ever lived. 从来就没有像他那么勇敢的人。本句意思是"海里的好鱼多的是。(强中更有强中手。)"所以正确答案应是 C。

52. [B] 根据句子意思,可断定这里要使用现在时,由此可以排除[C];remain 为系动词,一般不用进行时,由此可以排除[D]。All the President's Men 是书名,应该看为单数,所以[B]为正确答案,例如：*Wuthering Heights* is one of the most extraordinary books which human genius has ever produced. 《呼啸山庄》是人类的天才所创作出来的最优秀的作品之一。本句意思是"《总统班底》一书仍然是研究水门丑闻的历史学家重要的参考书。"所以正确答案应是 B。

53. [D] provided/providing that 可以引导条件状语从句,相当于 if,主句中一般使用 can + 动词原形,例如：You can fly to London this evening provided that you don't mind changing the plane in Paris. 只有你不介意在巴黎换机,你今晚就可以飞往伦敦。I believe that anyone can conquer fear by doing the things he fears to do, provided he keeps doing them until he gets a record of successful experiences behind him. 我相信任何人都可以通过干些使自己望而却步的事而战胜胆怯,但他必须持之以恒,直至他有了成功的经历。本句意思是"我对我的朋友说:"如果你能妥善保管我的笔记,我就可以借给你。""所以正确答案应是 D。

54. [A] 在这里虽然从句时态和主句时态出现了不一致,但却合乎情理,表示过去的虚拟条件,可能导致一个虚拟的现在结果,例如：If they had been more careful then, they would get better results now. 如果他们当时更仔细些,他们现在就会

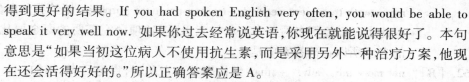

得到更好的结果。If you had spoken English very often, you would be able to speak it very well now. 如果你过去经常说英语,你现在就能说得很好了。本句意思是"如果当初这位病人不使用抗生素,而是采用另外一种治疗方案,他现在还会活得好好的。"所以正确答案应是 A。

55. [B] 当 hope, mean, intend, expect 或 be 的过去式后跟不定式的完成时时,表示主语的愿望没有实现,或表示某事未曾发生过,例如:I meant to have called on you, but something urgent prevented me from coming. 我本打算去拜访你,可惜有件急事使我没有去成。You were to have been kind to the old man. 你们本应该对那位老人仁慈些。另外,start 为短暂性动词,一般不用在进行时,由此可以排除[D]。本句意思是"琳达本应该一个月前就开始这项试验,但是她在最后一刻却改变了主意。"所以正确答案应是 B。

56. [D] must have done 用来表示对过去某动作的肯定推测,如:He must have been to England for he knows so much about that country. 他一定去过英国,因为他了解那么多有关那个国家的事情。She must have seen spring up before her a great hope. 她当时一定是看见眼前出现了很大的希望。本句意思是"我在研讨会上第一次见到她时,她肯定有 50 岁左右。"所以正确答案应是 D。

57. [C] 句型 not so much A as B 意为"与其说 A,不如说 B",例如:Oceans don't so much divide the world as unite it. 与其说海洋分割了世界,不如说海洋联结了世界。He is not so much a writer as a reporter. 与其说他是一位作家,不如说他是一个记者。本句意思是"与其说是书中的语言倒不如说是背景知识使得这本书难以理解。"所以正确答案应是 C。

58. [D] 根据句子结构,这里表示公路建设项目中所出现的问题早就在委员会预料之中,例如:We have anticipated the resistance to our plan that we have met. 我们的计划遇到了一些人的反对,这是我们早就预料到的。本句意思是"这条道路施工过程所出现的问题,这个委员会都已提前预料到了。"所以正确答案应是 D。

59. [A] 根据主句时态,我们可以肯定这里需要使用过去时;根据句意,可断定这里要用完成体,例如:I shuddered when I recalled the danger I had been in at that time. 想到那时我所处的危险境地,我不禁毛骨悚然。本句意思是"那个学生说,他发现这篇文章中有好几个地方难以理解。"所以正确答案应是 A。

60. [C] but (that) 可作"若不,除非"讲,可以引导假设状语从句,要注意的是,尽管主句谓语动词要使用虚拟语气,但是从句谓语动词只能用陈述语气,因为从句的内容的真实的,例如:But that the friction was great, the pump would not have been damaged. 如果摩擦不那么大,这台水泵就不会坏了。There would be no air around the earth, but that there is gravity. 如果没有地球吸引力,地球周围就不会有空气。本句意思是"如果不是当初不得不辍学找工作养活家人,他本来就可以完成大学学习了。"所以正确答案应是 C。

61. [B] 在这里,than 是连词,和 more 搭配;同时 than 也是关系代词,引导一个定语从句,修饰先行词 money,than 在定语从句中作主语,例如:He drank a little more than was good for him. 他喝酒喝过了量。She gave me the impression of having

more teeth than were necessary for any practical purpose. 她给我的印象是,她长着比实际需要更多的牙齿。本句意思是"这项研究需要的资金要比已经投入的多。"所以正确答案应是 B。

62. [B] not more adj./adv. + than 结构表示否定前者,肯定后者,例如:He is not richer than his friend. 他不如他的朋友富有。而"no more adj./adv. + than"结构对前后两者都否定,例如:The heart is no more intelligent than the stomach, for they are both controlled by the brain. 心脏和胃一样,都不具有智力,因为它们二者都是由大脑控制的。本句意思是"人口过剩对人类构成了可怕的威胁,然而,与其说人口过剩对人类是一种威胁,倒不如说是对环境是一种破坏。"所以正确答案应是 B。

63. [D] 在这里,可把 for there to be sth. 看作是不定式复合结构"for + n./ pron. + to do sth."的变体,例如:I don't want for there to be any more mistakes in your composition. 我不希望在你的作文里再有任何错误。It isn't cold enough for there to be a frost tonight, so I can leave Jim's car out quite safely. 今晚天不太冷,不会下霜,因此我可把吉姆的小汽车放在户外,而不必担心安全问题。本句意思是"老年人和年轻人之间的交流问题并非罕见。"所以正确答案应是 D。

64. [B] 在这里短语动词 look at 和句子主语 the situation 是逻辑动宾关系,因此为了避免出现悬垂结构,因此要使用被动语态或过去分词,由此可以排除[A]和[D];另外,look at 在这里表示"观察"之意义,不强调动作的延续性,由此可以排除[C]。例如:Written in a terse, lucid style, the book describes the author's childhood experiences in Louisiana just before the outbreak of the Civil War. 这本书以简明、透彻的文体,描述了作者于南北战争前,在路易斯安娜州的童年生活。本句意思是"在他看来,目前的形势看起来并不是毫无希望。"所以正确答案是 B。

65. [C] 与 essential, imperative, anxious, vital, advisable, preferable, desirable, insistent, natural, important, necessary, urgent 等形容词相关的名词性从句中,谓语要使用动词原形或"should + 动词原形":例如:It is essential that theory should be closely connected with practice. 理论必须紧密联系实际。Don't you think it essential that the new technique should be popularized at once? 难道你不认为应该立即推广这项新技术吗?本句意思是"极其重要的是,威廉姆要克服学习中的困难继续他的学业。"所以正确答案应是 C。

66. [C] crude 意为"粗糙的,粗制的,未经提炼的",如:The production of crude oil this year has increased by 10%. 今年原油的产量增长了10%。man-made 意为"人造的,合成的",指完全由人工制造的,并不含有"仿造"以及真伪对比的意义,例如:Man-made skin is experimental, and more clinical testing will be needed before it is available for widespread use. 人造皮肤仍处于实验阶段,还需要进行更多的临床实验,才能被广泛应用。natural 意为"自然的,天然的,与生俱来的",例如:Natural abilities are like natural plants that need pruning by study. 天然的能力犹如天然的植物,需要通过学习来精心修剪。Let early education be a sort

of amusement; you will then be better able to find out the natural bent. 让早期教育作为一种娱乐,这样就更容易发现一个人的天赋。real 意为"具体的,客观存在的",用以表示"非虚构的,实在的",可说明实情、实况、实物等,例如:Some artificial flowers resemble real flowers so closely that it is very hard to distinguish one from another. 有些人造花像真花一样,很难区分。本句意思是"他几天前在街头市场上买的那幅画只不过是一件粗劣的赝品。"所以正确答案应是 C。

67. ［A］ turn one's back on sb. 短语动词"背弃,抛弃,不理睬",例如:I was deeply hurt by the way she just turned her back on me. 她根本不理睬我,这深深刺痛了我的心。He felt guilty at turning his back on friends in the forest. 他对在林中抛弃朋友一事深感内疚。本句意思是"她对一直很好——我不能在她需要我帮助时候抛开她不管。"所以正确答案应是 A。

68. ［B］ exclusive 意为"独占的,惟一的,排外的",例如:He moves in exclusive social circles and belongs to the most exclusive clubs. 他活动于社交甚严的社交圈内,而且属于那些最不愿吸收外人的俱乐部。而 extensive 意为"广阔的,大量的,大规模的",如:The storm has brought about extensive damage. 暴风雨造成了巨大的损失。inclusive 作"包含……在内的"讲,例如:The monthly rent is $200 inclusive of everything. 月房租总共200美元,包括一切费用在内。comprehensive 意为"综合的,广泛的,理解的",例如:The boys' and girls' schools have been amalgamated to form a new comprehensive. 男校和女校联合而组成了一所新的综合中学。本句意思是"俱乐部的酒吧只供俱乐部成员使用。"所以正确答案应是 B。

69. ［D］ affordable 作"支付得起的,不太昂贵的",例如:The company penetrated the home-computer market with an affordable new model. 这家公司以大众可承受的新机型打入家用电脑市场。而 approachable 意为"可接近的,可与之打交道的",例如:The retreat in the mountains is approachable in winter only by helicopter. 山中的这处休养地冬天只能有靠直升飞机才可接近。payable 意为"可付的,应付的,有利益的",例如:Freight charges are payable on delivery. 货物运费于交货时支付。reachable 作"可触及的,可达到的,可获得的"讲,例如:The program for protocol verification mechanically generates all states reachable from a given initial state and checks the validity of user defined conditions in each state. 验证协议的程序,它从一个给定的初始状态机械地产生出一切可以到达的状态,并且审查每一状态下用户定义的条件的有效性。本句意思是"学费对低收入家庭的学生能够负担得起。"所以正确答案应是 D。

70. ［B］ 短语 in the aftermath of 作"在(灾难性的事件)发生后的一段时间内"讲,例如:In the aftermath of the terrorist attack on the World Trade Centre, engineers are trying hard to solve a question that a month ago would have been completely unthinkable. 在世界贸易中心遭受恐怖袭击后的一段时间内,工程师设法解决一个在一个月前根本就不可想象的问题。而短语 in consequence of(无定冠词)作"由

于……的缘故"讲,例如:Commerce is seriously paralyzed in consequence of a se-vere earthquake. 由于发生强烈地震,商业严重瘫痪。短语 as a result of 意为"由于,出于……原因",例如:Her heart was slightly damaged as a result of her long illness. 长期生病使她的心脏受到轻度损伤。短语 in effect 作"实际上(事实上,在实行中)"讲,例如:He said he graduated from Oxford, while in effect, he never went to college. 他说他是牛津毕业的,但实际上他从没上过大学。本句意思是"医疗专家们告诫当局,要警惕地震后一段时间内发生疫情的危险。"所以正确答案应是 B。

71. [A]和[B]　become 有 be right or fitting, befit 之意,作"与……相称,适宜,适于"讲,例如:This new dress becomes you. 这件新衣服很合你身。He used language that does not become a man of his education. 他所用的字眼与一个受过他这样的教育的人不相称。fit 也可作"适合,与……相匹配"讲,例如:Words should be only the clothes, carefully custom-made to fit the thought. 语言应该只是精心定做的与思想适应的衣服。We might as well require a man to wear still the coat which fitted him when a boy, as civilized society to remain ever under the regime of their barbarous ancestors. 如果要求文明社会袭用蒙昧的祖先的制度,那就等于叫一个大人还穿童年的衣裳。而 support 意为"支持,支撑",如:It is not e-nough to help the feeble up, but to support him after. 仅仅把弱者扶起来是不够的,还要在他站起来之后支持他。improve 意为"改良,改善,使……进步",例如:Art improves nature. 艺术使本质更完美。本句意思是"在大庭广众之下作出这样粗俗的举动对处在你这种位置的人来说是不合适的。"所以正确答案应是 A 和 B。

72. [B]　incidentally 相当于 by the way,作"顺便提一下,顺便说一下"讲,在讲话中用来引入新话题,例如:And, incidentally, it is a chronic complaint of wives that their husbands do not notice new dresses, new hats, and changes in household arrange-ments. 而且,顺便说一句,妻子们经常抱怨,他们的丈夫不注意新衣服、新帽子和家庭摆设的变化。而 accidentally 意为"意外地,偶然地",如:We accidentally found an ideal solution. 我们意外地找到了一个理想的解决办法。eventually 意为"最后,最终",如:He studied hard at college so that he could e-ventually reach his goal of being a good teacher. 他在大学里刻苦学习,为的是能实现当一名好教师的最终目标。naturally 作"自然地,当然地"讲,例如:Don't aim for success if you want it; just do what you love and believe in, and it will come naturally. 如果你想成功,不要去追求它。做你喜欢的工作并相信它,成功自然会到来。本句意思是"我现在必须走了,顺便说一下,如果你想要那本书,我下次就给你带来。"所以正确答案应是 B。

73. [D]　短语 get round to doing sth. 作"(在处理完较重要的事情后)处理某事",例如:I'm very busy at the moment but I hope to get round to answering your letter next week. 我现在很忙,希望下周能抽出时间给你回信。而 get away with 意思是"摆脱惩罚,不受批评",如:Those who lie and cheat will never get away with it.

那些撒谎和欺骗别人的人决不会逃脱惩罚。get back at sb. 的意思是"报复"，例如：I'll get back at her for landing me in trouble. 她给我带麻烦，我会报复的。get by 意为"通过，混过"，例如：I have no formal clothes for the occasion. Perhaps I can get by in a dark suit? 我没有适合那种场合的礼服，也许穿深色西服还行吧？ How does she get by on such a small salary? 她靠那麽一点儿薪水怎么过活？本句意思是"在耽搁了很长一段时间后，她设法给我回了电子邮件。"所以正确答案应是 D。

74. [C] readily 意为"毫不迟疑，欣然；容易地"，如：He readily promised to help us. 他毫不犹豫地答应帮助我们。Most plastics do not readily conduct heat or electricity. 大多数塑料不易传热或导电。而 promptly 意为"敏捷地，快捷地"，如：Paying bills promptly is regarded as a good financial practice. 当场支付账单被认为是良好的理财习惯。instantly 意为"立即地，即刻地"，例如：Gas flowing through the pipes burns instantly but can be kept under control easily by opening or closing the pipes. 通过管子的煤气会瞬间燃烧起来，但我们凭开关管道很容易控制它。quickly 作"迅速地，快地"讲，例如：I quickly laugh at everything for fear of having to cry. 我对任何事情都迫不及待地给以笑容，生怕不得不哭出来。本句意思是"个人电脑对普通人再也不是可望不可及的了，现在很容易就能买到。"所以正确答案应是 C。

75. [A] basics 作名词，意思为"基本因素，基本原理，概要"，例如：Some people think that the first basics of Marxism-Leninism have gone out of style. 有些人认为马列主义的基本原理已经过时了。而 basic 则是形容词，意为"基本的，基础，首要的"，例如：We feel anger, love, sadness—all the basic emotions. 我们有喜怒哀乐等一切基本感情。elementary 作"基础的，基本的"讲，例如：How can you expect to exceed without even the most elementary knowledge of the field? 你在这个领域连一点基础知识都没有，还想取得成功？element 意为"元素，要素"，例如：Silence is the element in which great things fashion themselves. 沉默是造就伟大事业的因素。本句意思是"在我读大学一年级时，我就学了新闻专业的基础知识。"所以正确答案应是 A。

76. [D] 请注意区别这四个单词的不同搭配。短语 at the rate of 作"以……速度或比率"讲，例如：The future is something which everyone reaches at the rate of sixty minutes an hour, whatever he does, whoever he is. 未来是这样一件东西，每个人都以每小时 60 分钟的速度朝它走去，不管它做什么，也不管他是谁。而短语"by percent"则表示"以……百分比"，例如：Total industrial output value increased by 8.9 percent. 工业总产值增加了 8.9%。Against the American dollar its value increased by more than 8 percent. 与美元相比它的价值增加了 8% 以上。in proportion to 表示"与……成比例"，例如：A man is often bigoted in proportion to his folly. 一个人往往越愚蠢越固执。in the ratio of 意为"以……比例"，例如：Men outnumber women here in the ratio of three to one. 当地男子数量以三比一超过女子。本句意思是"根据新的税法，任何超出这一标准的资金

收入都必须按 59% 的税率纳税。"所以正确答案应是 D。

77. ［C］ spectator 指"看的人"，例如看展览、表演、体育比赛、马戏、杂技的人，因为这些娱乐活动的重点在"看"不在"听"，例如：The spectators at the football match were rather noisy. 看足球比赛的观众实在太吵了。而 audience 在字面上指的是"听的人"，比如听课、听音乐会的人，即"听众"。但看戏剧、看电影、看电视的人一般也用 audience 来表示，另外，这个词是集合名词，例如：The audience was（were）enthusiastic on the opening night of the play. 在那出戏首次公演的夜晚，观众非常热情。participant 作"参与者，参加者"讲，而 observer 则意为"旁观者"，例如：Husbands and wives are not audience, but participant observers in each other's lives. This law of lasting love instructs us to look with instead of for love. 夫妻并非彼此生活的观众，而是参与对方生活的观察者。持久爱情的这一法则教导我们用充满爱意的眼神去看自己的伴侣，而不是用寻找爱的眼神去看。本句意思是"体育场里成千上万的观众起立对这场精彩的表演表示敬意。"所以正确答案应是 C。

78. ［C］ stretch 强调线性的延伸，而 expanse 则表示面积的扩展，根据句中的"gazing out over"，可以断定 stretch 更为合适，例如：This is much the worst stretch of motorway in the country. 这是这个国家最最糟糕的一段路。A vast expanse of rice fields was laid out before us. 大片稻田展现在我们面前。本句意思是"我们静静地站着，凝望着沙漠那无尽的边沿。"所以正确答案应是 C。

79. ［C］ sense 意为"隐隐约约地感到"，强调通过直觉而产生的感觉，所以 sense 后面不能接"冷，饿，快乐"等表示清晰感觉的词，例如：The horse sensed danger and stopped. 那匹马意识到危险便停了下来。I sensed that there was someone in the room with me. 我感觉到房间里有人。He was at last beginning to sense what the trouble was. 他终于开始意识到问题之所在。本句意思是"医生经常能本能感觉到他们的病人的焦虑。"所以正确答案应是 C。

80. ［A］ 短语 smack one's lips 表示"咂嘴，馋涎欲滴，津津有味地吃"，例如：I couldn't bear to sit with him at the same table, because he smacked his lips as he ate his food. 我受不了与吉姆同桌吃饭，因为他吃东西时老是津津有味地咂嘴。本句意思是"玛丽在餐桌旁坐下，一边看着盘子，一边咂着嘴，馋涎欲滴。"所以正确答案应是 A。

1996 年英语专业四级考试阅读理解参考答案与解析

Part VI   Reading Comprehension

TEXT   A

66. ［B］ 文章第一段第二句就是本文的主题句"The greatest of these have probably been in the economic lives of women."，由此可以断定［B］正确。选项［A］范围太大。［C］范围太小，只涉及到第四段部分内容。［D］也仅仅涉及到第三段部分内容。

67. [D] 就为什么越来越多的已婚妇女能够重新工作,作者在第三段最后给出了原因:"related to this(Women are involved in child-rearing for a much shorter time),there has been a rapid increase in the number of women with young children who return to work when the children are old enough not to need constant care and attention."可见[D]正确答案。

TEXT B

68. [D] 根据第一段中的描述,我们不难看出这是一段非常生动的图画,[D]为正确答案。这不是什么"现场报道"[A],也不是"戏剧性的描写"[B],更不是什么"吹牛大话"[C]。

69. [A] 根据全文,尤其是第一段的描写,可知这是一场破坏性极强的、使数千人丧生的灾难,我们不难看出[A]正确。

70. [A] 综观全文,我们可知这篇文章通过发生在"秘鲁""山区""冰川"里的雪崩为例,向我们介绍了雪崩的形成和危害,由此可以肯定[A]而排除[B],[C]和[D]。如果读者注意到了本文的题目"Nature's Gigantic Snowplough",也就不难肯定 snowplough 在这里比喻的是雪崩。

TEXT C

71. [B] 作者为什么不知道自己的年龄,作者在第一段给出了答案:"never having seen any authentic record containing it",由此可以肯定[B]正确。

72. [A] 根据第一段"They seldom come nearer to it than planting-time, harvesting, spring-time, or falltime.",可以肯定[A]正确。

73. [C] 根据第三段"My mother and I were separated when I was but an infant—before I knew her as my mother.",就可断定[C]正确。

74. [D] 根据第三段中的"Frequently... its mother is taken from it, and hired out on some farm a considerable distance off"以及"My mother and I were separated when I was but an infant—before I knew her as my mother",可肯定[D]正确。

75. [A] 根据第三段中"My mother and I were separated when I was but an infant—before I knew her as my mother",可推断出作者和母亲在一起的时间不长。文章未说明或暗示出他与主人、祖父、祖母生活在一起的时间,所以选项[B],[C]和[D]均可排除。

76. [B] 作者在第三段指出,当母亲被买到别的地方后,"the child is placed under the care of an older woman",由此可断定[B]正确。

TEXT D

77. [B] 根据第一段"For the 1992 Winter Games, French organizers constructed a new motorway, parking lots and runs for skiing in the Alps. Environmentalists screamed 'Disaster!'",就可断定[B]正确。另外,根据下文相关内容,我们就不难排除[A],[C]和[D]。

78. [D] 根据第三段"there are still too many billboards for strict green tastes",便可肯定[D]正确。根据第一段中"energy(is)efficient",就可排除[A]。根据第二段

最后"Smoking has been banned outdoors as well as in, with enforcement by polite requests",就可排除[B]。根据第三段"after the Games, athlete housing will be converted into vacation homes or shipped to the northlands for student dormitories",就可排除[C]。

79. [A] 根据第三段中的"the I.O.C. claims that green awareness is now entrenched——along with sport and culture——as a permanent dimension of the Olympic Charter",就可肯定[A],而排除[B]。另外,[C]和[D]在文中未提及。

80. [D] 根据最后一段中的"Salt Lake City, bidding for the 2002 Games",就可断定[D]正确。根据本文,我们还知道,Calgary 是 1988 年奥运会主办地,Sydney 是 2000 年夏季奥运会举办地,而 Oslo 只是 1994 年 Lillehammer 冬奥会东道国挪威的首都,因此可排除[A],[B]和[C]。

1997 年英语专业四级考试阅读理解参考答案与解析

Part Ⅵ   Reading Comprehension

TEXT   A

66. [C] 根据第二段第二句"Arts students may well find that their official contact with teachers is less than this average, while science and engineering students may expect to be timetabled for up to 20 hours per week.",我们可以断定[C]正确。而[A],[B]和[D]在文中未提及,也推理不出,因此可以排除。

67. [A] 根据第二段中的"Lectures, seminars and tutorials are all one hour in length",就可肯定[A]正确。

68. [A] 根据第二段第一句"An undergraduate course consists of a series of lectures, seminars and tutorials and, ... laboratory classes",可以肯定[B],[C]和[D]都是教学形式,但不全面,正确答案为[A]。

TEXT   B

69. [C] 就 Dan Eckberg 和他的学生用什么方法了解非洲,作者在第二段第一句给出了答案"using computers, satellite hookups, and telephone hotlines",由此可以断定[C]正确。

70. [A] 通观全文,尤其是根据第一段第一句,我们知道这篇文章介绍的是如何了解"a country you can't visit",就可肯定[A]是正确答案。根据第一段最后一句"They're seeing countries and learning about cultures with the aid of electronic communications",就可排除[B]。根据第九段"Ten lesson plans——on topics ranging from the Maya language to the Maya creation myth——have been developed for the interactive expedition."可以排除[C]。根据第七段中的"students can make research proposals"和"and through the online activities, an answer will be found——a discovery!"可以排除[D]。

TEXT C

71. [C] 根据第一段第三句"Their number decreases as the depth increases.",就可排除[A]和[D]。根据第一段倒数第二句中的"the yearly average does not vary much",就可排除[B],根据第一段,尽管"about 460 miles one earthquake occurs only every few years.",但并不能由此而断定460英里以下的地方就不会发生地震,可见[C]正确。

72. [A] 第二段先是用了一个形象的类比,通过这个比方,作者希望说明不坚固的建筑承受不起小的震动。接着作者又指出 Agadir 发生的地震尽管小,但是却摧毁了整个城市,由此可以推断出城市遭到破坏的原因是低质量的建筑,所以[A]为正确答案。

73. [B] 根据第三段最后一句"If followed, these suggestions will make disastrous earthquakes almost a thing of the past.",就不难看出[B]正确。

74. [C] 根据最后一段中的"*tsunamis* travel fairly slowly...An adequate warning system is in use to warn all shores likely to be reached by the waves.",可见[C]正确。同时可知 warning systems 早就"开发"出来了,并已经投入了"应用",由此可以排除[D]。根据最后一句"There is no way to stop the oncoming wave."可以排除[B]。根据第四段中的"The waves are not noticeable out at sea because of their long wave length.",就可以排除[A]。

TEXT D

75. [C] 根据第一段,我们了解到,在妇女的解放运动中男人也得到了解放,因为他们不再需要 pay women the old-fashioned courtesies ,因此[C]正确。

76. [A] 由于此前的一切都很"自然"(when she pulled the chair out I sat on it, quite naturally, since it happened to be the chair I wanted to sit in),所以当妻子说:"你又那样做了"时,丈夫显得很困惑。由此可以肯定[A]正确。

77. [C] 根据"I had got there first, after all."可以排除[A]和[D]。根据"it happened to be the chair I wanted to sit in",可以排除[B]。只有[C]未提及,是正确答案。

78. [A] 文章最后给出了作者先于妇女上车的原因是"In times like these, there might be attackers hidden about",[A]正确。

79. [A] 从作者的叙述方式看,作者在论述举止风度和妇女解放问题时,以及在举例说明时,明显地带有调侃的语气,[A]正确。

80. [B] 这篇文章重点强调了对旧有礼节的突破以及人们观点的更新,但并不是说现在就不需要礼节了,女士就不需要男士的帮助和尊重了。[A],[C]和[D]都太绝对,歪曲了作者的意图。根据全文,尤其是第五段第一和第二句,可以肯定[B]正确。不过需要注意的是,即使选项[B]也有太过宽泛之嫌,文章仅限于男士对女士礼节方面的讨论。

1998 年英语专业四级考试阅读理解参考答案与解析

Part Ⅵ　Reading Comprehension

TEXT　A

66. [D]　作者在第一段最后指出：或许这些绘画者认为这些图画会有助于他们捕捉猎物，能够帮助他们叙述故事，可见[D]为正确答案。

67. [C]　作者在第四段中指出了 Greek alphabet 和 Egyptian system 相比较所具有的长处，根据"The signs they used were very easy to write"，就可排除[A]。根据"there were fewer of them than in the Egyptian system"，就可排除[B]。根据"each sign, or letter, represented only one sound in their language"，可排除[D]。而[C]在文中未提及。

68. [A]　根据第二段最后一句"The signs these people used became a kind of alphabet."，就可肯定[A]为正确答案。文章第三段中只指出了在现代人眼里，"Some of these pictures are like modern comicstrip stories."，而并不是说，这些古人喜欢创作 comicstrip stories，由此可排除[B]。第四段最后一句"The Romans copied the idea (Greek Alphabet), and the Roman alphabet is now used all over the world."告诉我们[C]和[D]错误。

69. [C]　根据最后一段中的"But we still need pictures of all kinds. . . . We find them everywhere"，就可肯定[C]正确。而[A], [B]和[D]在本文中未被提及。

TEXT　B

70. [D]　[A]陈述了一个事实，与题目无关。文章提及了使用工具"helped to develop human intelligence"，而不是"developed human capabilities"，由此可排除[B]。[C]中内容未被提及，可予以排除。根据第二段最后一句中的"it was the key to the success of mankind"，可以断定[D]正确。

71. [B]　作者在文章最后一段指出生活正在发生着更快的变化。变化如此之快，人们不知道 20 年后的生活将会是什么样子，也不知道 200 万年后的世界将是什么样子，由此可见[B]正确。

TEXT　C

72. [A]　作者在第三段中指出，Farwell 受伤是由于"a switchman's negligence"，由此可以排除[B]，并且肯定[A]正确。根据段中"The court reasoned that since Farwell had taken the job of an engineer voluntarily at good pay, he had accepted the risk."，就可排除[C]。可根据本段最后"In effect a railroad could never be held responsible for injury to one employee caused by the mistake of another."将[D]排除。

73. [A]　根据第四段最后内容"But the court . . . argued that the railroad's negligence was the immediate cause of damage only to the nearest buildings. Beyond them the connection was too remote to consider."，可见铁路只需要赔偿附近建筑的损失。由此可见[A]正确。

74. ［C］ 根据最后一段中的"public sentiment began to turn against the railroads—against their economic and political power and high fares as well as against their callousness toward individuals."就可排除［A］，［B］和［D］，而肯定［C］。需要注意的是，如果题目像这样限定一下，可能会更明确些：The following aroused public resentment against the railroad EXCEPT _____.

75. ［D］ 根据第四段可以排除［A］和［C］。文章只涉及到了与美国铁路有关的诉讼，由此可以排除［B］，而肯定［D］。

TEXT D

76. ［D］ 根据常识，就可排除［B］。根据第二段第一句中的"Hawaii's native peoples have fared worse than any of its other ethnic groups"，我们就可知 native peoples 包括在 Hawaii's ethnic groups 中，更何况 native minority 呢？可见 Hawaii's native minority 和 Hawaii's ethnic groups 外延不对等，因此可以排除［A］。根据第四段第一句"However, the Hawaiian natives are not united in their demands"，我们可以肯定在这一段作者讨论的是不同的土著集团的不同态度，因此可以断定 the Ka Lahui group 只是土著少数民族的一个组织，而不是全体土著人，由此可以排除［C］。另外，第 78 题的题干"Which of the following groups holds a less radical attitude on the matter of sovereignty?"也有助于我们排除［C］。根据第五段最后一句"The state authorities only count as native those people with more than 50 per cent Hawaiian blood."可以看出［D］比较接近事实，但是不够准确：文章指出有"50% 以上血统"的夏威夷人才能被称为土著人，而［D］中只是说有"50% 血统"的夏威夷人，那么 50% 以上血统的人应不应该算土著人，虽然答案是显而易见的，但是题目还是不够准确。

77. ［C］ 根据第二段中的"They make up over 60 per cent of the state's homeless"，可以排除［A］。根据"their life span is five years less than the average Hawaiians"，可将［B］排除。本段最后一句"They are the only major US native group without some degree of autonomy"，可以帮助我们排除［D］。根据"Hawaii's native peoples have fared worse than any of its other ethnic groups"，可知［C］正确。

78. ［C］和［D］ 答案在第三段。根据"Hawaii's first native governor"，可以排除［A］。根据"a sovereignty advisory committee set up by ... John Waihee"，可以排除［B］。要注意"recommending that the Hawaiian natives decide by themselves"是 a sovereignty advisory committee 做的事情，可见［C］是正确答案。而［D］在文章中没有被提及，由此可见［D］正确与否难以确定。

79. ［B］ 答案在第四段。文章未提及美国印第安人对主权和独立的任何要求，所以［A］不正确。根据第一句，我们了解到夏威夷土著人的意见要求不一致，由此可以排除［D］。根据最后一句"the Ka Lahui group... declared itself a new nation in 1987 and wants full, official independence from the US"，可以排除［C］。根据"Office of Hawaiian Affairs（OHA）... has now become the moderate face of the native sovereignty movement."，可以断定［B］正确。

80. ［B］ 首先，读者应该格外注意题干中的"various native Hawaiians"。根据第四段第二句"Some just want greater autonomy within the state",可以排除［A］。根据第六段第二句"They also want their claim on 660,000 hectares of Hawaiian crown land to be accepted.",可排除［C］。根据第四段最后一句中的"the Ka Lahui group...wants full, official independence from the US.",可以排除［D］。文章未提到［B］,所以为正确答案。

1999 年英语专业四级考试阅读理解参考答案与解析

Part Ⅵ Reading Comprehension

TEXT A

66. ［B］ 文章开篇指出,人们不知道有多少生病的儿童在医院中能够继续接受教育,更不用说,了解医院所能提供的教育的内容和质量了,由此可见［B］正确。

67. ［D］ 根据第三段中的"the extent and type of hospital teaching available differ a great deal across the country",可断定［A］错误。根据"half the hospitals in England which admit children have no teacher",可以排除［B］和［C］。根据"half the hospitals have no teacher"和"A further quarter have only a part-time teacher",只可推知"剩下的四分之一的学校有数位兼职教师,或一位全职教师,或数位全职教师"(请特别注意 only 一词),这也与［D］不甚相符。只可以说［D］比较接近事实。

68. ［B］ 根据第六段中的"Children tend to rely on concerned school friends to keep in touch with school work",就可断定［B］正确

69. ［C］ 通观全文,就不难发现作者对医院为生病儿童提供教育的现状不满意,正确答案为［C］。

TEXT B

70. ［D］ 首先,我们不难排除［A］和［C］。而选择项［B］比较具有迷惑性,它似乎与文章中的某些内容相一致,第二段最后中的"to bring computers to the people",但是读者要清楚,这只是一种表象,而非实质。根据第三段最后"help the children discover about computers in their own way",以及根据第四段最后"they are not told what to do, they find out."就可肯定［D］正确。

71. ［B］ 通读全文,尤其是根据第三段中的"Albrecht had started a project called Computertown USA in the local library",就可断定［B］为正确答案。

72. ［C］ 根据第四段第一句"Over here, in Britain, Computertowns have taken off in a big way, and there are now about 40 scattered over the country",可以排除［A］。根据第四段"The clubs cater for the enthusiasts... non-experts, ... are happier going to Computertowns",可以排除［B］。根据第四段"they are most successful when tied to a computer club",可以排除［D］,而肯定［C］。

73. ［A］ 根据第四段最后一句中的"with experts available to encourage them and answer any questions",以及第五段第二句"The computer experts ... have to be able to explain the answers to the questions that people really want to know",可以排除

[B]。根据同一段第五句中的"there are computers available for them to experiment on",可以排除[C]和[D]。根据第五段第二句中的"The computer experts have to learn not to tell people about computers",可以肯定[A]为正确答案。

TEXT C

74. [D] 第一段第一句"There must be few questions on which responsible opinion is so utterly divided as on that of how much sleep we ought to have",可以肯定[D]正确,[B]错误。误选[A]的读者,很可能是因为没有注意到 issue(问题)和 opinion(看法,观点)的差别。[C]中的内容未在文中提及。

75. [A] 根据第一段中的"They are alert ... sleepy when it is time to get up",可以肯定[A]正确。根据第一段最后内容"this may have nothing to do with how fatigued their bodies are, or how much sleep they must take to lose their fatigue",可以排除[B]和[C]。[D]只是描述性的句子,与文章无关。

76. [D] 根据文章最后"It would be a pity to retard our development by holding back those people who are gifted enough to work and play well with less than the average amount of sleep, if indeed it does them no harm",可以推定[D]正确。而[A]和[B]的内容都过于武断。根据本段中"the majority sleep too much",可以肯定[C]亦过武断。

77. [A] 通读全文,可知作者在各段中均叙述了一个别人的观点,并加以评论。第一种观点认为睡眠可由身体自我调节;第二种观点认为现在的趋势是人们的睡眠越来越少;第三种观点认为现在人睡得太多。由此可见[A]正确。

TEXT D

78. [C] 根据第三段中的"Most often these(pull factors)are economic",可以排除[A],并肯定[C]。作者在第二段最后指出,只有在极端个别情况下,push factors 比 pull factors 更重要,除此,作者并未对这两种因素进行重要性方面的对比,由此可以排除[B]和[D]。

79. [B] 根据第五段中的"because of their varying abilities and personalities",可以排除[A]和[D]。根据同一段中的"The prospect... may appear interesting and challenging to an unmarried young man and appallingly difficult to a slightly older man with a wife and small kids",可以排除[C]。正确答案为[B]。作者在文章中并未提及教育对移民的影响。

80. [B] 通观全文,不难看出作者在文中介绍了国际间移民的决定性因素,由此可以肯定[B]正确。而[D]的范围太大。

2000 年英语专业四级考试阅读理解参考答案与解析

Part Ⅵ Reading Comprehension

TEXT A

66. [C] 第一段指出:"A great deal of communicating is performed on person-to-person ba-

sis",而且如果我们"travel in buses, buy things in shops, or eat in restaurants"我们就必须交流,另外,"give information or opinions, receive news or comment"也需要交流,因此,我们可以肯定本段主要介绍了 communications 的重要性。

67. [D] 第二段最后一句指出:"Secondly, speed has revolutionized the transmission and reception of communications"以至于地方新闻的传播速度经常比国内新闻慢,而国内新闻又比国际新闻慢,由此可以推断出国际新闻的传播速度最快,可见[D]正确答案。

68. [B] 根据第三段第一句"No longer is the possession of information confined to a privileged minority"可以肯定[A]是正确陈述。根据第四段中第一句"Communication is no longer merely concerned with the transmission of information",可见[C]为正确陈述。根据同段第二句"The modern communication industry influences the way people live in society and broadens their horizons",可知[D]为正确叙述。文章第三段确实提及"but today there are public libraries",但并不能说明现在已经没有了私人图书馆,另外有常识的人也非常了解这一点,所以[B]为正确答案。

69. [D] 根据最后一段,我们可以看出作者同时也认识到现代通讯网络也可能被滥用,因此我们不能说作者对此漠不关心,由此可排除[A],肯定[D]。最后一段讲到了媒体提供的信息很重要,没有提到传媒巨变,由此可以排除[B]。文章最后指出"However, the mass media are with us for better, for worse, and there is no turning back",可见作者对媒体的未来并不悲观。

TEXT B

70. [C] 第一段第一和第二句告诉我们:"The men and women of Anglo-Saxon England normally bore one name only. Distinguishing epithets were rarely added",在这里 distinguishing epithets 指的就是 surname,可见[C]为正确答案。

71. [C] 根据本段中最后一句中的"for many years after that (the 13th and 14th centuries), the degree of stability in family names varied considerably in different parts of the country",我们可以断定尽管13和14世纪后姓氏才固定下来,但是有些人在不断地改变其姓氏,因此[C]正确。

72. [A] 在第二段中作者指出姓氏可分为四类:patronymic, occupational, descriptive and local。在接下来的四个段落中,作者分别对这四个类别进行了分析。根据第三段中的介绍,我们可以肯定[A]为正确答案。

73. [A] [A]陈述的是人们对 occupational names 的看法,而不事实,为正确答案。[B]在文章第五段中被提及,[C]在第五段第一句被提及,[D]在第六段中被提及,均可予排除。

TEXT C

74. [B] 文章第一段明确指出了瑞士银行引以为豪的是"their system of banking secrecy and numbered accounts",可见[B]为正确答案,另外,有一定国际金融知识的人都知道瑞士银行以为储户保密而闻名于世。有人误选了[C],但只要注意区别"mysterious（神秘的）"和"secret（保密的,秘密的）"的不同意义,就可避免之。

75. [D] 作者在文章最后指出,银行认为"this secrecy was ever given up, foreigners would fall over themselves in the rush to withdraw money, and the Swiss banking system would virtually collapse overnight",作者指出这种观点"contributing to the mystique",可见银行在"捍卫"其做法,所以[D]为正确答案。

76. [C] 文章最后指出银行并不必"inform of a client to anyone, including the Swiss government",而且"To some extent, therefore, the principle of secrecy had been maintained."可见变化并非实质性的,所以[C]为正确答案。而[A]和[B]错误。作者并未就"是否需要更多的变化"发表自己的意见,由此可以排除[D]。

TEXT D

77. [D] 根据文中的"worked monotonously"以及"smoke trailed themselves for ever and ever",就可将[A]排除。根据"river... ran purple with ill-smelling dye","there could have been no such blotch upon the view without a town"等,可以排除[B]。根据"there was a rattling and a trembling all day long",就可以排除[C]。

78. [A] 根据文中的"It was a town of machinery and tall chimneys, out of which smoke trailed themselves for ever and ever.","the piston of the steam-engine worked monotonously up and down","Workers emerged from low underground doorways into factory yards"以及"the whirr of shafts and wheels"等信息,就可肯定这是一个工业城镇。

79. [C] 作者在第三段中指出"But no temperature made the mad elephants more mad or more sane. Their wearisome heads went up and down at the same rate, in hot weather and in cold, wet weather and dry, fair weather and foul.",如果再回过头去看看作者在第一段中的那个比喻"the piston of the steam-engine worked monotonously up and down like the head of an elephant in a state of madness",就不难肯定[C]是正确答案。

80. [B] 通读全文,我们看到是空气污染、环境污染、噪音污染、水污染等,不难看出[B]为正确答案。

2001 年英语专业四级考试阅读理解参考答案与解析

Part VI Reading Comprehension

TEXT A

66. [B] 第一段中的 clatter 一词作"(转动时)发出急促的敲击声"讲,可知火车在路过火车站时,没有停下来,可将[D]排除。根据第二段第一句中的"Then it began suddenly to slow down",可知[A]和[C]错误。而[B]为正确答案。

67. [A] 综观全文,我们不难发现 Mrs. McGillicuddy 是一个很爱观察周围情况的人,所以[A]正确答案。

68. [D] 根据第五段的描写,我们可知对面火车上有一男子在"扼杀"一个妇女,而且作者在第七段还指出，what she had seen at such close quarters 对 Mrs. McGillicuddy 来说是"horror"，使她 paralysed，可见[D]正确答案。

69. [B] 就 Mrs. McGillicuddy 为什么没有 ring the communication cord，作者通过她的心理活动"After all, what use would it be ringing the cord of the train in which she was travelling?"告诉我们这样做是没有任何用处的。所以[B]为正确答案。

TEXT B

70. [C] 根据第一段第一句"I am one of the many city people"以及第二句中虚拟条件从句"if it weren't for my job"，可知作者现在在城里工作，[C]为正确答案。

71. [A] 可从第二段中找到正确答案。根据段中的"The sense of belonging to a community tends to disappear"，可以排除[B]。根据"noisy, dirty and impersonal" "massive tower blocks"以及"All you can see from your window is sky, or other blocks"，可以排除[C]。根据"Children become ... cooped up at home all day"，以及"their mothers feel isolated"，可以排除[D]。有的读者只是根据本段第一句中的"Cities can be frightening places"，就排除了[A]，需要注意的是，frightening 的东西未必使人"恐惧"，另外从文中也找不到人们有任何恐惧症状。故[A]是正确答案。

72. [C] 根据第三段倒数第二句中的"for anything slightly out of the ordinary you have to go on an expedition to the nearest large town"，以及我们的常识，可知 daily necessities, fresh fruits 和 fresh vegetables 都是 ordinary things，而只有 designer clothes 才称得上是"anything slightly out of the ordinary"，可见[C]是正确答案

73. [D] 作者在第五段指出："They generally have about as much sensitivity as the plastic flowers they leave behind"，当然塑料花没有任何"敏感性"，可见作者认为这些人都 insensitive，不体贴他人。这一点从最后一句中也可得到证明：这些人将他们奇怪的观点强加在"当地的""不情愿接受的"居民身上。

74. [B] 在第一段中，作者首先表示非常希望到乡下去住，但是认为这个想法是否现实还有待证明(But how realistic is the dream?)。作者接着分析了城市生活和乡村生活各自的优势与弊端。最后，通过他的小猫 Toby 的可能的反应(he would rather have the electric imitation-coal fire any evening)间接地表达了自己的观点：呆在城里。

TEXT C

75. [B] 根据第四段最后一句中的"they must spend enough time on separate interests with separate people to preserve and develop their separate personalities and keep their relationship fresh"，就可推断出[B]为正确答案。

76. [D] 根据第三段中的"Married couples are likely ... to fall into dull exhausted silence when the guests have gone"，就可断定[D]正确。

77. [C] 在最后一段中，作者指出"the children are allowed to command all time and attention, allowing the couple no time to develop liking and friendship, as well as love, allotting them exclusive parental roles"，可知[C]正确，并排除[A], [B]和[D]。

TEXT D

78. ［D］ 作者在文章开头就说明,在英国送孩子上学很难,接着就指出原因是"there are very many choices to make",可见［D］正确。

79. ［A］ 作者指出,一些做父母的人在心中都在考虑"whether the child should be compelled to go to school at all",原因是他们对传统教育不满意(dissatisfaction with conventional education)。

80. ［B］ 根据文章最后的"any parent who is interested enough can insist that as many choices as possible be made open to him, and the system is theoretically supposed to provide them",就可断定［B］正确。有些读者认为［D］也是正确的,错误的原因是他们没有注意到文章中的"some parents may ... send their child to the only school available in the immediate neighbourhood"和选项中的"Most parents usually send their children to the schools nearby"。

2002 年英语专业四级考试阅读理解参考答案与解析

Part Ⅵ Reading Comprehension

TEXT A

66. ［B］ 根据第一句中的"Many of the home electric goods which are advertised as liberating the modern woman tend to have the opposite effect"和第三句中"but the time saved does not really amount to much",可见［B］正确。

67. ［A］ 文中提到,将衣服拿到洗衣店,不但更省心,而且未必更费钱,原因是什么呢? 当然是,不买洗衣机,省了一大笔钱,可见 capital investment 是花在买洗衣机上的钱。［A］是正确答案。

68. ［D］ 根据文中的"but instead foster her sense of her own usefulness, emphasizing the creative aspect of her function as a housewife",可知［D］为正确答案。

TEXT B

69. ［C］ 根据第一段中的第二句"A country's standard of living, therefore, depends first and foremost on its capacity to produce wealth.",所以［C］为正确答案。

70. ［A］ 根据第二段,可知［D］不是正确选择。根据第三段,可知［B］和［C］非正确答案。正确答案只能是［A］。

71. ［D］ 根据最后一段,可推知［D］为正确答案。特别需要一提的是,要注意题干中的 equally 一词,根据该词和第一段,就可以排除另外三个选项。

TEXT C

72. ［C］ 根据第一段,就可发现［A］,［B］和［D］错误,而［C］为正确答案。

73. ［A］ 根据第二段中第二句"If we do (dress in a certain way or behave in a certain manner), they tell us, we will be able to meet new people with confidence and deal with every situation confidently and without embarrassment",可见 fashion 可以使我们信心十足。

74. [B] 第三段第二句指出了时尚的三个原因：convenience，practical necessity 和 the fancy of an influential person，可见[B]是正确答案。

75. [D] 在第五段中，作者指出：在今天的社会里，人们在着装、发型的选择方面可以"you can dress as you like or do your hair the way you like instead of the way you should"，不难看出这是"个性"使然。

76. [A] 根据最后一段的主题句"At the same time，appearance is still important in certain circumstances and then we must choose our clothes carefully"，就可知[A]为正确答案。而其他三个选项错误。

TEXT D

77. [C] 第一段最后一句"We are witnessing a globalization of our sporting culture"，是本段的主题句，是对本段例子的总结，根据本段提供的一些例子我们可知[C]正确。

78. [B] 根据第三段第二句"Peugeot，Michelin and Panasonic are multi-national corporations that want worldwide returns for the millions they invest in teams"，可以排除[A]。另据第四段第一句"This is undoubtedly an economic-based revolution we are witnessing here，one made possible by communications technology，but made to happen because of marketing considerations."，可以排除[C]和[D]。另外，[B]在文中未提及。

79. [D] 作者在第六段指出，这种观点很"无耻"，只是一心为了得到更多的广告收入，而根本不考虑体育运动的连贯性。可见作者的态度是 critical。

80. [B] 在最后一段，我们了解到"our choice of sports as consumers also grows"，既然我们都成了体育消费者，所以体育自然就是"消费品"了。可见[B]正确。

2003 年英语专业四级考试阅读理解参考答案与解析

Part VI Reading Comprehension

TEXT A

66. [B] 就早期移民的生活方式为什么发生了变化，作者在第一段明确给出了原因"With the development of ideas about individualism"，由此可见[B]为正确答案。

67. [B] 根据第一段第一句和第二段第一句，我们就可以排除[A]。根据第一段最后一句以及第二段就可排除[C]。根据这两个段落的后半部分，可以排除[D]。尽管文章第一句指出"The way in which people use social space reflects their social relationships and their ethnic identity."但是文章并未谈论人们之间的关系，由此可以肯定[B]为正确答案。

TEXT B

68. [C] 根据第五和第六段，我们就可肯定[C]为正确答案。

69. [B] 根据本文倒数第三段，就不难断定[B]正确。

70. [A] 根据文章最后四段作者对数字13的讲述，尤其是最后一段，我们可以看出作

者对迷信的态度是不赞成的，

TEXT C

71. [A] 根据第一段中"Psychologists view the subject either as a matter of frustration or a joke."可知心理学家放弃了对这个课题的研究。根据"Now the biologists have moved into this minefield"，可知，生物学家开始了这个课题的研究，由此可以断定[A]正确。根据第一段最后一句"But being different...is not the same as being better or worse."可以排除[B]。根据第三段中的"This is the first time that a structural difference has been found between the brains of women"，就可排除[D]。

72. [D] 首先需要指出的是，该题题干中的"brain differences"似乎应为"the differences between man and woman in thinking and behavior"。这样，根据第三段倒数第二句"We tend to think that is the influence of society that produces these differences."就可断定[D]为正确答案。

73. [A] 由于本段谈论的是男生和女生在学业上的不同表现，由此我们就不难肯定[A]为正确答案。

74. [B] 根据最后一段"We should be looking for differences in intellectual processing"，我们就可推理出作者建议我们要进一步研究这部分大脑的工作机理，由此可以肯定[B]正确。

75. [A] 通读全文，我们就不难发现，本文主要介绍了大脑结构方面的研究发现，由此可以肯定[A]正确。[B]，[C]和[D]的内容都只是文章的一个方面，而不是主要内容，均可排除。

TEXT D

76. [D] 根据第二段，可以排除[A]和[B]。根据第三段，可以排除[C]。而只有[D]未提及，为正确答案。

77. [A] 作者在本段中指出，人们在电脑拥有比例方面的差异在逐渐缩小，同时我们都知道计算机是一种"数字"产品，由此可以肯定[A]为正确答案。

78. [A] 根据第九段，我们可知[A]是错误叙述，但为正确答案。而[B]，[C]和[D]为正确陈述，皆为错误答案。

79. [C] 通读全文，就不难肯定文章讨论了将来的职业、未来工作的性质以及未来的学校和图书馆，由此可以排除[A]，[B]和[D]。另外文章只谈论了不同种族在计算机拥有率方面的差异，而并未讨论种族差异，由此可以断定[C]为正确答案。

80. [C] 根据最后一段，尤其是本段第一句，同时也是本段的主题句"Even entry-level workers and those in formerly unskilled positions require a growing level of education"，可以肯定[C]正确。

2004 年英语专业四级考试阅读理解参考答案与解析

Part Ⅵ   Reading Comprehension

TEXT   A

66. [B]　细节题。根据第三段最后一句"Many employers, for example, will overlook occasional inefficiencies from their secretary provided she has a pleasant personality."就可断定[B]为正确答案。

67. [C]　作者在第一段提出了本文讨论的话题,接着在第二和第三段分别介绍了对"面试"的两种截然相反的态度,在第四段中作者谈及了面试中存在的问题,最后作者指出了成功面试者和失败面试者之间的性格差别。由此,可见作者对面试的态度是比较客观的。正确答案为[C]。

68. [C]　作者在第三段中指出"...an employer is concerned not only with a candidate's ability, but with the suitability of his or her personality for the particular work situation.",可见不同的人之所以对"面试"有不同的看法,是因为他们判断面试者能力的标准是不同的,因此正确答案应为[C]。

69. [A]　作者在最后一段比较了成功面试者和失败面试者之间不同的"个性",由此,并结合全文,我们不难推测出作者目的在于,指出成功的面试和面试者个性之间的关系。所以[A]为正确答案。

TEXT   B

70. [D]　作者在第一段最后明确指出"have to pay higher prices when they go to the shops"的原因是 a result of this "shrinkage",而这里的"shrinkage"指的就是"由于失盗而造成的损失",所以[D]为正确答案。

71. [C]　根据第四段第一句中的"who gives way to a sudden temptation",就可肯定[C]正确。根据"this kind of shop-lifter is rarely poor",可以排除[D]。[A]在文章中未被提及,也可以排除。本段指出的"countless others who, because of age, sickness or plain absent-mindedness, simply forget to pay for what they take from the shops",并不属于"shoplifters",由此可以排除[B]。

72. [B]　根据第四段第一句中的"the person who gives way to a sudden temptation and is in all other respects an honest and law-abiding citizen",可以断定[B]为正确答案。并且排除[C]。根据"this kind of shop-lifter is rarely poor",可以排除[A]。[D]在文章中未被提及,可以排除。

73. [A]　根据第二段最后一句中的"they (the professionals) account for only a small percentage of the total losses due to shop-lifting",可以肯定[A]为错误陈述,因此是正确答案。根据第三段中的"they are dealt with severely by the courts",可以排除[B]。根据第四段中的"Contrary to what one would expect, this kind of shop-lifter is rarely poor.",可以排除[C]。根据第二段中的"The professionals do not pose much of a problem for the store detectives",可以排除[D]。

74. [？] 作者在最后一段以"劫机"为例来说明"入店行窃"给普通顾客带来的麻烦和不便。作者最后指出,长此以往,顾客将不得不忍受比"存包"更为不便的"搜身",由此,可见[A],[B],[C]和[D]均不是正确答案。

TEXT　C

75. [C] 根据第一段中的"the ache is bad enough it keeps me from sleeping",就可断定[C]正确。有的读者可能会根据"My bones have been aching again, as they often do in humid weather."选择[A]。需要注意的是,"天气潮湿"是骨头痛的原因,而不是作者睡不着觉的直接原因。根据"There are sleeping pills, of course, but the doctor has warned me against them."可以排除[B]。在本段中未提及[D],可以排除之。

76. [A] 根据第二段中的"I made do with some peanut butter",可以排除[B]。根据"There was nothing much I wanted to eat: the remains of a bunch of celery, a blue-tinged heel of bread, a lemon going soft.",可以肯定[A]正确。

77. [C] 根据第二段中的"feeling my way in the faint street light that came through the window.",可以排除[A]。根据全文可以肯定作者在这座房子已经住了很久了,可以排除[B]。根据最后一段中的"My various possessions were floating in their own pools of shadow",就可排除[D]。所以,正确答案为[C]。另外,根据全文所述和我们的常识,也可断定[C]正确。

TEXT　D

78. [B] 作者在第三段首先指出"he (an English driver) will not go until he receives the lawful signal.",接着,作为对比,作者指出"Brazilians view the thing quite differently.",巴西人对信号灯视而不见,有时即使注意到了信号灯,也只是将其作为一种毫无意义的装饰,由此,可见[B]正确。

79. [C] 根据第二段中的"One of the greatest gulfs separating the driving nations is the Atlantic Ocean. More precisely, it is the mental distance between the European and the American motorist",注意此处的American指的是"美洲人"。作者在第三段分别以英国人和巴西人为例说明欧洲驾驶员和美洲驾驶员之间的差别,因此[C]为正确答案。

80. [C] 短语"by moving off prematurely"正是对"anticipate the green light"的解释,由此可以断定[C]正确。

2005 年英语专业四级考试阅读理解参考答案与解析

Part Ⅵ　Reading Comprehension

TEXT　A

81. [C] 根据第一段中的"We watched TV every night."以及"After supper, we'd sprawl on Mom's bed and stare for hours at the tube.",就可断定[C]正确。根据"I didn't know enough to really care (about my marks).",可以排除[B]和[D];文

English

章只提及"My marks in school were miserable"而未提到作者哥哥的学业情况，由此可以排除[A]。

82. [A]　根据第一段中的"My older brother and I lived with Mom"，可以排除[B]；根据第二段中的"She had noticed something in the suburban houses she cleaned-books."可以排除[C]；根据同一段中的"Our mother had only been able to get through third grade."可以排除[D]。只有[A]在文章既未提及，也无从推理出来，因此是正确答案。

83. [D]　根据第二段中的"she . . . snapped off the TV"中的动词短语 snapped off，就可以看出作者母亲态度非常坚决、果断，因此[D]正确。

84. [B]　根据第三段中的"We moaned and complained about how unfair it was."以及第四段中的"I wandered reluctantly among the children's books."，可以知[B]正确。

TEXT　B

85. [C]　根据第六段中的"There were images forming in my mind instead of before my eyes."，可以排除[A]和[B]。根据同段中的"the experience was quite different from watching TV"，可以排除[D]。只有[C]在文中未提及，也无从推理出来，是正确选择。

86. [A]　根据第二段中的"he single-handedly pioneered the concepts of branding and mer-chandising"，可以排除[B]；根据"his greatest skills were his insight and his man-agement ability"，可以排除[C]；根据"the man. . . built the company from noth-ing"，可以排除[D]。根据"Ironically, he could not draw particularly well."就可断定[A]为正确答案。

87. [B]　根据第四段最后一句中的"(not only did his cartoons celebrate America,) but, during World War Ⅱ, studios made training films for American soldiers"，可以肯定[B]为正确答案。

88. [D]　Disney was more or less the genuine article 是本段的主题句(topic sentence)，作者是通过以下几个 supporting details 来支持本主题句的："he was very definitely on the side of ordinary people"，"he voted for Franklin Roosevelt, . . . a leader of the workers"，"he was suspicious of large, bureaucratic organizations"，通过这些细节，我们可以看出 Disney 同情普通人，所以[D]为正确答案。

89. [B]　通读全文，我们可以看出作者在介绍 Disney 的优点和长处的同时，也指出了他的缺点与不足，因此作者的写作态度是客观的。

TEXT　C

90. [B]　根据段中的"Answers to this question would be many and diverse"，即可断定[B]为正确答案。

91. [A]　根据本段中的"This book explores ways of achieving these objectives. It deals, of course, with the techniques of music, but only in order to show how technique is directed toward expressive aims in music and toward the listener's musical experi-ence."可得知[A]正确。

92. [D]　根据第二段前两句"For many, the enjoyment of music does not remain at a stand-

still. We feel that we can get more satisfaction from the musical experience. "可知 [D]为正确选择。

93. [C] 在第三段作者首先指出"there is a common ground from which all musical experiences grow",然后指出"That source is sound itself.",据此,我们可以断定 [C]正确。

94. [D] 根据最后一段中的"All music moves; and because it moves, it is associated with a fundamental truth of existence and experience."以及"We are stirred by impressions of movement because our very lives are constantly in movement.",则可断定 [D]正确。

TEXT D

95. [B] 根据第三段第二句"Gut feelings can occur without a person being consciously aware of them."可知[B]是正确选择。

96. [D] 根据第五段"Emotional self-awareness is the building block of the next fundamental of emotional intelligence: being able to shake off a bad mood."以及文章的后半部分,我们可知"one may control them",所以[D]正确。

97. [A] 如果我们分别用四个选项替代 spice,便不难发现[A]是最好的选择,而且该选择和 spice 的名词形式有共同的语义场(香料,调味品;意味,风味)。

98. [C] 根据第七段中的"But we can have some say in how long that emotion will last."可知[C]正确。

99. [B] 作者在第九段指出"'reframing'... means consciously reinterpreting a situation in a more positive light."据此可以断定[B]正确。

100. [B] [A]只概括了第一段的内容;[C]仅总结了最后两段的内容;[D]概括了第七段内容。只有[B]能够概括出整篇文章的内容,为正确答案。

2006 年英语专业四级考试阅读理解参考答案与解析

Part Ⅵ　Reading Comprehension

TEXT A

81. [B] 根据文章第三最后的"Now, however, a night out can be arranged on the run."和 "It is no longer 'see you there at 8', but 'text me around 8 and we'll see where we all are'"可以肯定[B]正确。

82. [D] 文章第五段明确指出"the mobile phone's individuality and privacy gave texters the ability to express <u>a whole new outer personality</u>."而且手机短消息"allowed texters to present a setf-image that differed from the one familiar to those who knew them well",由此可以断定[D]为正确答案。

83. [A] 根据第五段中的"texting allowed texters to present a self-image that differed from the one familiar to those who knew them well."以及"the mobile phone's individuality and privacy gave texters the ability to express <u>a whole new outer personality</u>"

可以推理出[A]正确。

84. [C]　根据第六段中的最后一句"there is the 'spacemaker': these people focus on themselves and keep out other people."可以肯定[C]正确。

85. [B]　[A]仅能够包括文章第四和第五段内容;[D]只涉及到文章第六段内容;文章未来涉及到[C]中内容,均可以排除,因此正确答案为[B]。另外,根据文章第一段中的"Recent research indicates that the mobile phone is changing not only our culture, but our very bodies as well."可知作者在这里要讨论手机对我们文化和身体两方面的影响,根据第二段中的"First. Let's talk about culture."可知作者在这里只讨论了手机对我们文化的影响。由此可以进一步肯定[B]为正确选择。

TEXT　B

86. [C]　根据第二段中的"As a result of this (the working-class tended to be paid less than middle-class people, such as teachers and doctors) and also of the fact that workers' jobs were generally much less secure, distinct differences in life-styles and attitudes came into existence."可以断定[C]正确。

87. [A]　根据第三段第一句"The stereotype of what a middle-class man did with his money was perhaps nearer the truth."就可以肯定[A]正确。

88. [D]　根据第三段中的"Both of these (buying a house as a top priority 和 the education of his children) provided him and his family with security."可以排除[A];根据"He was—and still is—inclined to take a longer-term view."可以排除[B];根据"Not only did he regard buying a house as a top priority, but he also considered the education of his children as extremely important."可以排除[C],由此可以肯定[D]为正确选择。

89. [B]　"Social security and laws to improve job-security, combined with a general rise in the standard of living since the mid-fifties of the 20th century, have made it less necessary than before to worry about 'tomorrow'."可以排除[A],[C]和[D],并肯定[B]为正确答案。

90. [A]　根据第五段中的"They generally tend to share very similar tastes in music and clothes, they spend their money in having a good time, and save for holidays or longer-term plans when necessary. There seems to be much less difference than in previous generations."可以排除[B];根据"As long as this gap (between the well-paid and the low-paid) exists, there will always be a possibility that new conflicts and jealousies will emerge, or rather that the old conflicts will re-appear, but between different groups."可以排除[C];根据"In fact there has been a growing tendency in the past few years for the middle-classes to feel slightly ashamed of their position."可以排除[D]。据此可以肯定[A]为正确选择。另外,根据第一段中的"Ideas about social class—whether a person is 'working-class' or 'middle-class'—are one area in which changes have been extremely slow."就可以推断出并不是所有的领域的变化都是缓慢的,因此也可以排除[A]。

TEXT C

92. 〔A〕 凭借我们的语法和词汇知识,根据第二段中的"when he would sometimes pass me coldly, and sometimes bow and smile",可以肯定〔A〕正确。

93. 〔D〕 Mr. Rochester 说的"you criticize my appearance"指的是 Miss Eyre 在回答他自己是否帅气时所的说的"No, sir."(第四段);因此 Mr. Rochester 接下来所说的"and then you stab me in the back",应该指 Miss Eyre 接下来说的"Sir, I'm sorry. I should have said that beauty doesn't matter, or something like that."由此,可肯定〔D〕正确。

94. 〔A〕 在第八段中 Mr. Rochester 自问("Why do I tell you all this?")自答"Because you're the sort of person people tell their problems and secrets to, because you're sympathetic and give them hope."由此可以断定〔A〕正确。

95. 〔D〕 在文章最后,Mr. Rochester 为 Miss Eyre 回顾了过去("perhaps because of the effect Lowood school has had on you"),总结了现在("You don't relax or laugh very much.""You're like a bird in a cage."),并展望了美好的未来("But in time you will be more natural with me, and laugh, and speak freely. ...When you get out of the cage, you'll fly very high.")据此可以肯定〔D〕正确。

TEXT D

96. 〔D〕 根据第一段中的"The machine would not be a passive participant but would add its own suggestions, information, and opinions"以及"it would sometimes take the initiative in developing or changing the topic",就可以排除〔A〕;根据第三段中的"The computer's own personality would be lively and impressive",可以排除〔B〕;根据第一段中的"The ideal companion machine... would also be programmed to behave in a pleasant manner."可以排除〔C〕。由此可以肯定〔D〕为正确选择。另外,根据第一段中的"the machine would remain slightly unpredictable and therefore interesting."也可以肯定〔D〕正确。

97. 〔D〕 根据第二段中的"Friendships are not made in a day, and the computer would be more acceptable as a friend if it imitated the gradual changes that occur when one person is getting to know another."和"The whole process would be accomplished in a subtle way"以及"After experiencing a wealth of powerful, well-timed friendship indicators",就可以推断出〔D〕为正确答案。

100. 〔C〕 选项〔A〕范围太广,涉及包括人和计算机之间的关系之内的所有 artificial relationships,因此〔A〕可以排除;选项〔B〕中 intimate relationships 还包括人与人之间、人与动物之间、人与计算机之间的亲密关系,因此〔B〕概括的内容也太宽泛,可以排除;本文重点讨论了计算机 artificial intelligence,而不均衡地讨论人和计算机之间的关系,由此可以排除〔D〕。所以正确答案为〔C〕。

2007 年英语专业四级考试阅读理解参考答案与解析

Part Ⅴ   Reading Comprehension

TEXT A

81. [C]   根据第一段中的"the bad ones who terrorize their guests and overcharge them at the slightest opportunity",可知[A]和[B]指的是 bad landladies,因此都过于片面。第一段中的"Good landladies... are figures as popular in fiction as the bad ones"表示好的女房东和坏的房东在小说中都同样常见,而是表示她们都受房客欢迎,因此可以排除[D]。根据第一段后半部分内容,可以推断出女房东基本上都是合格的,[C]为正确答案。

82. [A]   根据第二段中的"with the added difficulties that arise from deciding who pays for what, and in what proportion",可以断定[A]正确。同时,根据第一段中的"house rules may restrict the freedom to invite friends to visit","shared cooking and bathroom facilities"和"tidy and untidy guests are living under the same roof"可知[B],[C]和[D]都不是"additional disadvantage",均可以排除。

TEXT B

83. [D]   根据第三段中的"flat sharing can be very cheap",可以排除[A];根据"there will always be someone to talk to and go out with",可以排除[B];根据"the chores, in theory, can be shared",可以排除[C]。由此可以断定正确答案为[D]。

84. [C]   根据第三段中的"The kindness or curiosity of strangers took me all over Europe, North America, Asia and southern Africa. Some of the lift-givers became friends, many provided hospitality on the road",可以肯定[A]正确。根据第四段中的"Not only did you find out much more about a country than when traveling by train or plane, but there was that element of excitement about where you would finish up that night."可以肯定[B]正确,因此正确答案为[C]。

85. [A]   根据第七段中的"hitchhiking was clearly still alive and well in some places",基本可以肯定[A]。另外,同段中的"the general feeling was that throughout much of the west it was doomed",可以排除[B];根据第六段中的"Rural Ireland was recommended as a friendly place for hitching, as was Quebec, Canada",并结合第五段中的"A few years ago",可以排除[C];根据第九段中的"In Poland in the 1960s... Everyone was hitchhiking then",可以排除[D]。

86. [D]   根据第 10 段中的"Surely this is a good idea for society."尤其是第一个单词"Surely",就可肯定[D]正确。

87. [B]   根据第三中的"Some of the lift-givers became friends, many provided hospitality on the road."和第十段中的"Hitchhiking would increase respect by breaking down barriers between strangers."可以排除[A];根据第 10 段中的"It would help fight global warming by cutting down on fuel consumption as hitchhikers would be using

existing fuels."可以排除[C];根据第 10 段中的"It would also improve educational standards by delivering instant lessons in geography, history, politics and sociology."可以排除[D],由此可以断定[B]为正确答案。

88. [D]　最后一段中的"someone who is trying to travel hopefully with thumb outstretched"指那些在路边伸着大拇指希望搭便车旅行的人,根据"either...or..."结构,可以推断出"put it to the test yourself"的意思是亲自实践一下"To travel hopefully",也就是做一个搭便车的人,所以正确答案为[D]。

TEXT　C

89. [B]　根据第三段中的"She moved with the same ease and loveliness I often saw in the women of Laos. Her long black hair was as shiny as the black silk of the skirts she was selling."和第六段中的"She smiled, more with her eyes than with her lips."可以断定[B]正确。另外,根据第四段中的"I don't speak Laotian very well",可以排除[A];根据第三段中的"She was selling skirts."可以排除[C];综观全文,没有任何细节暗示作者和 the woman in the marketplace 相识,因此可以排除[D]。

90. [A]　根据第五段中的"It is the custom to bargain in Asia."可以排除[B];根据"In Laos bargaining is done in soft voices and easy moves with the sort of quiet peacefulness."可以排除[C];根据"We shook our heads in disagreement over the price; then, immediately, we made another offer and then another shake of the head."可以排除[D]。由此可以断定[A]是正确答案。

91. [C]　根据第六段中的"She was so pleased that unexpectedly, she accepted the last offer I made. But it was too soon. The price was too low. She was being too generous and wouldn't make enough money."可以肯定[C]正确。

92. [C]　根据第六段中的"that way I was able to pay her three times as much before she had a chance to lower the price for the larger purchase."可以断定[C]正确。

93. [A]　根据第八段中的"without knowing it, I have also learned to defend myself against what is soft and what should be easy."可以断定[A]为正确答案。

94. [C]　根据最后一段中的"There is no defense against a generous spirit, and this time I cry, and very hard",可以推断出[C]正确。

TEXT　D

95. [B]　[A],[C]和[D]陈述的都是事实,可以排除。[B]项使用了矛盾修辞法(oxymoron),"They are school children without school."表达了一个似非而是的观点,这是些不上学的学龄儿童。

96. [A]　根据第三段中的"In 19th-century cities, schools were open seven or eight hours a day, 11 months a year. In rural America, the year was arranged around the growing season. ...but nearly all schools are scheduled as if our children went home early to milk the cows and took months off to work the crops."可知[A]正确。

97. [B]　通观全文,尤其是第三段和第五段内容,可以断定[B]为作者的观点,是正确答案。根据第三段最后中的"Now, three-quarters of the mothers of school-age

children work, but the calendar is written as if they were home waiting for the school bus."可以排除[A]和[D](注:该选项中的 valid 似乎应为 effective。)根据第三段中的"For much of our history, after all, Americans arranged the school year around the needs of work and family."可以排除[C]。

98. [D]　Dr. Boyer 认为"School...is educational."（第六段），而世人都认为"Schools are routinely burdened with the job of solving all our social problems."由此可以断定[D]正确。

99. [A]　选项[B]和[C]与本段内容没有任何关系。"the long summers"也就意味着学习时间的减少，也就是[D]项内容。短语 take a toll 的意思是"造成损失"，"the long summers of forgetting"则不但意味着学习时间的减少，而且长时间不学习带来的遗忘则更使学习进步变缓，所以正确答案应为[A]。

100. [C]　综观全文，整篇文章讨论了是现有的学校校历安排中存在的问题，因此[C]正确。